big NATE

GAME ON!

by LINCOLN PEIRCE

**Andrews McMeel
Publishing, LLC**

Kansas City • Sydney • London

Big Nate is distributed internationally by Universal Uclick.

Big Nate: Game On! copyright © 2013 by United Feature Syndicate. All rights reserved. Printed in China. No part of this book may be used or reproduced in any manner whatsoever without written permission except in the case of reprints in the context of reviews.

Andrews McMeel Publishing, LLC
an Andrews McMeel Universal company
1130 Walnut Street, Kansas City, Missouri 64106

www.andrewsmcmeel.com

13 14 15 16 17 SDB 10 9 8 7 6 5 4 3

ISBN: 978-1-4494-2777-1

Library of Congress Control Number: 2012952339

Made by:
Shenzhen Donnelley Printing Company Ltd.
Address and location of production:
No.47, Wuhe Nan Road, Bantian Ind. Zone,
Shenzhen China, 518129
3rd Printing—6/10/13

Big Nate can be viewed on the Internet at
www.comics.com/big_nate

ATTENTION: SCHOOLS AND BUSINESSES

Andrews McMeel books are available at quantity discounts with bulk purchase for educational, business, or sales promotional use. For information, please e-mail the Andrews McMeel Publishing Special Sales Department:
specialsales@amuniversal.com

SWISH!

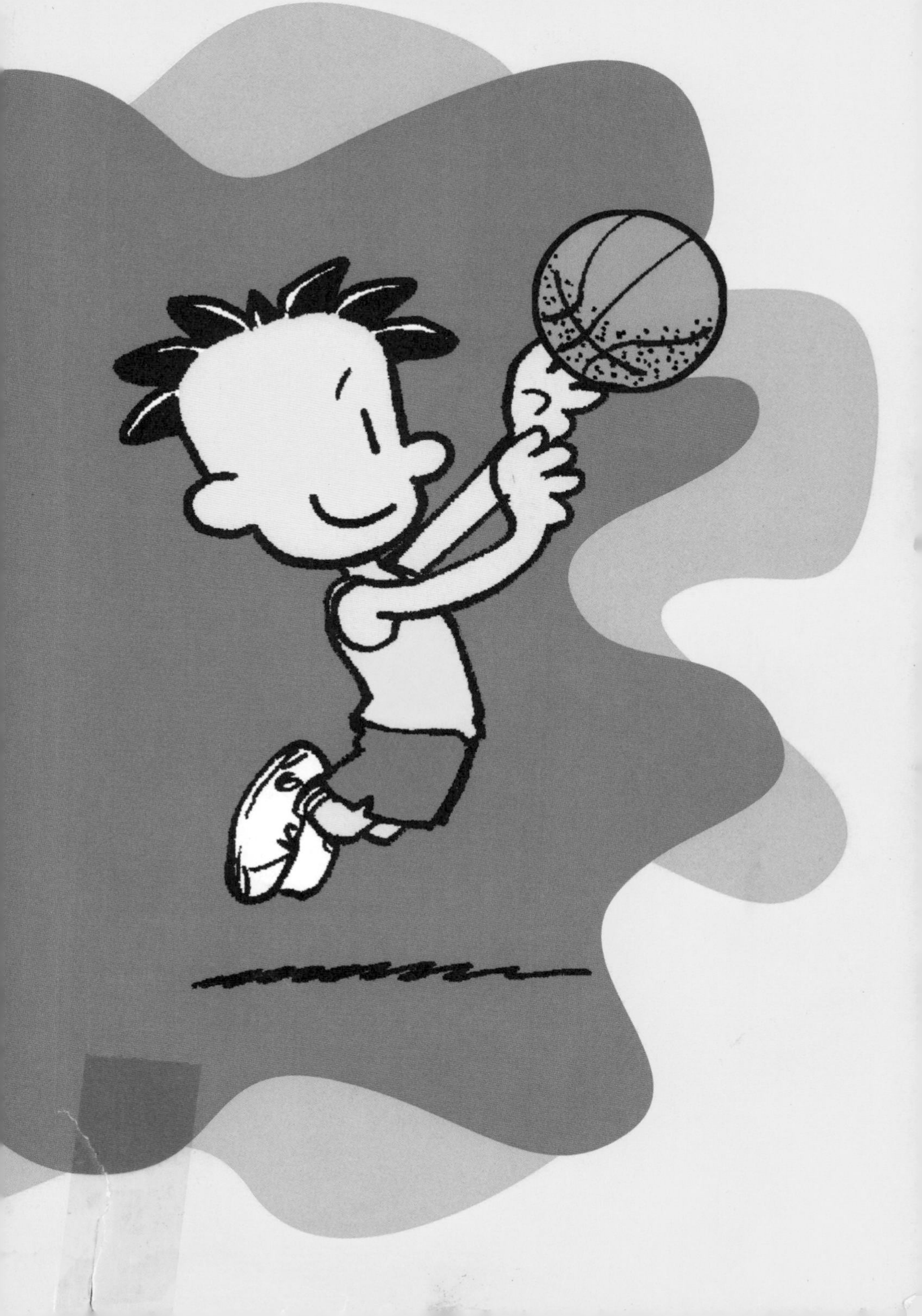

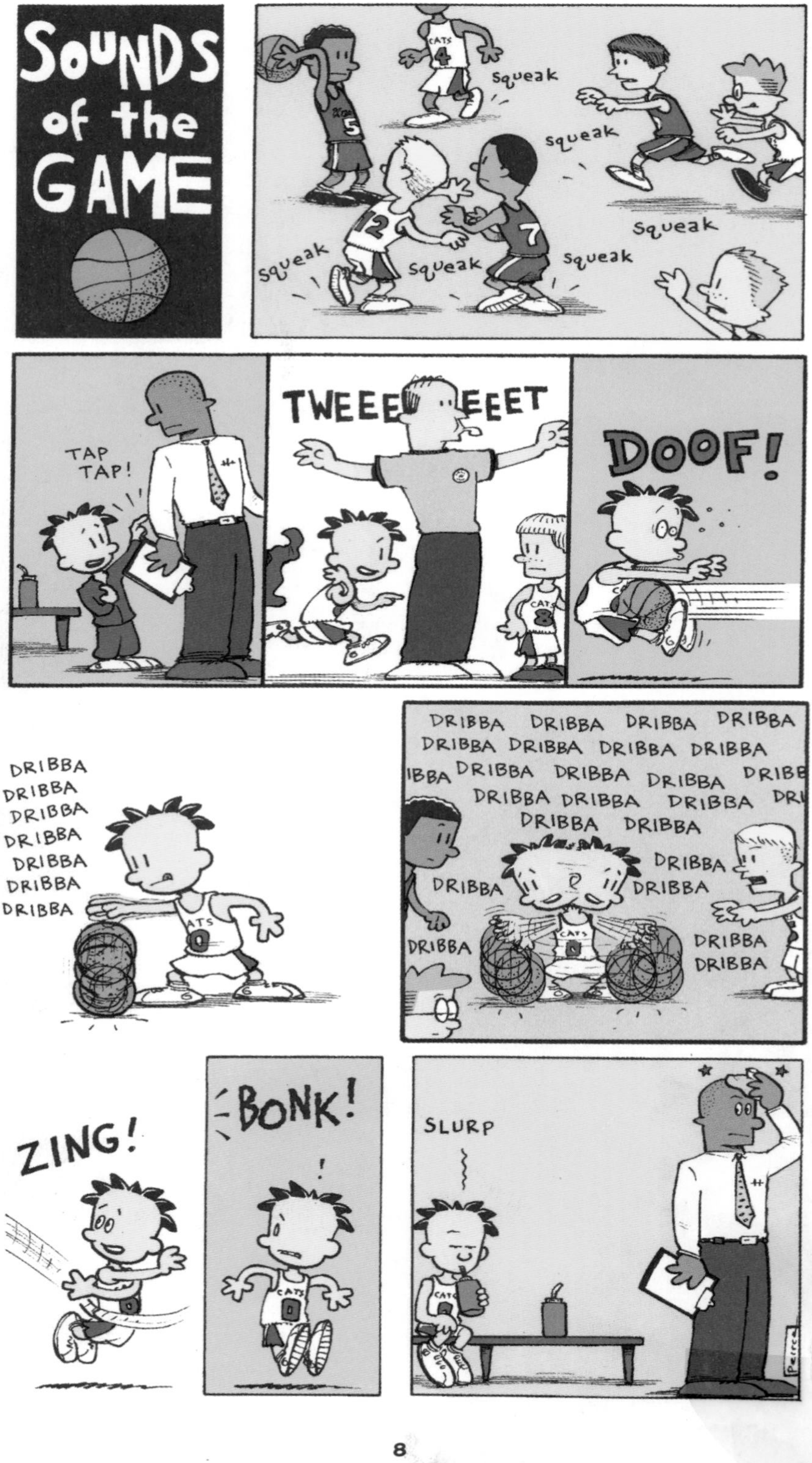
SOUNDS of the GAME
squeak
squeak
squeak
squeak
squeak
squeak
TAP TAP!
TWEEEEEEET
DOOF!
DRIBBA DRIBBA DRIBBA DRIBBA DRIBBA DRIBBA DRIBBA
DRIBBA DRIBBA
ZING!
BONK!
!
SLURP

HOLD IT! FOUL!

THAT'S A FOUL, NATE! IF YOU DO THAT IN A GAME, YOU'LL GET CALLED EVERY TIME!

WHAT? NO WAY!

I DIDN'T BUMP HIM, I DIDN'T GRAB HIM, I DIDN'T TRIP HIM!... TECHNICALLY, I DIDN'T EVEN **TOUCH HIS BODY!**

NEVERTHELESS...

MAY I GO TO THE LOCKER ROOM TO "ADJUST" MYSELF?

Peirce

BIG GAME TODAY, MEN! THESE GUYS ARE UNDEFEATED. THIS'LL BE A TOUGH, TOUGH GAME.

THEY'RE TALLER, THEY'RE MORE SKILLED. BUT IF YOU HANG IN THERE, TRY TO STAY CLOSE... WELL, ANYTHING CAN HAPPEN!

DON'T OVERFOCUS ON THE FINAL OUTCOME. DO YOUR BEST, AND I'LL BE PROUD OF YOU NO MATTER WHAT!

CLAP
CLAP
CLAP

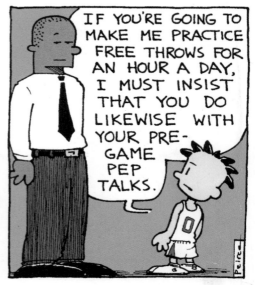

IF YOU'RE GOING TO MAKE ME PRACTICE FREE THROWS FOR AN HOUR A DAY, I MUST INSIST THAT YOU DO LIKEWISE WITH YOUR PRE-GAME PEP TALKS.

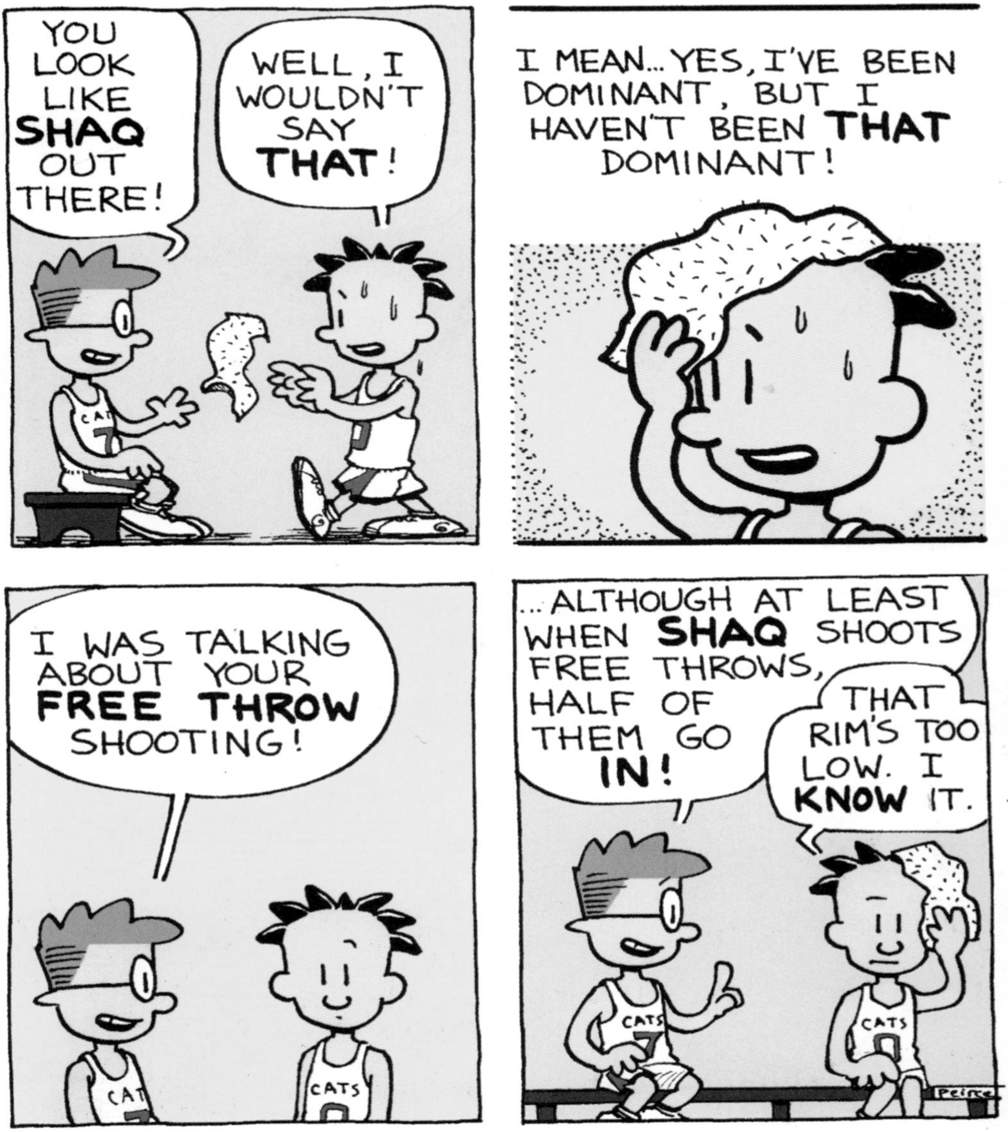
YOU LOOK LIKE **SHAQ** OUT THERE!
WELL, I WOULDN'T SAY **THAT**!
I MEAN... YES, I'VE BEEN DOMINANT, BUT I HAVEN'T BEEN **THAT** DOMINANT!
I WAS TALKING ABOUT YOUR **FREE THROW** SHOOTING!
...ALTHOUGH AT LEAST WHEN **SHAQ** SHOOTS FREE THROWS, HALF OF THEM GO **IN**!
THAT RIM'S TOO LOW. I **KNOW** IT.

OKAY, THIS GUY'S A FOOT TALLER THAN I AM, BUT WHO CARES? I'VE GOT **QUICKNESS**! I'VE GOT **SPEED**!
I'LL SHOW HIM A CROSSOVER, A COUPLE OF HEAD FAKES, AND THEN I'LL BLOW BY HIM LIKE HE'S...
!
...SITTING STILL.
Peirce

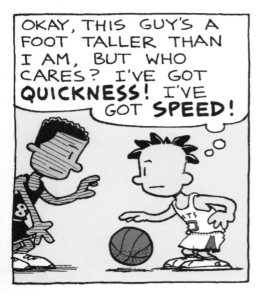

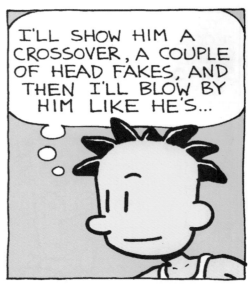

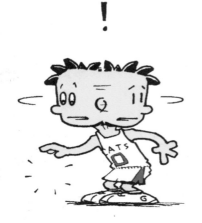

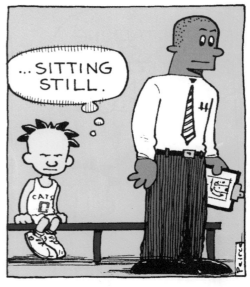

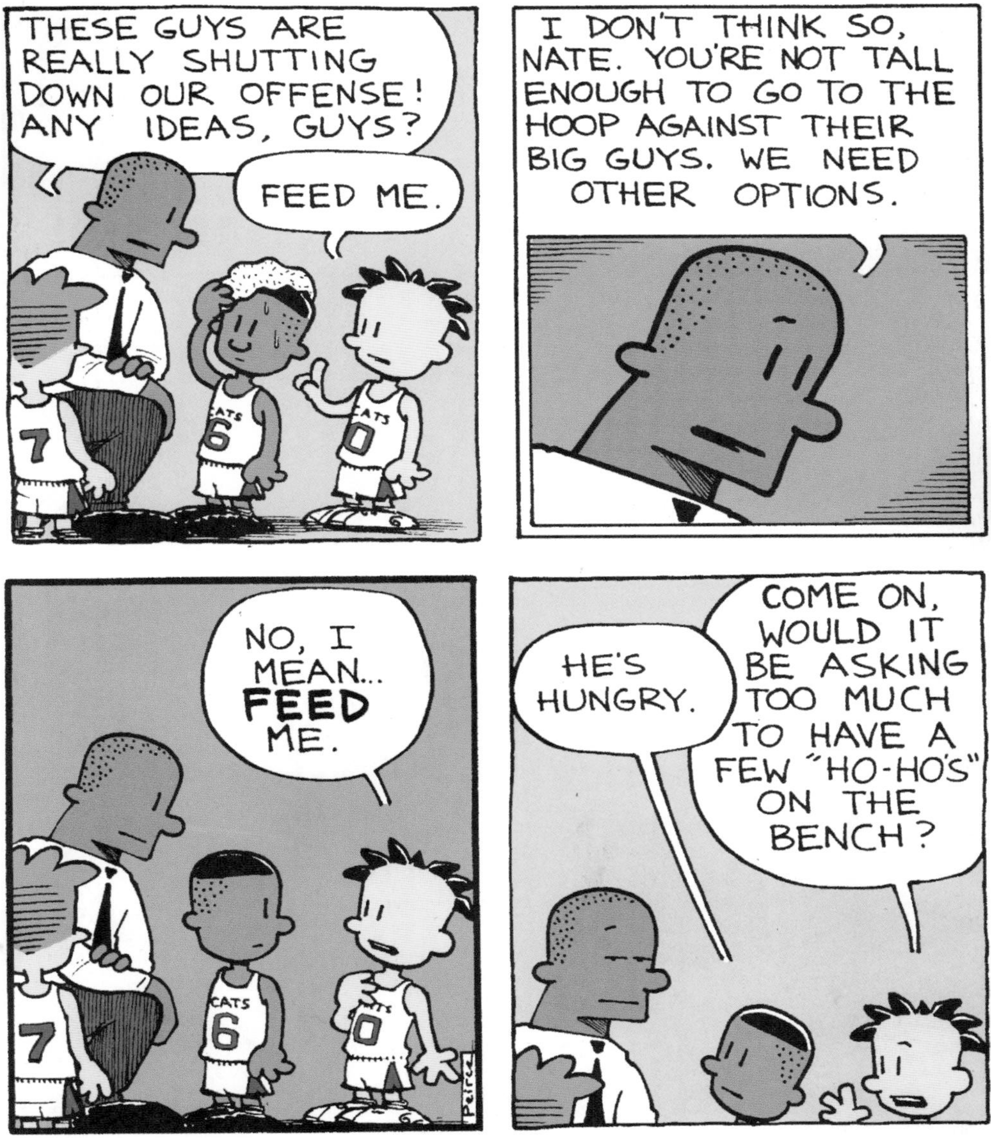
THESE GUYS ARE REALLY SHUTTING DOWN OUR OFFENSE! ANY IDEAS, GUYS?
FEED ME.
I DON'T THINK SO, NATE. YOU'RE NOT TALL ENOUGH TO GO TO THE HOOP AGAINST THEIR BIG GUYS. WE NEED OTHER OPTIONS.
NO, I MEAN... **FEED** ME.
HE'S HUNGRY.
COME ON, WOULD IT BE ASKING TOO MUCH TO HAVE A FEW "HO-HO'S" ON THE BENCH?

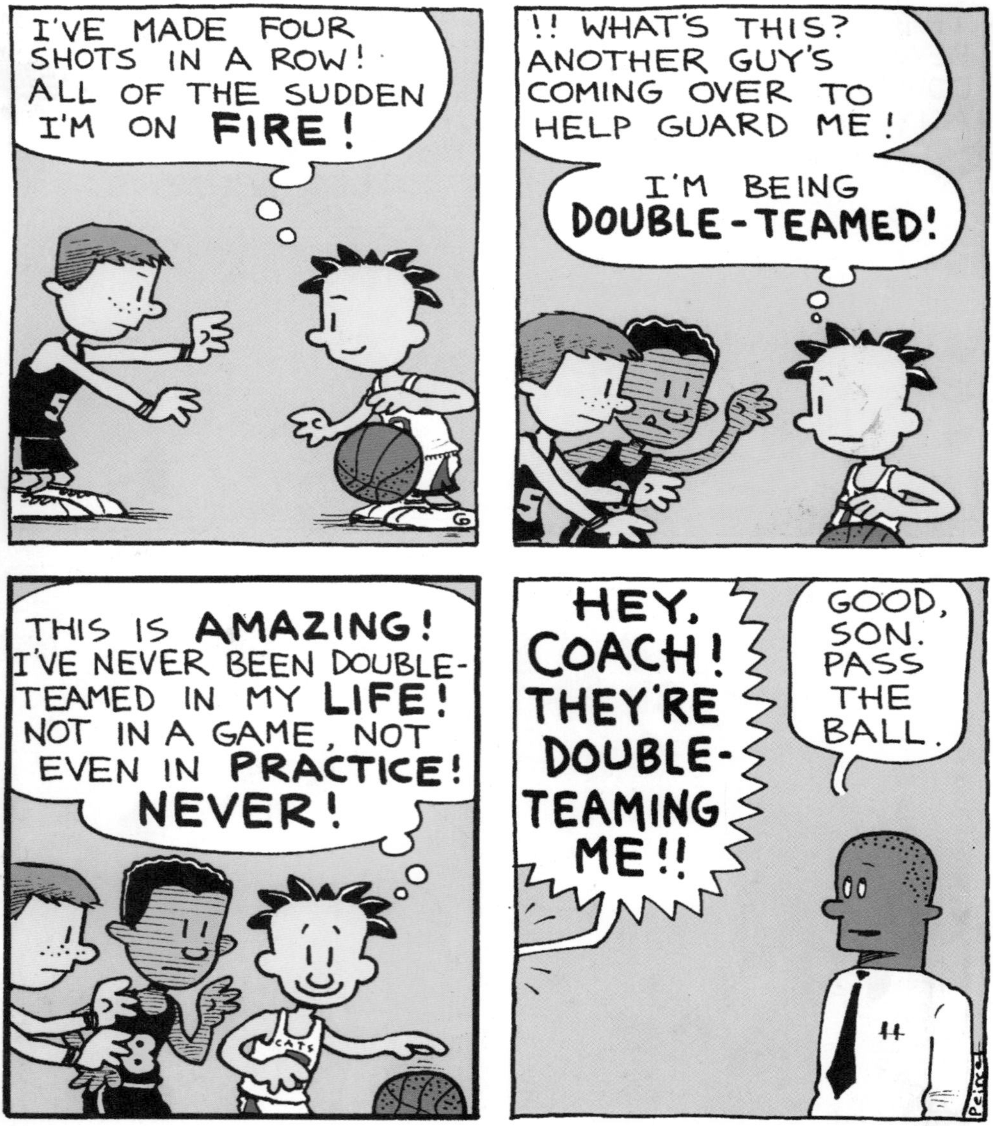

I'VE MADE FOUR SHOTS IN A ROW! ALL OF THE SUDDEN I'M ON FIRE!
!! WHAT'S THIS? ANOTHER GUY'S COMING OVER TO HELP GUARD ME!
I'M BEING DOUBLE-TEAMED!
THIS IS AMAZING! I'VE NEVER BEEN DOUBLE-TEAMED IN MY LIFE! NOT IN A GAME, NOT EVEN IN PRACTICE! NEVER!
HEY, COACH! THEY'RE DOUBLE-TEAMING ME!!
GOOD, SON. PASS THE BALL.

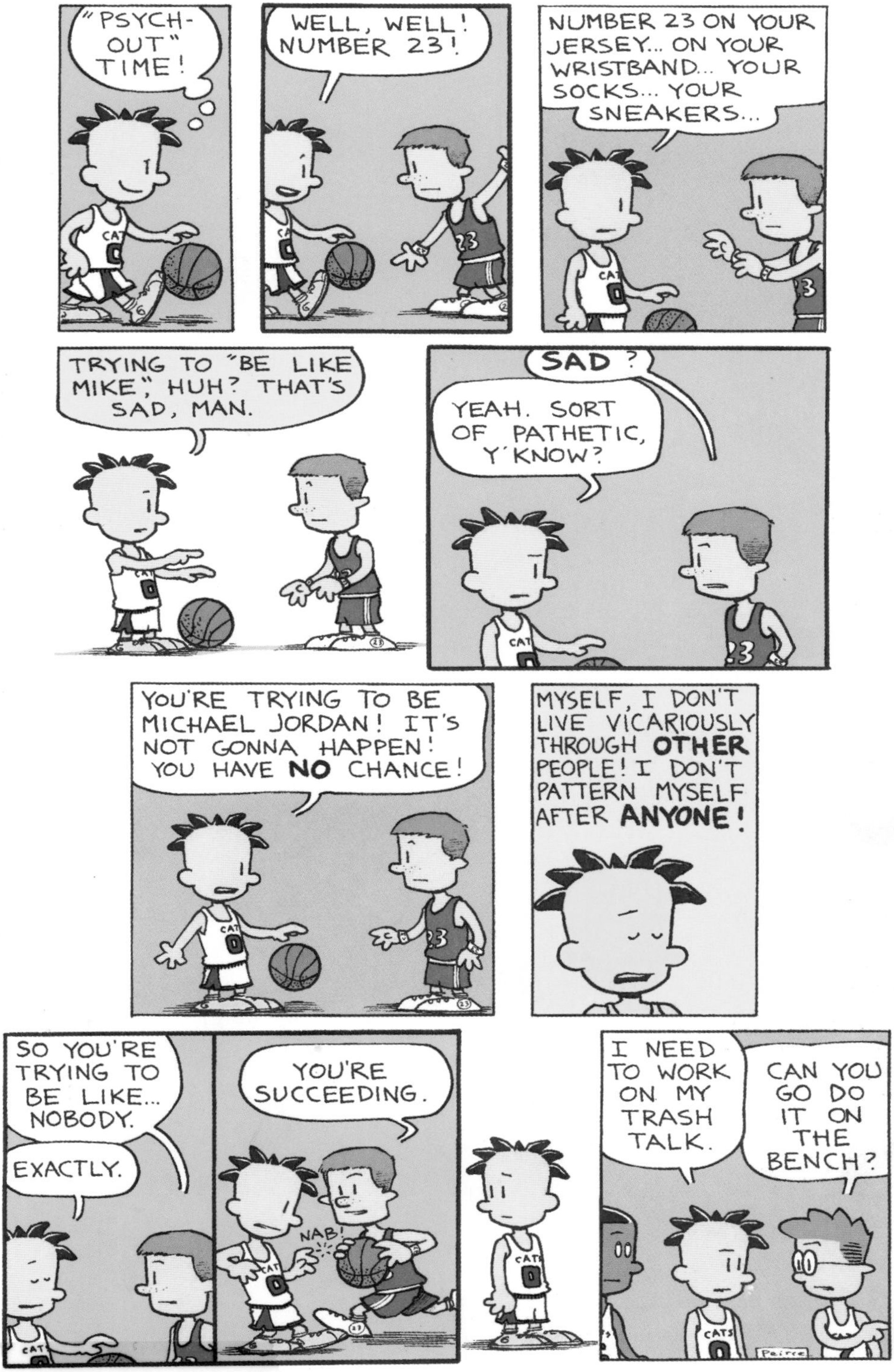
"PSYCH-OUT" TIME!
WELL, WELL! NUMBER 23!
NUMBER 23 ON YOUR JERSEY... ON YOUR WRISTBAND... YOUR SOCKS... YOUR SNEAKERS...
TRYING TO "BE LIKE MIKE," HUH? THAT'S SAD, MAN.
SAD?
YEAH. SORT OF PATHETIC, Y'KNOW?
YOU'RE TRYING TO BE MICHAEL JORDAN! IT'S NOT GONNA HAPPEN! YOU HAVE NO CHANCE!
MYSELF, I DON'T LIVE VICARIOUSLY THROUGH OTHER PEOPLE! I DON'T PATTERN MYSELF AFTER ANYONE!
SO YOU'RE TRYING TO BE LIKE... NOBODY.
EXACTLY.
YOU'RE SUCCEEDING.
NAB!
I NEED TO WORK ON MY TRASH TALK.
CAN YOU GO DO IT ON THE BENCH?
Peirce

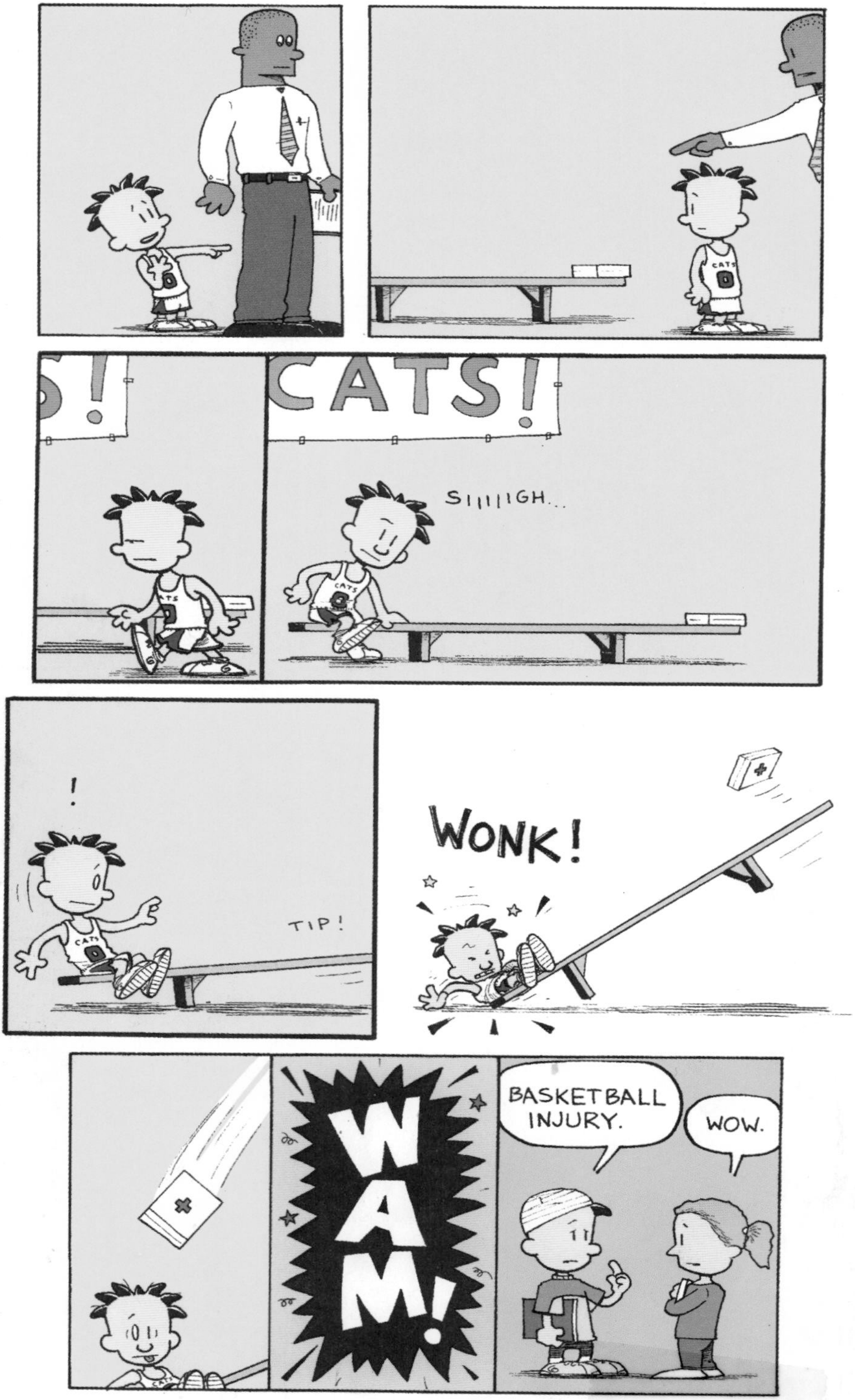
CATS!
SIIIIIGH...
!
TIP!
WONK!
WAM!
BASKETBALL INJURY.
WOW.

I AM GETTING **BODY-SLAMMED** OUT THERE! SOME OF THOSE GUYS OUTWEIGH ME BY **FIFTY POUNDS!**
I NEED TO GET BIGGER TO HOLD MY OWN AGAINST THOSE **GOONS** OUT THERE! I NEED TO **BULK UP!**
BY LIFTING WEIGHTS?
BY EATING.
AH.
"CHEEZ DOODLE"?
NARF
NARF
CHOMP
CHOMPF
NARF
Peirce

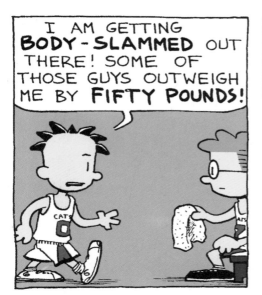

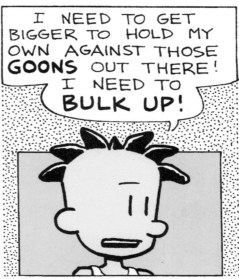

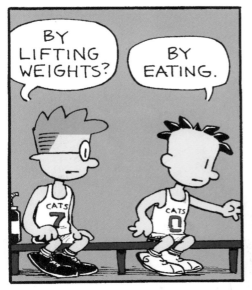

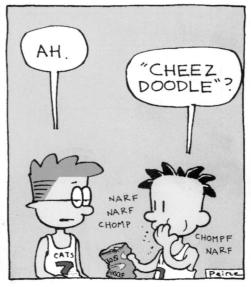

NATE, WHAT ON EARTH ARE YOU DOING?
I'M BEEFIN' UP, COACH!
CHOMP CHOMP NARF
CAT'S
I'M PUTTING ON WEIGHT SO I CAN BANG WITH THE BIG BOYS OUT THERE!
NARF NARF
NARF
NARF
TWEET!
LET'S GO, COACH! GET YOUR TEAM ON THE –
CHOMP
CHOMP
SLURP
NARF
NARF
GULP
DO I SMELL PASTRAMI?
HEY COACH! CAN I GO IN AS A "SUB"?
Peirce

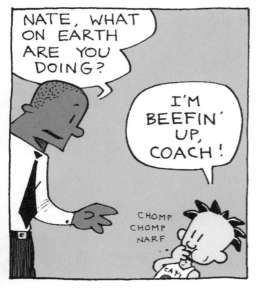

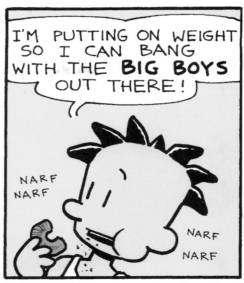

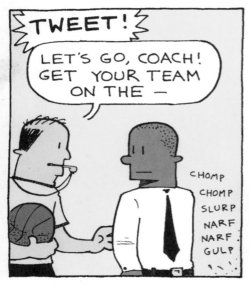

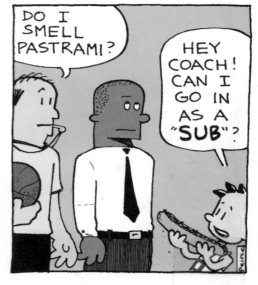

WITH A FEW EXTRA POUNDS ON ME, I'M GOING TO BE A **FORCE** OUT THERE!
MUNCH
CRUNCH
SMACK
NARF
NARF
THERE'LL BE NO STOPPING ME! I'LL BE A RUNAWAY TRUCK!
CHOMPF
CHOMPF
GULP
GLOMP
PAT!
PAT!
EVERY TRUCK NEEDS A SPARE TIRE!
PEIRCE

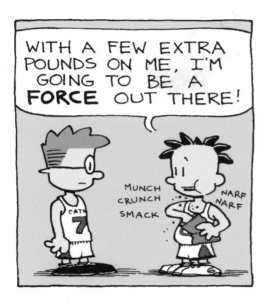

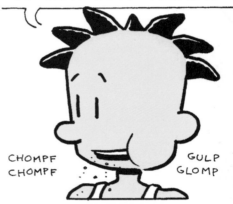

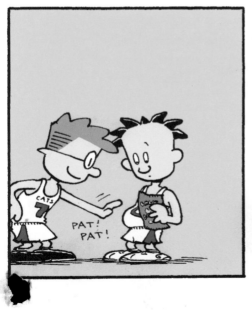

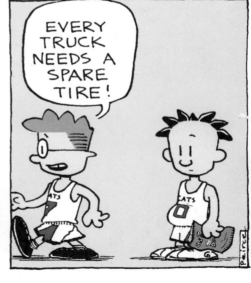

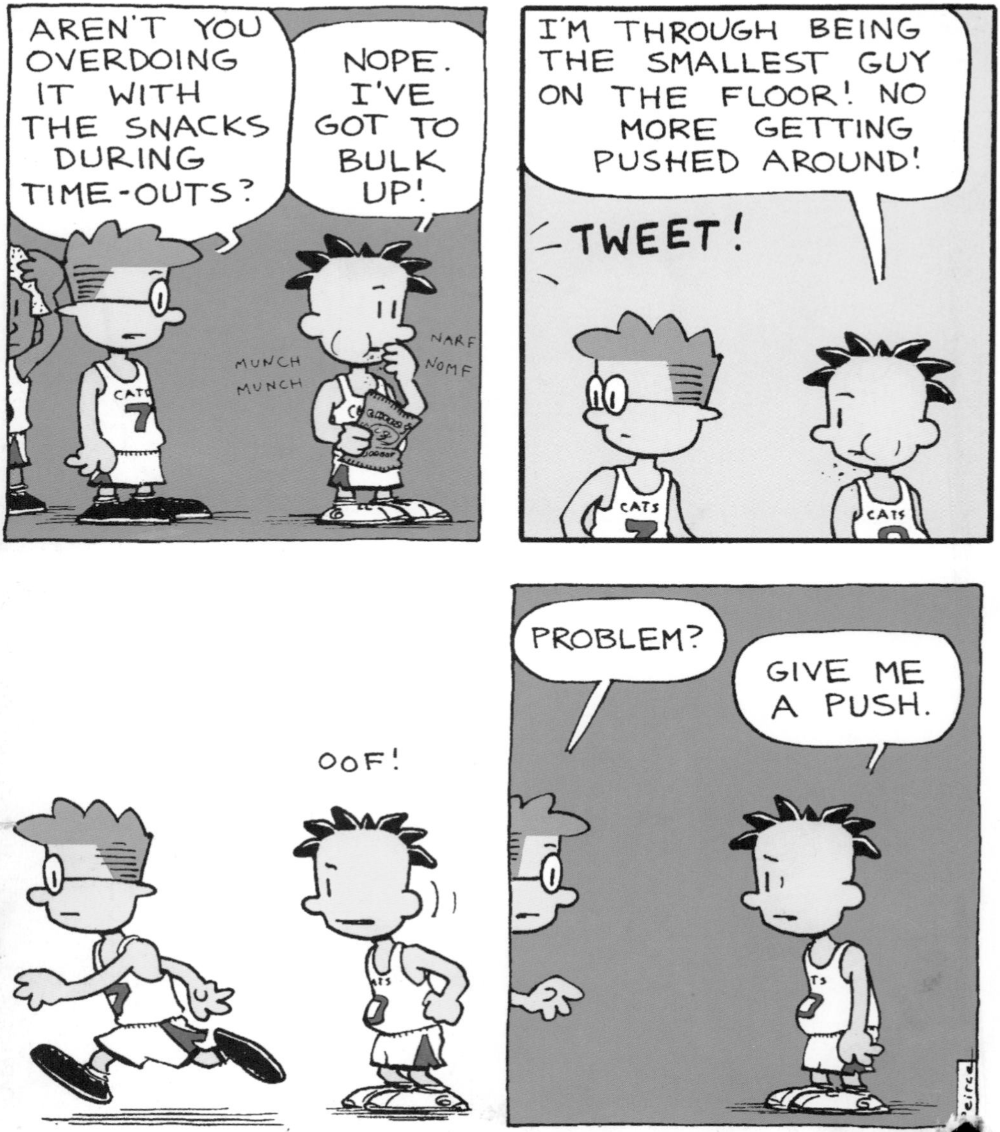
AREN'T YOU OVERDOING IT WITH THE SNACKS DURING TIME-OUTS?
NOPE. I'VE GOT TO BULK UP!
MUNCH MUNCH
NARF NOMF
I'M THROUGH BEING THE SMALLEST GUY ON THE FLOOR! NO MORE GETTING PUSHED AROUND!
TWEET!
OOF!
PROBLEM?
GIVE ME A PUSH.

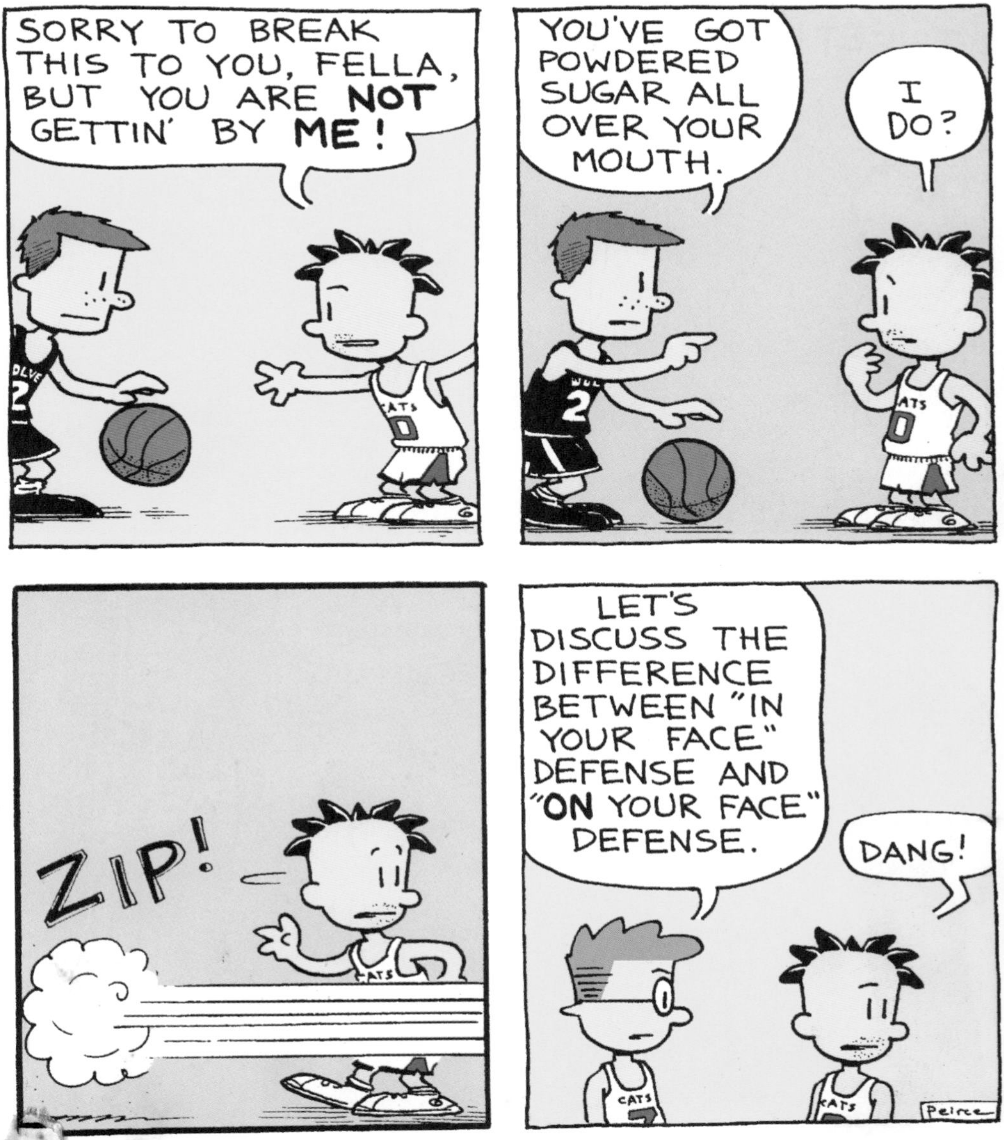
SORRY TO BREAK THIS TO YOU, FELLA, BUT YOU ARE **NOT** GETTIN' BY **ME**!
YOU'VE GOT POWDERED SUGAR ALL OVER YOUR MOUTH.
I DO?
ZIP!
LET'S DISCUSS THE DIFFERENCE BETWEEN "IN YOUR FACE" DEFENSE AND "**ON** YOUR FACE" DEFENSE.
DANG!
Peirce

TWEET!
FOUL!
ON ME? BUT I'VE ALREADY GOT FOUR FOULS!
SORRY, KID, BUT...
WAIT! LET'S BE REASON-ABLE ABOUT THIS! CAN'T WE TALK IT OVER? HERE! HERE!
WHAT'S THIS?
WHAT DOES IT LOOK LIKE?
A BRIBE.
WHA-? NO! NO! IT'S A "CHIPS AHOY!"
Peirce

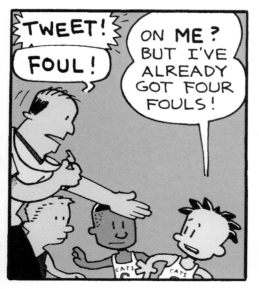

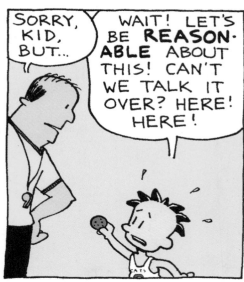

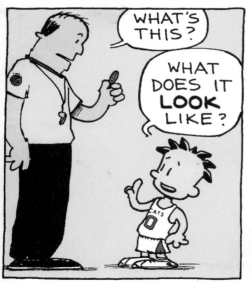

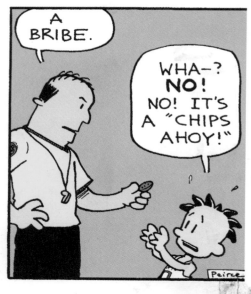

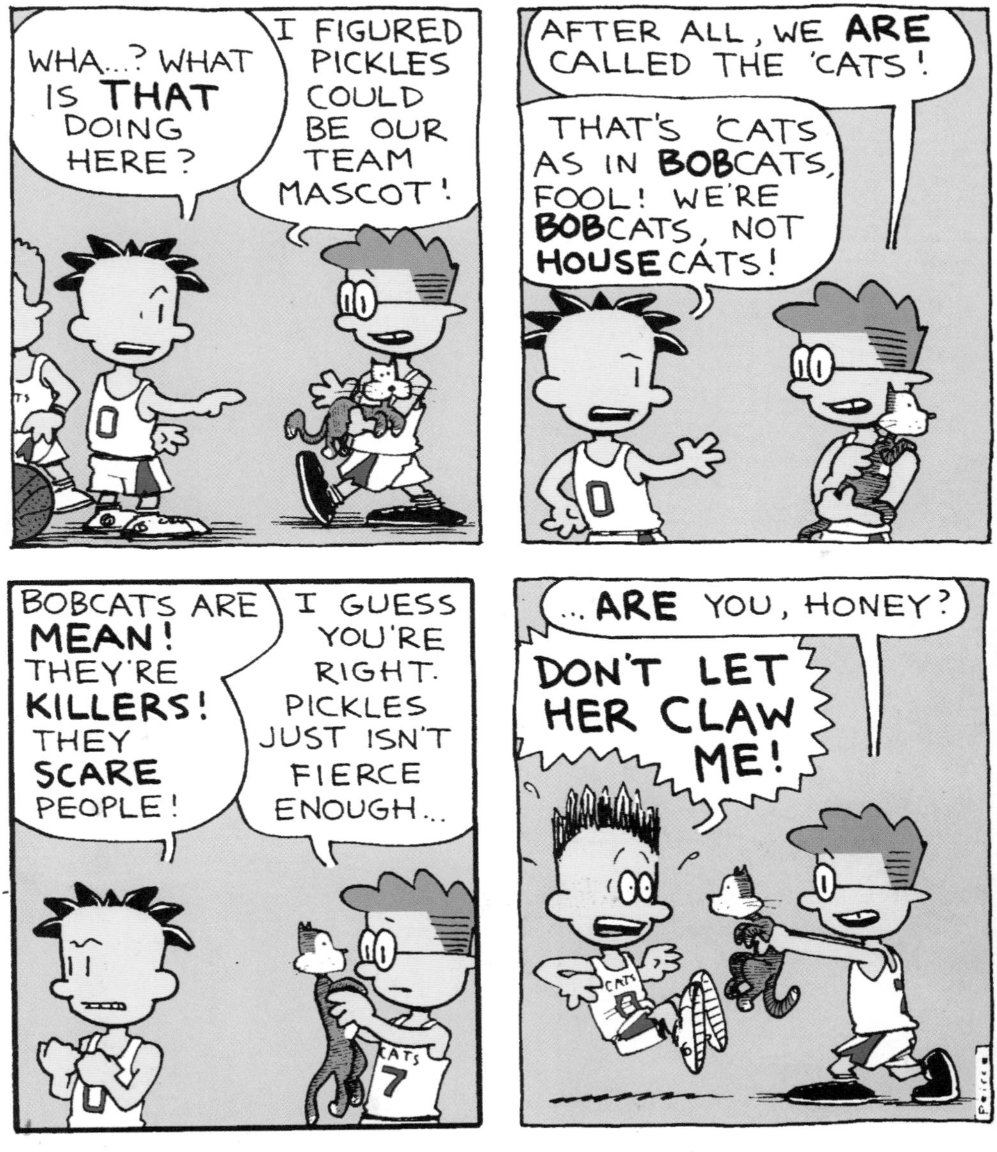
WHA...? WHAT IS THAT DOING HERE?
I FIGURED PICKLES COULD BE OUR TEAM MASCOT!
AFTER ALL, WE ARE CALLED THE 'CATS!
THAT'S 'CATS AS IN BOBCATS, FOOL! WE'RE BOBCATS, NOT HOUSECATS!
BOBCATS ARE MEAN! THEY'RE KILLERS! THEY SCARE PEOPLE!
I GUESS YOU'RE RIGHT. PICKLES JUST ISN'T FIERCE ENOUGH...
...ARE YOU, HONEY?
DON'T LET HER CLAW ME!

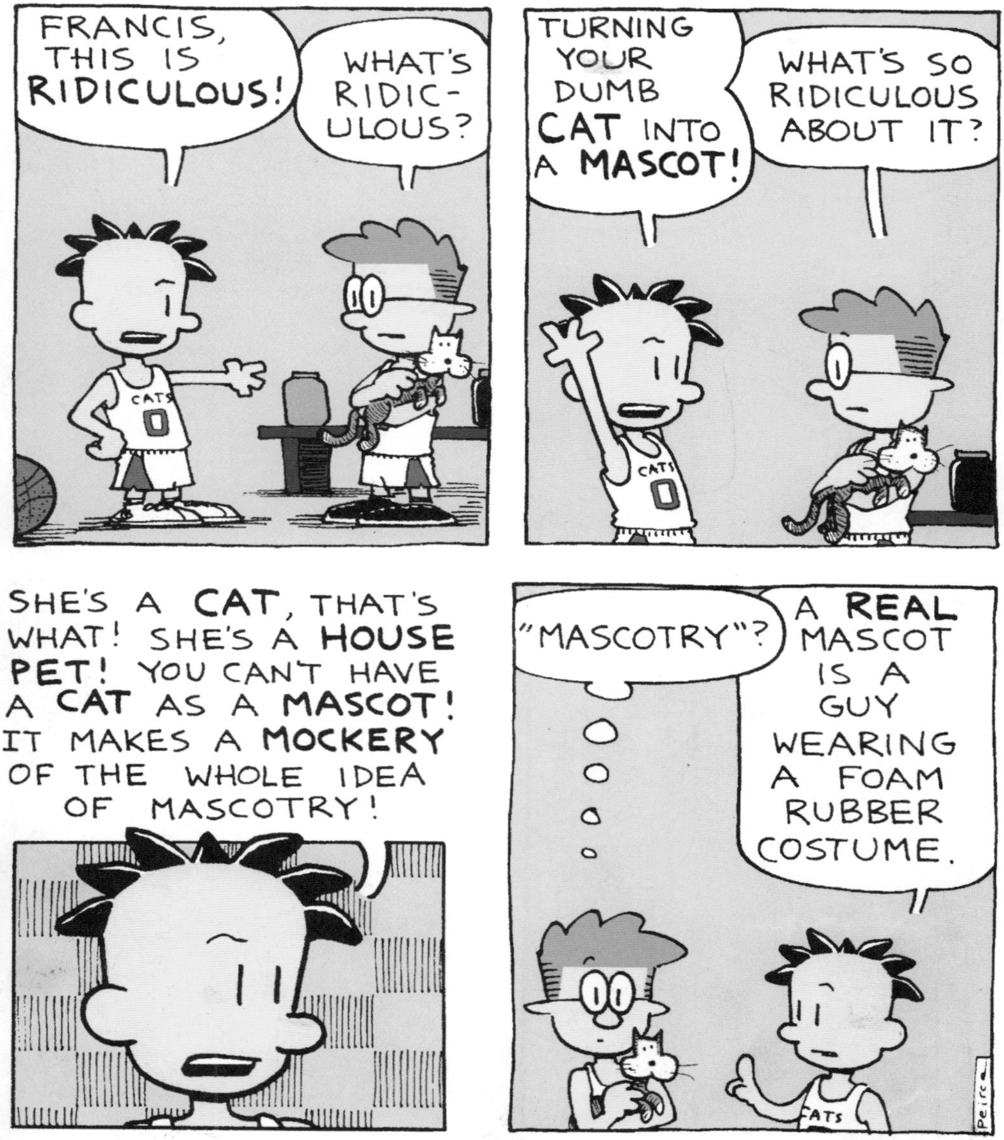
FRANCIS, THIS IS RIDICULOUS!
WHAT'S RIDIC-ULOUS?
CATS 0
TURNING YOUR DUMB CAT INTO A MASCOT!
WHAT'S SO RIDICULOUS ABOUT IT?
CATS 0
SHE'S A CAT, THAT'S WHAT! SHE'S A HOUSE PET! YOU CAN'T HAVE A CAT AS A MASCOT! IT MAKES A MOCKERY OF THE WHOLE IDEA OF MASCOTRY!
"MASCOTRY"?
A REAL MASCOT IS A GUY WEARING A FOAM RUBBER COSTUME.
CATS
Peirce

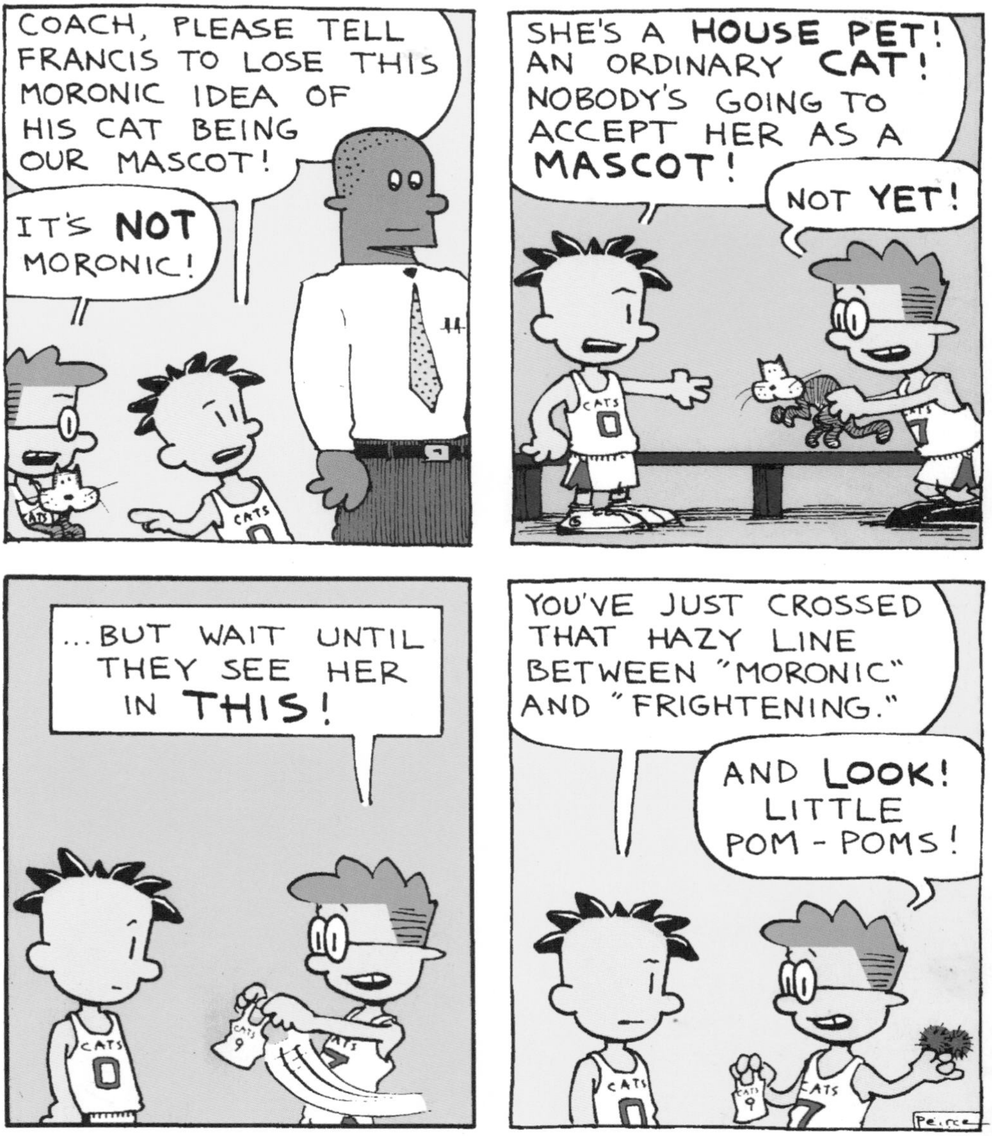
COACH, PLEASE TELL FRANCIS TO LOSE THIS MORONIC IDEA OF HIS CAT BEING OUR MASCOT!
IT'S **NOT** MORONIC!
SHE'S A **HOUSE PET**! AN ORDINARY **CAT**! NOBODY'S GOING TO ACCEPT HER AS A **MASCOT**!
NOT **YET**!
...BUT WAIT UNTIL THEY SEE HER IN **THIS**!
YOU'VE JUST CROSSED THAT HAZY LINE BETWEEN "MORONIC" AND "FRIGHTENING."
AND **LOOK**! LITTLE POM-POMS!
Peirce

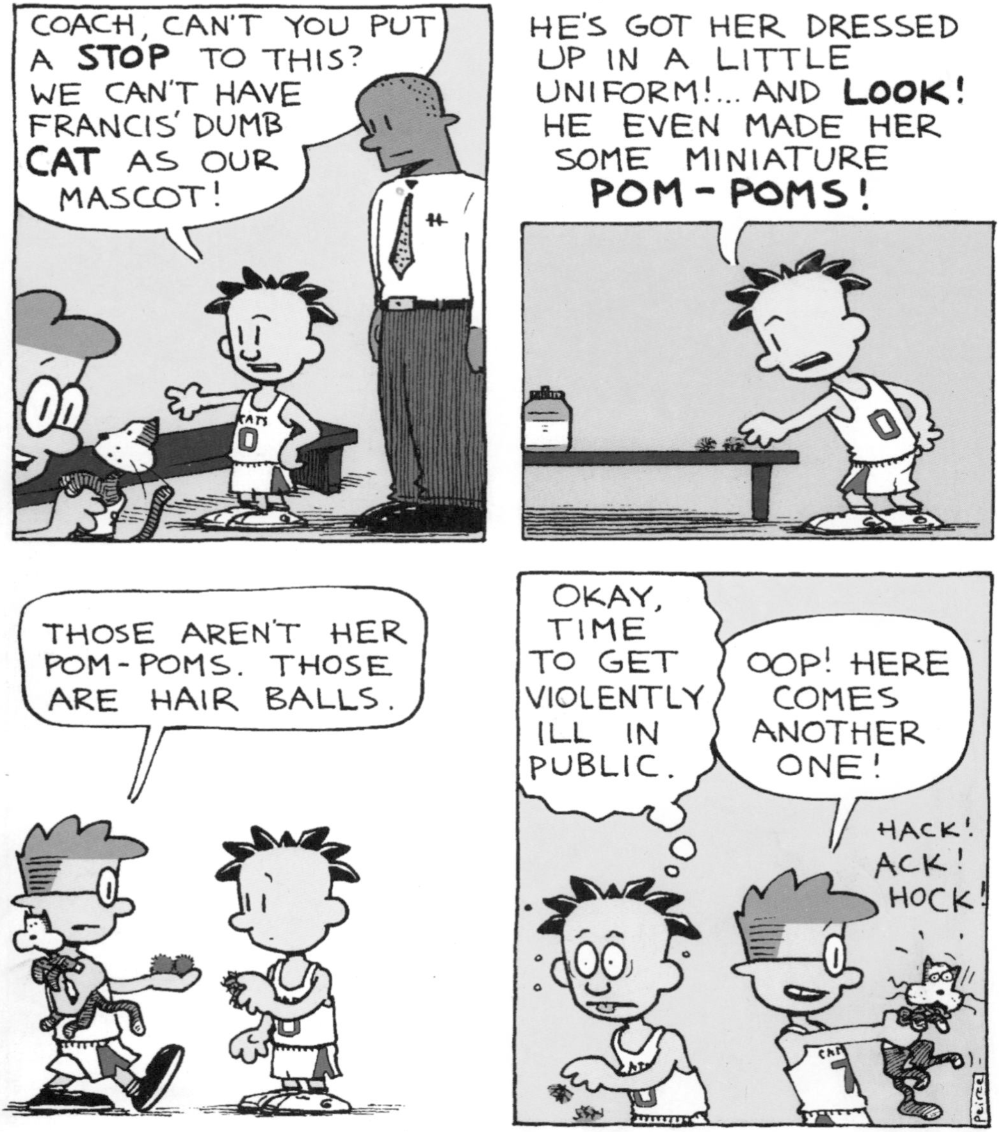
COACH, CAN'T YOU PUT A STOP TO THIS? WE CAN'T HAVE FRANCIS' DUMB CAT AS OUR MASCOT!
HE'S GOT HER DRESSED UP IN A LITTLE UNIFORM!... AND LOOK! HE EVEN MADE HER SOME MINIATURE POM-POMS!
THOSE AREN'T HER POM-POMS. THOSE ARE HAIR BALLS.
OKAY, TIME TO GET VIOLENTLY ILL IN PUBLIC.
OOP! HERE COMES ANOTHER ONE!
HACK! ACK! HOCK!
PEIRCE

FRANCIS!
ZING!
THUD!
MROWR!
PICKLES!
YOU DID THAT ON PURPOSE!
DID NOT!
I WONDER IF THIS EVER HAPPENED TO MIKE KRZYZEWSKI.

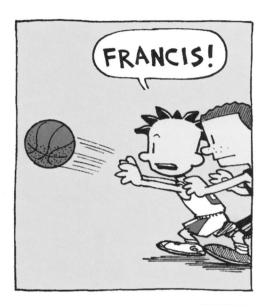

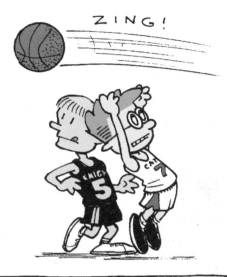

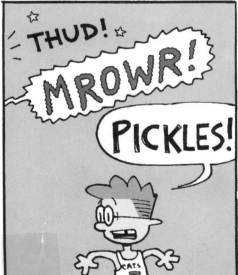

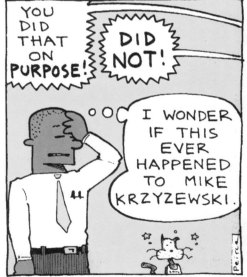

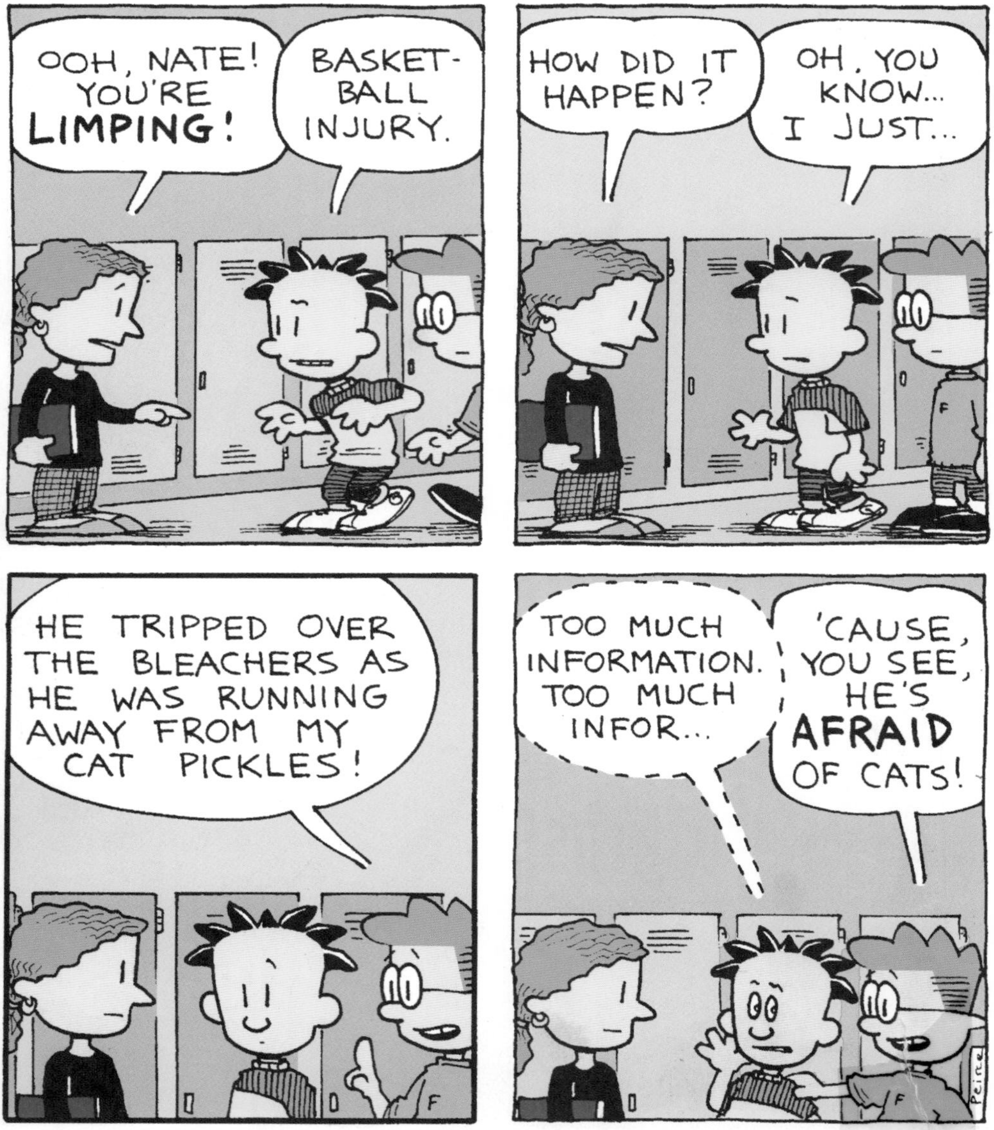
OOH, NATE! YOU'RE LIMPING!
BASKET-BALL INJURY.
HOW DID IT HAPPEN?
OH, YOU KNOW... I JUST...
HE TRIPPED OVER THE BLEACHERS AS HE WAS RUNNING AWAY FROM MY CAT PICKLES!
TOO MUCH INFORMATION. TOO MUCH INFOR...
'CAUSE, YOU SEE, HE'S AFRAID OF CATS!
Peirce

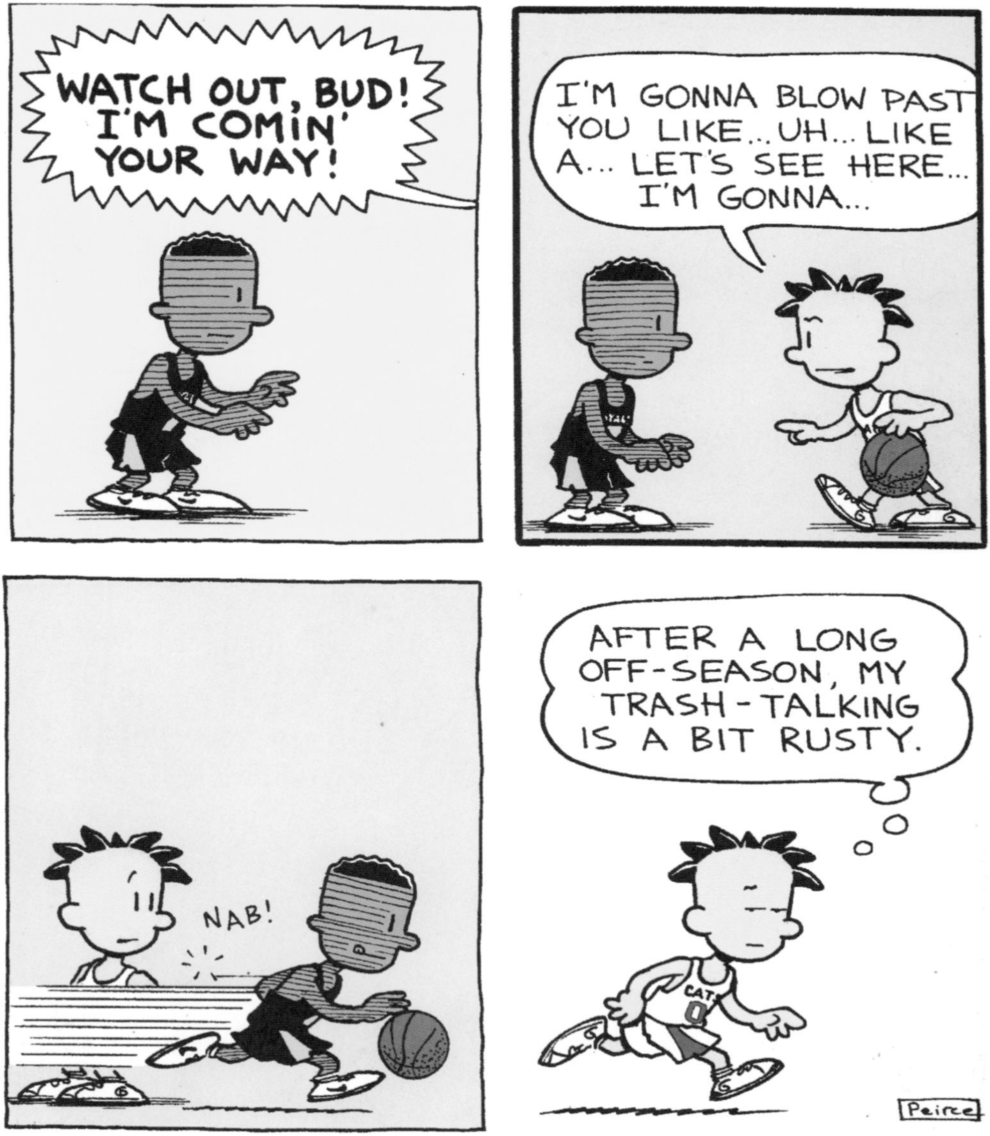
WATCH OUT, BUD! I'M COMIN' YOUR WAY!
I'M GONNA BLOW PAST YOU LIKE... UH... LIKE A... LET'S SEE HERE... I'M GONNA...
NAB!
AFTER A LONG OFF-SEASON, MY TRASH-TALKING IS A BIT RUSTY.
Peirce

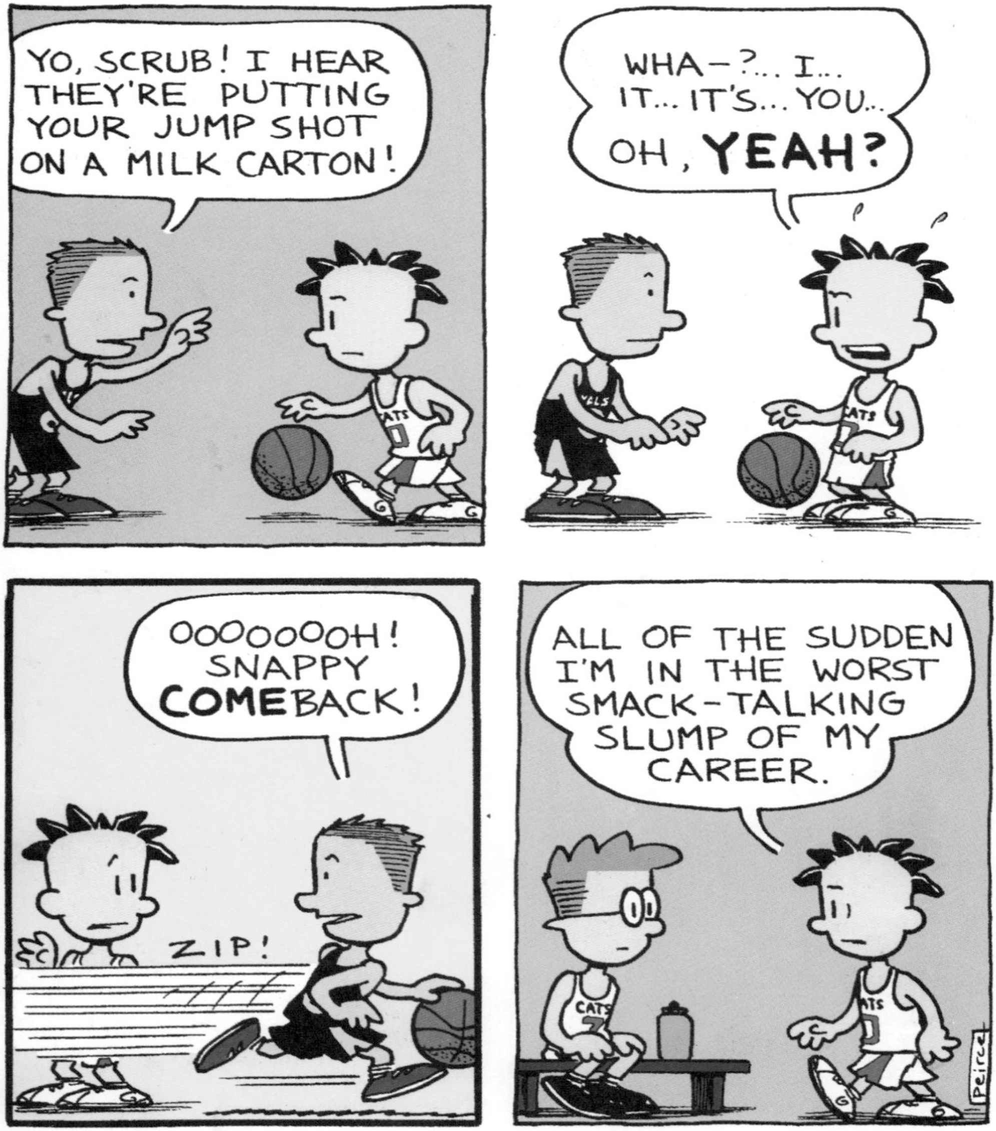
YO, SCRUB! I HEAR THEY'RE PUTTING YOUR JUMP SHOT ON A MILK CARTON!
WHA-?... I... IT... IT'S... YOU... OH, **YEAH?**
OOOOOOOOH! SNAPPY **COME**BACK!
ZIP!
ALL OF THE SUDDEN I'M IN THE WORST SMACK-TALKING SLUMP OF MY CAREER.
peirce

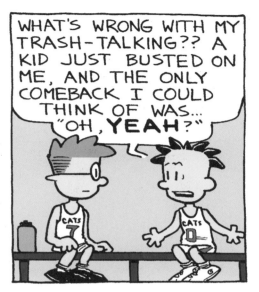

WHAT'S WRONG WITH MY TRASH-TALKING?? A KID JUST BUSTED ON ME, AND THE ONLY COMEBACK I COULD THINK OF WAS... "OH, YEAH?"
CATS 7
CATS 0
MY MIND IS A BLANK OUT THERE!
BUT AT LEAST YOU CAN STILL PLAY, RIGHT?
CATS 7
CATS 0
I CAN'T PLAY BALL WITHOUT TALKING SMACK! THAT'S LIKE SAMSON WITHOUT HIS HAIR! POPEYE WITHOUT HIS SPINACH! MOE AND LARRY WITHOUT CURLY!
SOONER OR LATER, IT ALWAYS COMES BACK TO THE THREE STOOGES.
I LIKE SHEMP!
CATS 7
CATS 13
Peirce

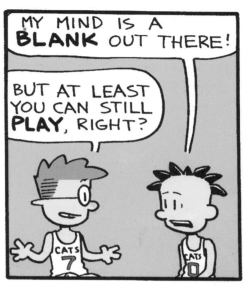

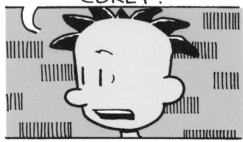

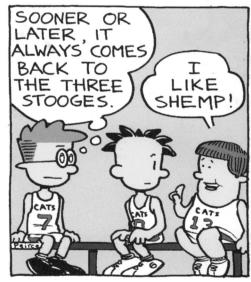

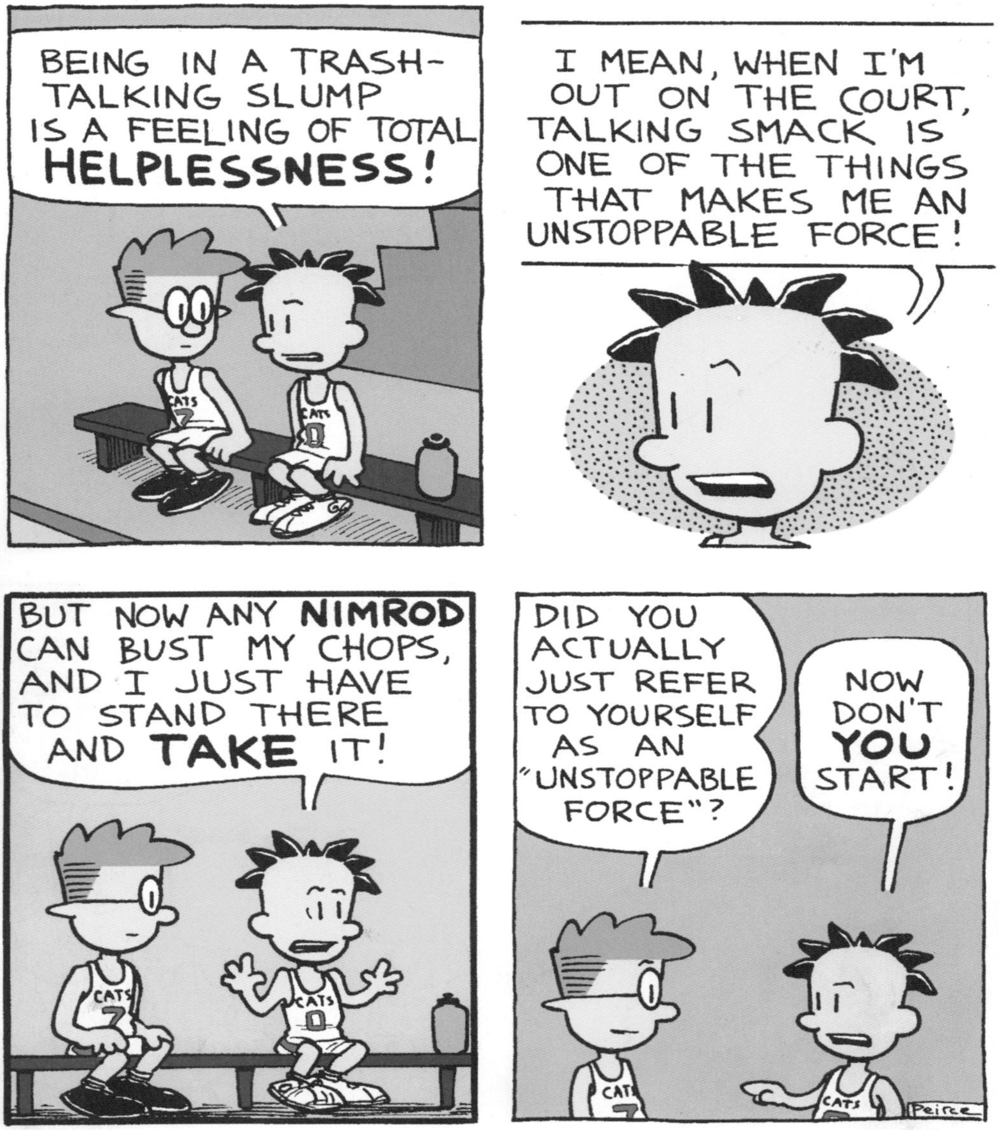
BEING IN A TRASH-TALKING SLUMP IS A FEELING OF TOTAL **HELPLESSNESS!**
CATS 7
CATS 0
I MEAN, WHEN I'M OUT ON THE COURT, TALKING SMACK IS ONE OF THE THINGS THAT MAKES ME AN UNSTOPPABLE FORCE!
BUT NOW ANY **NIMROD** CAN BUST MY CHOPS, AND I JUST HAVE TO STAND THERE AND **TAKE** IT!
CATS 7
CATS 0
DID YOU ACTUALLY JUST REFER TO YOURSELF AS AN "UNSTOPPABLE FORCE"?
NOW DON'T **YOU** START!
CATS
CATS
Peirce

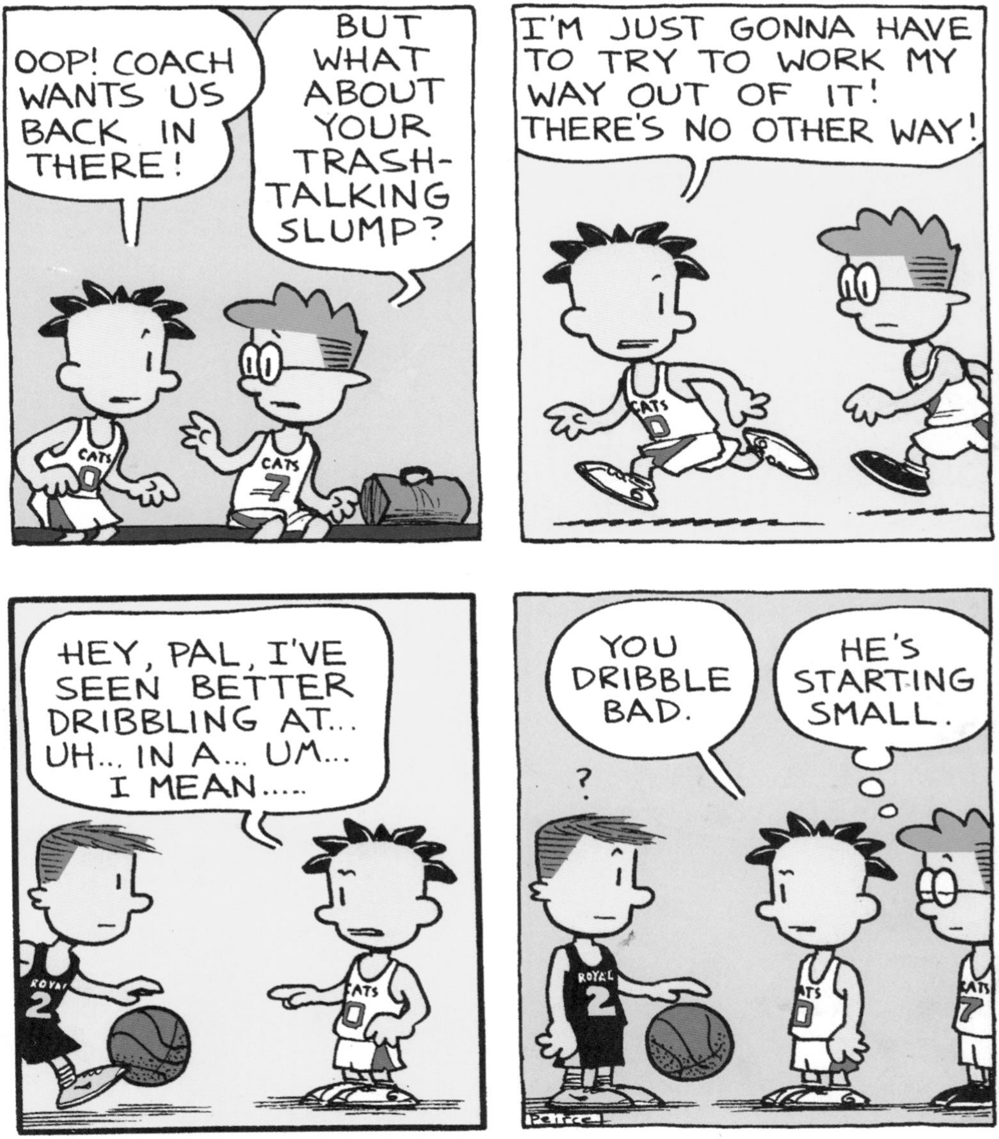
OOP! COACH WANTS US BACK IN THERE!
BUT WHAT ABOUT YOUR TRASH-TALKING SLUMP?
I'M JUST GONNA HAVE TO TRY TO WORK MY WAY OUT OF IT! THERE'S NO OTHER WAY!
HEY, PAL, I'VE SEEN BETTER DRIBBLING AT... UH... IN A... UM... I MEAN.....
?
YOU DRIBBLE BAD.
HE'S STARTING SMALL.

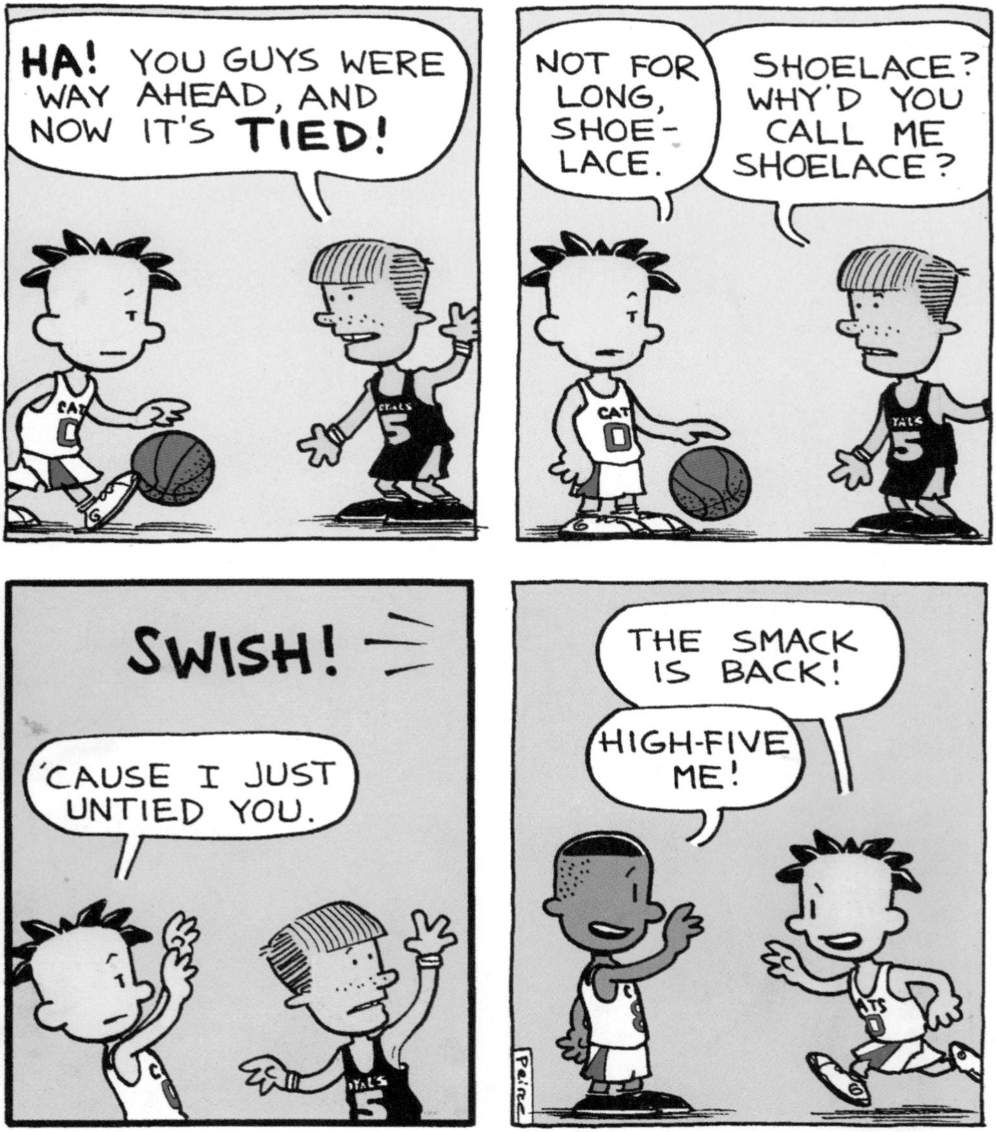
HA! YOU GUYS WERE WAY AHEAD, AND NOW IT'S TIED!
NOT FOR LONG, SHOE-LACE.
SHOELACE? WHY'D YOU CALL ME SHOELACE?
SWISH!
'CAUSE I JUST UNTIED YOU.
THE SMACK IS BACK!
HIGH-FIVE ME!
Peirce

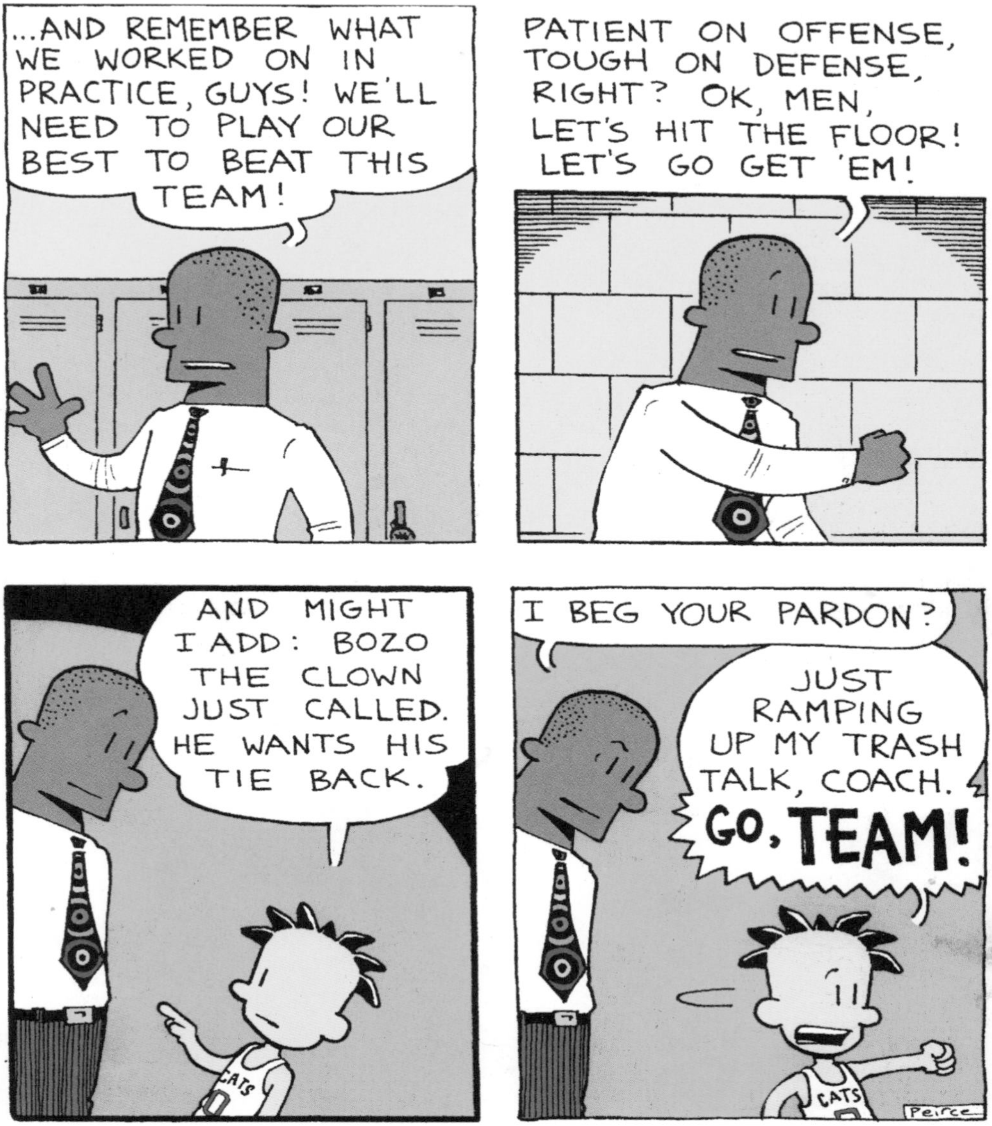
...AND REMEMBER WHAT WE WORKED ON IN PRACTICE, GUYS! WE'LL NEED TO PLAY OUR BEST TO BEAT THIS TEAM!
PATIENT ON OFFENSE, TOUGH ON DEFENSE, RIGHT? OK, MEN, LET'S HIT THE FLOOR! LET'S GO GET 'EM!
AND MIGHT I ADD: BOZO THE CLOWN JUST CALLED. HE WANTS HIS TIE BACK.
I BEG YOUR PARDON?
JUST RAMPING UP MY TRASH TALK, COACH.
GO, TEAM!
CATS
CATS
Peirce

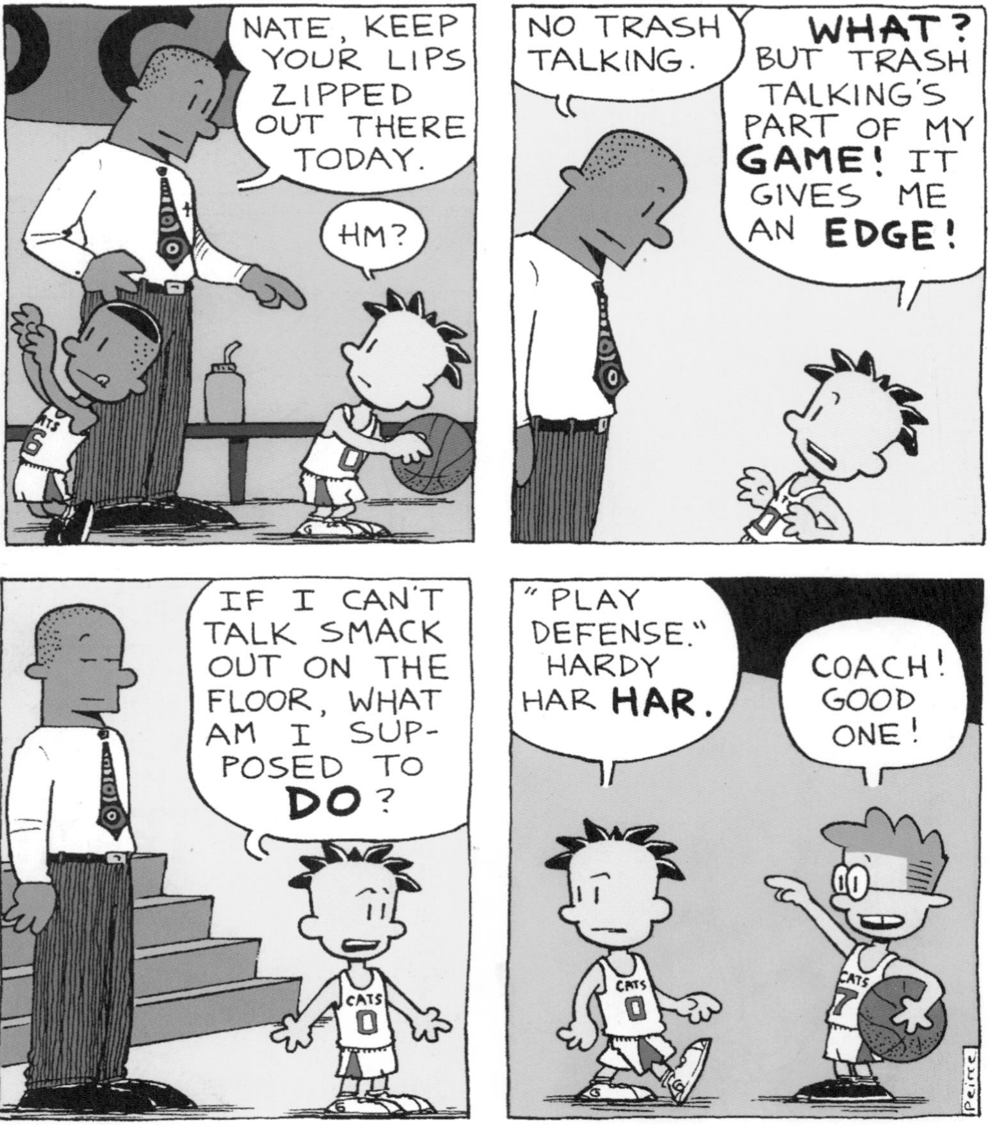
NATE, KEEP YOUR LIPS ZIPPED OUT THERE TODAY.
HM?
NO TRASH TALKING.
WHAT? BUT TRASH TALKING'S PART OF MY **GAME!** IT GIVES ME AN **EDGE!**
IF I CAN'T TALK SMACK OUT ON THE FLOOR, WHAT AM I SUP-POSED TO **DO**?
"PLAY DEFENSE." HARDY HAR **HAR**.
COACH! GOOD ONE!
Peirce

NATE, THE GAME'S ABOUT TO START! WHAT ON EARTH ARE YOU DOING?

JUST MAKING SOME CARDS, COACH.

YOU WON'T LET ME TRASH-TALK, SO DURING THE GAME I'M GOING TO HAND OUT SOME OF **THESE**!

"IS THAT YOUR MOM OVER THERE, OR HAS GOODYEAR COME OUT WITH A FLESH-COLORED BLIMP?"

✷ CHORTLE! ✷ THAT'S A GOODY!

RRRIP

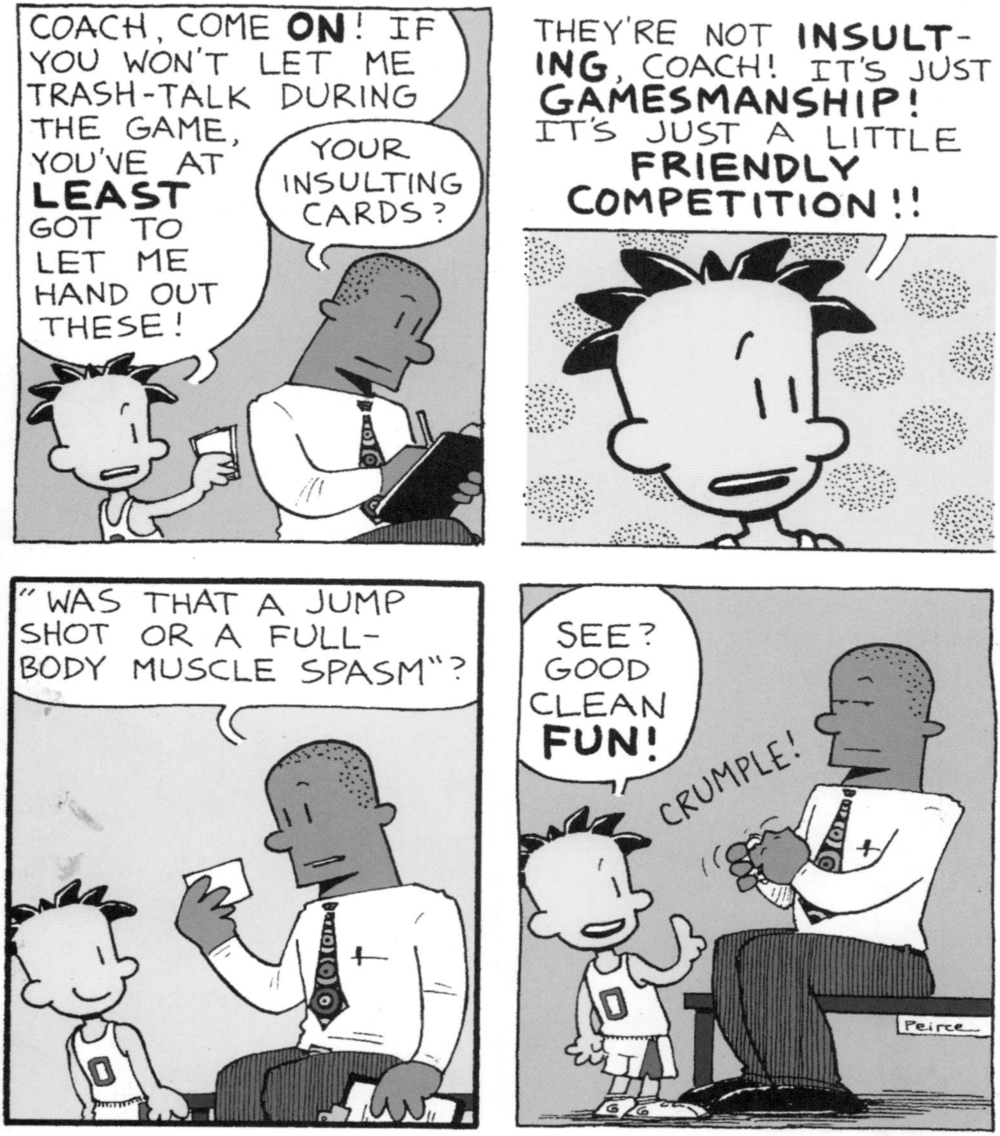
COACH, COME **ON**! IF YOU WON'T LET ME TRASH-TALK DURING THE GAME, YOU'VE AT **LEAST** GOT TO LET ME HAND OUT THESE!
YOUR INSULTING CARDS?
THEY'RE NOT **INSULTING**, COACH! IT'S JUST **GAMESMANSHIP!** IT'S JUST A LITTLE **FRIENDLY COMPETITION!!**
"WAS THAT A JUMP SHOT OR A FULL-BODY MUSCLE SPASM"?
SEE? GOOD CLEAN **FUN!**
CRUMPLE!
Peirce

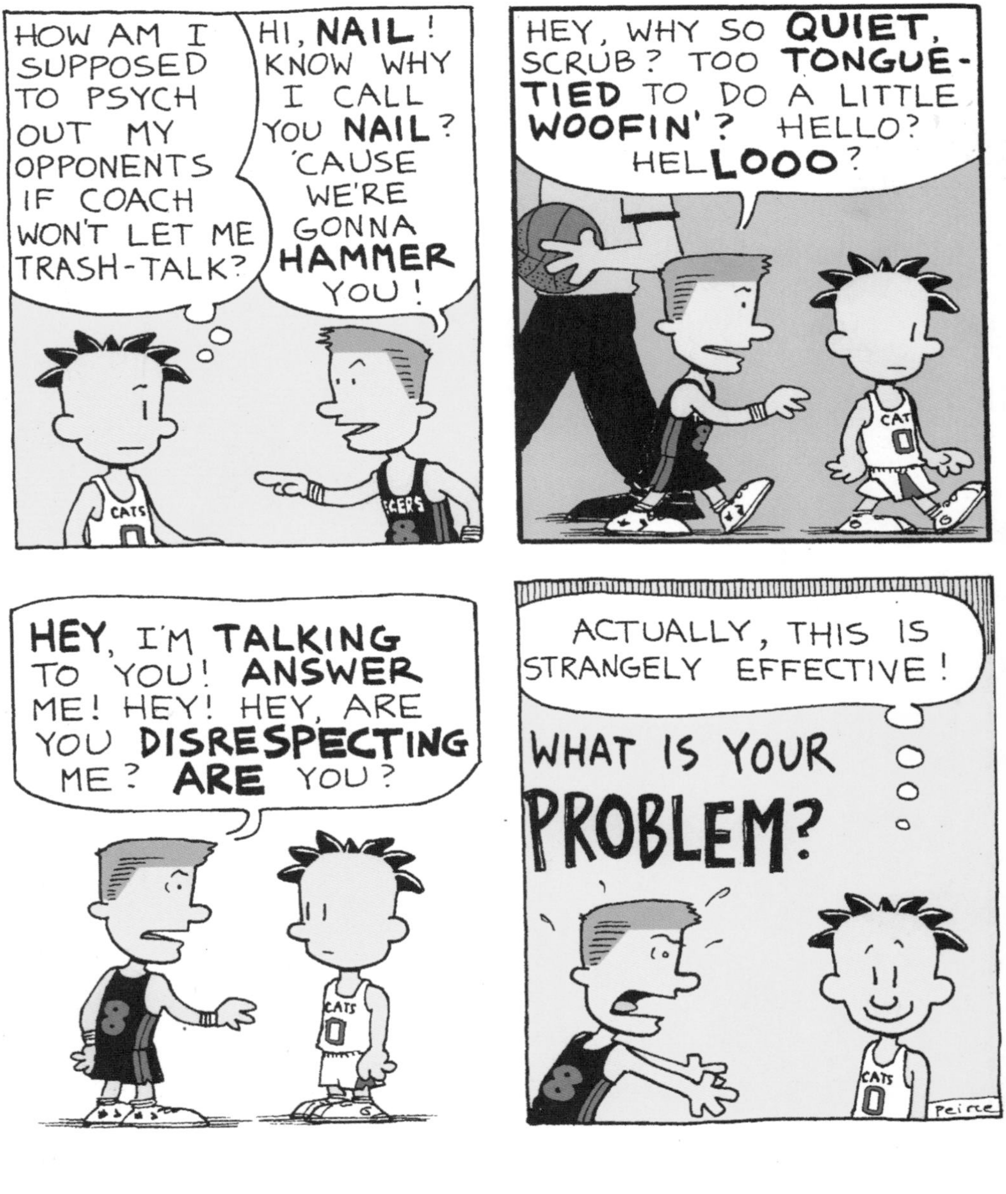
HOW AM I SUPPOSED TO PSYCH OUT MY OPPONENTS IF COACH WON'T LET ME TRASH-TALK?
HI, **NAIL**! KNOW WHY I CALL YOU **NAIL**? 'CAUSE WE'RE GONNA **HAMMER** YOU!
CATS
HEY, WHY SO **QUIET**, SCRUB? TOO **TONGUE-TIED** TO DO A LITTLE **WOOFIN'**? HELLO? HEL**LOOO**?
HEY, I'M **TALKING** TO YOU! **ANSWER** ME! HEY! HEY, ARE YOU **DISRESPECTING** ME? **ARE** YOU?
CATS
ACTUALLY, THIS IS STRANGELY EFFECTIVE!
WHAT IS YOUR **PROBLEM?**
CATS
Peirce

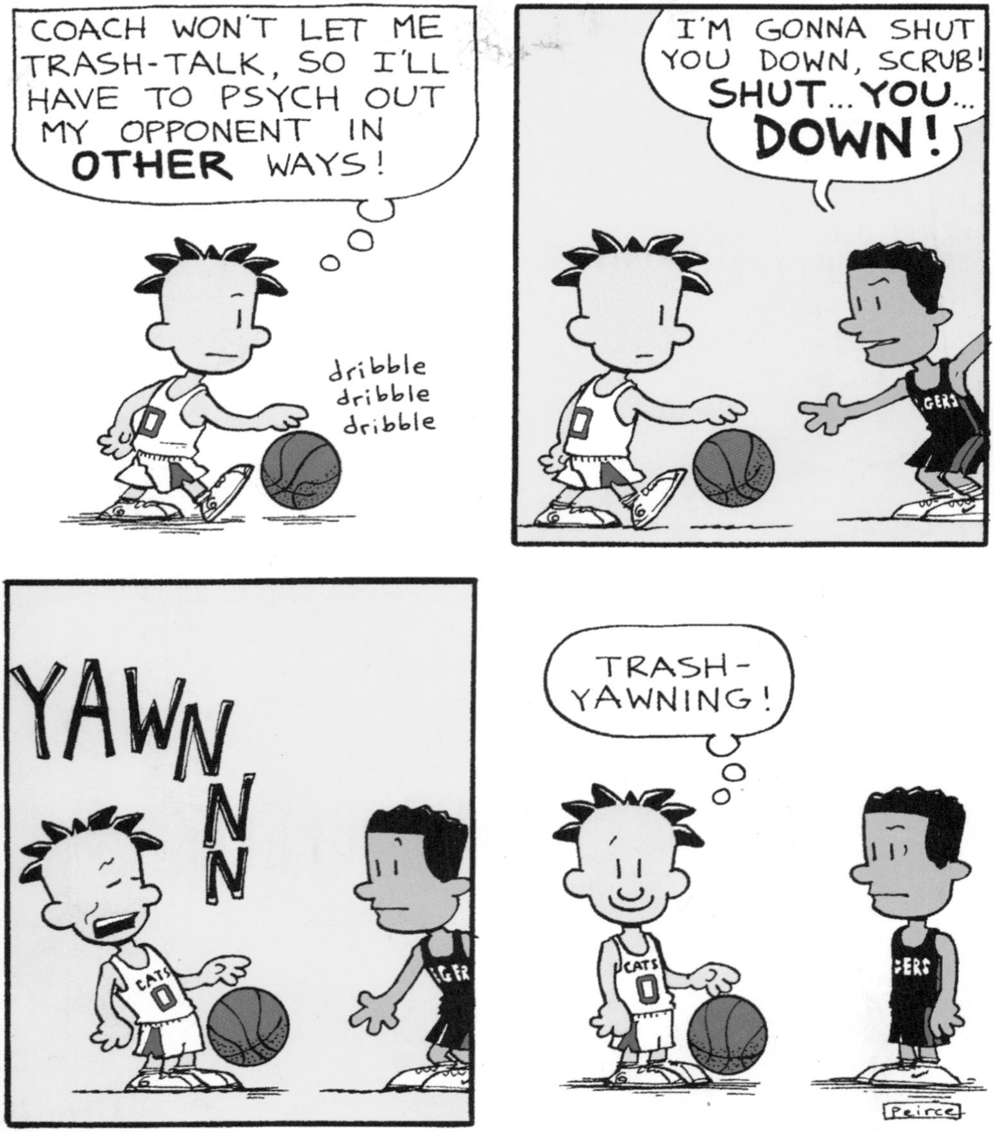
COACH WON'T LET ME TRASH-TALK, SO I'LL HAVE TO PSYCH OUT MY OPPONENT IN **OTHER** WAYS!
dribble dribble dribble
I'M GONNA SHUT YOU DOWN, SCRUB! **SHUT... YOU... DOWN!**
YAWNNNN
TRASH-YAWNING!
Peirce

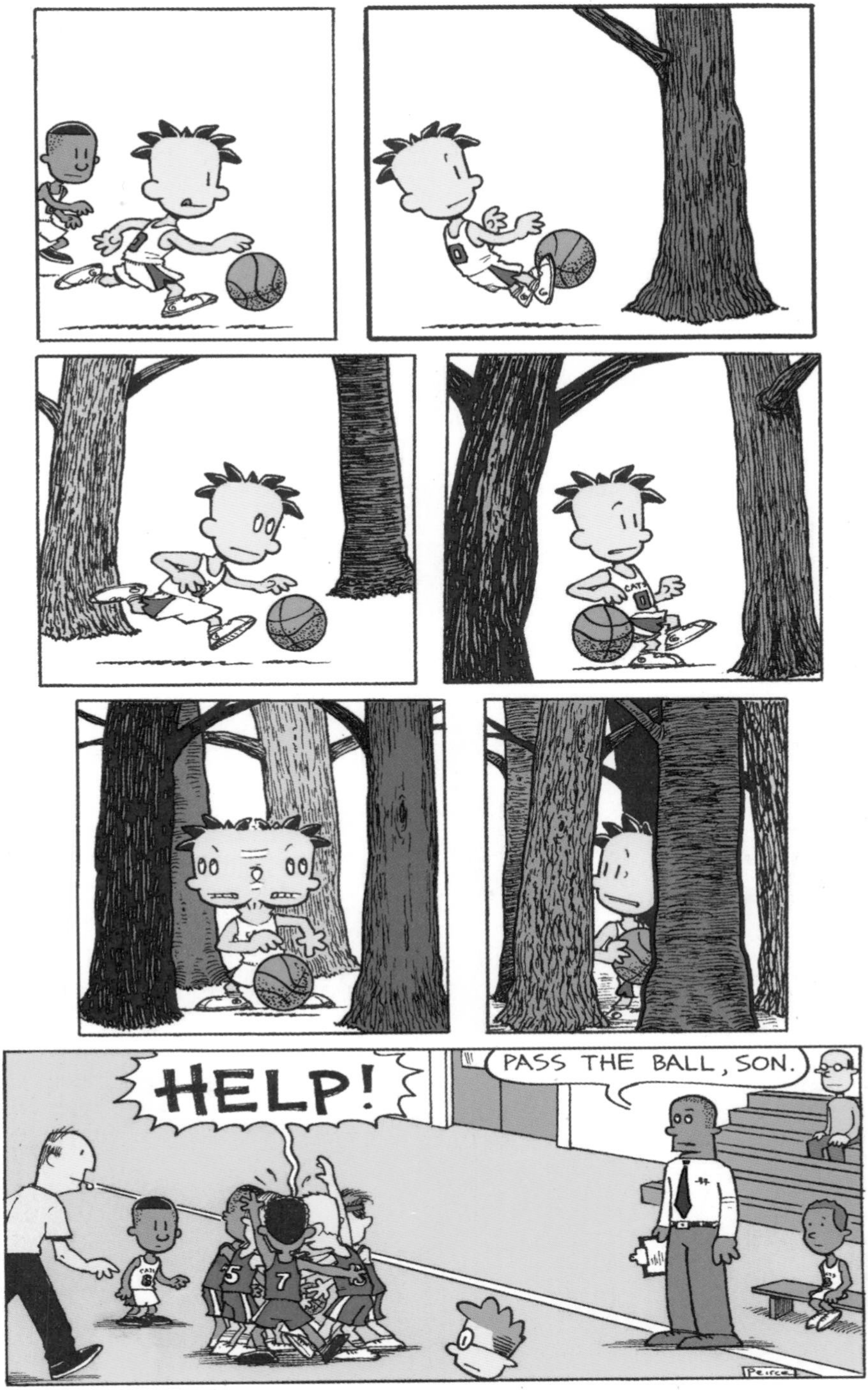
HELP!
PASS THE BALL, SON.

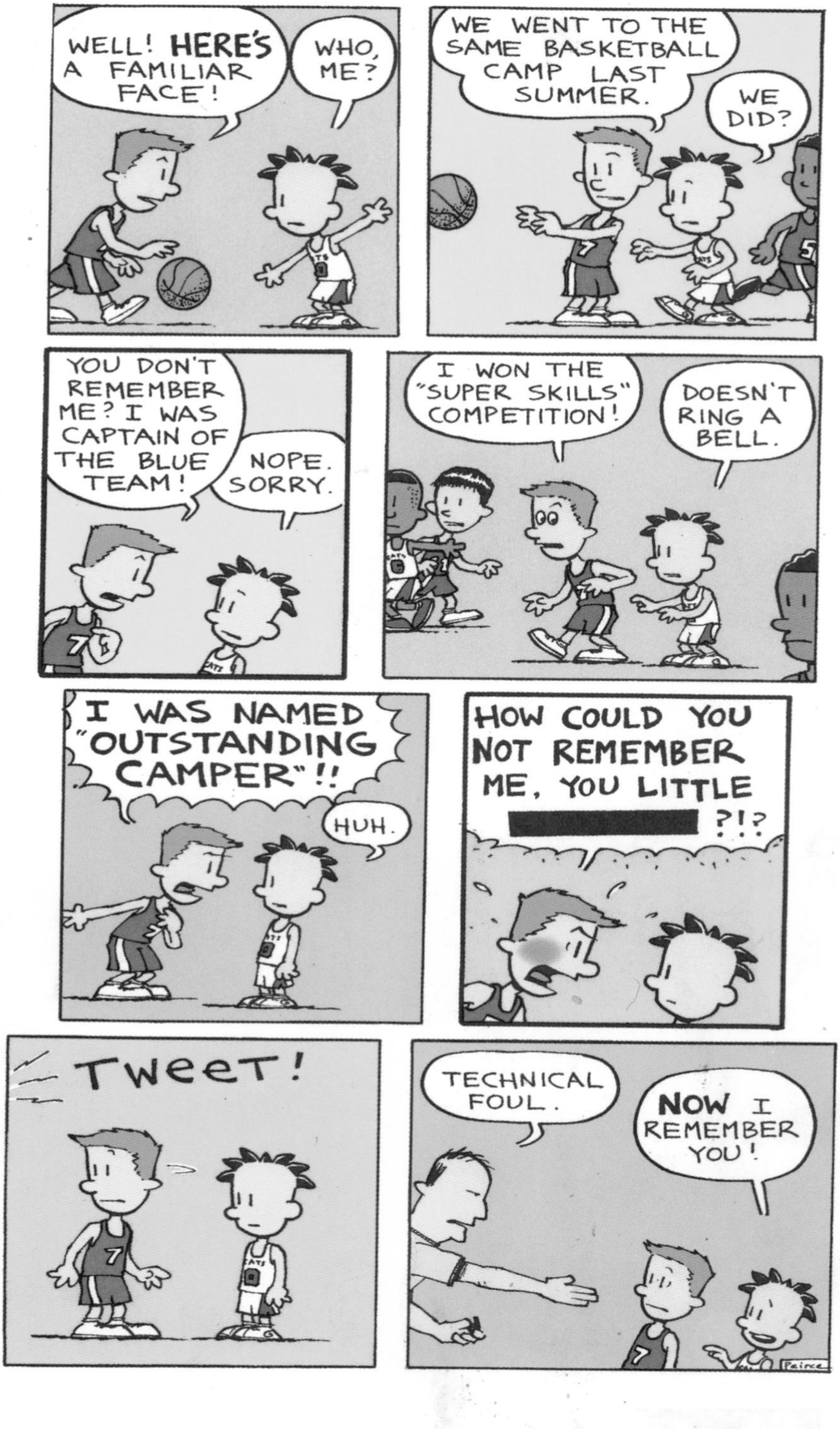
WELL! HERE'S A FAMILIAR FACE!
WHO, ME?
WE WENT TO THE SAME BASKETBALL CAMP LAST SUMMER.
WE DID?
YOU DON'T REMEMBER ME? I WAS CAPTAIN OF THE BLUE TEAM!
NOPE. SORRY.
I WON THE "SUPER SKILLS" COMPETITION!
DOESN'T RING A BELL.
I WAS NAMED "OUTSTANDING CAMPER"!!
HUH.
HOW COULD YOU NOT REMEMBER ME, YOU LITTLE [redacted] ?!?
TWEET!
TECHNICAL FOUL.
NOW I REMEMBER YOU!
Peirce

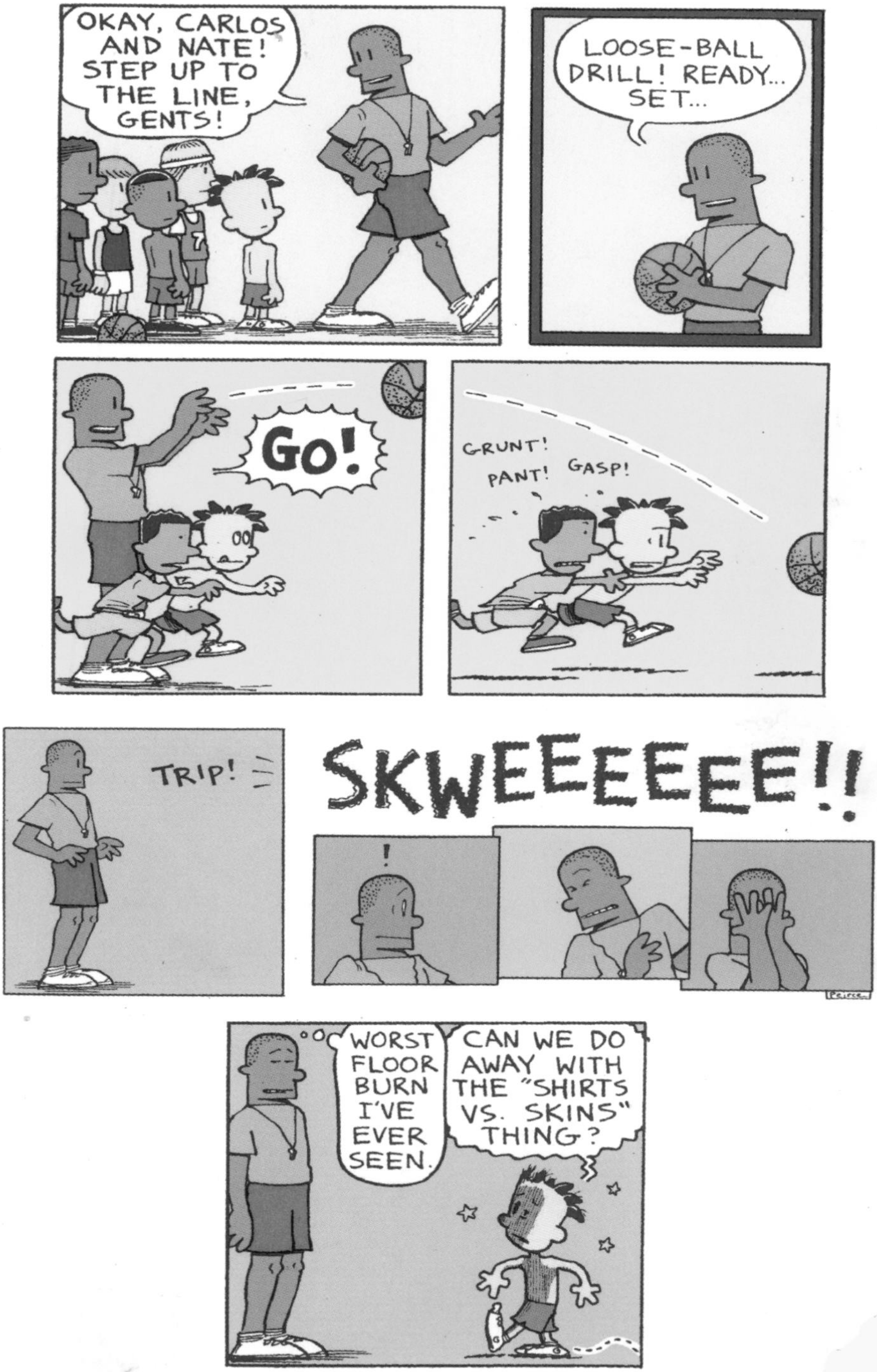
OKAY, CARLOS AND NATE! STEP UP TO THE LINE, GENTS!
LOOSE-BALL DRILL! READY... SET...
GO!
GRUNT!
PANT!
GASP!
TRIP!
SKWEEEEEEE!!
!
WORST FLOOR BURN I'VE EVER SEEN.
CAN WE DO AWAY WITH THE "SHIRTS VS. SKINS" THING?

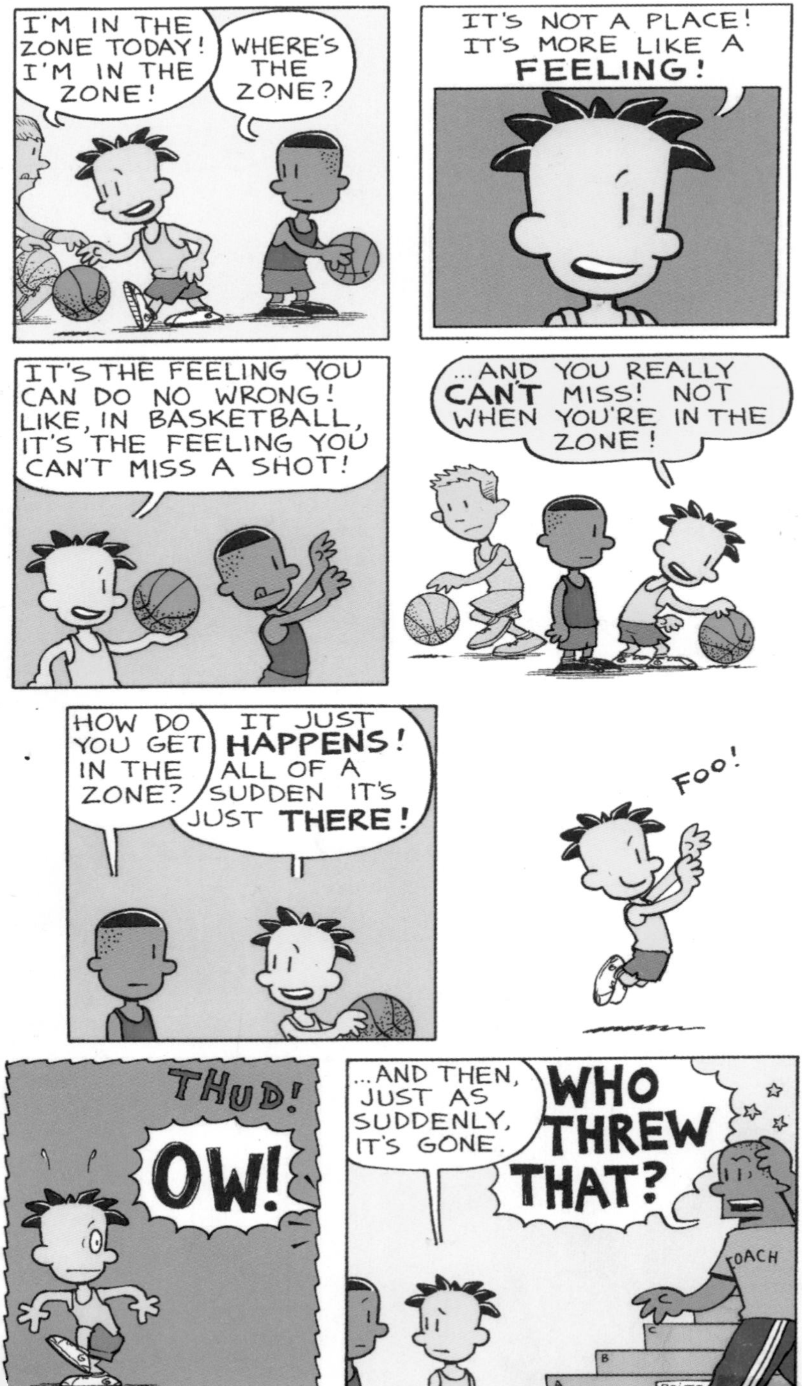
I'M IN THE ZONE TODAY! I'M IN THE ZONE!
WHERE'S THE ZONE?
IT'S NOT A PLACE! IT'S MORE LIKE A **FEELING!**
IT'S THE FEELING YOU CAN DO NO WRONG! LIKE, IN BASKETBALL, IT'S THE FEELING YOU CAN'T MISS A SHOT!
...AND YOU REALLY **CAN'T** MISS! NOT WHEN YOU'RE IN THE ZONE!
HOW DO YOU GET IN THE ZONE?
IT JUST **HAPPENS!** ALL OF A SUDDEN IT'S JUST **THERE!**
FOO!
THUD!
OW!
...AND THEN, JUST AS SUDDENLY, IT'S GONE.
WHO THREW THAT?
OACH
Peirce

NOBODY THINKS WE'LL BE ANY GOOD THIS SEASON, COACH, BUT I THINK WE'RE GONNA SURPRISE SOME PEOPLE!
WE COULD VERY WELL BE THE LEAGUE'S "SLEEPER" TEAM!
DRIBBA DRIBBA
FLING!
BONK!
OW!
THERE'S SLEEPING, AND THEN THERE'S COMA-TOSE.
SORRY, DUDE.
Peirce

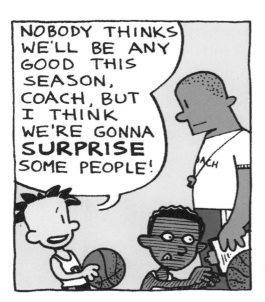

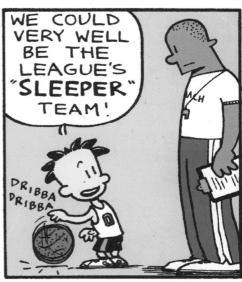

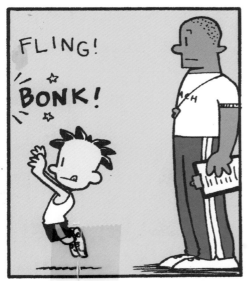

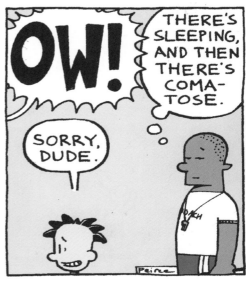

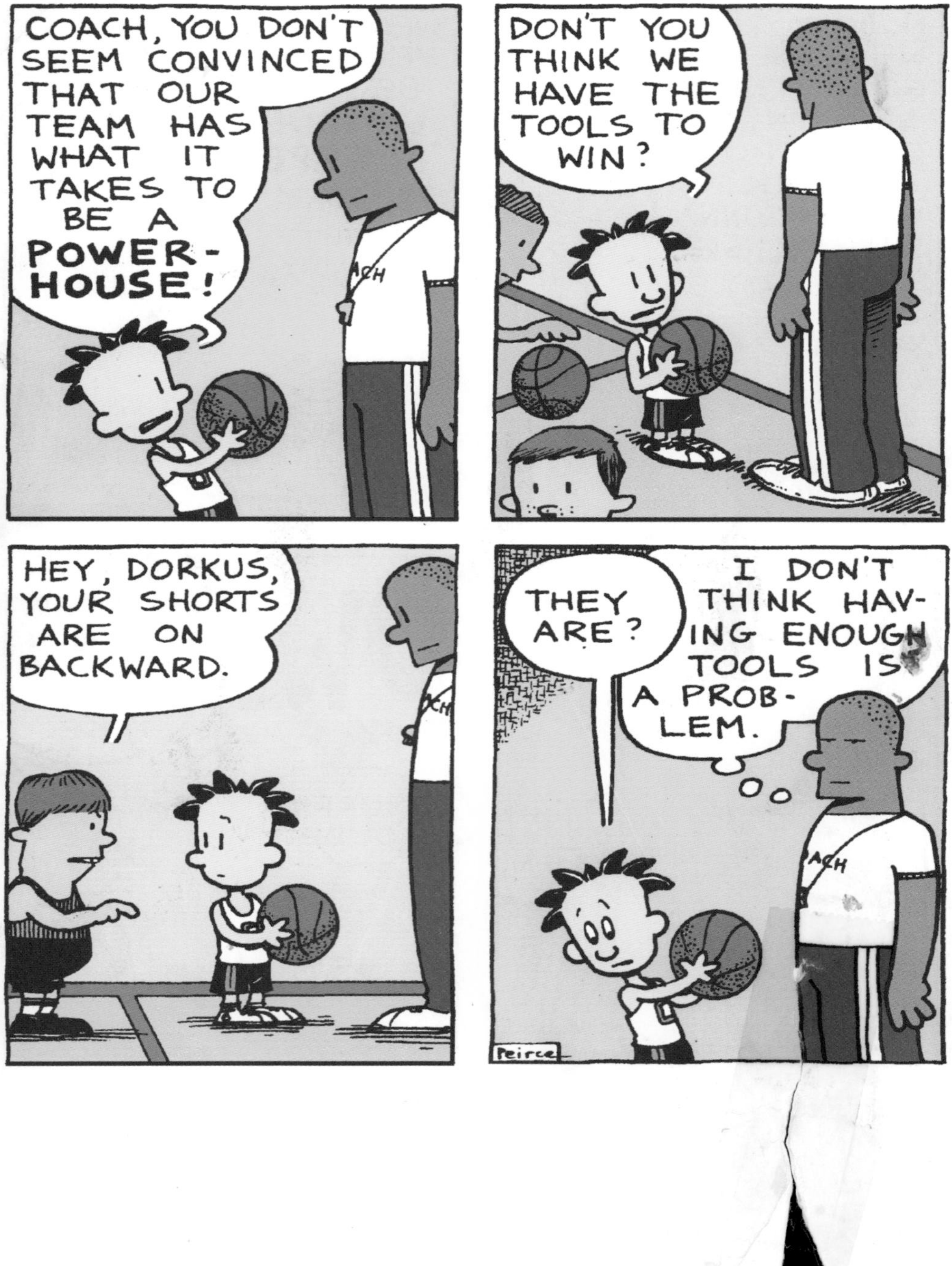
COACH, YOU DON'T SEEM CONVINCED THAT OUR TEAM HAS WHAT IT TAKES TO BE A **POWER-HOUSE!**
ACH
DON'T YOU THINK WE HAVE THE TOOLS TO WIN?
HEY, DORKUS, YOUR SHORTS ARE ON BACKWARD.
ACH
THEY ARE?
I DON'T THINK HAVING ENOUGH TOOLS IS A PROBLEM.
ACH
Peirce

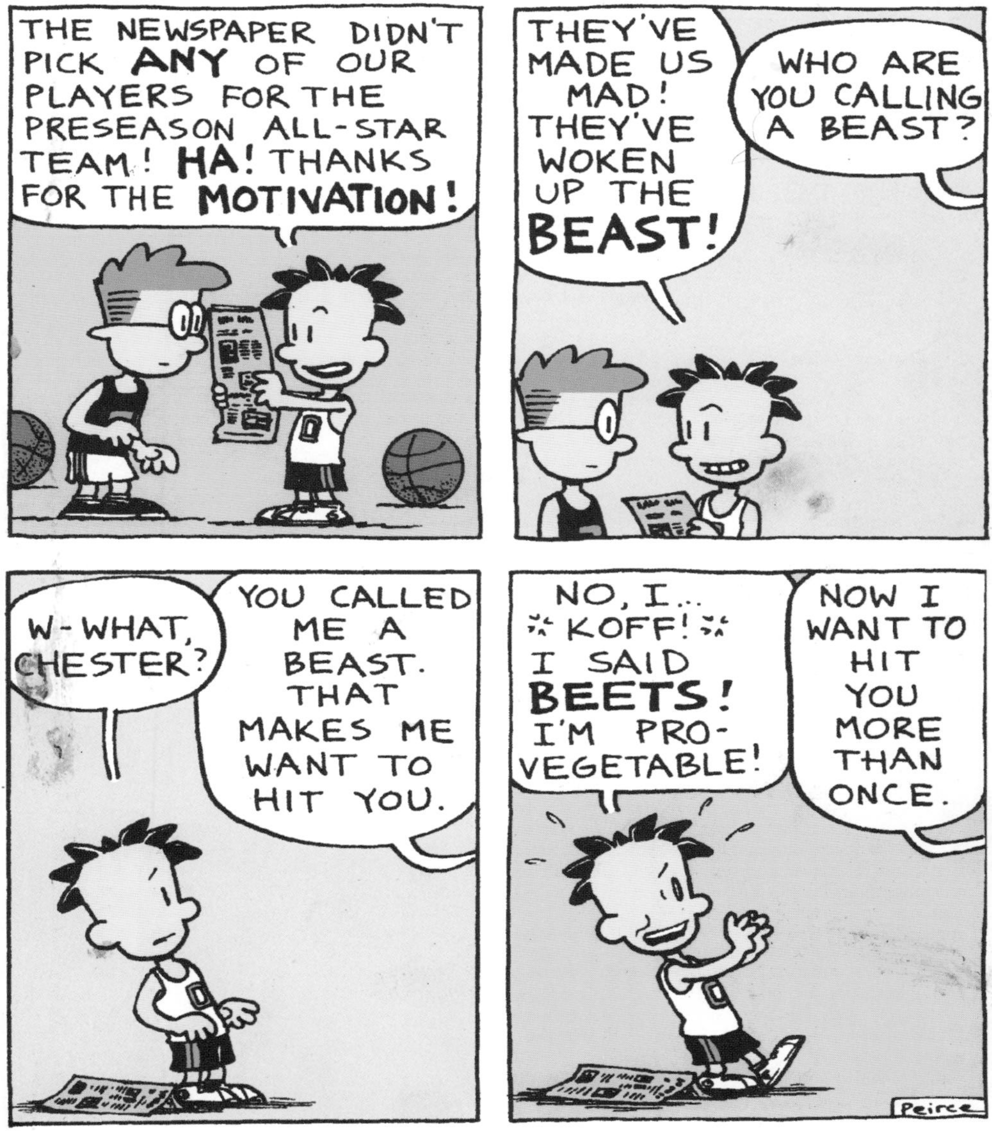
THE NEWSPAPER DIDN'T PICK ANY OF OUR PLAYERS FOR THE PRESEASON ALL-STAR TEAM! HA! THANKS FOR THE MOTIVATION!
THEY'VE MADE US MAD! THEY'VE WOKEN UP THE BEAST!
WHO ARE YOU CALLING A BEAST?
W-WHAT, CHESTER?
YOU CALLED ME A BEAST. THAT MAKES ME WANT TO HIT YOU.
NO, I... KOFF! I SAID BEETS! I'M PRO-VEGETABLE!
NOW I WANT TO HIT YOU MORE THAN ONCE.
Peirce

CHESTER, IF YOU WANT TO IMPROVE THIS SEASON, YOU'VE GOT TO LEARN THE DIFFERENCE BETWEEN GOOD, HARD-NOSED DEFENSE AND A FOUL.
WHAT DO YOU MEAN?
NATE, TRY TO DRIVE THE LANE ON CHESTER.
UH... OKAY.
SLAM!
THAT WAS A FOUL, SON.
BUT HE'S NOT BLEED-ING.
Peirce

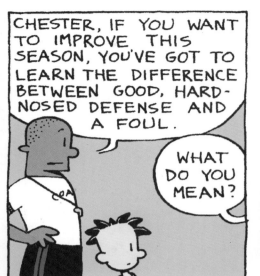

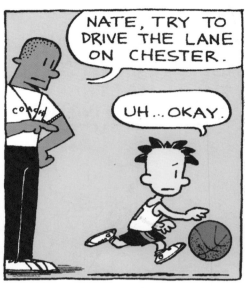

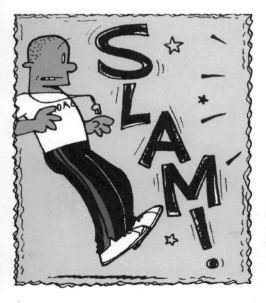

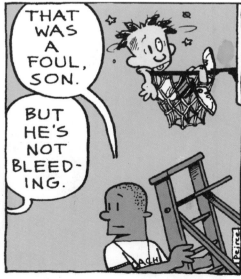

OKAY, GANG, WE'VE BEEN PRACTICING FOR TWO WEEKS, AND IT'S ALL BEEN LEADING UP TO **THIS**: OUR **FIRST GAME!**

UNFORTUNATELY, WE'RE PLAYING THE BEST TEAM IN THE STATE AND THEY'RE UNBEATEN IN SIX YEARS... BUT IT'LL BE A **GREAT** TEST FOR US!

TRY YOUR HARDEST, DO YOUR BEST... AND DON'T GET DISCOURAGED. KEEP YOUR HEADS UP, NO MATTER WHAT HAPPENS.

Peirce

MY ADRENAL GLANDS JUST COMPLETELY SHUT DOWN.

...AND HAVE **FUN** OUT THERE!

SORRY I'M LATE! WHAT DID I MISS?
OH, HEY DAD. IT'S HALF-TIME.
WELL, IT LOOKS LIKE QUITE A BATTLE! A DEFENSIVE STRUGGLE! 17 TO 12!
THE ONLY REASON IT SAYS "17" IS BECAUSE OUR SCORE-BOARD CAN'T DISPLAY 3-DIGIT NUMBERS.
SO IT'S... 170 TO 12?
NO, ONLY 117. THEY PUT IN THEIR SCRUBS.

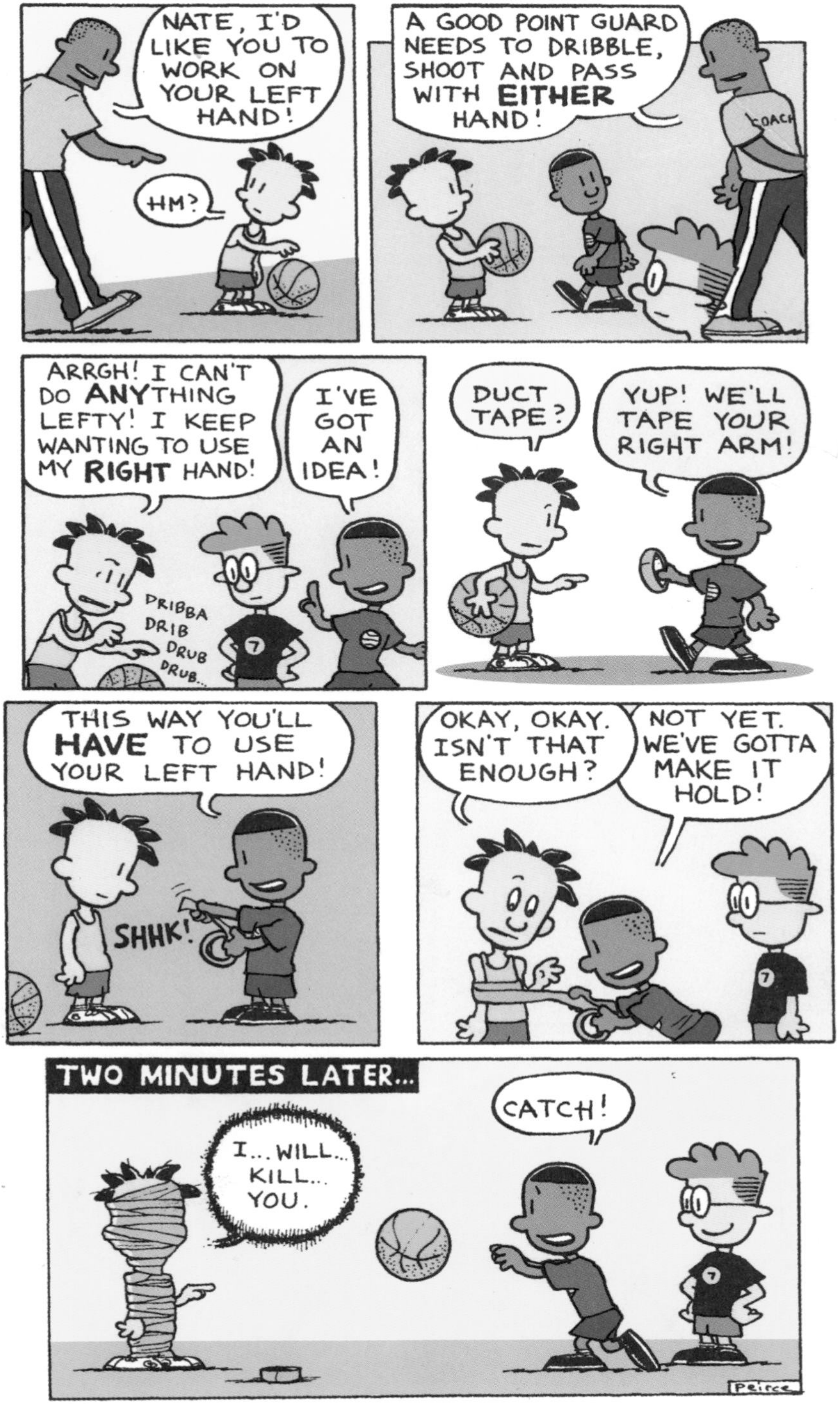
NATE, I'D LIKE YOU TO WORK ON YOUR LEFT HAND!
HM?
A GOOD POINT GUARD NEEDS TO DRIBBLE, SHOOT AND PASS WITH **EITHER** HAND!
COACH
ARRGH! I CAN'T DO **ANY**THING LEFTY! I KEEP WANTING TO USE MY **RIGHT** HAND!
I'VE GOT AN IDEA!
DRIBBA DRIB DRUB DRUB...
DUCT TAPE?
YUP! WE'LL TAPE YOUR RIGHT ARM!
THIS WAY YOU'LL **HAVE** TO USE YOUR LEFT HAND!
SHHK!
OKAY, OKAY. ISN'T THAT ENOUGH?
NOT YET. WE'VE GOTTA MAKE IT HOLD!
TWO MINUTES LATER...
I... WILL... KILL... YOU.
CATCH!
Peirce

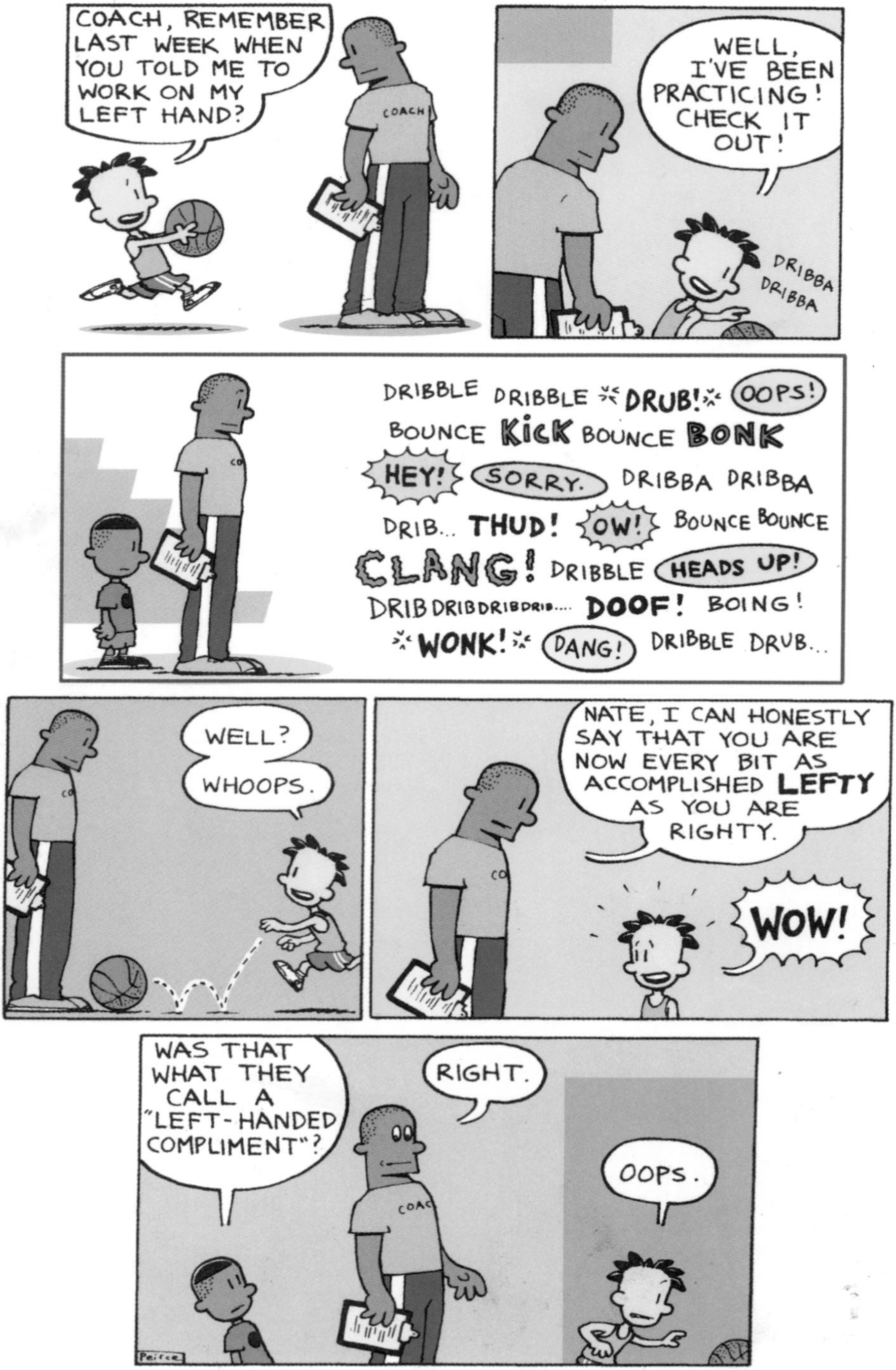
COACH, REMEMBER LAST WEEK WHEN YOU TOLD ME TO WORK ON MY LEFT HAND?
COACH
WELL, I'VE BEEN PRACTICING! CHECK IT OUT!
DRIBBA DRIBBA
DRIBBLE DRIBBLE DRUB! OOPS!
BOUNCE KICK BOUNCE BONK
HEY! SORRY. DRIBBA DRIBBA
DRIB... THUD! OW! BOUNCE BOUNCE
CLANG! DRIBBLE HEADS UP!
DRIB DRIB DRIB DRIB.... DOOF! BOING!
WONK! DANG! DRIBBLE DRUB...
WELL?
WHOOPS.
NATE, I CAN HONESTLY SAY THAT YOU ARE NOW EVERY BIT AS ACCOMPLISHED LEFTY AS YOU ARE RIGHTY.
WOW!
WAS THAT WHAT THEY CALL A "LEFT-HANDED COMPLIMENT"?
RIGHT.
OOPS.
COACH
Peirce

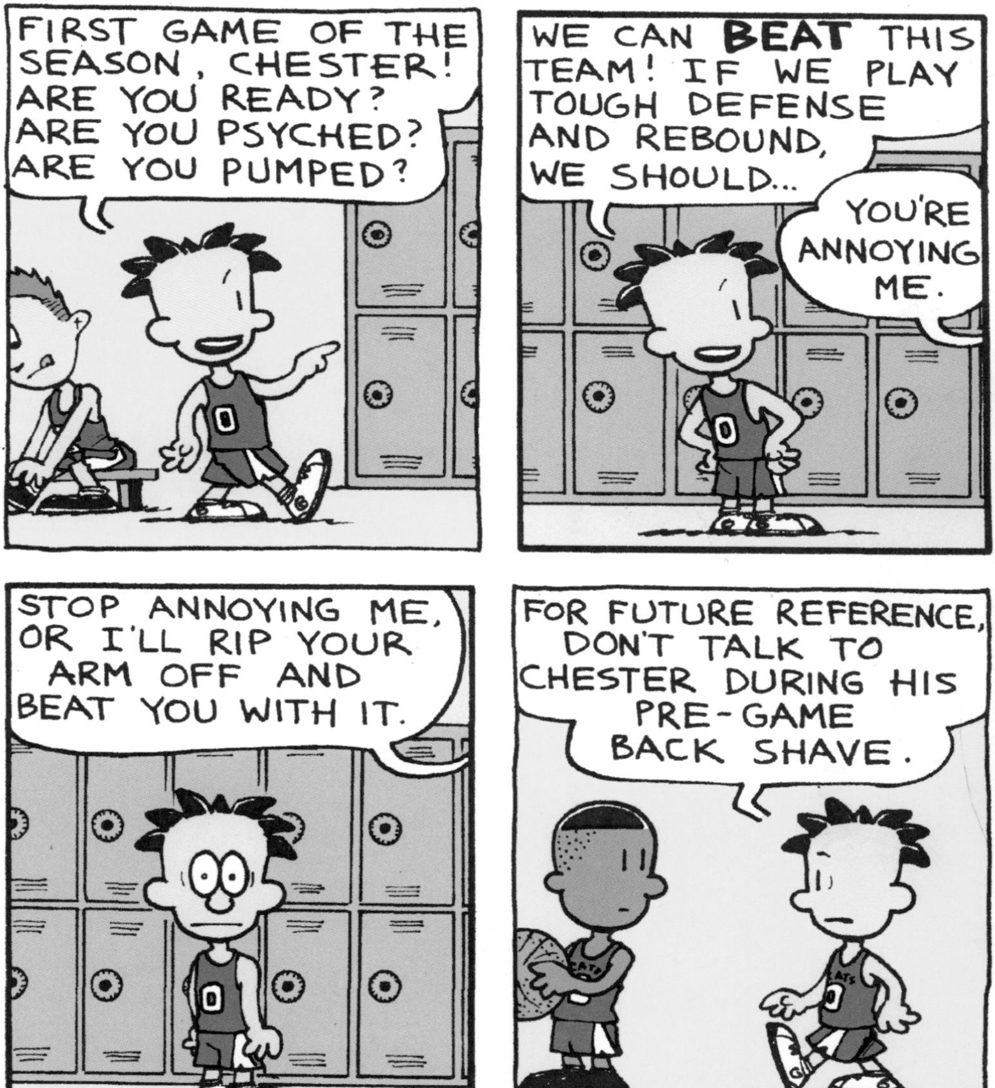
FIRST GAME OF THE SEASON, CHESTER! ARE YOU READY? ARE YOU PSYCHED? ARE YOU PUMPED?
WE CAN **BEAT** THIS TEAM! IF WE PLAY TOUGH DEFENSE AND REBOUND, WE SHOULD...
YOU'RE ANNOYING ME.
STOP ANNOYING ME, OR I'LL RIP YOUR ARM OFF AND BEAT YOU WITH IT.
FOR FUTURE REFERENCE, DON'T TALK TO CHESTER DURING HIS PRE-GAME BACK SHAVE.
Peirce

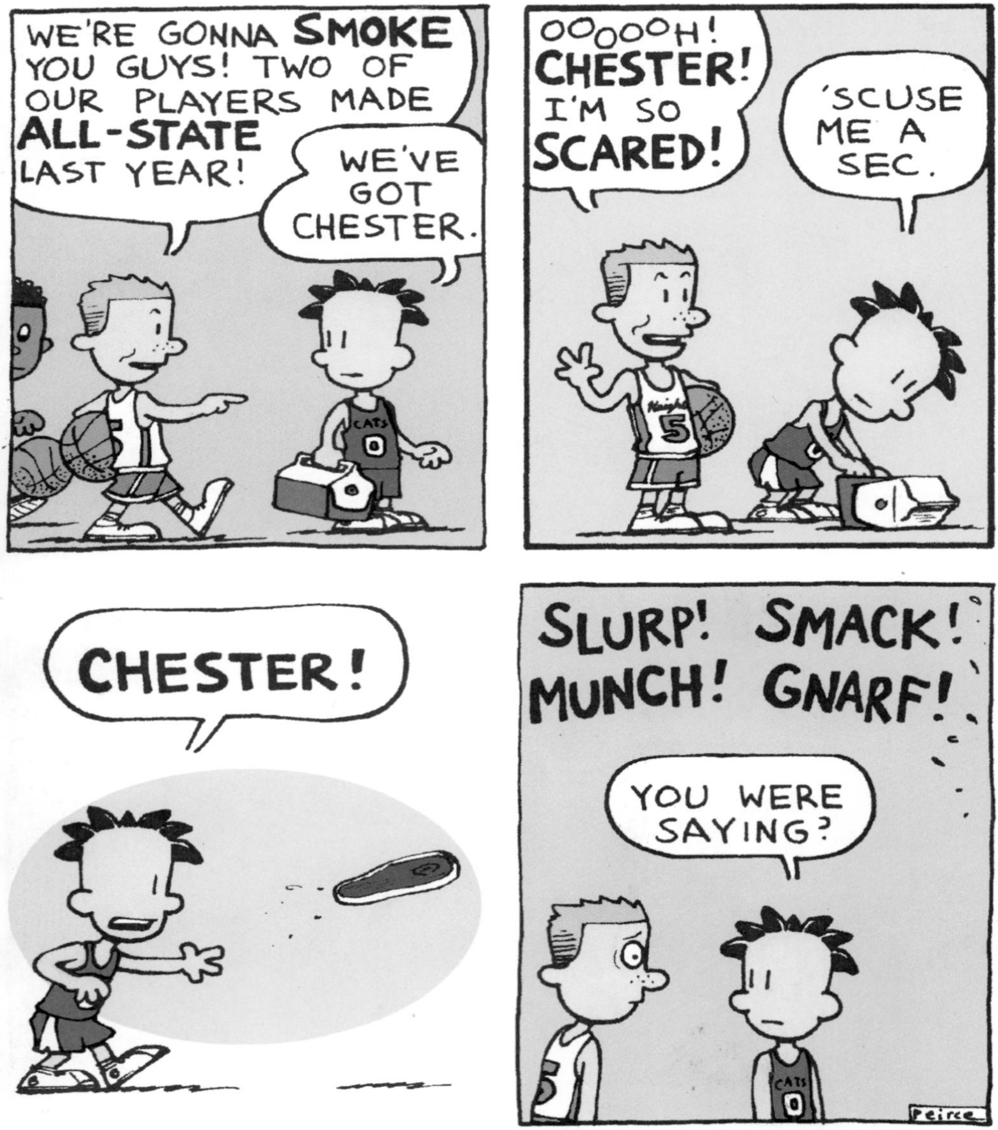
WE'RE GONNA SMOKE YOU GUYS! TWO OF OUR PLAYERS MADE ALL-STATE LAST YEAR!
WE'VE GOT CHESTER.
OOOOOOH! CHESTER! I'M SO SCARED!
'SCUSE ME A SEC.
CHESTER!
SLURP! SMACK! MUNCH! GNARF!
YOU WERE SAYING?
Peirce

CHESTER! TAKE IT **EASY!** YOU'VE ALREADY GOT THREE FOULS!
DON'T BOSS ME AROUND.
I'M NOT **BOSSING** YOU! I'M JUST SAYING WATCH THE FOULS!
YANK!
THAT WASN'T A FOUL, BUT CAN WE AGREE IT WASN'T GOOD FOR TEAM MORALE?
Peirce

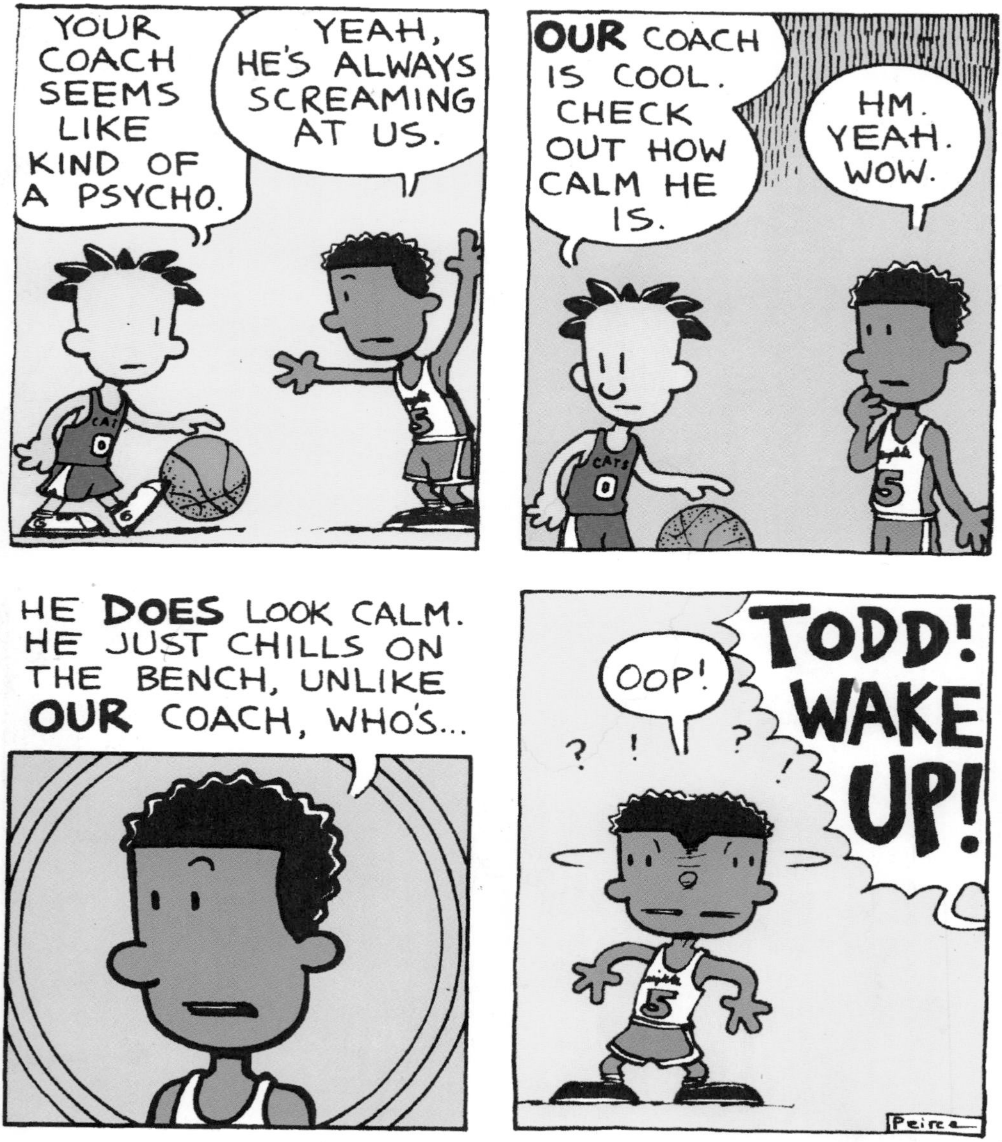

YOUR COACH SEEMS LIKE KIND OF A PSYCHO.
YEAH, HE'S ALWAYS SCREAMING AT US.
OUR COACH IS COOL. CHECK OUT HOW CALM HE IS.
HM. YEAH. WOW.
HE DOES LOOK CALM. HE JUST CHILLS ON THE BENCH, UNLIKE OUR COACH, WHO'S...
OOP!
? ! ? !
TODD! WAKE UP!
Peirce

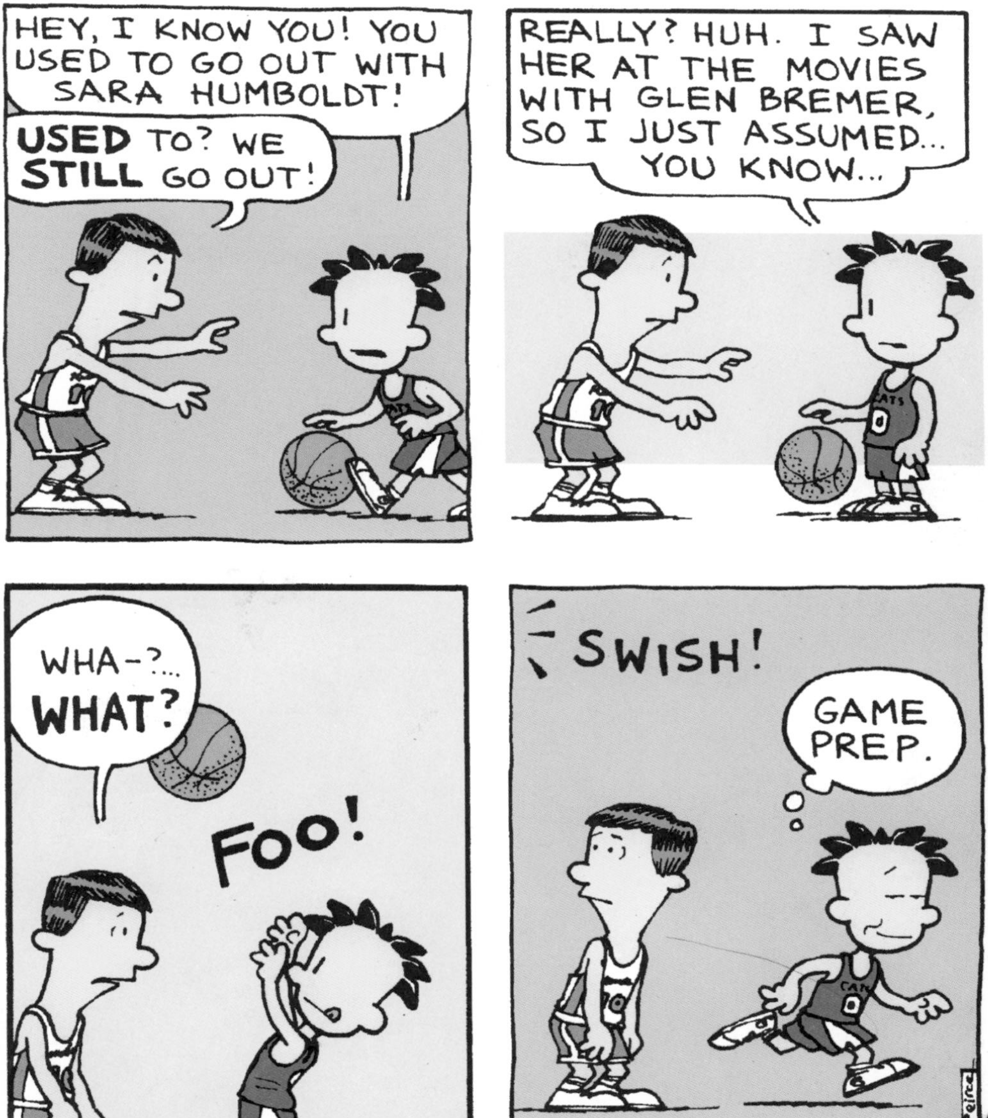
HEY, I KNOW YOU! YOU USED TO GO OUT WITH SARA HUMBOLDT!
USED TO? WE **STILL** GO OUT!
REALLY? HUH. I SAW HER AT THE MOVIES WITH GLEN BREMER, SO I JUST ASSUMED... YOU KNOW...
WHA-?... **WHAT?**
FOO!
SWISH!
GAME PREP.
Peirce

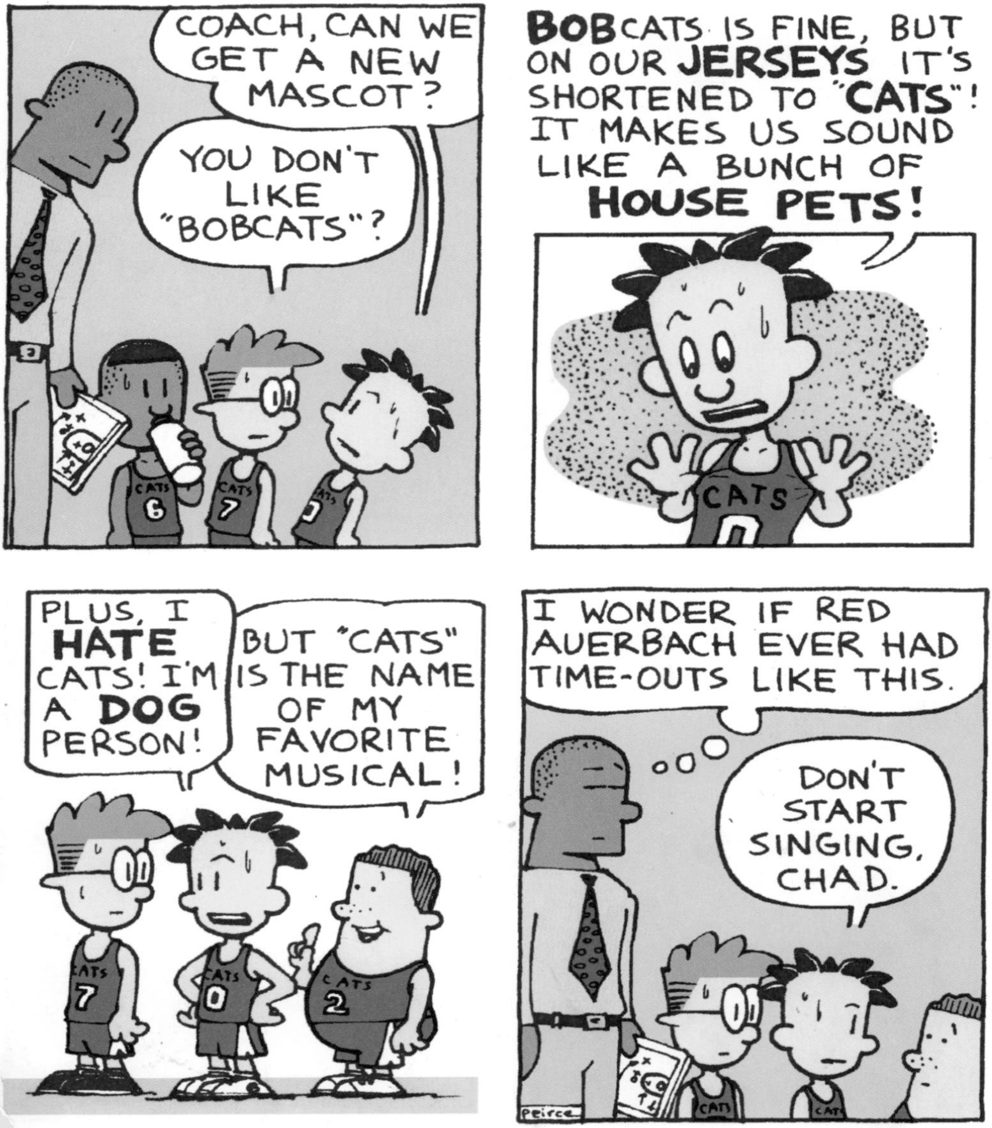
COACH, CAN WE GET A NEW MASCOT?
YOU DON'T LIKE "BOBCATS"?
CATS
6
CATS
7
BOBCATS IS FINE, BUT ON OUR JERSEYS IT'S SHORTENED TO "CATS"! IT MAKES US SOUND LIKE A BUNCH OF HOUSE PETS!
CATS
PLUS, I HATE CATS! I'M A DOG PERSON!
BUT "CATS" IS THE NAME OF MY FAVORITE MUSICAL!
CATS
7
CATS
0
CATS
2
I WONDER IF RED AUERBACH EVER HAD TIME-OUTS LIKE THIS.
DON'T START SINGING, CHAD.
Peirce

NATE, GET A MOVE ON! PRACTICE IS STARTING!

WHERE **ARE** THEY?

WHERE ARE WHAT?

MY **LUCKY SOCKS**! I CAN'T PLAY WITHOUT THEM! I WEAR THEM FOR EVERY PRAC-TICE! EVERY GAME!

THIS IS A **TRAGEDY**! A **DISASTER**! THIS CAN'T BE HAPPENING! NO!... **NO!**...

SOMETIMES I DON'T KNOW WHETHER I'M COACHING THE BASKET-BALL TEAM OR THE DRAMA CLUB.

NOOOOO

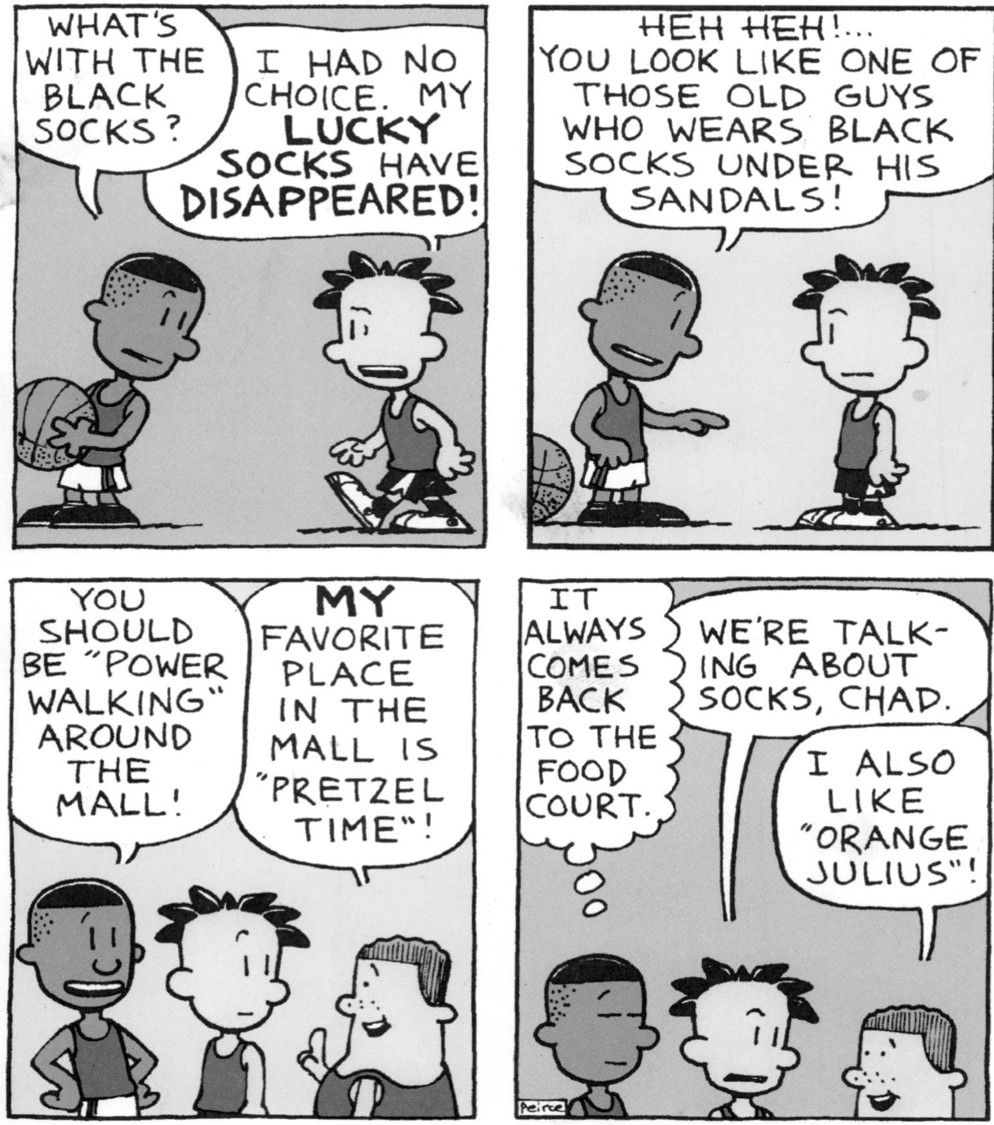
WHAT'S WITH THE BLACK SOCKS?
I HAD NO CHOICE. MY LUCKY SOCKS HAVE DISAPPEARED!
HEH HEH!... YOU LOOK LIKE ONE OF THOSE OLD GUYS WHO WEARS BLACK SOCKS UNDER HIS SANDALS!
YOU SHOULD BE "POWER WALKING" AROUND THE MALL!
MY FAVORITE PLACE IN THE MALL IS "PRETZEL TIME"!
IT ALWAYS COMES BACK TO THE FOOD COURT.
WE'RE TALKING ABOUT SOCKS, CHAD.
I ALSO LIKE "ORANGE JULIUS"!
Peirce

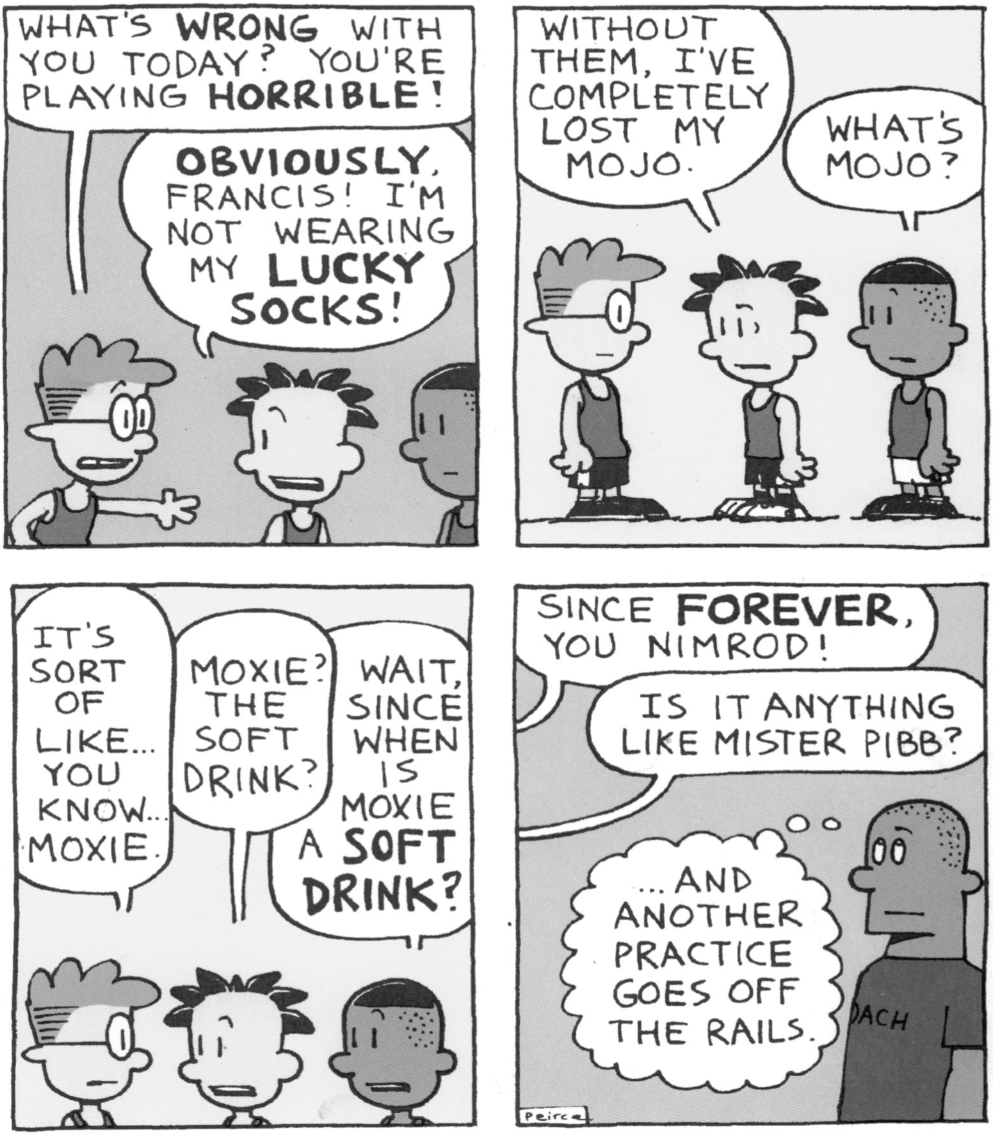
WHAT'S WRONG WITH YOU TODAY? YOU'RE PLAYING HORRIBLE!
OBVIOUSLY, FRANCIS! I'M NOT WEARING MY LUCKY SOCKS!
WITHOUT THEM, I'VE COMPLETELY LOST MY MOJO.
WHAT'S MOJO?
IT'S SORT OF LIKE... YOU KNOW... MOXIE.
MOXIE? THE SOFT DRINK?
WAIT, SINCE WHEN IS MOXIE A SOFT DRINK?
SINCE FOREVER, YOU NIMROD!
IS IT ANYTHING LIKE MISTER PIBB?
...AND ANOTHER PRACTICE GOES OFF THE RAILS.
Peirce

WHAT A LOUSY PRACTICE.
WE'D BETTER SHAPE UP BEFORE WE PLAY JEFFERSON.
IF I DON'T FIND MY LUCKY SOCKS, WE HAVE NO CHANCE.
JUST GET YOURSELF SOME NEW LUCKY SOCKS!
HEY, WHAT A GREAT IDEA, TEDDY! WHY DIDN'T I THINK OF THAT?
HELLO, ROOM SERVICE? SEND UP A PAIR OF ONE-OF-A-KIND LUCKY SOCKS, PLEASE!
HOW CAN A PAIR BE ONE-OF-A-KIND?
SIGH.

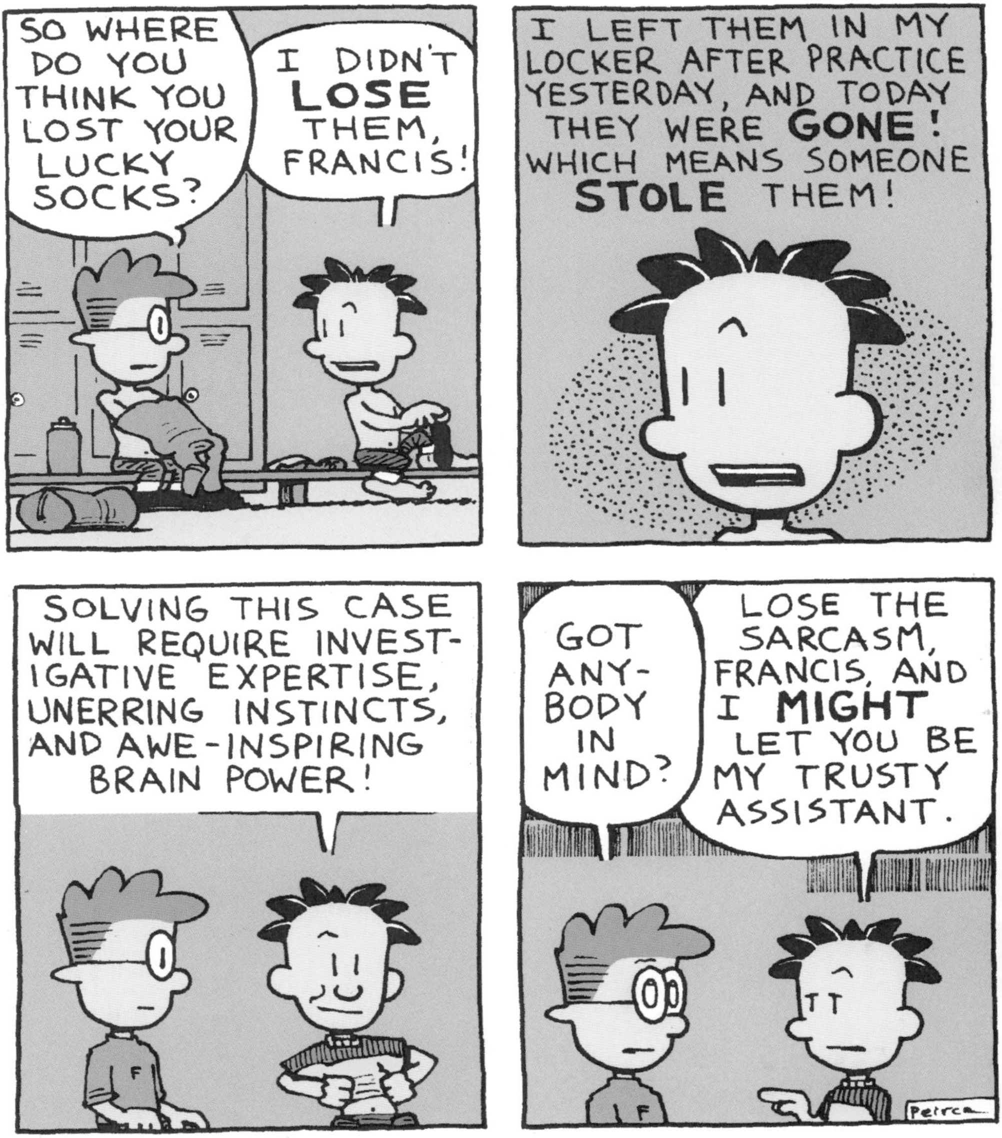
SO WHERE DO YOU THINK YOU LOST YOUR LUCKY SOCKS?
I DIDN'T **LOSE** THEM, FRANCIS!
I LEFT THEM IN MY LOCKER AFTER PRACTICE YESTERDAY, AND TODAY THEY WERE **GONE!** WHICH MEANS SOMEONE **STOLE** THEM!
SOLVING THIS CASE WILL REQUIRE INVEST-IGATIVE EXPERTISE, UNERRING INSTINCTS, AND AWE-INSPIRING BRAIN POWER!
GOT ANY-BODY IN MIND?
LOSE THE SARCASM, FRANCIS, AND I **MIGHT** LET YOU BE MY TRUSTY ASSISTANT.
F
F
Peirce

PLAY
BALL!

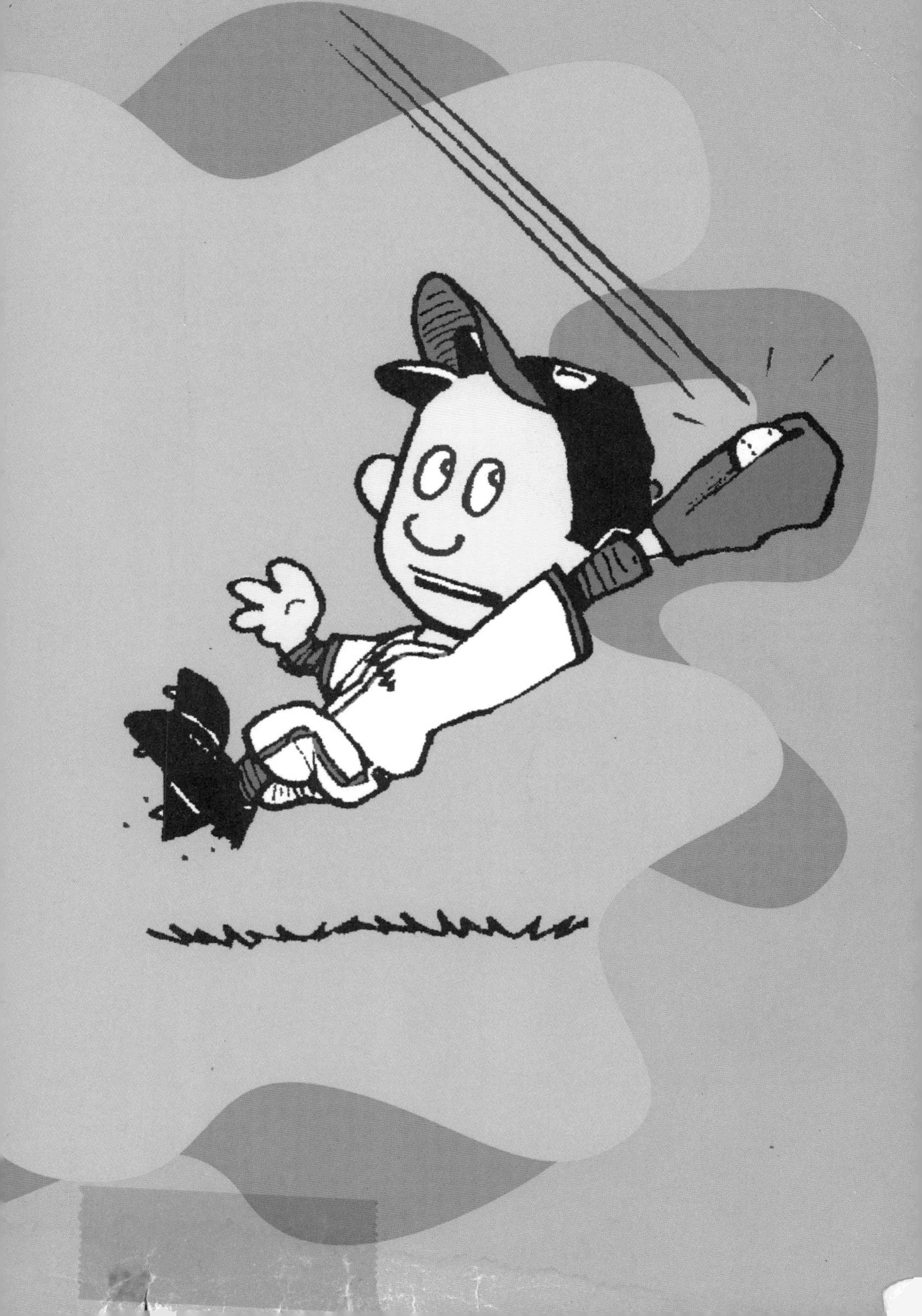

HELLO, NATE! READY FOR ANOTHER GREAT BASEBALL SEASON?

THAT DEPENDS.

IS OUR TEAM STILL GONNA BE CALLED "JOE'S TACOS"? THAT STUPID NAME WAS SO.... HEY, **WAIT** A MINUTE! WHAT'S **THAT?**

WHAT'S WHAT?

ON YOUR HAT! "CL"! WE HAVE A NEW NAME, DON'T WE? WHAT DOES "CL" STAND FOR?

OACH

"CHEZ LINDA"

OKAY, GANG, BRING IT IN!!

WHAT? WHOA! **HEY!** **WHAT??**

COA

Peirce

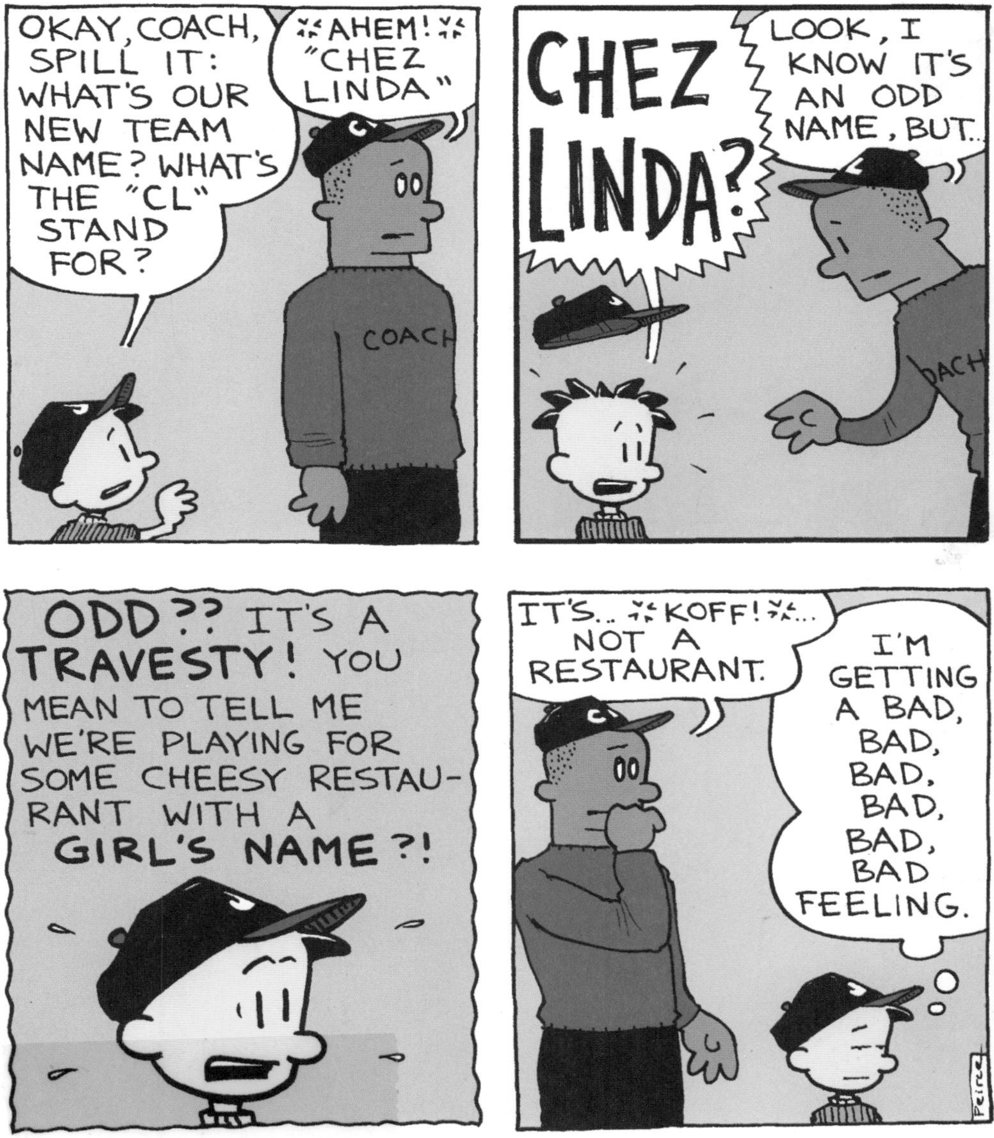
OKAY, COACH, SPILL IT: WHAT'S OUR NEW TEAM NAME? WHAT'S THE "CL" STAND FOR?
AHEM! "CHEZ LINDA"
COACH
CHEZ LINDA?
LOOK, I KNOW IT'S AN ODD NAME, BUT...
COACH
ODD?? IT'S A TRAVESTY! YOU MEAN TO TELL ME WE'RE PLAYING FOR SOME CHEESY RESTAU-RANT WITH A GIRL'S NAME?!
IT'S... KOFF! ... NOT A RESTAURANT.
I'M GETTING A BAD, BAD, BAD, BAD, BAD, BAD FEELING.
Peirce

SO THE "CHEZ LINDA" THAT'S SPONSORING OUR TEAM **ISN'T** A RESTAURANT?

UH... NO...

WELL, WHAT **IS** IT, THEN? WHAT'S THE BIG SECRET? IF IT'S NOT SOME LAME RESTAURANT, THEN...

!!...HEY, **WAIT** A MINUTE!! IT'S SOME SORT OF **DIVE**, ISN'T IT? A SLEAZY LOUNGE OR SOMETHING!!

NO, OF COURSE IT...

HEY GUYS! GREAT NEWS!!

Peirce

SO OUR NEW TEAM SPONSOR, "CHEZ LINDA," ISN'T A RESTAURANT...
NO
COACH
AND IT ISN'T A SLEAZY LOUNGE...
NO!
WELL, JUST TELL ME WHAT IT IS! HOW BAD CAN IT BE?
IT'S A BEAUTY PARLOR.
A BEAUTY PARLOR?!
Peirce

LOOK, GANG, I KNOW YOU'RE NOT HAPPY TO BE PLAYING ON A TEAM CALLED "CHEZ LINDA", BUT IT'S JUST A **NAME**!

WHAT **REALLY** MATTERS IS PLAYING HARD AND TO THE BEST OF YOUR ABILITY! AND YOU GUYS HAVE A **LOT** OF ABILITY!

PLAY LIKE YOU'RE CAPABLE AND YOU'LL MAKE "CHEZ LINDA" THE MOST **FEARED** NAME IN THE ENTIRE **LEAGUE**!

THEY'RE NOT BUYING THIS.

LISTEN TO YOURSELF, MAN.

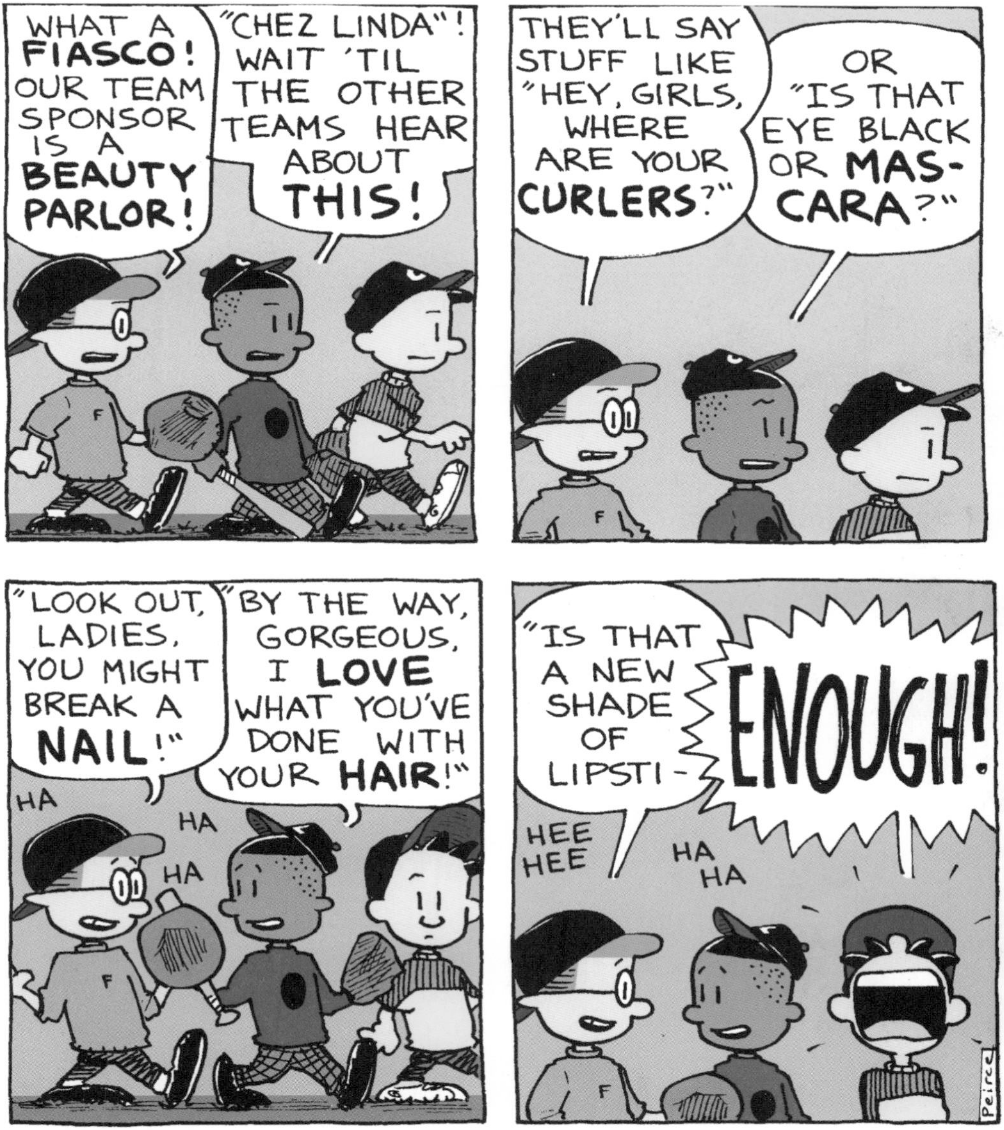

WHAT A FIASCO! OUR TEAM SPONSOR IS A BEAUTY PARLOR!
"CHEZ LINDA"! WAIT 'TIL THE OTHER TEAMS HEAR ABOUT THIS!
THEY'LL SAY STUFF LIKE "HEY, GIRLS, WHERE ARE YOUR CURLERS?"
OR "IS THAT EYE BLACK OR MASCARA?"
"LOOK OUT, LADIES, YOU MIGHT BREAK A NAIL!"
"BY THE WAY, GORGEOUS, I LOVE WHAT YOU'VE DONE WITH YOUR HAIR!"
HA HA HA
"IS THAT A NEW SHADE OF LIPSTI-
ENOUGH!
HEE HEE
HA HA
Peirce

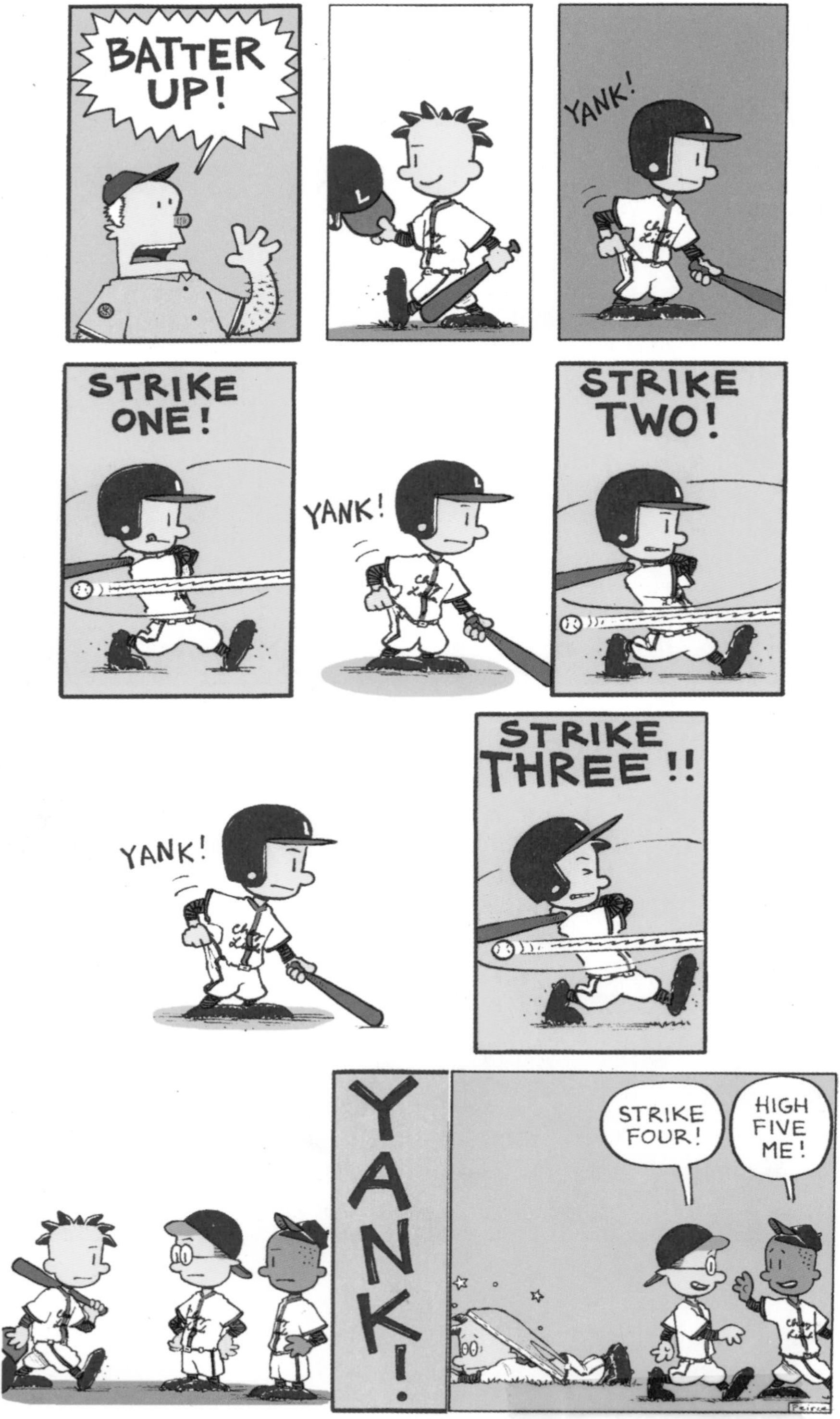
BATTER UP!
YANK!
STRIKE ONE!
YANK!
STRIKE TWO!
YANK!
STRIKE THREE!!
YANK!
STRIKE FOUR!
HIGH FIVE ME!
Peirce

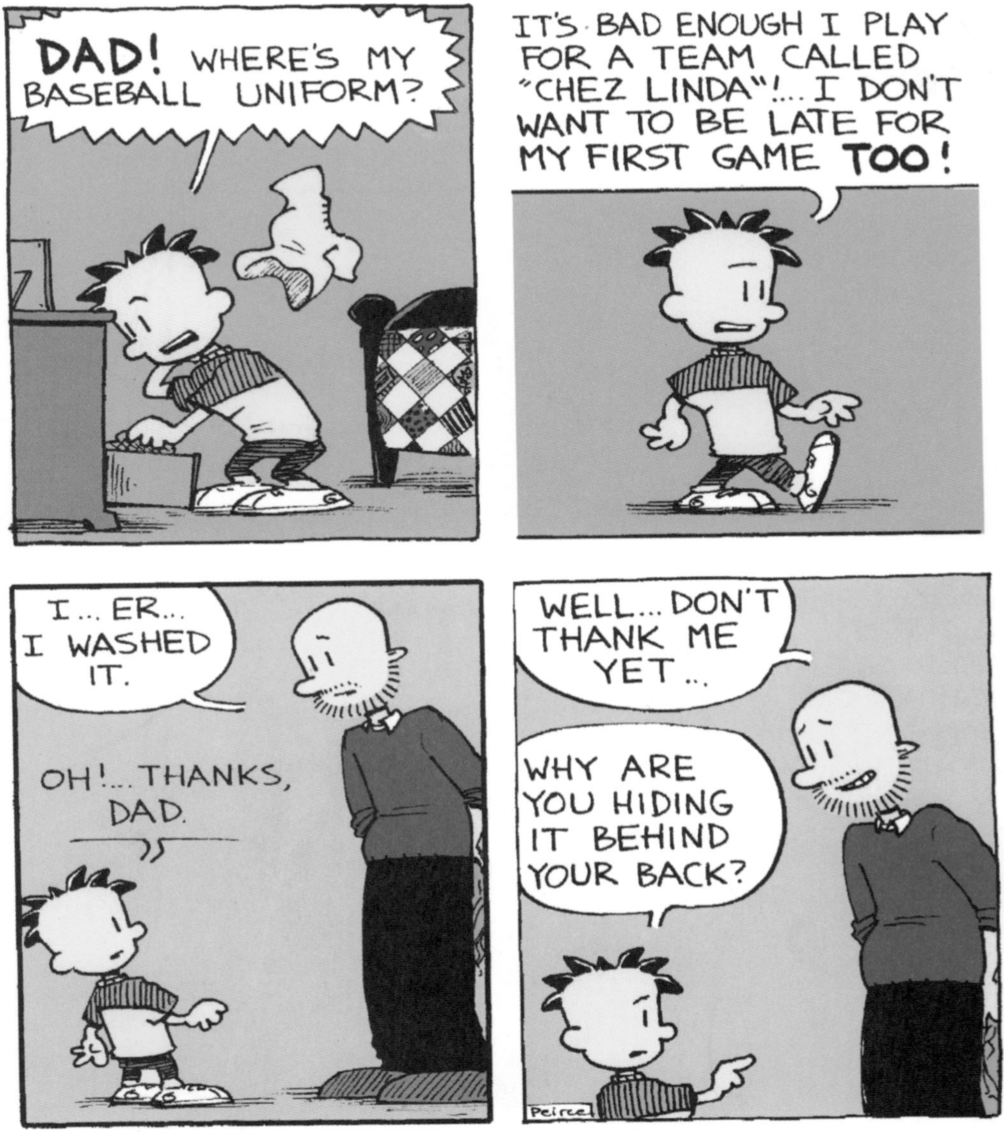
DAD! WHERE'S MY BASEBALL UNIFORM?
IT'S BAD ENOUGH I PLAY FOR A TEAM CALLED "CHEZ LINDA"!... I DON'T WANT TO BE LATE FOR MY FIRST GAME TOO!
I... ER... I WASHED IT.
OH!... THANKS, DAD.
WELL... DON'T THANK ME YET...
WHY ARE YOU HIDING IT BEHIND YOUR BACK?
Peirce

IS THAT MY BASE-BALL UNIFORM BEHIND YOUR BACK?
ER... YES.
I THOUGHT I'D WASH IT, SO YOU'D LOOK SHARP FOR YOUR FIRST GAME OF THE SEASON...
BUT... AHEM!... SOMEHOW MY RED SWEAT-SHIRT GOT MIXED IN WITH THE WHITES, AND...
IT'S PINK!
WELL, TECH-NICALLY, I'D CALL IT MORE OF A "SALMON."

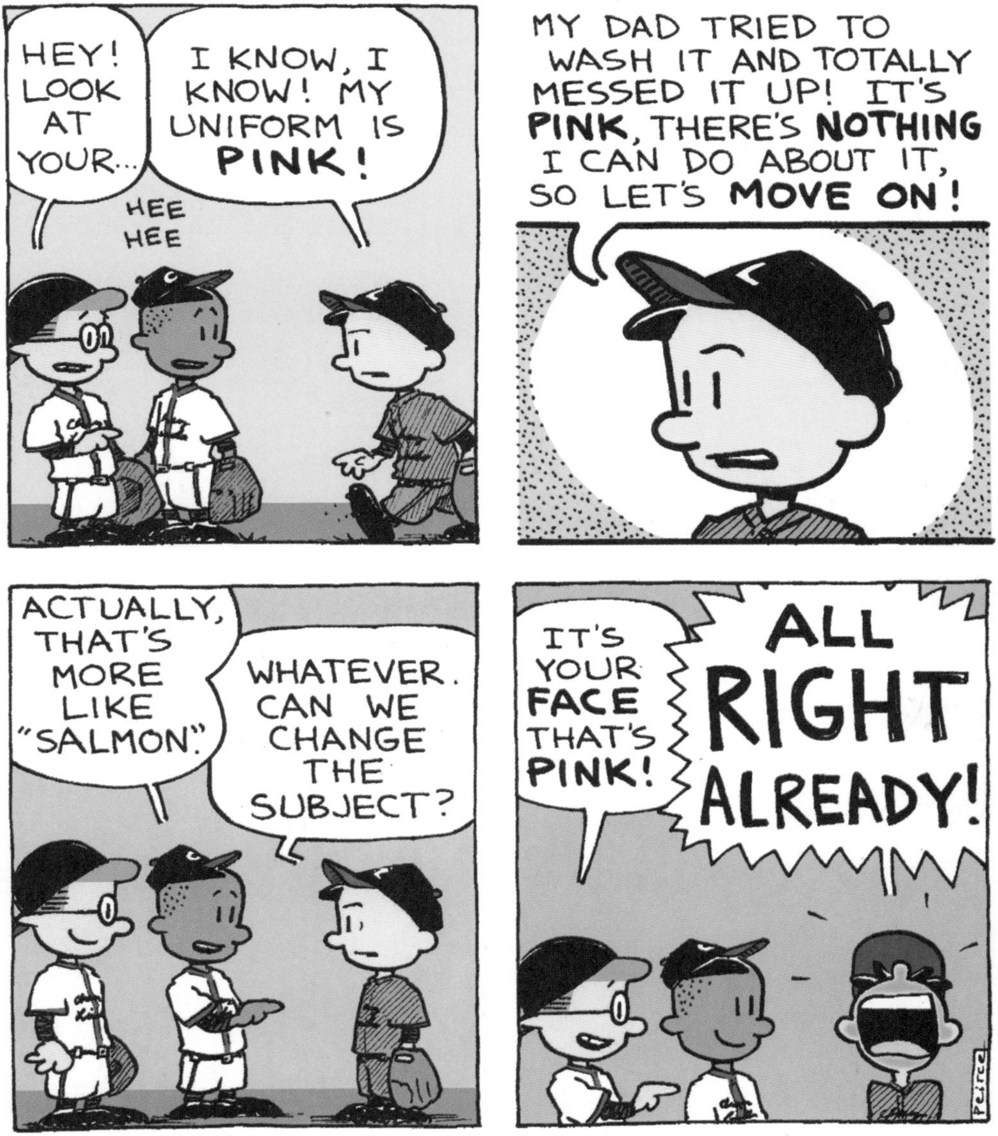
HEY! LOOK AT YOUR...
I KNOW, I KNOW! MY UNIFORM IS PINK!
HEE HEE
MY DAD TRIED TO WASH IT AND TOTALLY MESSED IT UP! IT'S PINK, THERE'S NOTHING I CAN DO ABOUT IT, SO LET'S MOVE ON!
ACTUALLY, THAT'S MORE LIKE "SALMON."
WHATEVER. CAN WE CHANGE THE SUBJECT?
IT'S YOUR FACE THAT'S PINK!
ALL RIGHT ALREADY!
PEIRCE

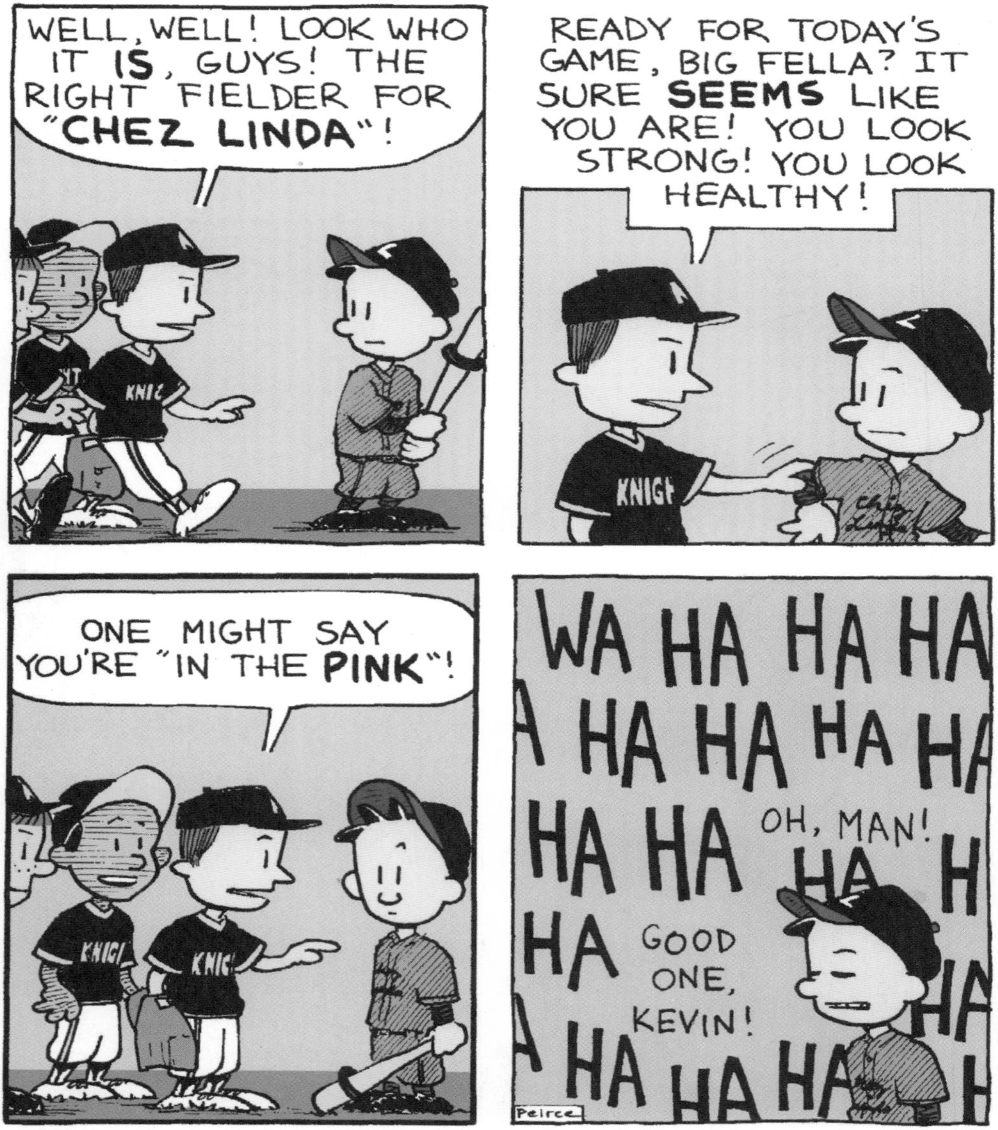
WELL, WELL! LOOK WHO IT **IS**, GUYS! THE RIGHT FIELDER FOR "**CHEZ LINDA**"!
READY FOR TODAY'S GAME, BIG FELLA? IT SURE **SEEMS** LIKE YOU ARE! YOU LOOK STRONG! YOU LOOK HEALTHY!
ONE MIGHT SAY YOU'RE "IN THE **PINK**"!
WA HA HA HA HA HA HA HA HA HA HA HA HA HA HA HA HA HA HA HA HA
OH, MAN!
GOOD ONE, KEVIN!
Peirce

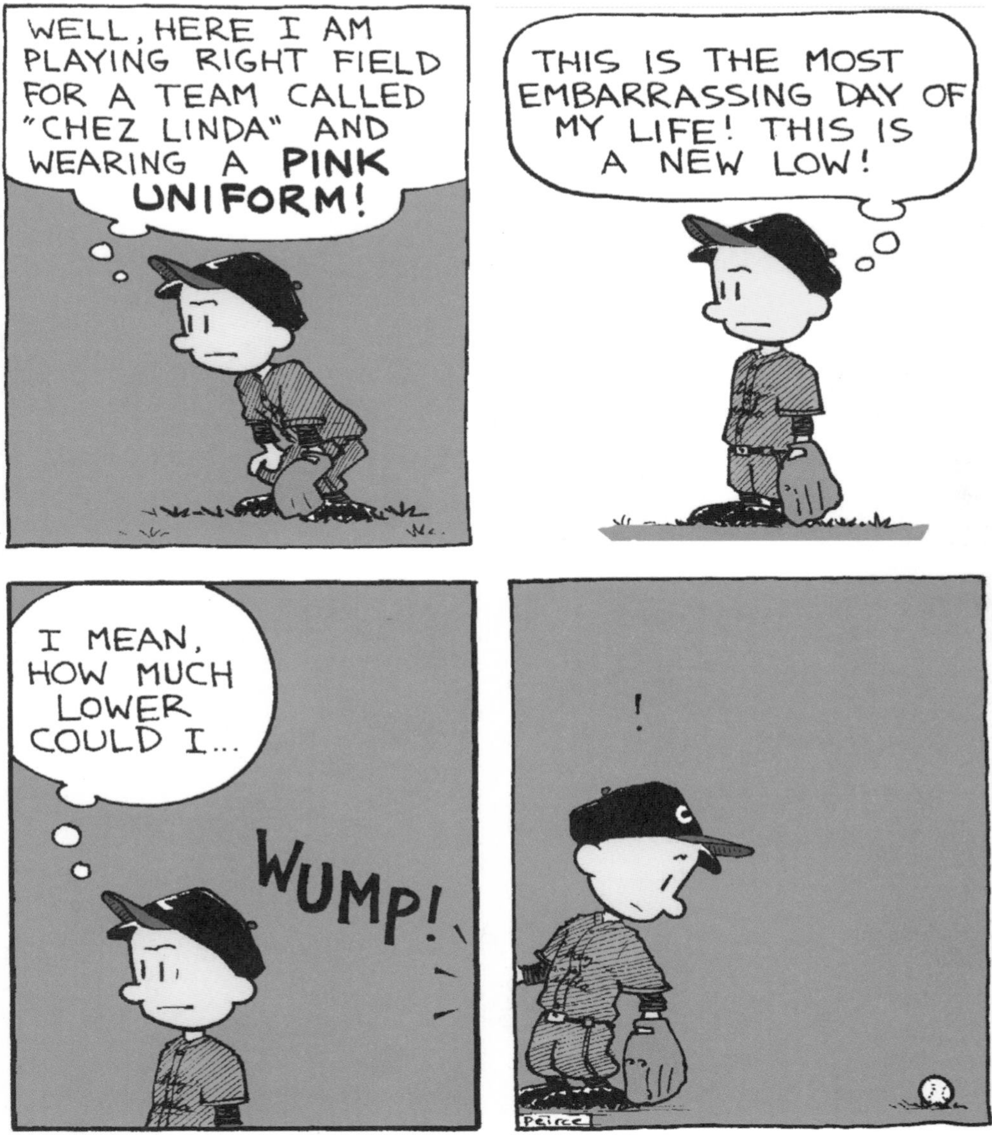
WELL, HERE I AM PLAYING RIGHT FIELD FOR A TEAM CALLED "CHEZ LINDA" AND WEARING A **PINK UNIFORM!**
THIS IS THE MOST EMBARRASSING DAY OF MY LIFE! THIS IS A NEW LOW!
I MEAN, HOW MUCH LOWER COULD I...
WUMP!
!
Peirce

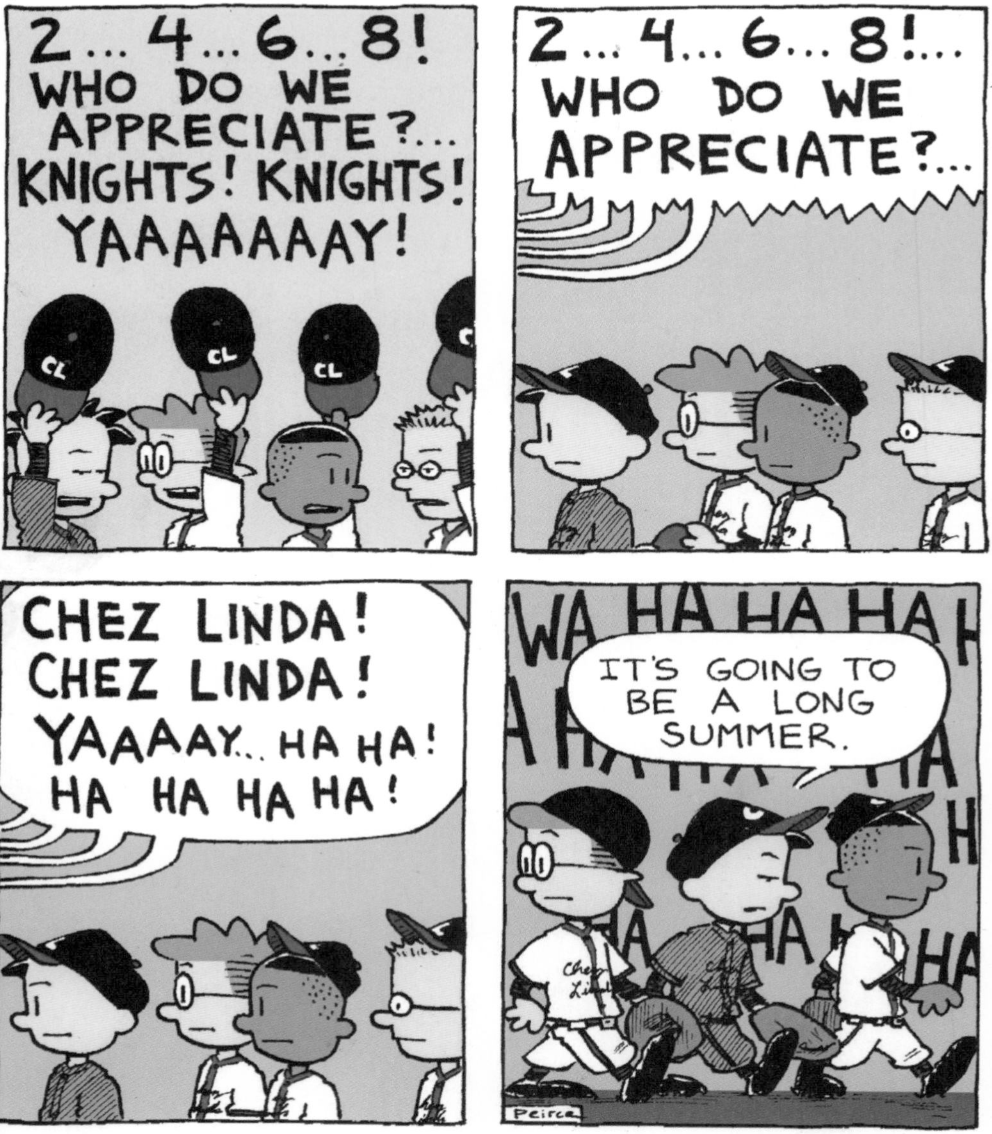
2... 4... 6... 8! WHO DO WE APPRECIATE?... KNIGHTS! KNIGHTS! YAAAAAAAY!
CL
2... 4... 6... 8!... WHO DO WE APPRECIATE?...
CHEZ LINDA! CHEZ LINDA! YAAAAY... HA HA! HA HA HA HA!
WA HA HA HA
IT'S GOING TO BE A LONG SUMMER.
Peirce

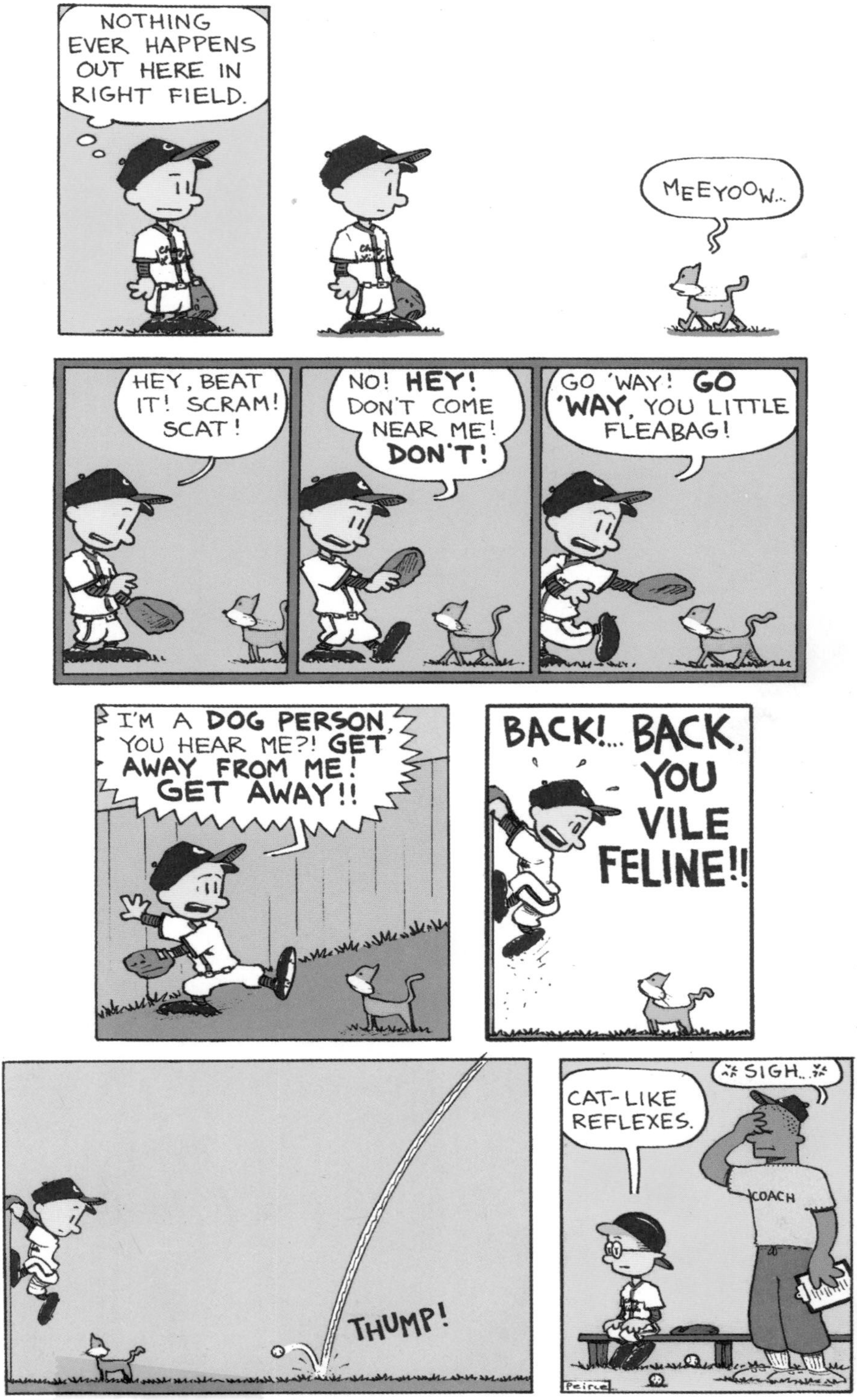
NOTHING EVER HAPPENS OUT HERE IN RIGHT FIELD.
MEEYOOW...
HEY, BEAT IT! SCRAM! SCAT!
NO! HEY! DON'T COME NEAR ME! DON'T!
GO 'WAY! GO 'WAY, YOU LITTLE FLEABAG!
I'M A DOG PERSON, YOU HEAR ME?! GET AWAY FROM ME! GET AWAY!!
BACK!... BACK, YOU VILE FELINE!!
THUMP!
CAT-LIKE REFLEXES.
SIGH...
COACH
Peirce

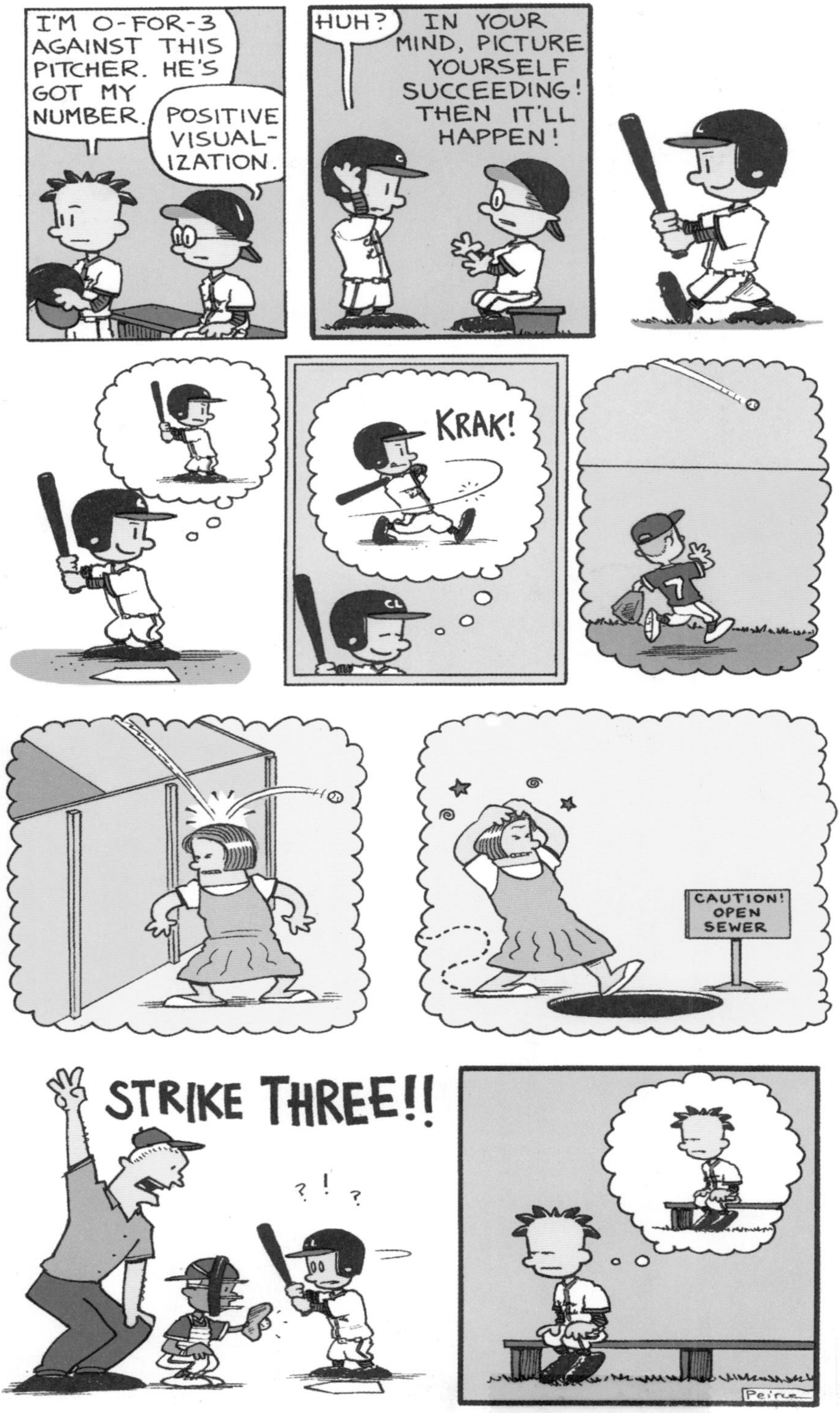

I'M 0-FOR-3 AGAINST THIS PITCHER. HE'S GOT MY NUMBER.
POSITIVE VISUALIZATION.
HUH?
IN YOUR MIND, PICTURE YOURSELF SUCCEEDING! THEN IT'LL HAPPEN!
KRAK!
7
CAUTION! OPEN SEWER
STRIKE THREE!!
?!?
Peirce

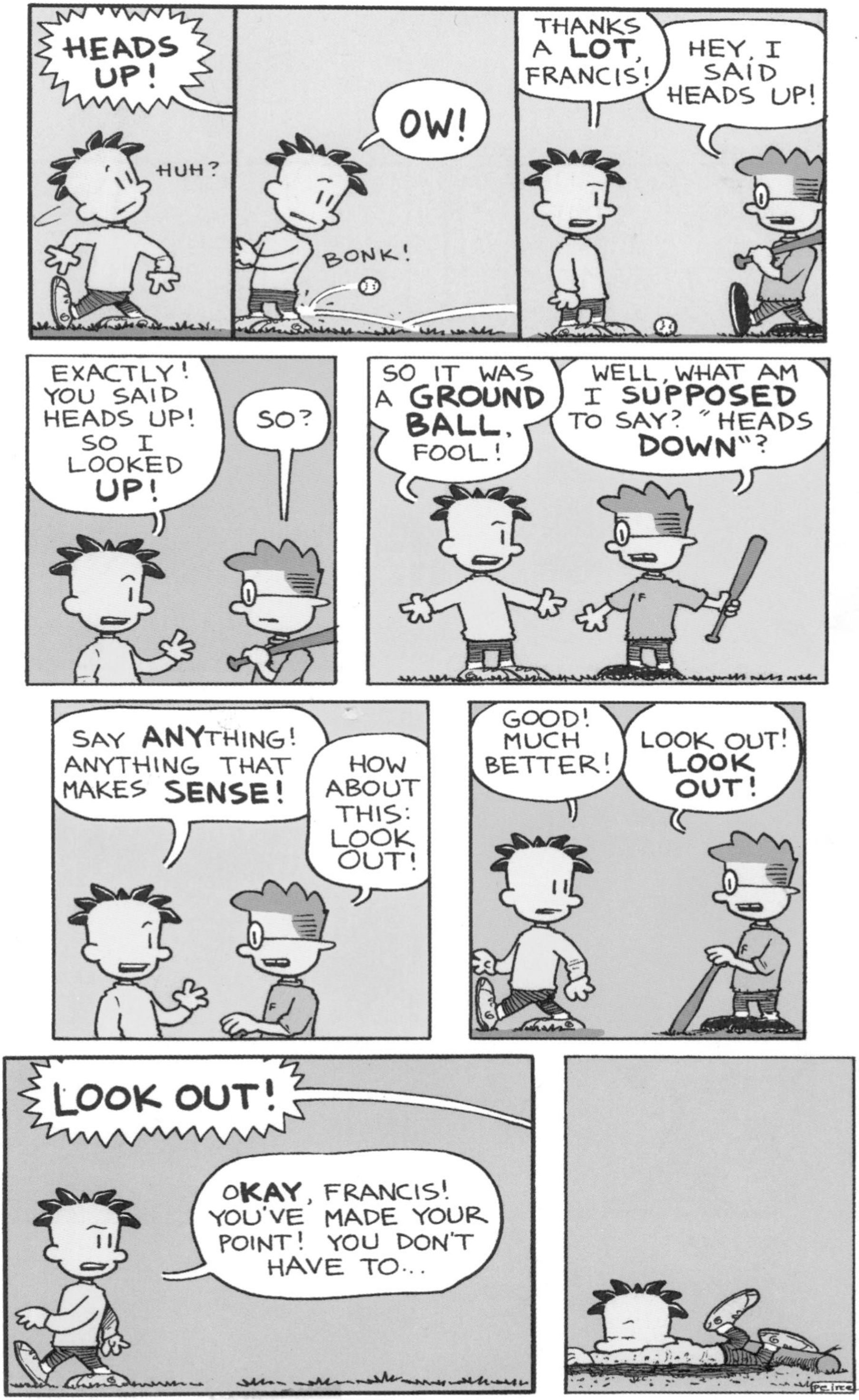
HEADS UP!
HUH?
OW!
BONK!
THANKS A LOT, FRANCIS!
HEY, I SAID HEADS UP!
EXACTLY! YOU SAID HEADS UP! SO I LOOKED UP!
SO?
SO IT WAS A GROUND BALL, FOOL!
WELL, WHAT AM I SUPPOSED TO SAY? "HEADS DOWN"?
SAY ANYTHING! ANYTHING THAT MAKES SENSE!
HOW ABOUT THIS: LOOK OUT!
GOOD! MUCH BETTER!
LOOK OUT! LOOK OUT!
LOOK OUT!
OKAY, FRANCIS! YOU'VE MADE YOUR POINT! YOU DON'T HAVE TO...
PEIRCE

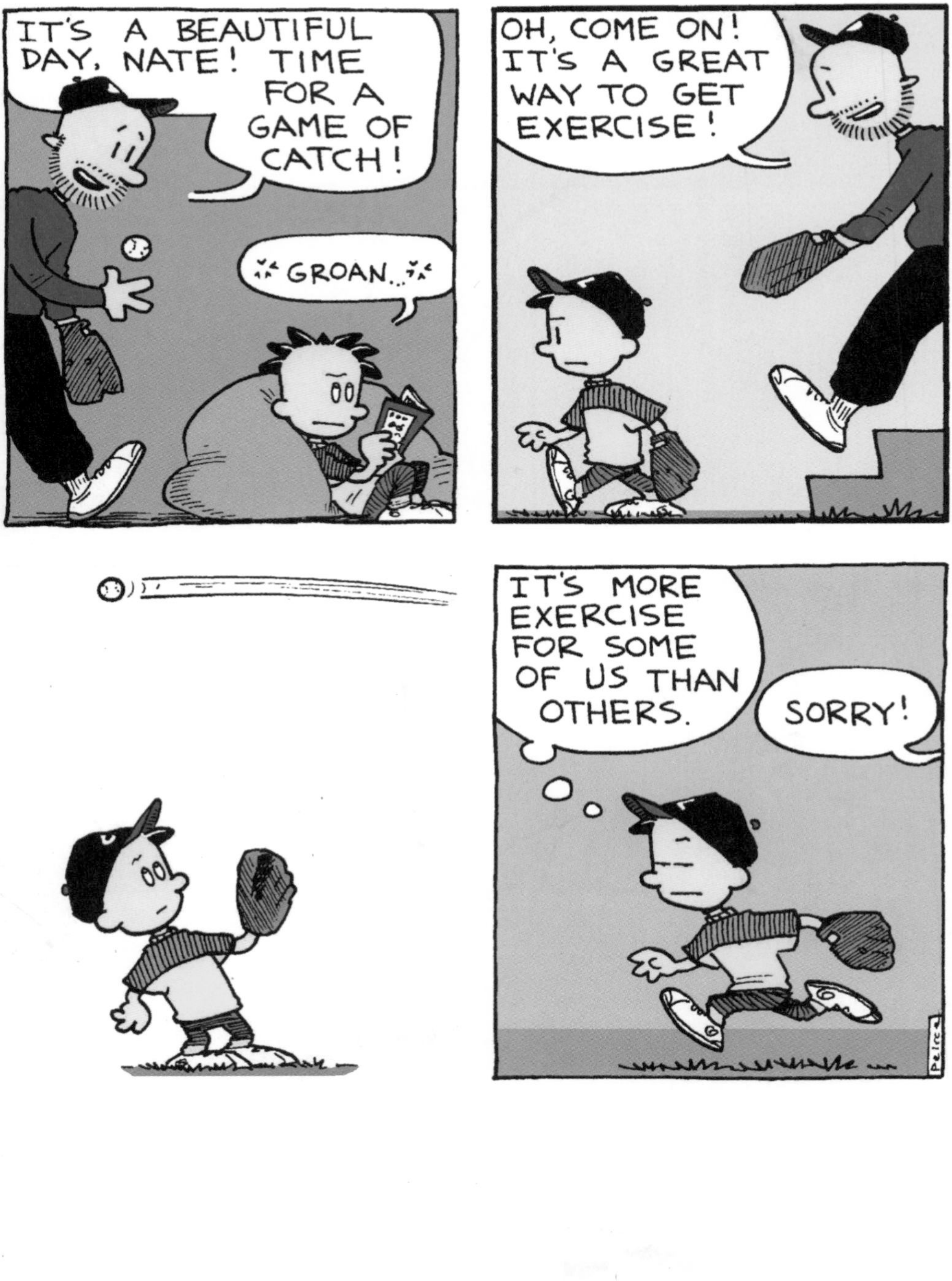
IT'S A BEAUTIFUL DAY, NATE! TIME FOR A GAME OF CATCH!
GROAN...
OH, COME ON! IT'S A GREAT WAY TO GET EXERCISE!
IT'S MORE EXERCISE FOR SOME OF US THAN OTHERS.
SORRY!

sigh...
CAN'T FIND IT, DAD! LOOKS LIKE THAT BALL'S HISTORY!
OH, WELL! GUESS WE CAN'T PLAY CATCH ANYMORE!
THERE IT IS!
GREAT.
THAT'S THE PROBLEM WITH YOU KIDS! YOU GIVE UP TOO EASILY!
peirce

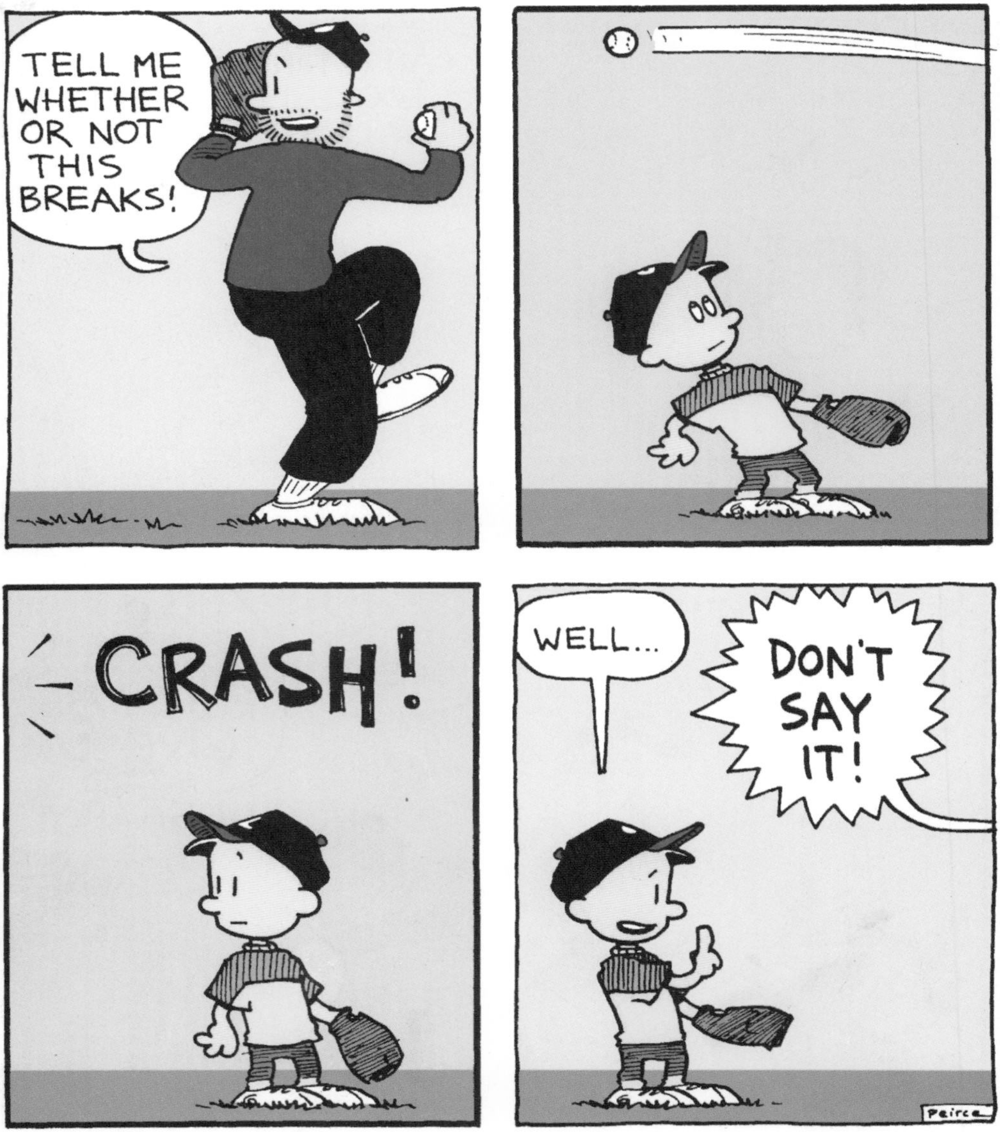
TELL ME WHETHER OR NOT THIS BREAKS!
CRASH!
WELL...
DON'T SAY IT!
Peirce

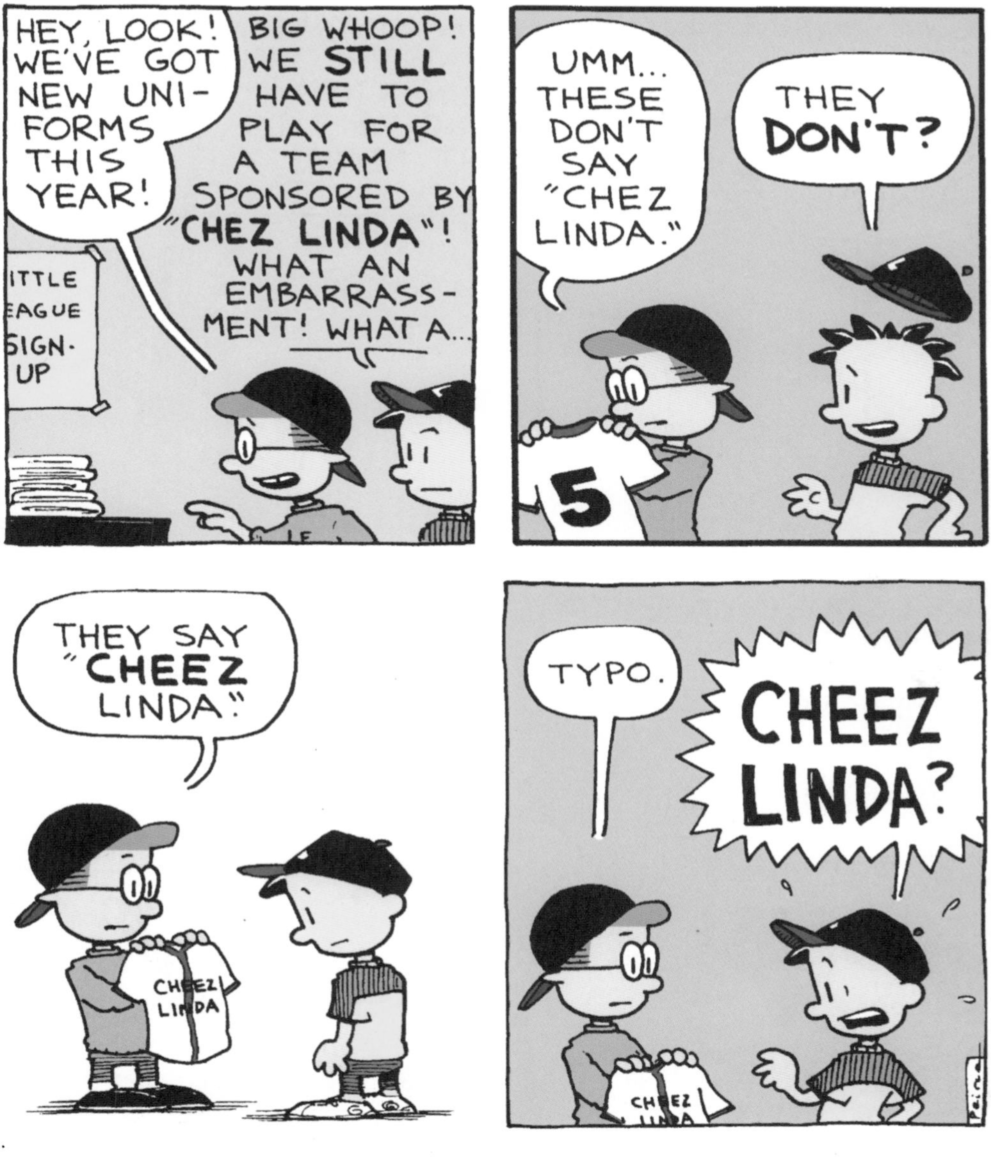
HEY, LOOK! WE'VE GOT NEW UNIFORMS THIS YEAR!
BIG WHOOP! WE STILL HAVE TO PLAY FOR A TEAM SPONSORED BY "CHEZ LINDA"! WHAT AN EMBARRASSMENT! WHAT A...
LITTLE LEAGUE SIGN-UP
UMM... THESE DON'T SAY "CHEZ LINDA."
THEY DON'T?
5
THEY SAY "CHEEZ LINDA."
CHEEZ LINDA
TYPO.
CHEEZ LINDA?

COACH! WHAT IS GOING **ON**? OUR UNIFORMS SAY "**CHEEZ** LINDA"!
I KNOW, I KNOW.
COACH
A MISTAKE WAS MADE AT THE PRINT SHOP. UNFORTUNATELY, THERE'S NO TIME TO CORRECT IT BEFORE THE SEASON STARTS!
WE'LL JUST HAVE TO MAKE THE BEST OF IT. NOW COME OVER HERE FOR TEAM PICTURES.
Peirce
SAY "CHEEZ." HA HA
SHUT UP.
CHEEZ LINDA! WE SOUND LIKE SOME SORT OF MUTANT SNACK FOOD!
CHEEZ LINDA

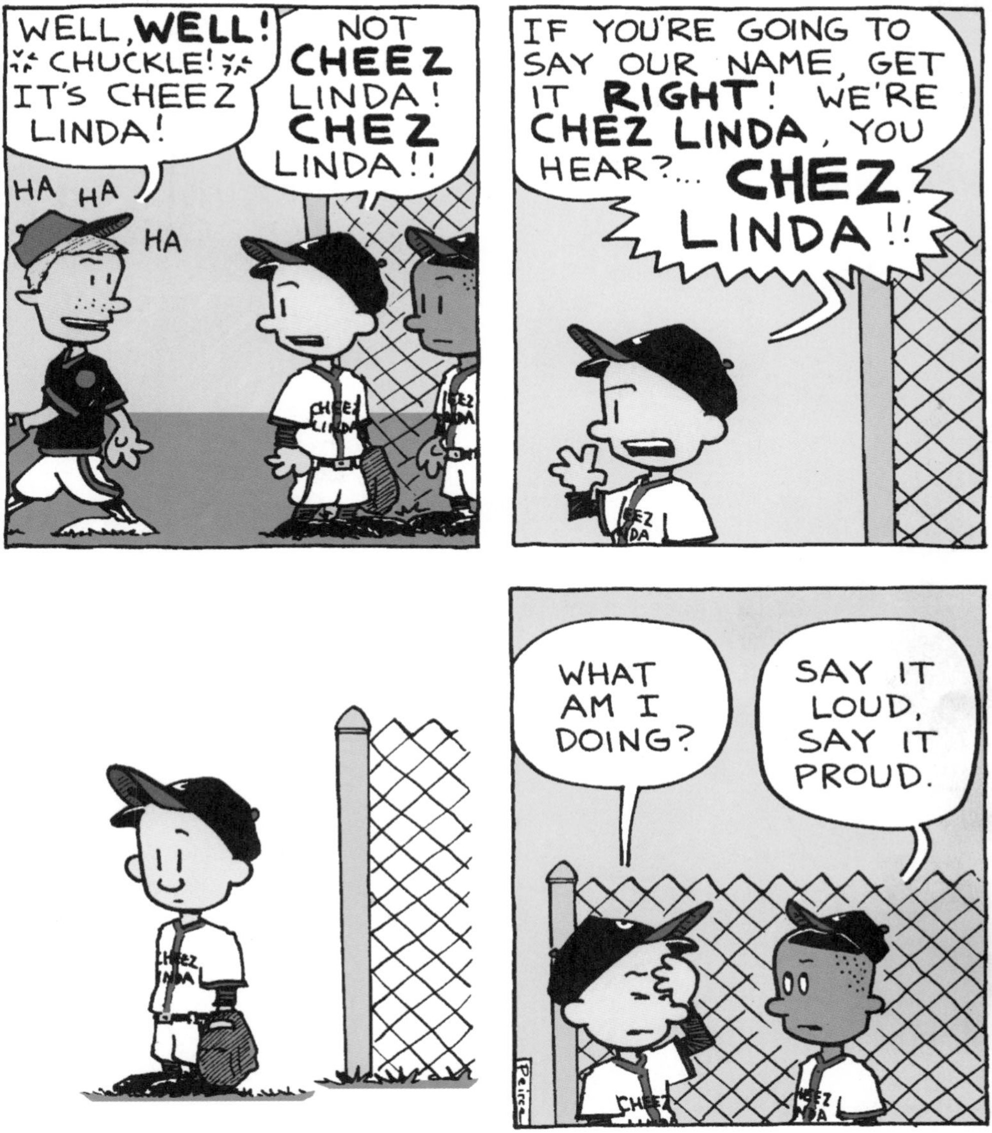
WELL, **WELL**! CHUCKLE! IT'S CHEEZ LINDA!
HA HA HA
NOT **CHEEZ** LINDA! **CHEZ** LINDA!!
CHEEZ LINDA
IF YOU'RE GOING TO SAY OUR NAME, GET IT **RIGHT**! WE'RE **CHEZ LINDA**, YOU HEAR?... **CHEZ LINDA**!!
WHAT AM I DOING?
SAY IT LOUD, SAY IT PROUD.
Peirce

YOU'VE GOT A TOUGH JOB, COACH.

YOU'VE GOT TO INSPIRE AND MOTIVATE A TEAM CALLED "CHEZ LINDA" WHICH NOW, BECAUSE OF SOME STUPID PRINTING ERROR, IS CALLED "**CHEEZ LINDA**"!

WHAT WOULD KNUTE ROCKNE HAVE DONE?

I THINK WE CAN SAFELY ASSUME THAT KNUTE ROCKNE NEVER WOULD HAVE FOUND HIMSELF IN THIS SITUATION.

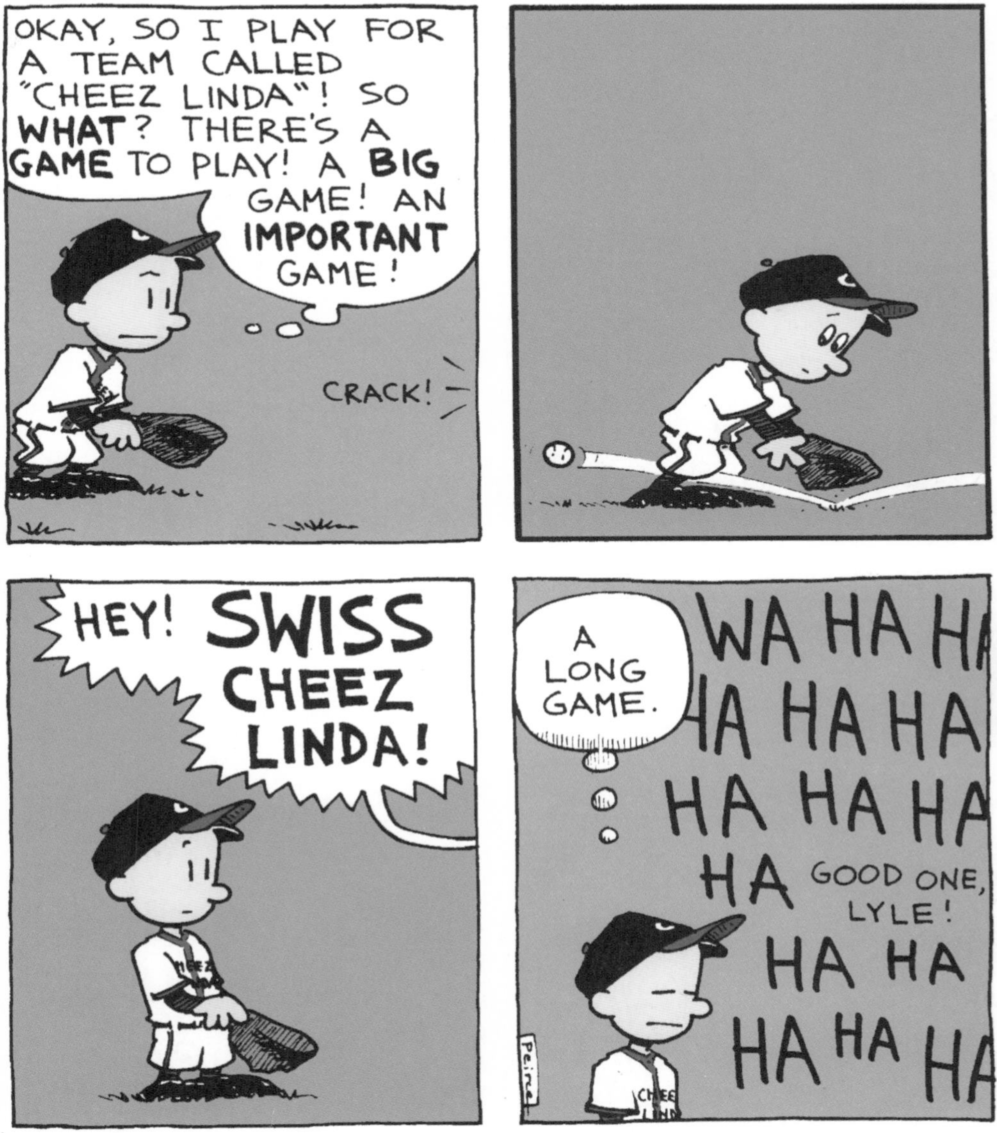
OKAY, SO I PLAY FOR A TEAM CALLED "CHEEZ LINDA"! SO **WHAT**? THERE'S A **GAME** TO PLAY! A **BIG** GAME! AN **IMPORTANT** GAME!
CRACK!
HEY! SWISS CHEEZ LINDA!
A LONG GAME.
WA HA HA HA HA HA HA HA HA HA HA
GOOD ONE, LYLE!
HA HA HA HA HA
Peirce

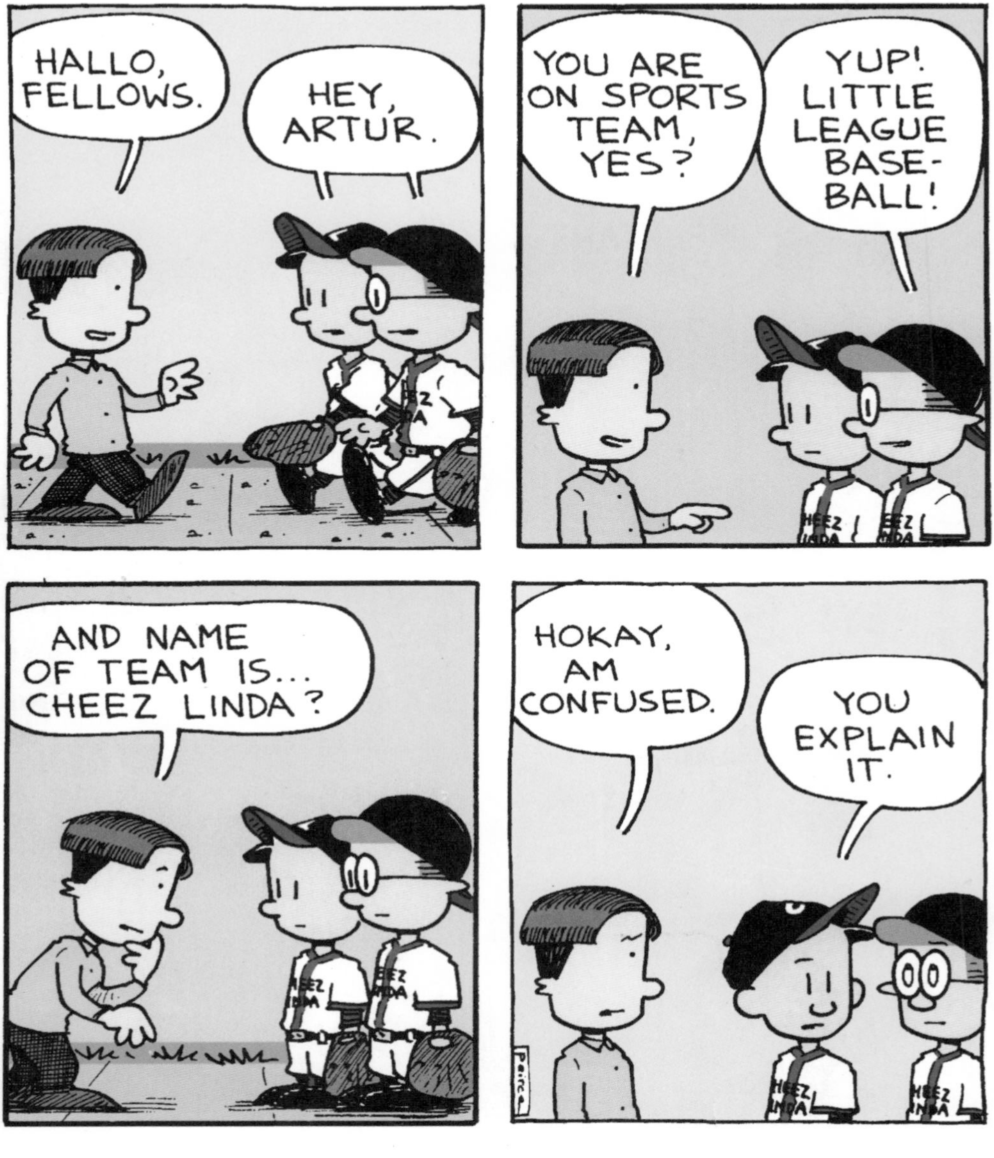
HALLO, FELLOWS.
HEY, ARTUR.
YOU ARE ON SPORTS TEAM, YES?
YUP! LITTLE LEAGUE BASE-BALL!
AND NAME OF TEAM IS... CHEEZ LINDA?
HOKAY, AM CONFUSED.
YOU EXPLAIN IT.
Peirce

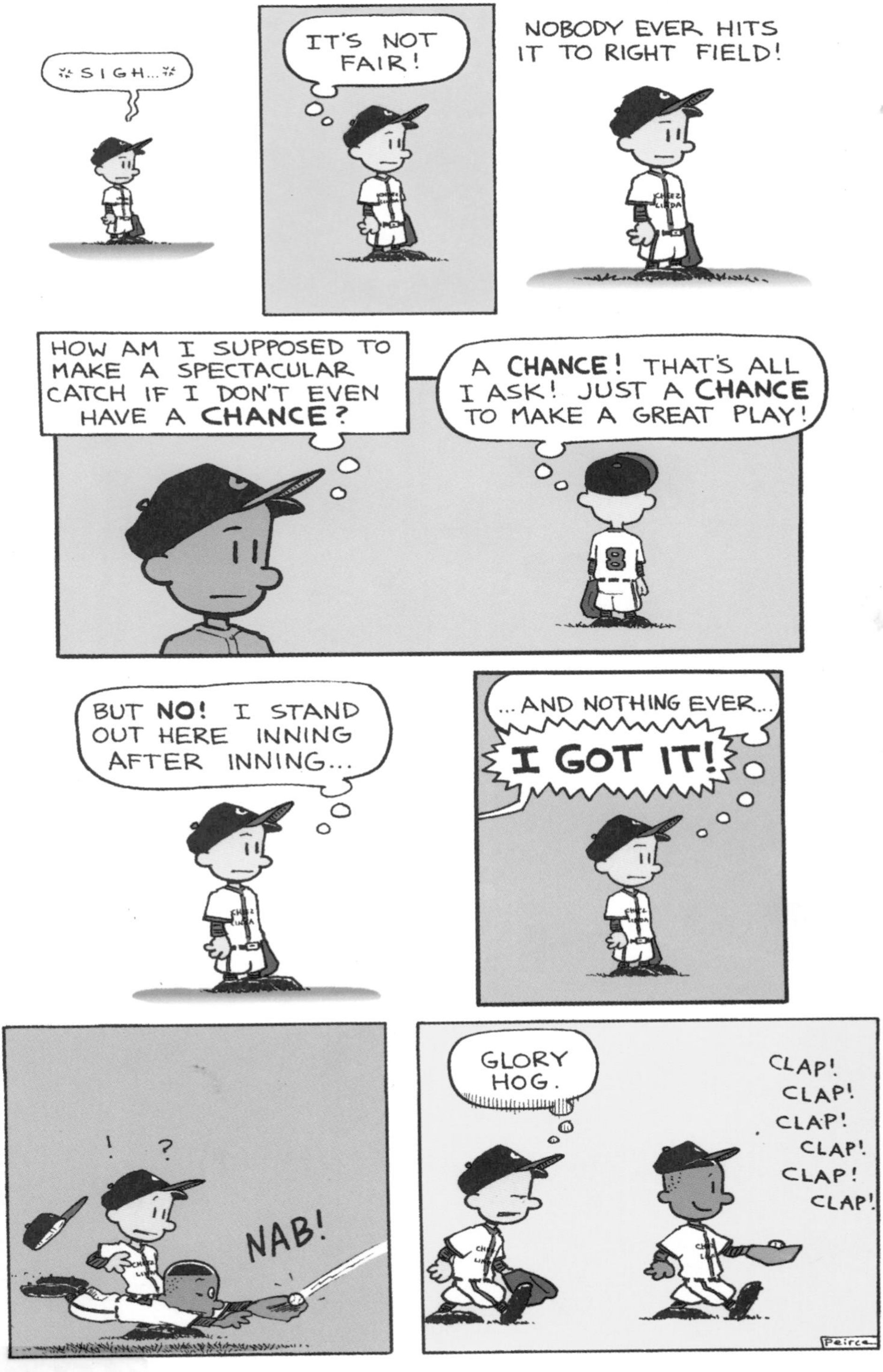
SIGH...
IT'S NOT FAIR!
NOBODY EVER HITS IT TO RIGHT FIELD!
HOW AM I SUPPOSED TO MAKE A SPECTACULAR CATCH IF I DON'T EVEN HAVE A **CHANCE**?
A **CHANCE**! THAT'S ALL I ASK! JUST A **CHANCE** TO MAKE A GREAT PLAY!
BUT **NO**! I STAND OUT HERE INNING AFTER INNING...
...AND NOTHING EVER...
I GOT IT!
! ?
NAB!
GLORY HOG.
CLAP! CLAP! CLAP! CLAP! CLAP! CLAP!
Peirce

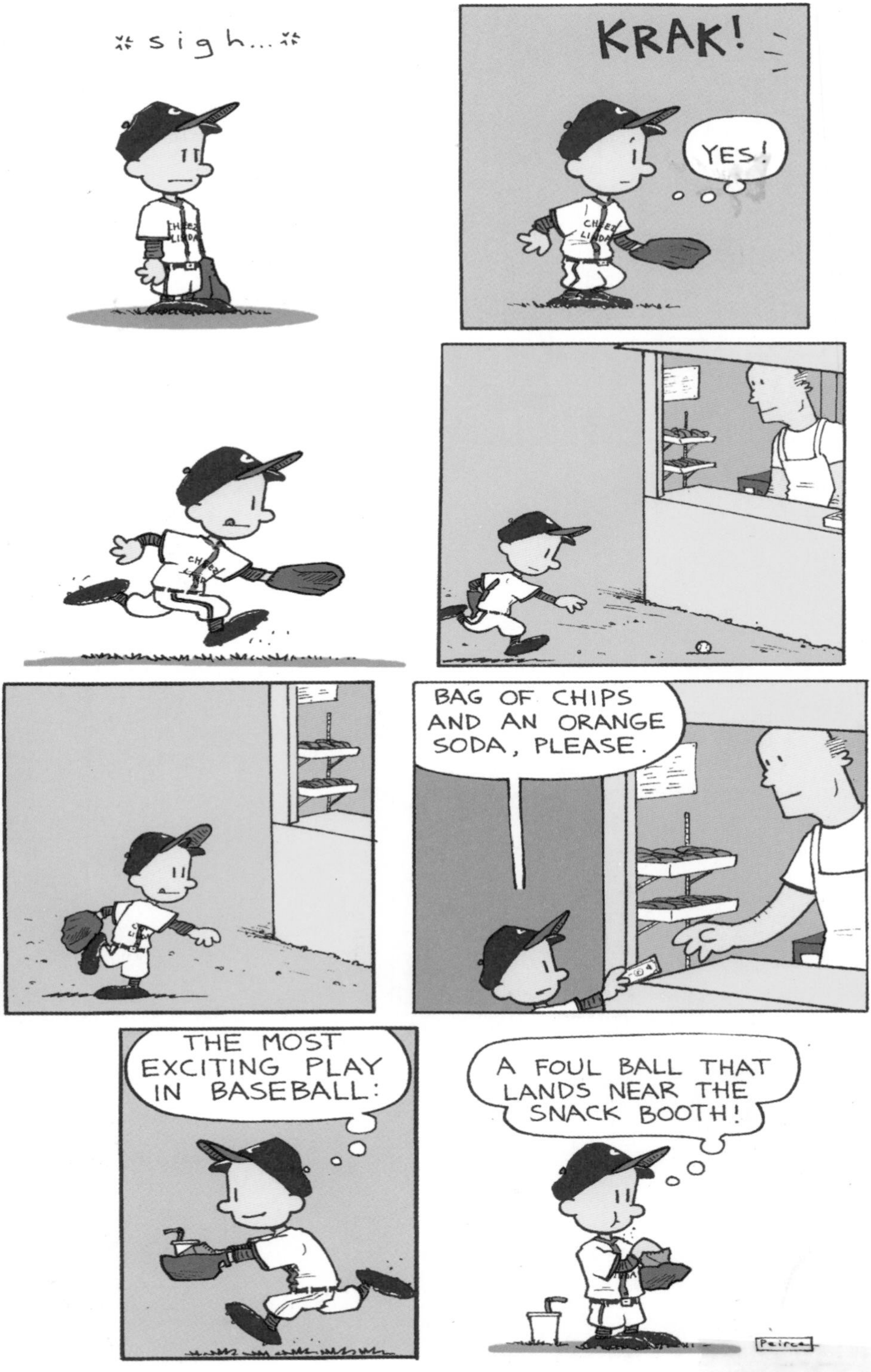
sigh...
KRAK!
YES!
BAG OF CHIPS AND AN ORANGE SODA, PLEASE.
THE MOST EXCITING PLAY IN BASEBALL:
A FOUL BALL THAT LANDS NEAR THE SNACK BOOTH!
Peirce

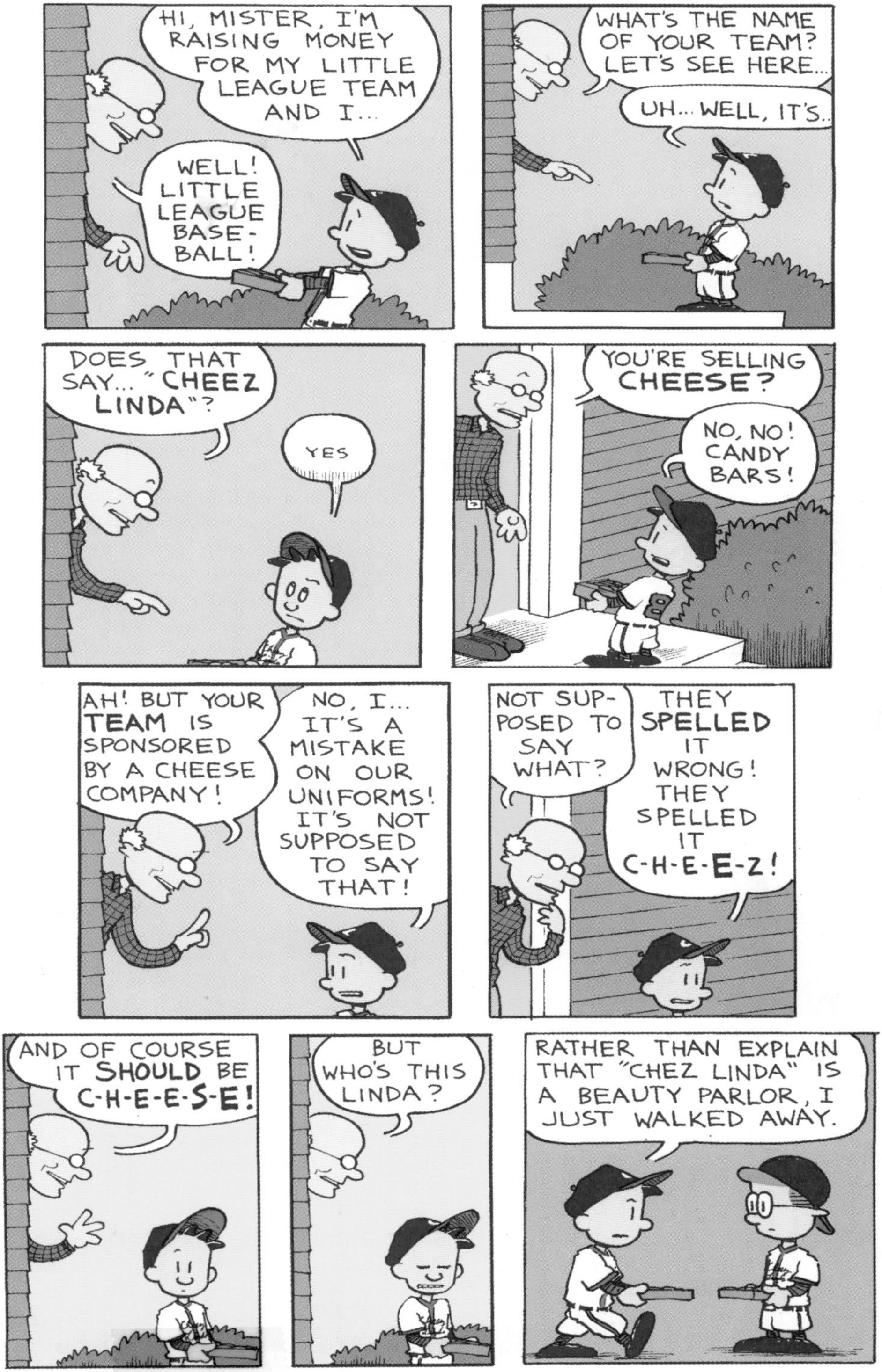
HI, MISTER, I'M RAISING MONEY FOR MY LITTLE LEAGUE TEAM AND I...
WELL! LITTLE LEAGUE BASE-BALL!
WHAT'S THE NAME OF YOUR TEAM? LET'S SEE HERE...
UH... WELL, IT'S...
DOES THAT SAY... "CHEEZ LINDA"?
YES
YOU'RE SELLING CHEESE?
NO, NO! CANDY BARS!
AH! BUT YOUR TEAM IS SPONSORED BY A CHEESE COMPANY!
NO, I... IT'S A MISTAKE ON OUR UNIFORMS! IT'S NOT SUPPOSED TO SAY THAT!
NOT SUP-POSED TO SAY WHAT?
THEY SPELLED IT WRONG! THEY SPELLED IT C-H-E-E-Z!
AND OF COURSE IT SHOULD BE C-H-E-E-S-E!
BUT WHO'S THIS LINDA?
RATHER THAN EXPLAIN THAT "CHEZ LINDA" IS A BEAUTY PARLOR, I JUST WALKED AWAY.

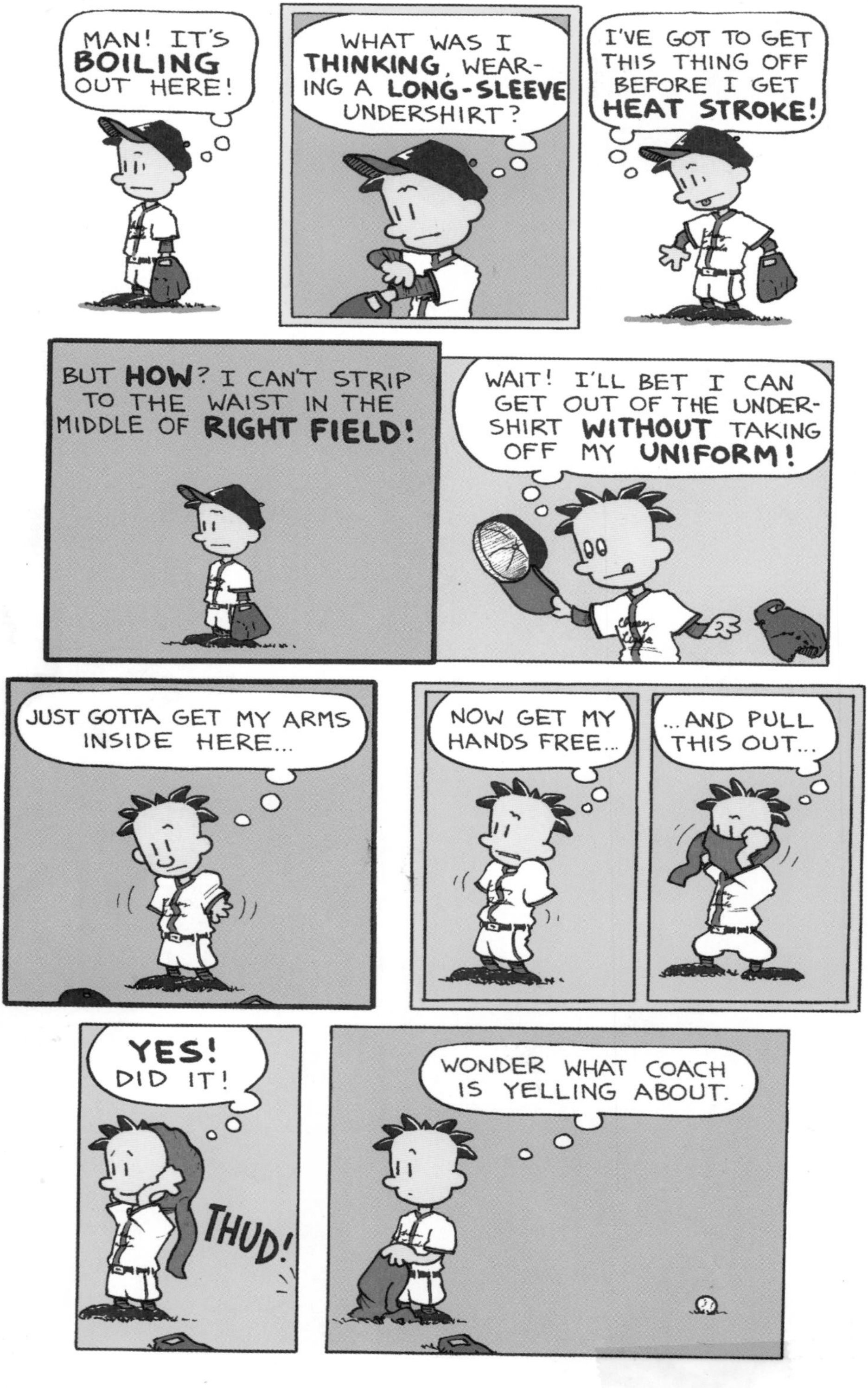
MAN! IT'S **BOILING** OUT HERE!
WHAT WAS I **THINKING**, WEARING A **LONG-SLEEVE** UNDERSHIRT?
I'VE GOT TO GET THIS THING OFF BEFORE I GET **HEAT STROKE!**
BUT **HOW**? I CAN'T STRIP TO THE WAIST IN THE MIDDLE OF **RIGHT FIELD!**
WAIT! I'LL BET I CAN GET OUT OF THE UNDERSHIRT **WITHOUT** TAKING OFF MY **UNIFORM!**
JUST GOTTA GET MY ARMS INSIDE HERE...
NOW GET MY HANDS FREE...
...AND PULL THIS OUT...
YES! DID IT!
THUD!
WONDER WHAT COACH IS YELLING ABOUT.

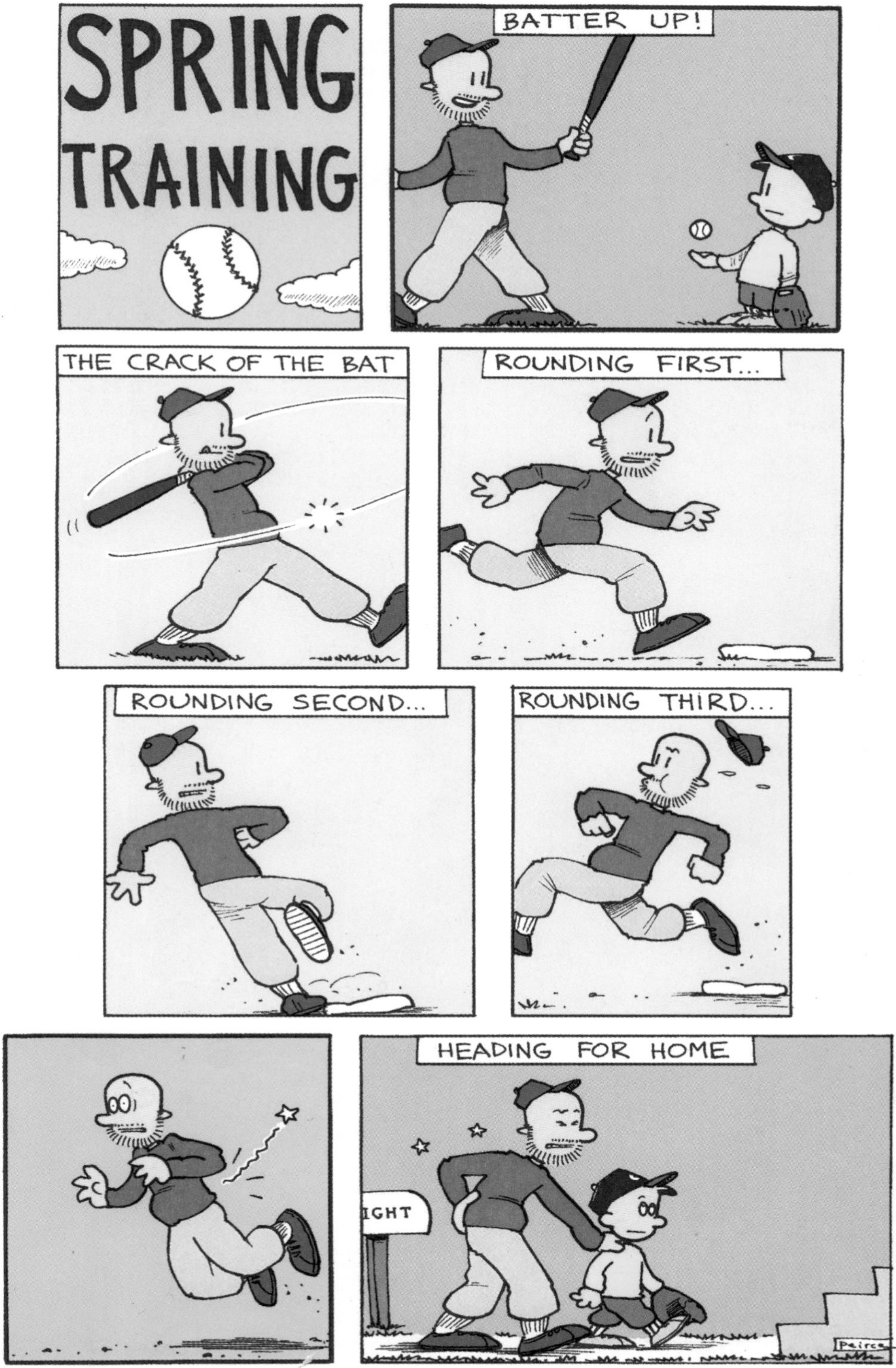
SPRING TRAINING
BATTER UP!
THE CRACK OF THE BAT
ROUNDING FIRST...
ROUNDING SECOND...
ROUNDING THIRD...
HEADING FOR HOME
IGHT
Peirce

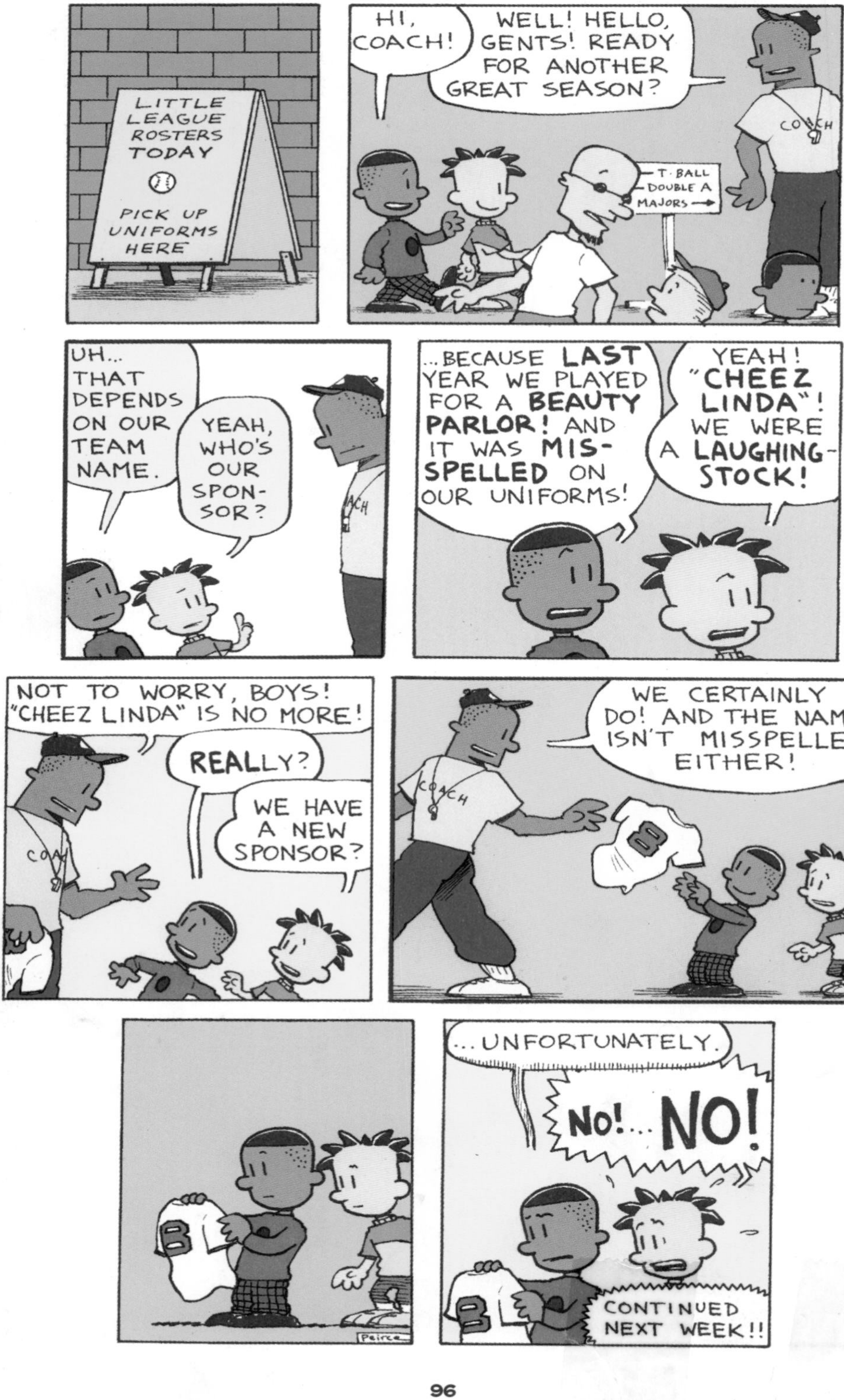

LITTLE LEAGUE ROSTERS TODAY
PICK UP UNIFORMS HERE
HI, COACH!
WELL! HELLO, GENTS! READY FOR ANOTHER GREAT SEASON?
COACH
T-BALL
DOUBLE A
MAJORS →
UH... THAT DEPENDS ON OUR TEAM NAME.
YEAH, WHO'S OUR SPON-SOR?
...BECAUSE LAST YEAR WE PLAYED FOR A BEAUTY PARLOR! AND IT WAS MIS-SPELLED ON OUR UNIFORMS!
YEAH! "CHEEZ LINDA"! WE WERE A LAUGHING-STOCK!
NOT TO WORRY, BOYS! "CHEEZ LINDA" IS NO MORE!
REALLY?
WE HAVE A NEW SPONSOR?
WE CERTAINLY DO! AND THE NAME ISN'T MISSPELLED, EITHER!
Peirce
...UNFORTUNATELY.
NO!... NO!
CONTINUED NEXT WEEK!!

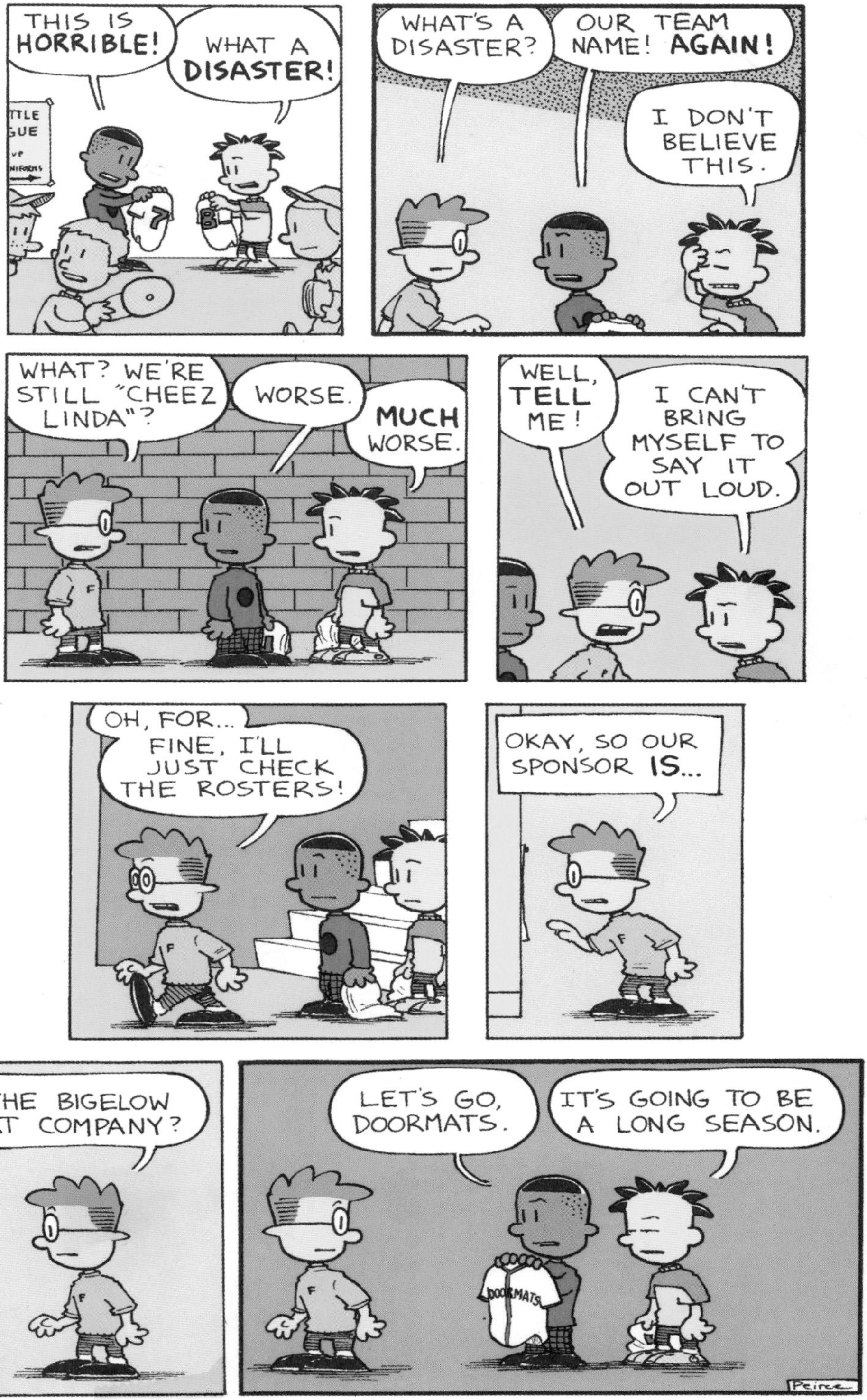
THIS IS HORRIBLE!
WHAT A DISASTER!
WHAT'S A DISASTER?
OUR TEAM NAME! AGAIN!
I DON'T BELIEVE THIS.
WHAT? WE'RE STILL "CHEEZ LINDA"?
WORSE.
MUCH WORSE.
WELL, TELL ME!
I CAN'T BRING MYSELF TO SAY IT OUT LOUD.
OH, FOR...
FINE, I'LL JUST CHECK THE ROSTERS!
OKAY, SO OUR SPONSOR IS...
...THE BIGELOW MAT COMPANY?
LET'S GO, DOORMATS.
IT'S GOING TO BE A LONG SEASON.
DOORMATS
Peirce

HOME! HOME!! PLAY AT THE PLATE!

WUMP!

HOLY SMOKES! THIS GUY'S COMIN' FAST!... AND HE'S **HUGE!**

I'M GONNA GET FLATTENED LIKE A PANCAKE!

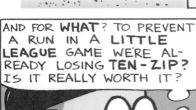

AND FOR **WHAT**? TO PREVENT A RUN IN A **LITTLE LEAGUE** GAME WE'RE ALREADY LOSING **TEN-ZIP**? IS IT REALLY WORTH IT?

I DON'T THINK SO.

SAFE!

HEY, STAN! YOU FORGOT TO WIPE YOUR FEET!

HA HA HA HA HA HA HA

PLAYING FOR THE "DOORMATS" IS BECOMING A SELF-FULFILLING PROPHECY.

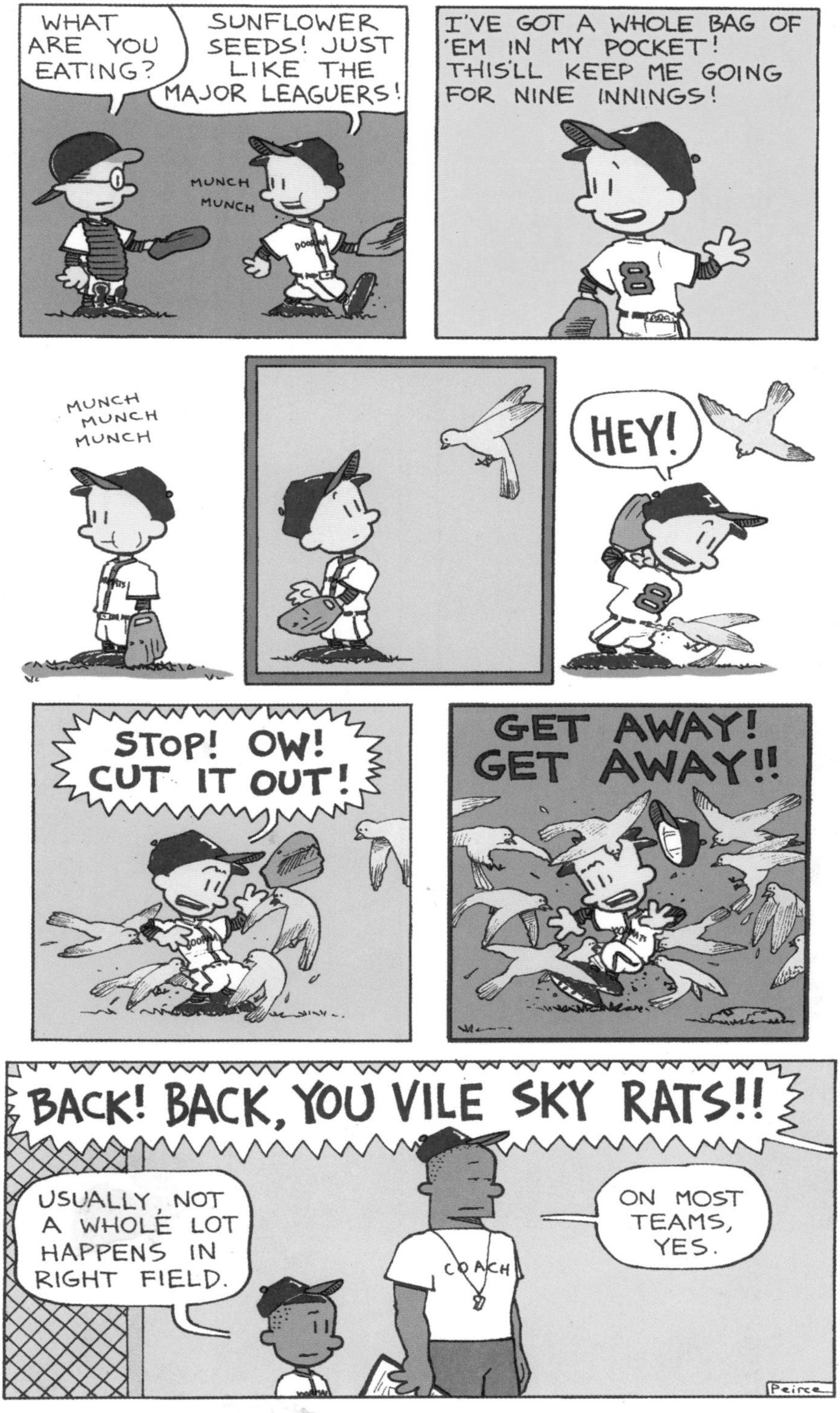
WHAT ARE YOU EATING?
SUNFLOWER SEEDS! JUST LIKE THE MAJOR LEAGUERS!
MUNCH MUNCH
I'VE GOT A WHOLE BAG OF 'EM IN MY POCKET! THIS'LL KEEP ME GOING FOR NINE INNINGS!
MUNCH MUNCH MUNCH
HEY!
STOP! OW! CUT IT OUT!
GET AWAY! GET AWAY!!
BACK! BACK, YOU VILE SKY RATS!!
USUALLY, NOT A WHOLE LOT HAPPENS IN RIGHT FIELD.
ON MOST TEAMS, YES.
COACH
Peirce

GANG, I WON'T BE ABLE TO RUN TODAY'S PRAC- TICE BECAUSE I HAVE TO ATTEND A COACHES' CLINIC!
COACH
...BUT I'M LEAVING YOU IN GOOD HANDS! COACH JOHN IS GOING TO HANDLE THINGS!
COACH
YOU ALL REMEMBER COACH JOHN!
COACH
...AS ONE REMEMBERS A VIOLENT BOUT OF THE STOMACH FLU.
NO SLOUCH- ING, SCRUBS!
Peirce

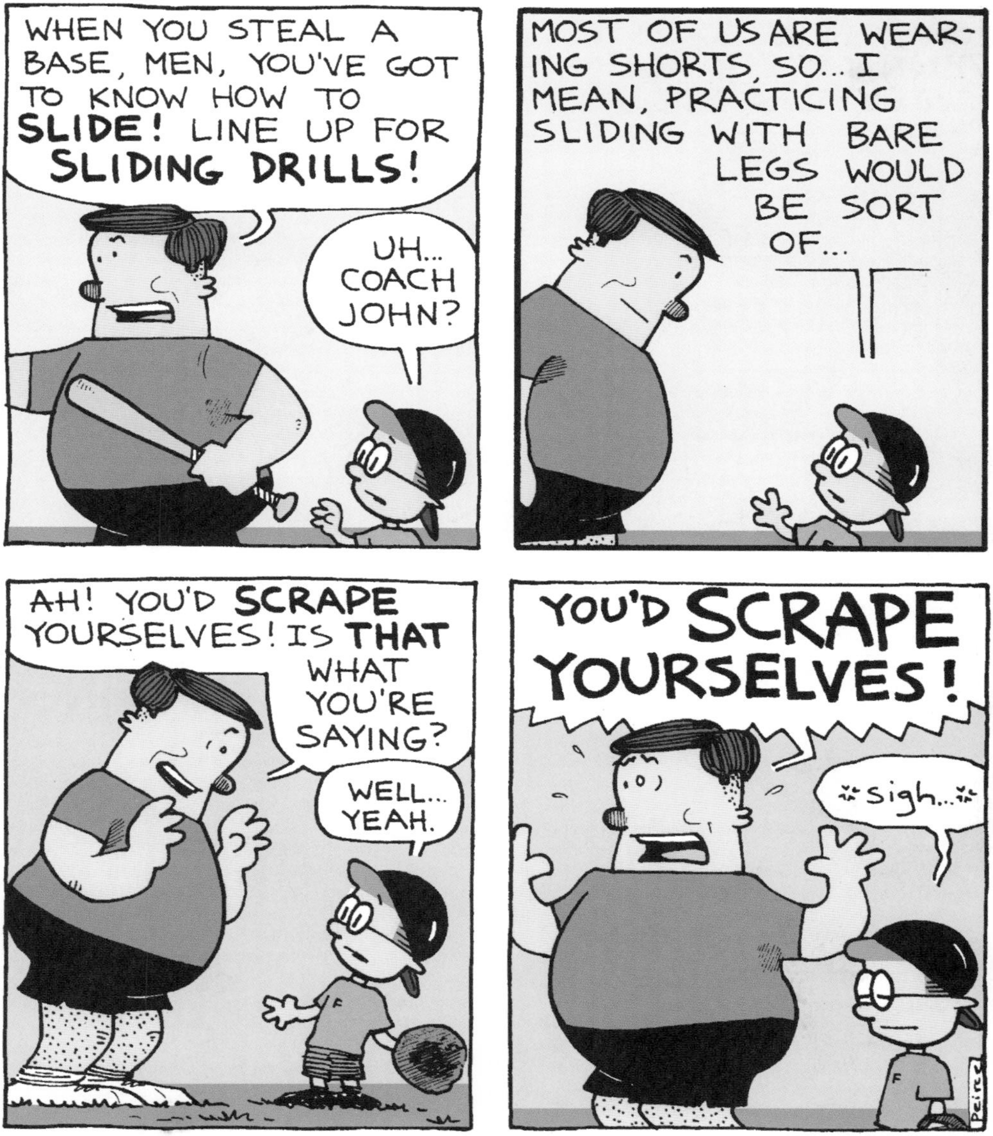
WHEN YOU STEAL A BASE, MEN, YOU'VE GOT TO KNOW HOW TO SLIDE! LINE UP FOR SLIDING DRILLS!
UH... COACH JOHN?
MOST OF US ARE WEARING SHORTS, SO... I MEAN, PRACTICING SLIDING WITH BARE LEGS WOULD BE SORT OF...
AH! YOU'D SCRAPE YOURSELVES! IS THAT WHAT YOU'RE SAYING?
WELL... YEAH.
YOU'D SCRAPE YOURSELVES!
sigh...
PEIRCE

OKAY, HERE COMES A **BUNT!** **CHARGE** THE BALL! **CHARGE** IT!
KA-
POW!
FAKED YOU OUT! ASSUME **NOTHING**, SOLDIERS!!
MY ENTIRE LIFE JUST FLASHED BEFORE MY EYES.
Peirce

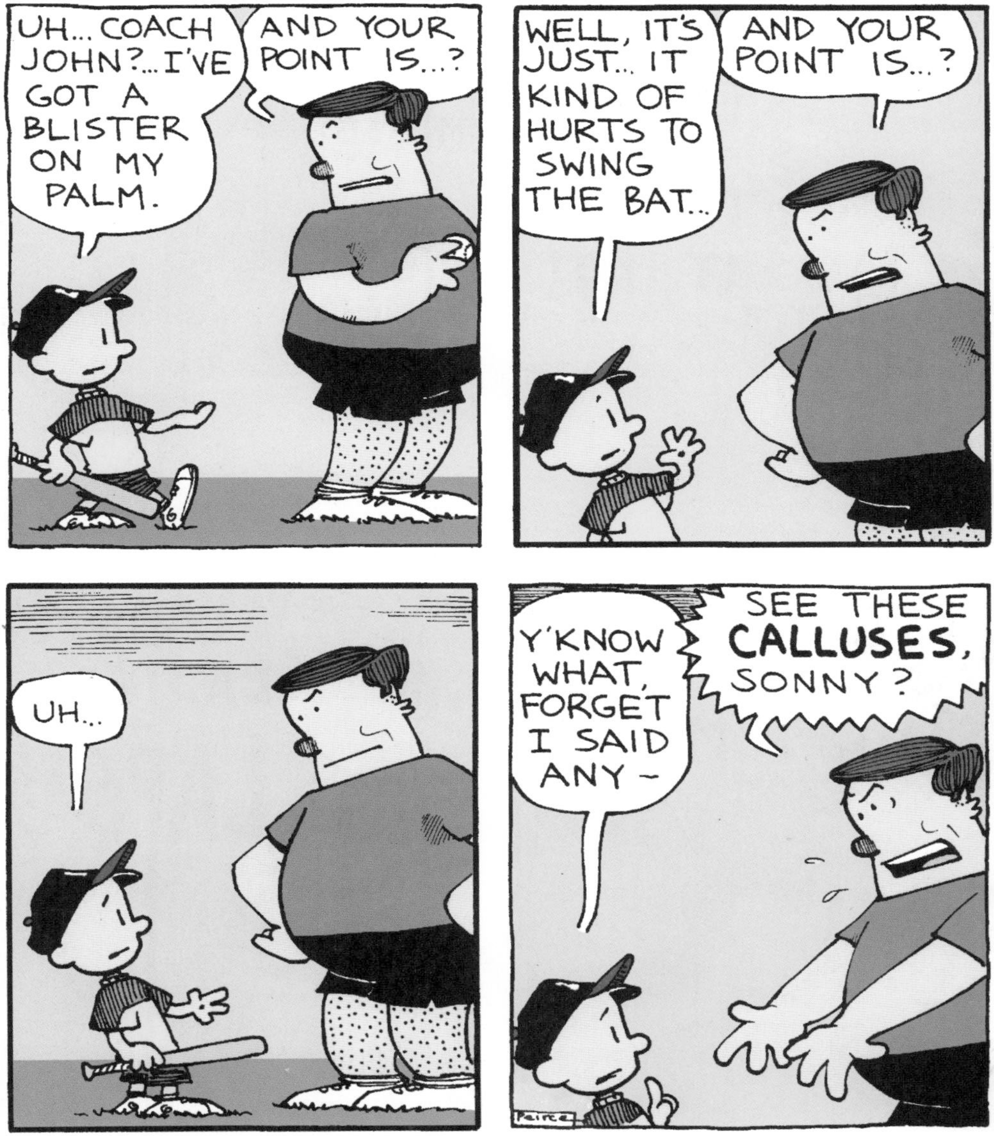
UH... COACH JOHN?... I'VE GOT A BLISTER ON MY PALM.
AND YOUR POINT IS...?
WELL, IT'S JUST... IT KIND OF HURTS TO SWING THE BAT...
AND YOUR POINT IS...?
UH...
Y'KNOW WHAT, FORGET I SAID ANY–
SEE THESE **CALLUSES**, SONNY?
PEIRCE

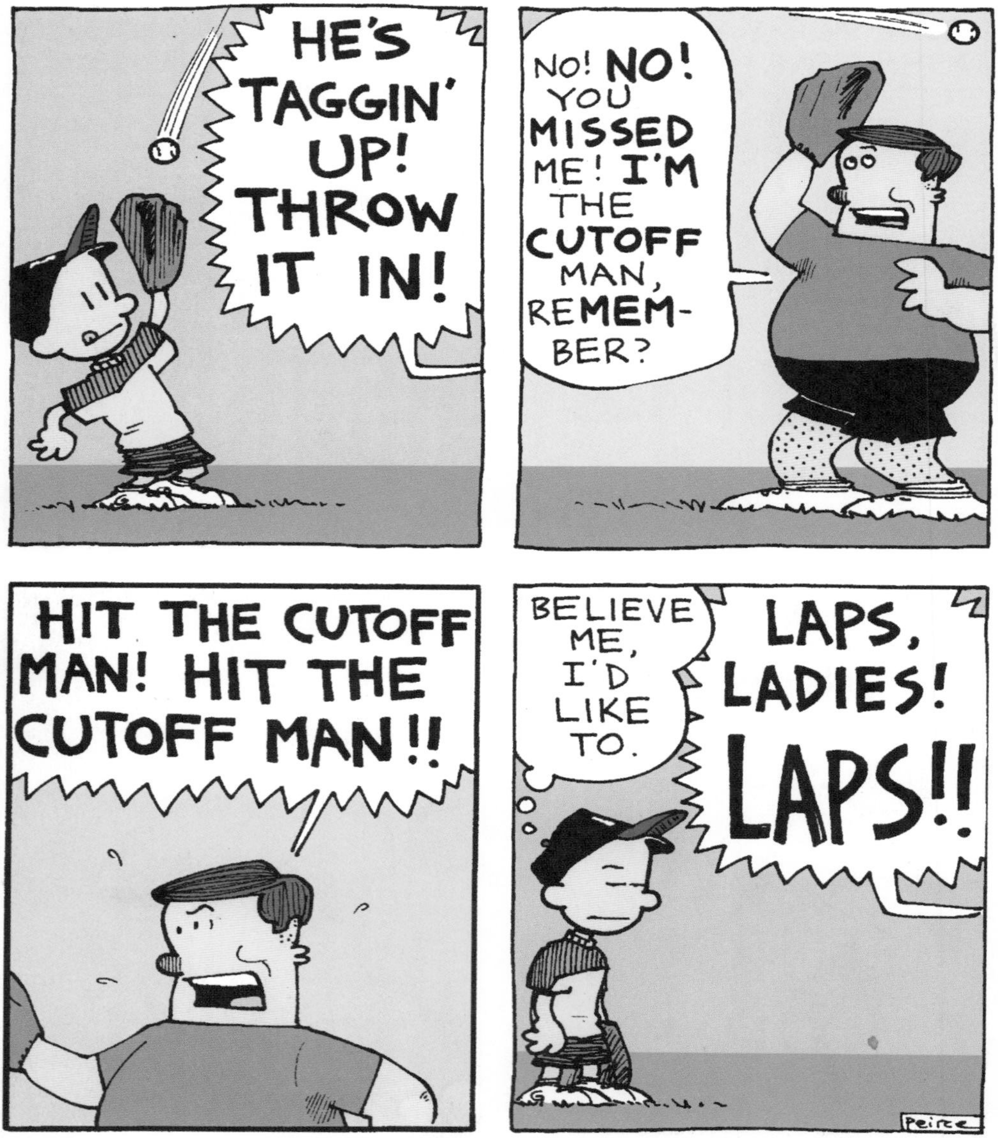
HE'S TAGGIN' UP! THROW IT IN!
NO! NO! YOU MISSED ME! I'M THE CUTOFF MAN, REMEMBER?
HIT THE CUTOFF MAN! HIT THE CUTOFF MAN!!
BELIEVE ME, I'D LIKE TO.
LAPS, LADIES! LAPS!!
Peirce

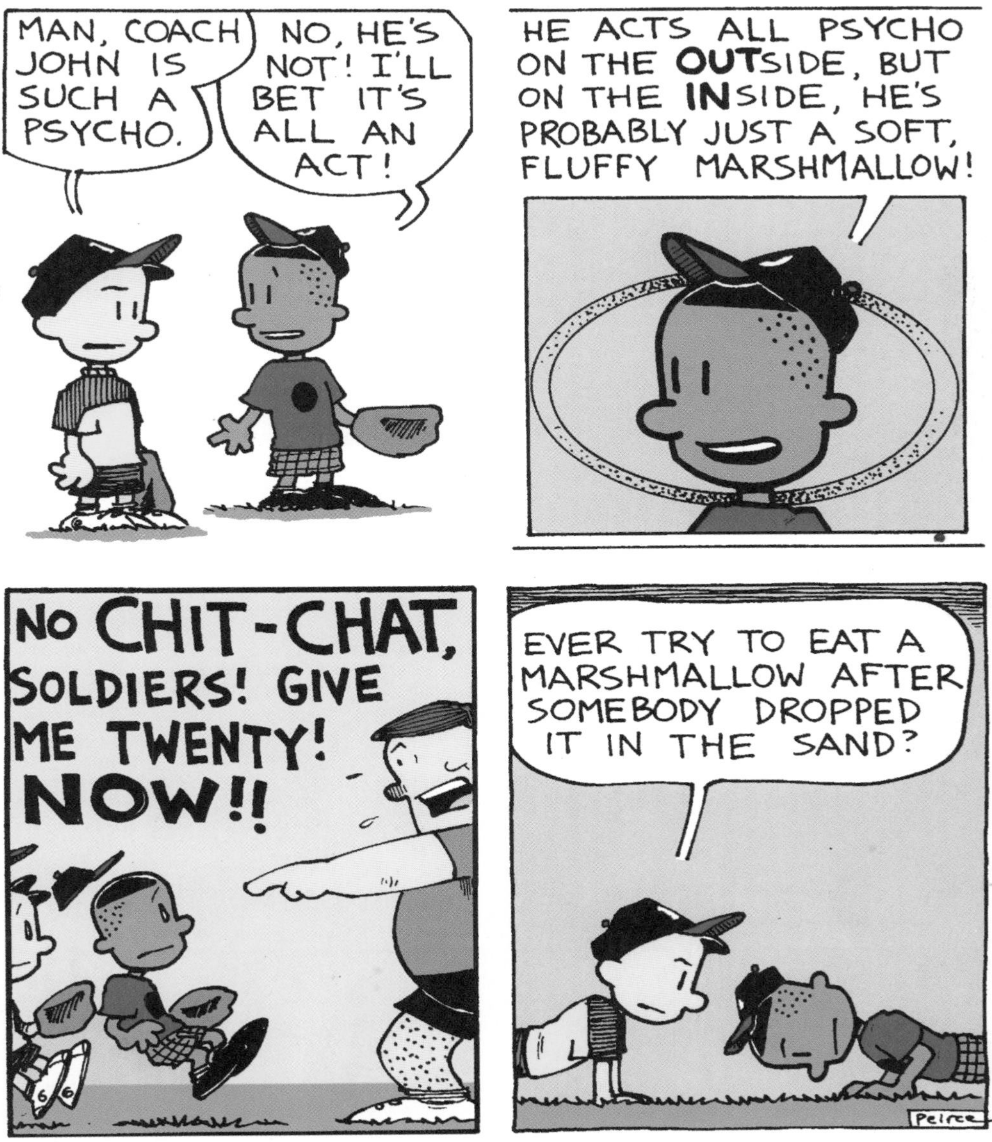
MAN, COACH JOHN IS SUCH A PSYCHO.
NO, HE'S NOT! I'LL BET IT'S ALL AN ACT!
HE ACTS ALL PSYCHO ON THE OUTSIDE, BUT ON THE INSIDE, HE'S PROBABLY JUST A SOFT, FLUFFY MARSHMALLOW!
NO CHIT-CHAT, SOLDIERS! GIVE ME TWENTY! NOW!!
EVER TRY TO EAT A MARSHMALLOW AFTER SOMEBODY DROPPED IT IN THE SAND?
PEIRCE

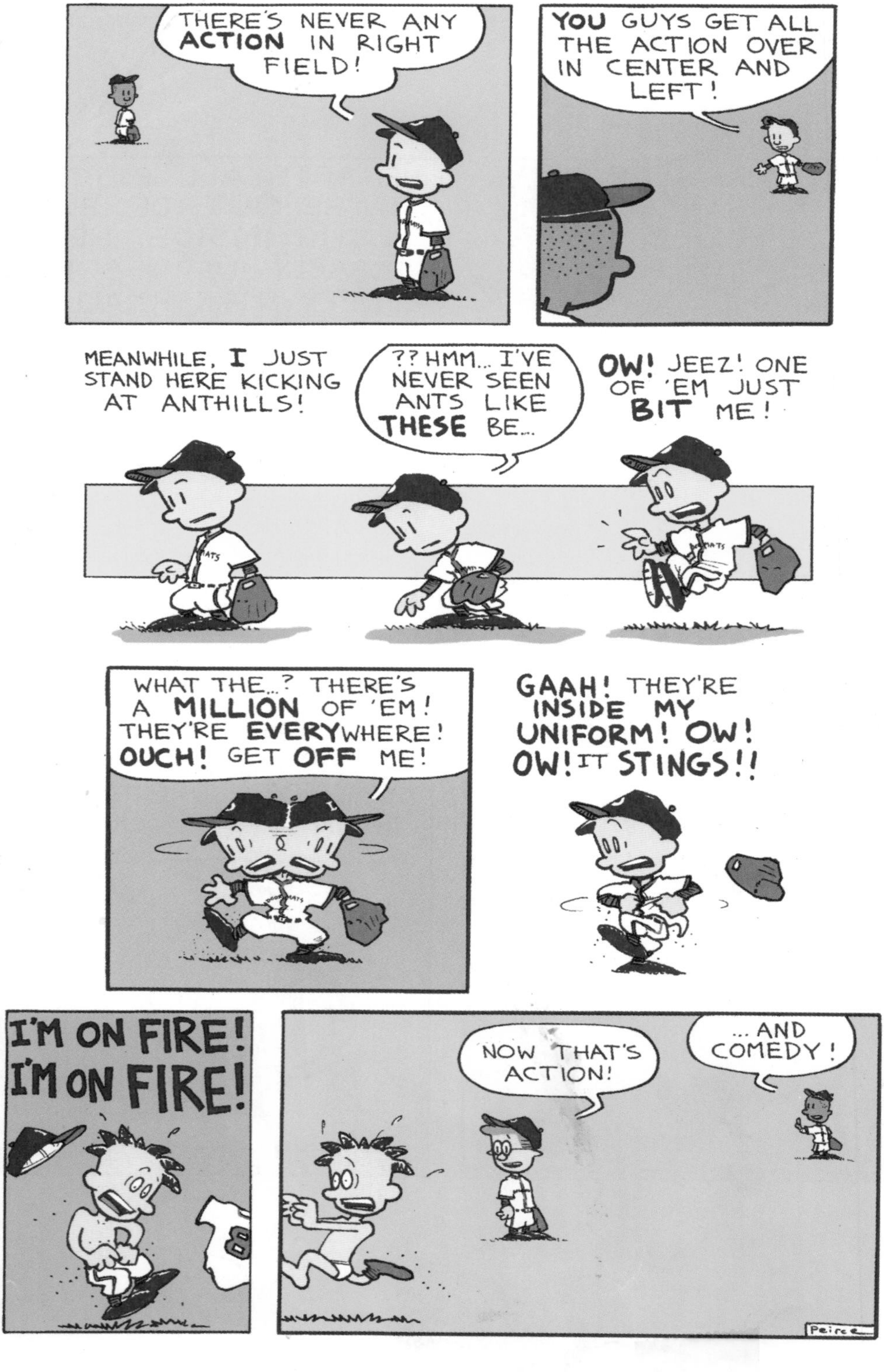
THERE'S NEVER ANY ACTION IN RIGHT FIELD!
YOU GUYS GET ALL THE ACTION OVER IN CENTER AND LEFT!
MEANWHILE, I JUST STAND HERE KICKING AT ANTHILLS!
?? HMM... I'VE NEVER SEEN ANTS LIKE THESE BE...
OW! JEEZ! ONE OF 'EM JUST BIT ME!
WHAT THE...? THERE'S A MILLION OF 'EM! THEY'RE EVERYWHERE! OUCH! GET OFF ME!
GAAH! THEY'RE INSIDE MY UNIFORM! OW! OW! IT STINGS!!
I'M ON FIRE! I'M ON FIRE!
NOW THAT'S ACTION!
...AND COMEDY!
Peirce

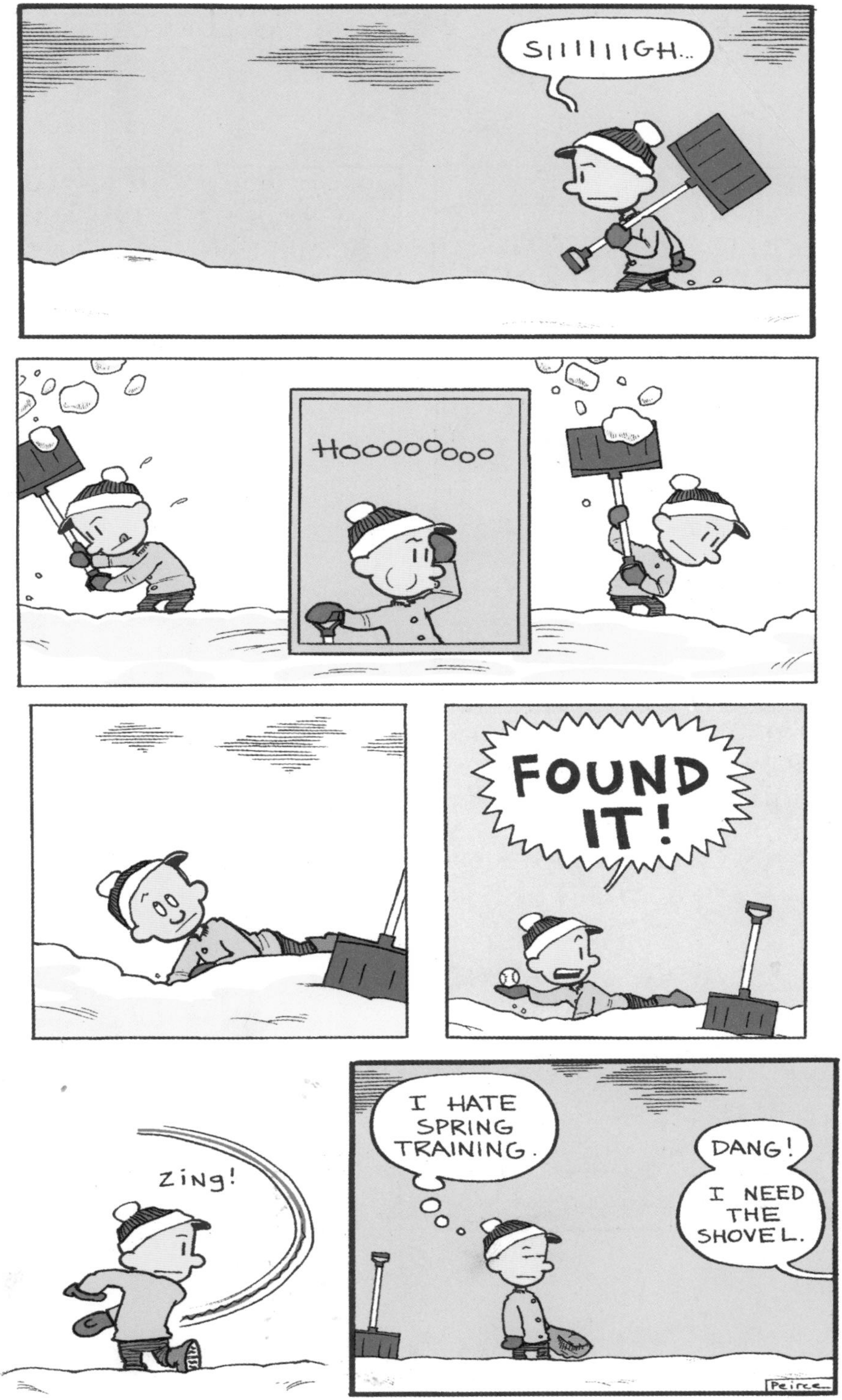
SIIIIIGH...
HOOOOOOOO
FOUND IT!
ZING!
I HATE SPRING TRAINING.
DANG!
I NEED THE SHOVEL.
Peirce

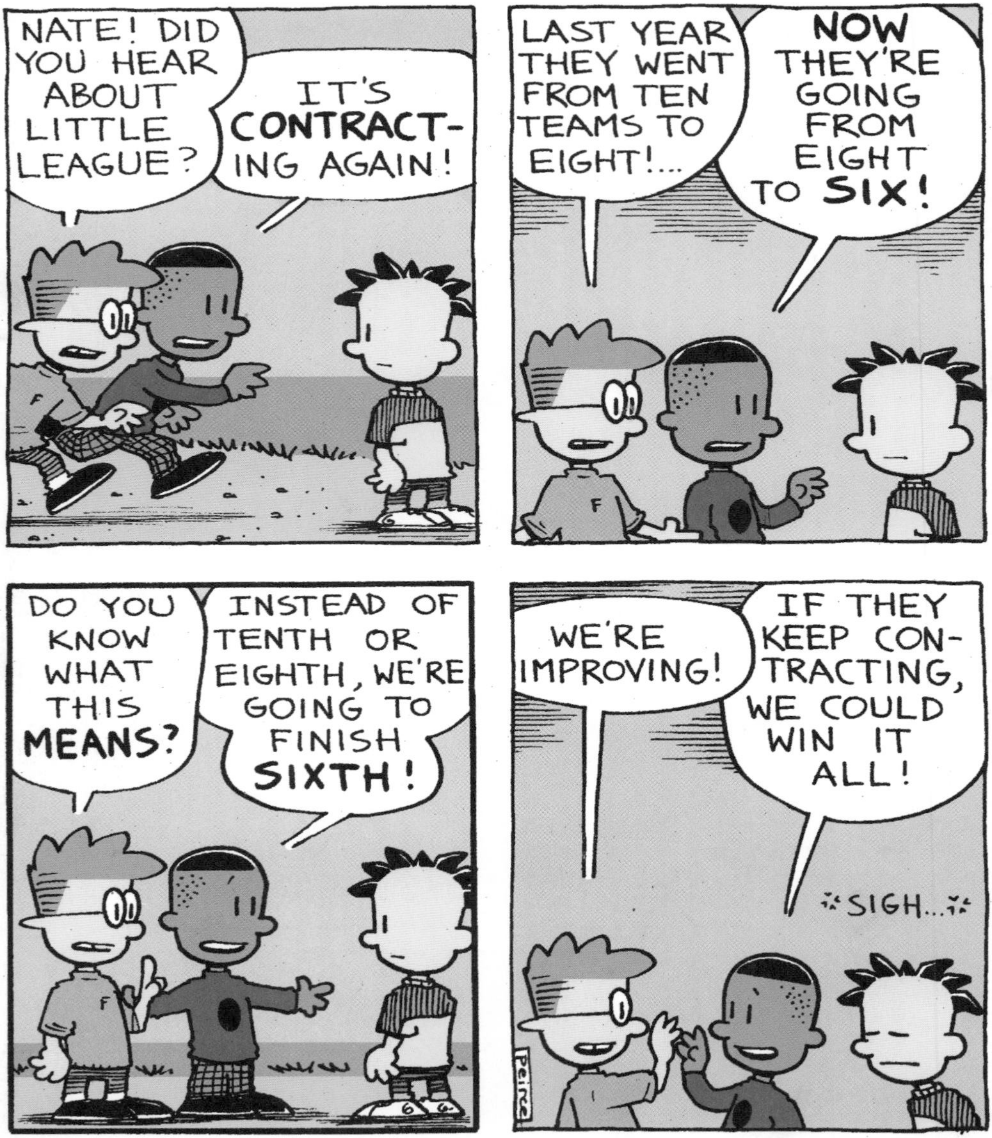
NATE! DID YOU HEAR ABOUT LITTLE LEAGUE?
IT'S CONTRACTING AGAIN!
LAST YEAR THEY WENT FROM TEN TEAMS TO EIGHT!...
NOW THEY'RE GOING FROM EIGHT TO SIX!
DO YOU KNOW WHAT THIS MEANS?
INSTEAD OF TENTH OR EIGHTH, WE'RE GOING TO FINISH SIXTH!
WE'RE IMPROVING!
IF THEY KEEP CONTRACTING, WE COULD WIN IT ALL!
SIGH...
Peirce

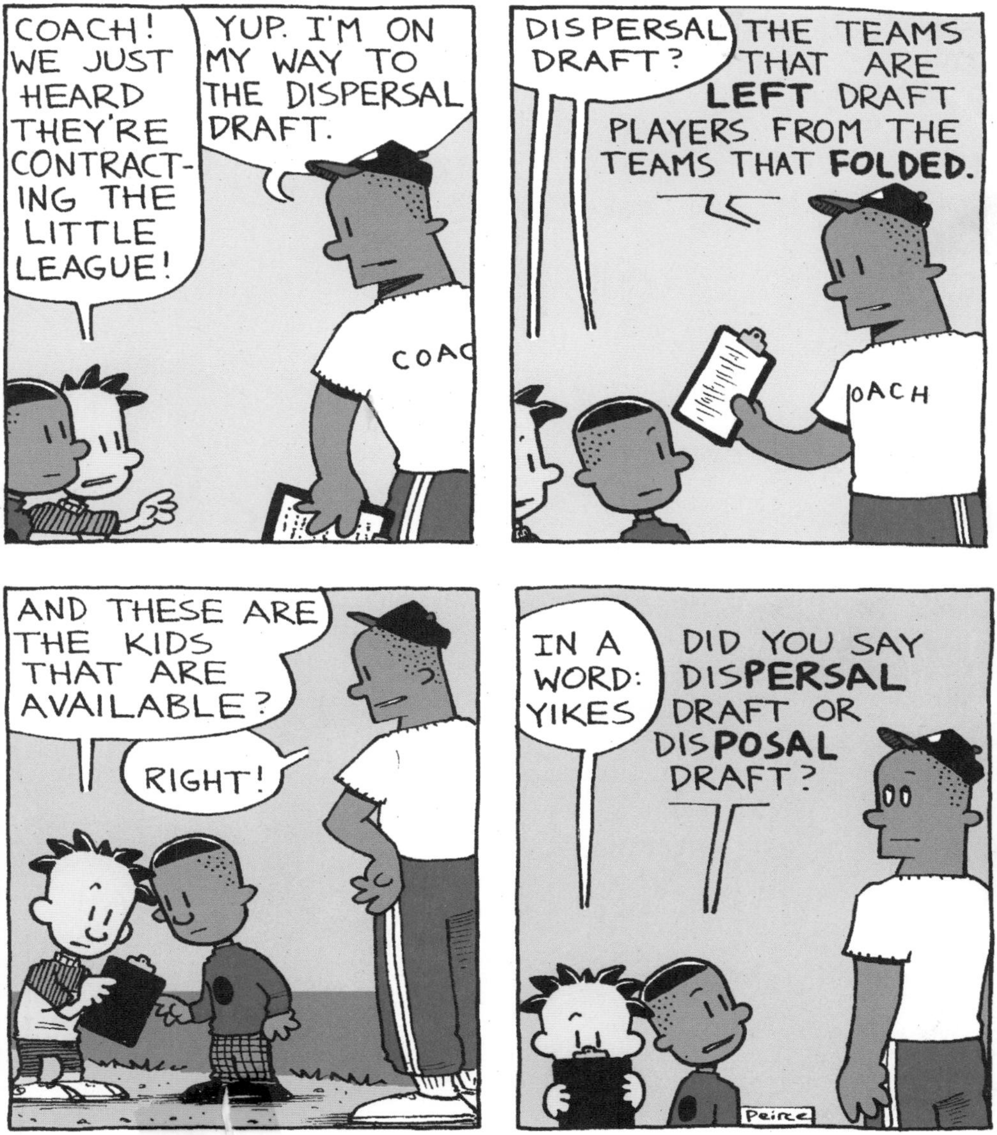
COACH! WE JUST HEARD THEY'RE CONTRACTING THE LITTLE LEAGUE!
YUP. I'M ON MY WAY TO THE DISPERSAL DRAFT.
COAC
DISPERSAL DRAFT?
THE TEAMS THAT ARE **LEFT** DRAFT PLAYERS FROM THE TEAMS THAT **FOLDED.**
OACH
AND THESE ARE THE KIDS THAT ARE AVAILABLE?
RIGHT!
IN A WORD: YIKES
DID YOU SAY DIS**PERSAL** DRAFT OR DIS**POSAL** DRAFT?
Peirce

SO YOU'RE OFF TO THE DISPERSAL DRAFT, EH, COACH?
YUP!
WELL, DON'T DRAFT ANYONE WHO PLAYS RIGHT FIELD! THAT'S **MY** POSITION!
OR **CENTER** FIELD! THAT'S WHERE **I** PLAY!
AND DON'T PROMISE MY **NUMBER** TO SOME OTHER KID! **I'M** NUMBER EIGHT!
AND **I'M** NUMBER **SIX**!
THERE'S NO "I" IN TEAM.
AND DON'T DRAFT ANY DORKS!
YEAH, WE'VE GOT AN **IMAGE** TO KEEP UP!
Peirce

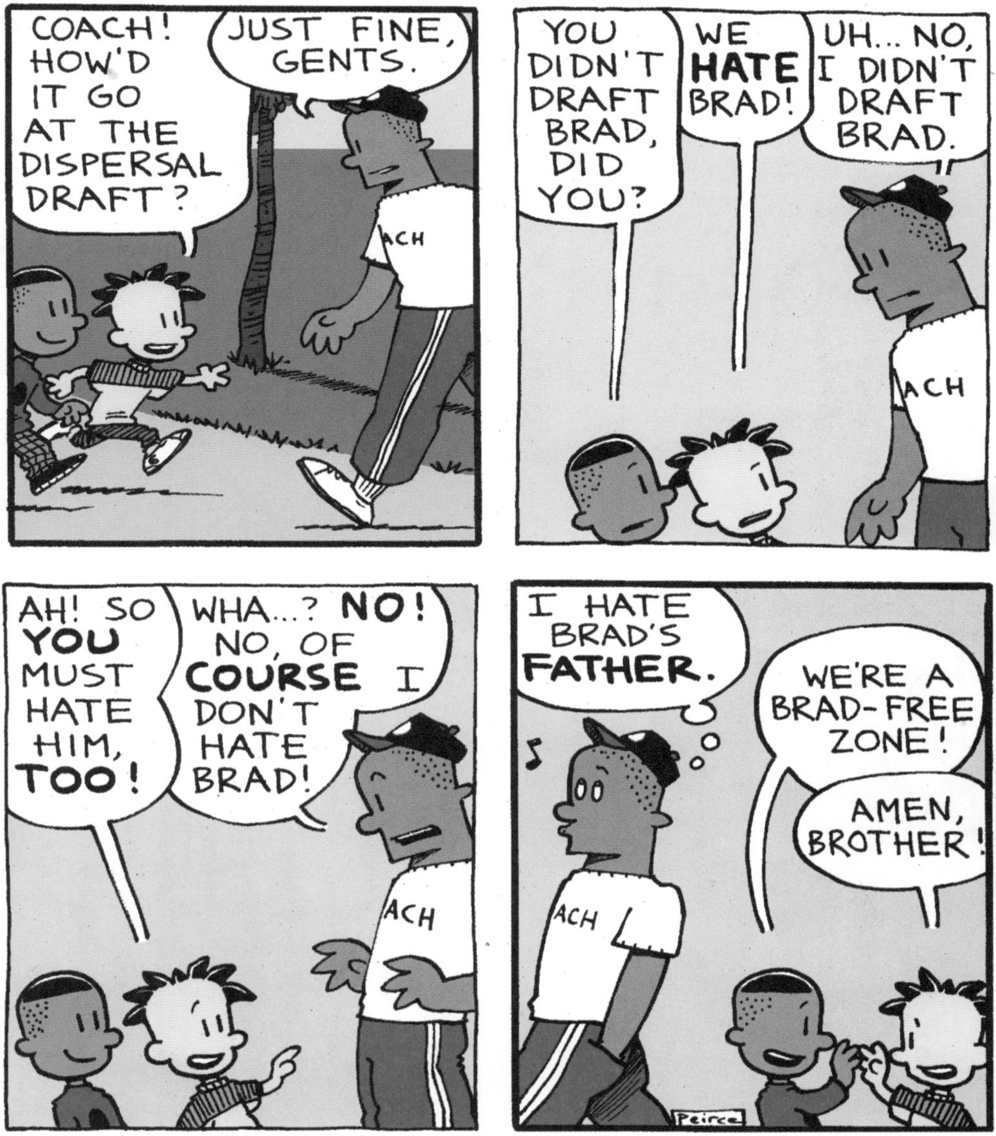
COACH! HOW'D IT GO AT THE DISPERSAL DRAFT?
JUST FINE, GENTS.
ACH
YOU DIDN'T DRAFT BRAD, DID YOU?
WE **HATE** BRAD!
UH... NO, I DIDN'T DRAFT BRAD.
ACH
AH! SO **YOU** MUST HATE HIM, **TOO**!
WHA...? **NO!** NO, OF **COURSE** I DON'T HATE BRAD!
ACH
I HATE BRAD'S **FATHER**.
WE'RE A BRAD-FREE ZONE!
AMEN, BROTHER!
ACH
Peirce

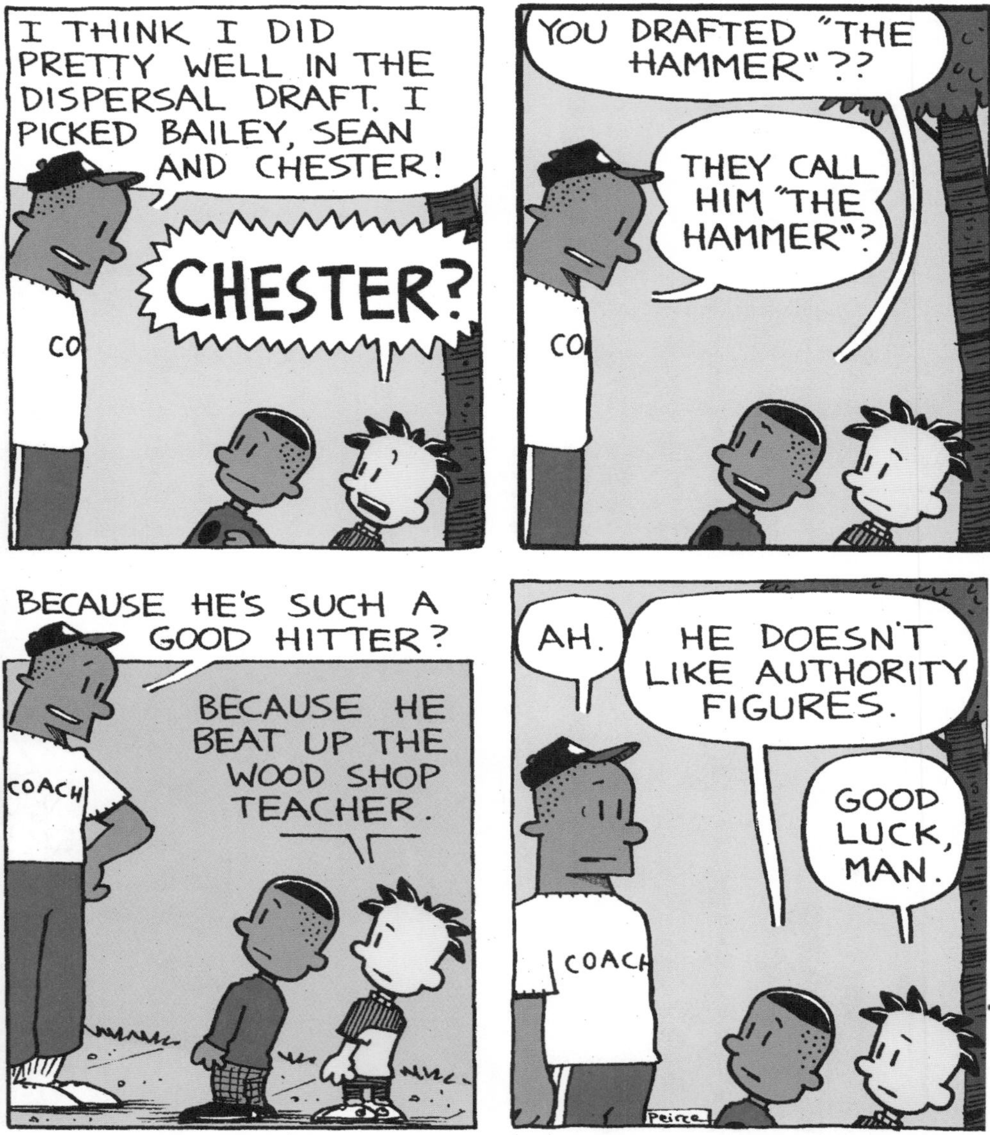
I THINK I DID PRETTY WELL IN THE DISPERSAL DRAFT. I PICKED BAILEY, SEAN AND CHESTER!
CHESTER?
CO
YOU DRAFTED "THE HAMMER"??
THEY CALL HIM "THE HAMMER"?
CO
BECAUSE HE'S SUCH A GOOD HITTER?
BECAUSE HE BEAT UP THE WOOD SHOP TEACHER.
COACH
AH.
HE DOESN'T LIKE AUTHORITY FIGURES.
GOOD LUCK, MAN.
COACH
Peirce

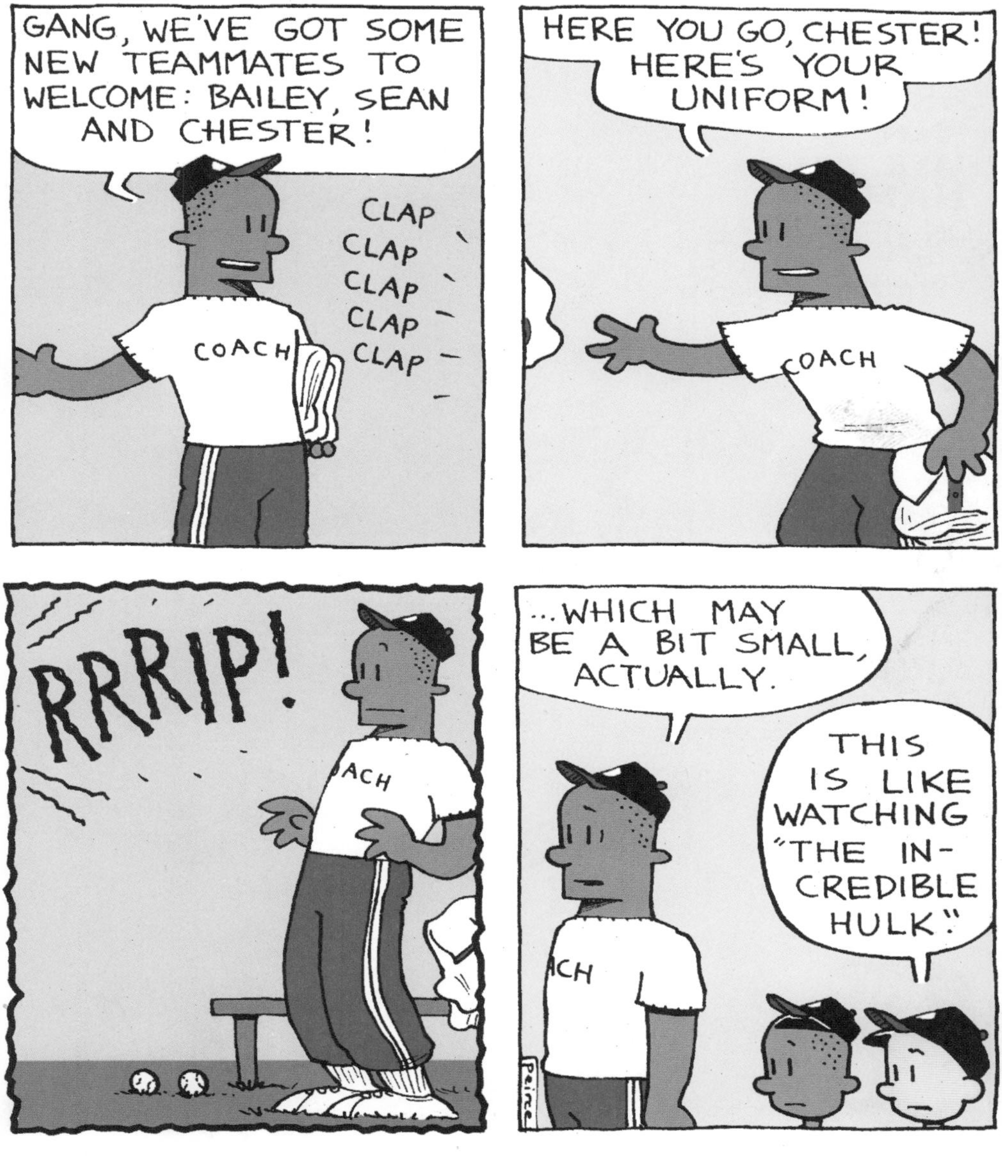
GANG, WE'VE GOT SOME NEW TEAMMATES TO WELCOME: BAILEY, SEAN AND CHESTER!
CLAP CLAP CLAP CLAP CLAP
COACH
HERE YOU GO, CHESTER! HERE'S YOUR UNIFORM!
COACH
RRRIP!
...WHICH MAY BE A BIT SMALL, ACTUALLY.
THIS IS LIKE WATCHING "THE INCREDIBLE HULK."
Peirce

COACH! OUR JERSEYS DON'T HAVE A NAME ON 'EM!
WE HAVE NO NAME!
OACH
THAT'S ONE REASON THE LEAGUE CONTRACTED! WE'VE LOST SOME OF OUR SPONSORS!
OACH
SO WHO ARE WE, THEN?
I GUESS WE'RE... THE NOTHINGS!
"LET'S GO, NOTHINGS"?
I'M PINING FOR THE GOOD OL' DAYS OF "LET'S GO, CHEZ LINDA."
Peirce

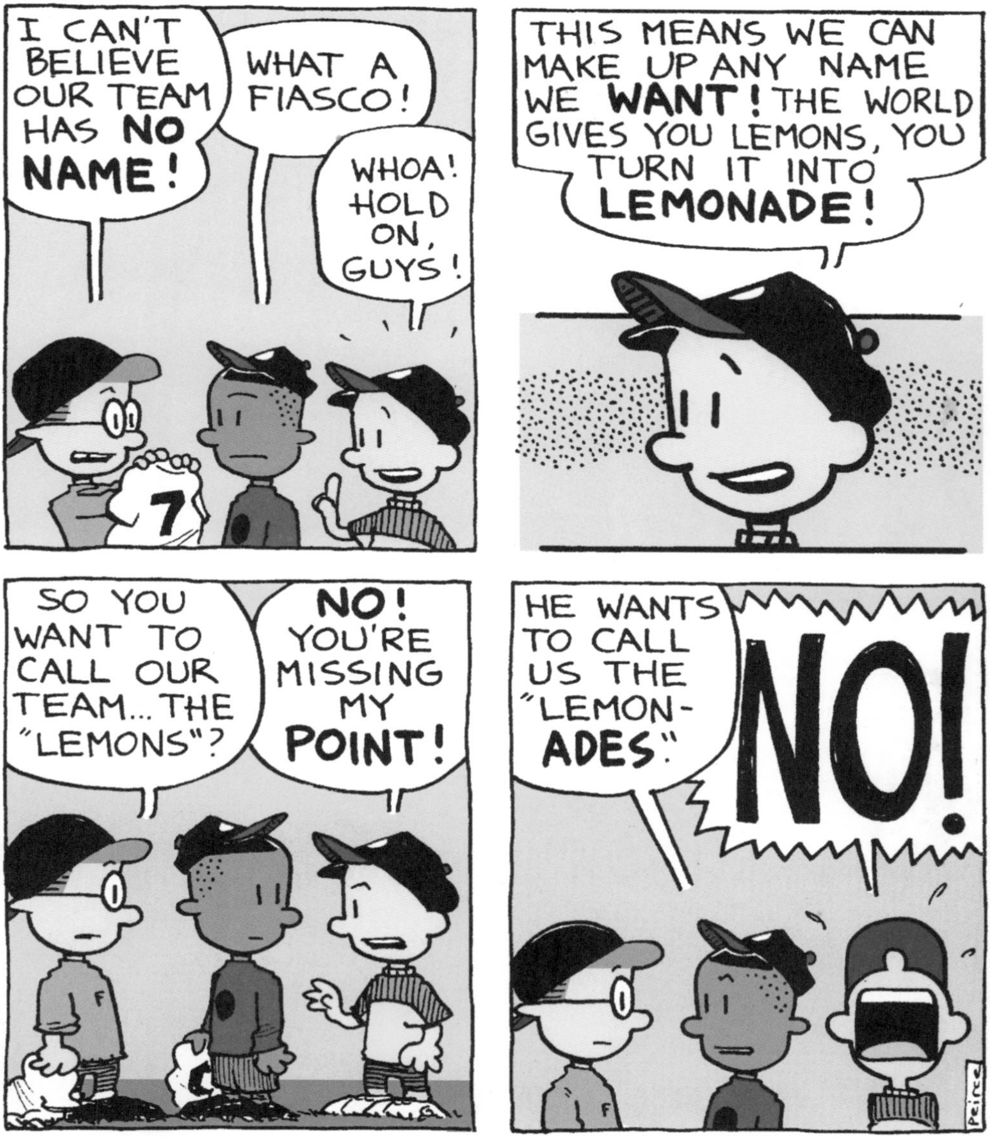
I CAN'T BELIEVE OUR TEAM HAS NO NAME!
WHAT A FIASCO!
WHOA! HOLD ON, GUYS!
7
THIS MEANS WE CAN MAKE UP ANY NAME WE WANT! THE WORLD GIVES YOU LEMONS, YOU TURN IT INTO LEMONADE!
SO YOU WANT TO CALL OUR TEAM... THE "LEMONS"?
NO! YOU'RE MISSING MY POINT!
HE WANTS TO CALL US THE "LEMON-ADES."
NO!
Peirce

COACH, SINCE THE **LEAGUE** DIDN'T GIVE US A TEAM NAME, CAN **WE** MAKE ONE UP?
SURE!
COACH
HOW 'BOUT THE YANKEES?
NO! THE RED SOX!
YANKEES!
RED SOX!
YANKEES!
RED SOX!!
1918!
JETER STINKS!!
PERSONALLY, I'M A TIGERS FAN.
ACH
Peirce

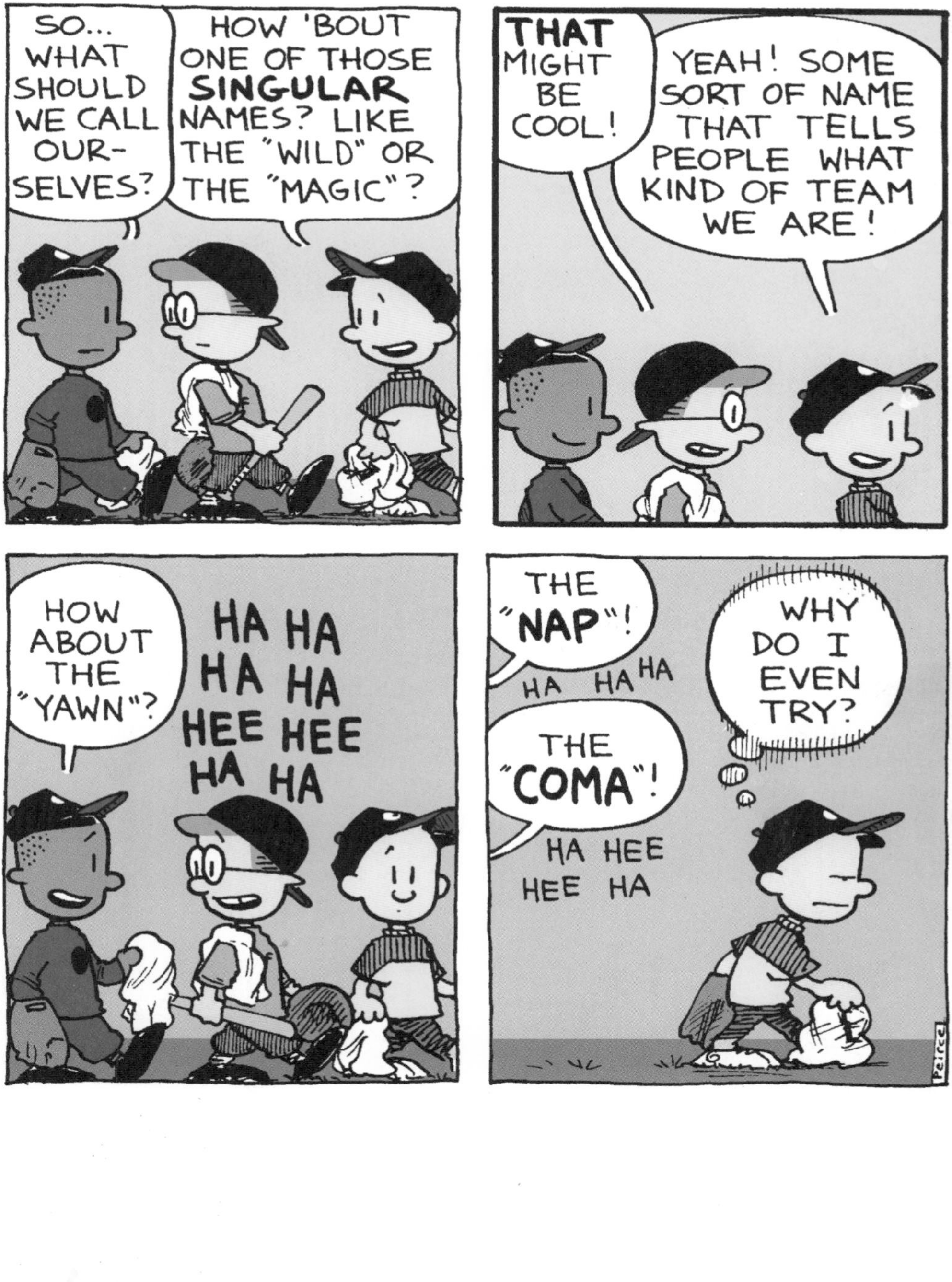
SO... WHAT SHOULD WE CALL OURSELVES?
HOW 'BOUT ONE OF THOSE **SINGULAR** NAMES? LIKE THE "WILD" OR THE "MAGIC"?
THAT MIGHT BE COOL!
YEAH! SOME SORT OF NAME THAT TELLS PEOPLE WHAT KIND OF TEAM WE ARE!
HOW ABOUT THE "YAWN"?
HA HA HA HA HEE HEE HA HA
THE "**NAP**"!
HA HA HA
THE "**COMA**"!
HA HEE HEE HA
WHY DO I EVEN TRY?
Peirce

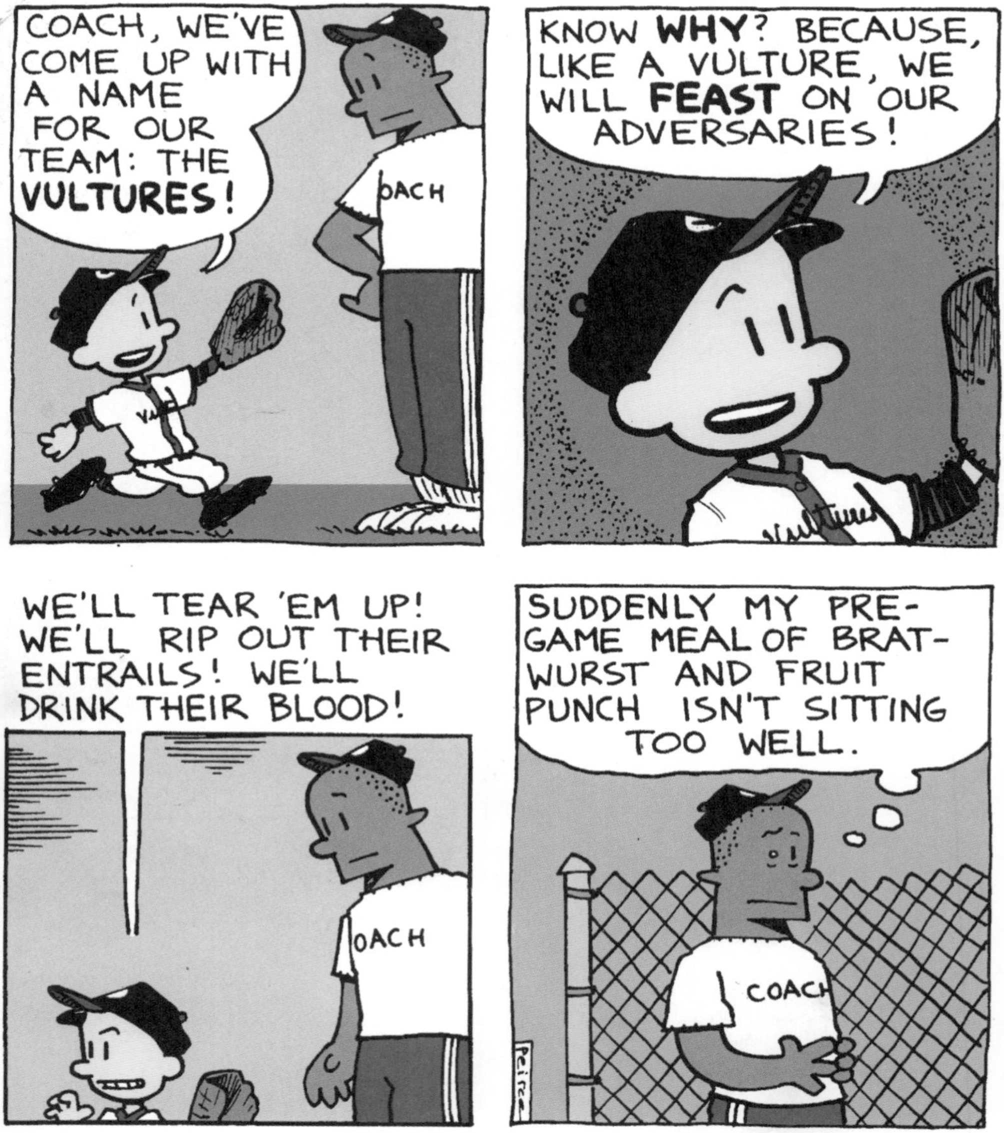
COACH, WE'VE COME UP WITH A NAME FOR OUR TEAM: THE **VULTURES**!
OACH
KNOW **WHY**? BECAUSE, LIKE A VULTURE, WE WILL **FEAST** ON OUR ADVERSARIES!
WE'LL TEAR 'EM UP! WE'LL RIP OUT THEIR ENTRAILS! WE'LL DRINK THEIR BLOOD!
OACH
SUDDENLY MY PRE-GAME MEAL OF BRAT-WURST AND FRUIT PUNCH ISN'T SITTING TOO WELL.
COACH
Peirce

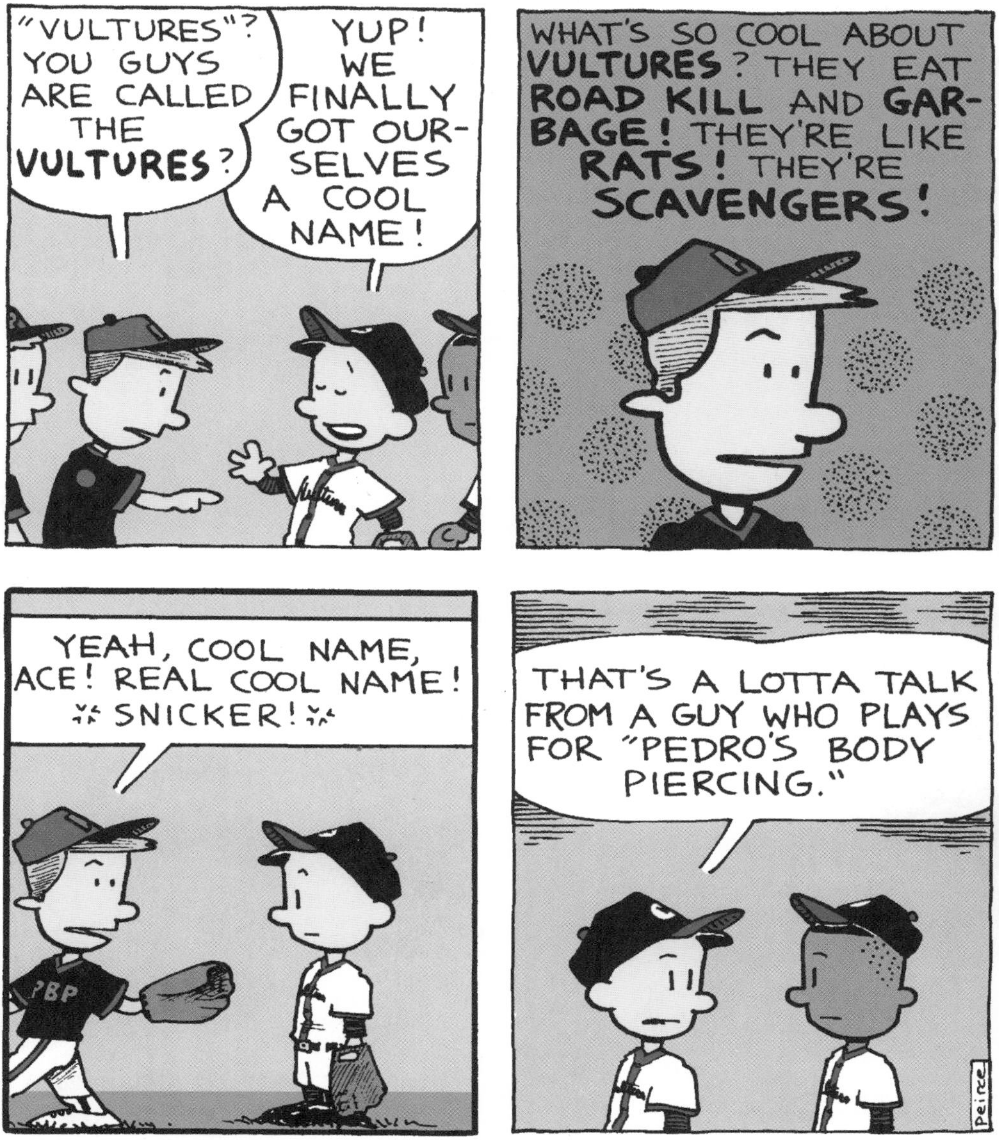
"VULTURES"? YOU GUYS ARE CALLED THE VULTURES?
YUP! WE FINALLY GOT OURSELVES A COOL NAME!
WHAT'S SO COOL ABOUT VULTURES? THEY EAT ROAD KILL AND GARBAGE! THEY'RE LIKE RATS! THEY'RE SCAVENGERS!
YEAH, COOL NAME, ACE! REAL COOL NAME! SNICKER!
PBP
THAT'S A LOTTA TALK FROM A GUY WHO PLAYS FOR "PEDRO'S BODY PIERCING."
peirce

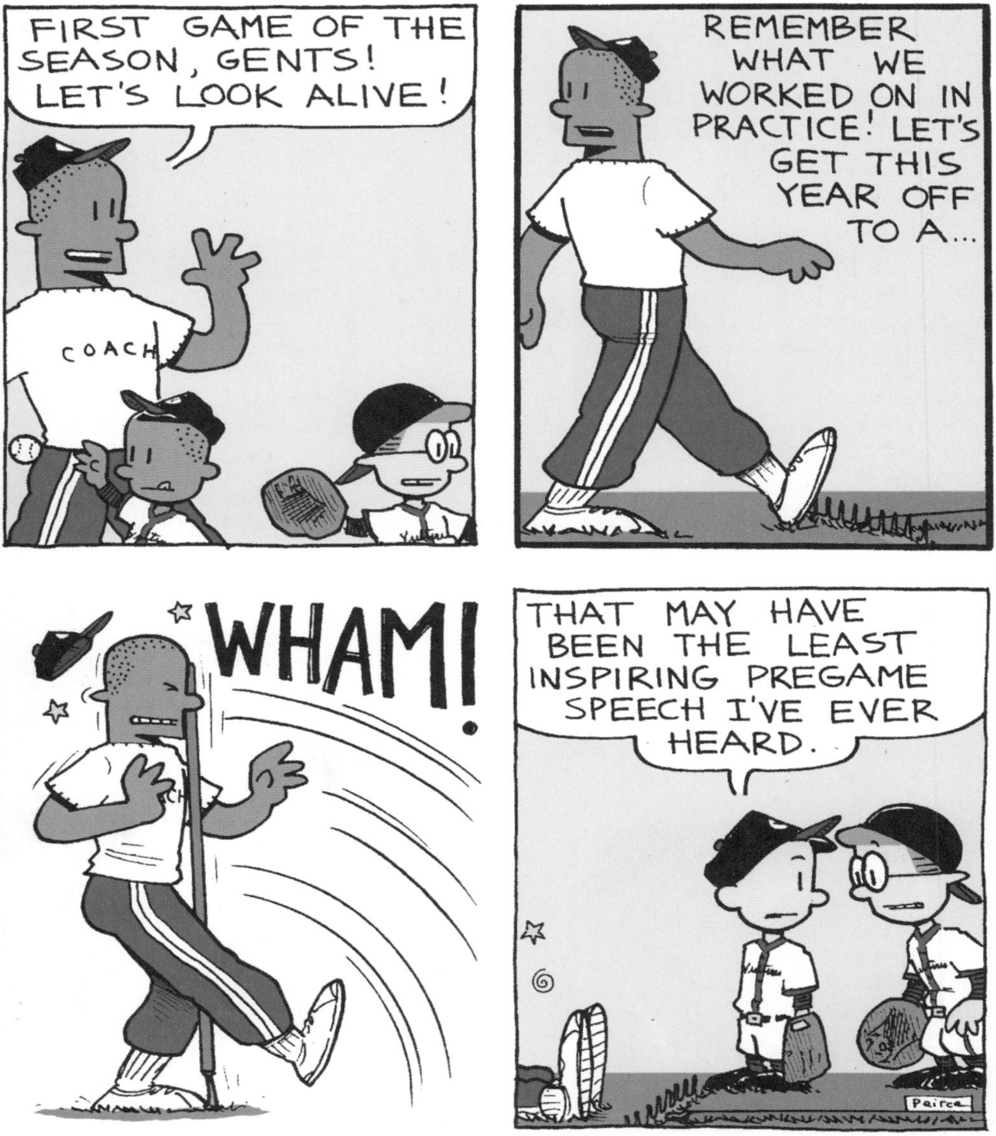
FIRST GAME OF THE SEASON, GENTS! LET'S LOOK ALIVE!
COACH
REMEMBER WHAT WE WORKED ON IN PRACTICE! LET'S GET THIS YEAR OFF TO A...
WHAM!
THAT MAY HAVE BEEN THE LEAST INSPIRING PREGAME SPEECH I'VE EVER HEARD.
Peirce

THE FIRST INNING OF THE FIRST GAME OF THE SEASON!
COME ON, CHESTER! LITTLE BINGO!
CRACK!
BOOM!
UNTIL NOW, I'VE NEVER SEEN A HOME RUN BREAK THE SOUND BARRIER!
I THINK IT'S GONNA BE A GOOD YEAR!
Peirce

GIMME THAT DOUGHNUT.
THIS DOUGHNUT? SURE, CHESTER.
HERE
CHOMPF! CHOMPF! MUNCH! CRUNCH! CHOMP!
BURP!
THIS IS LIKE BEING TEAMMATES WITH THE TAZMANIAN DEVIL.
Peirce

HOLY COW!! THAT'S CHESTER'S THIRD HOME RUN OF THE GAME!
HE'S EN FUEGO!
CHESTER! HIGH FIVE!
WHUMP!
FOR FUTURE REFERENCE, IT'S PROBABLY BETTER TO JUST PAT HIM ON THE BACK.
Peirce

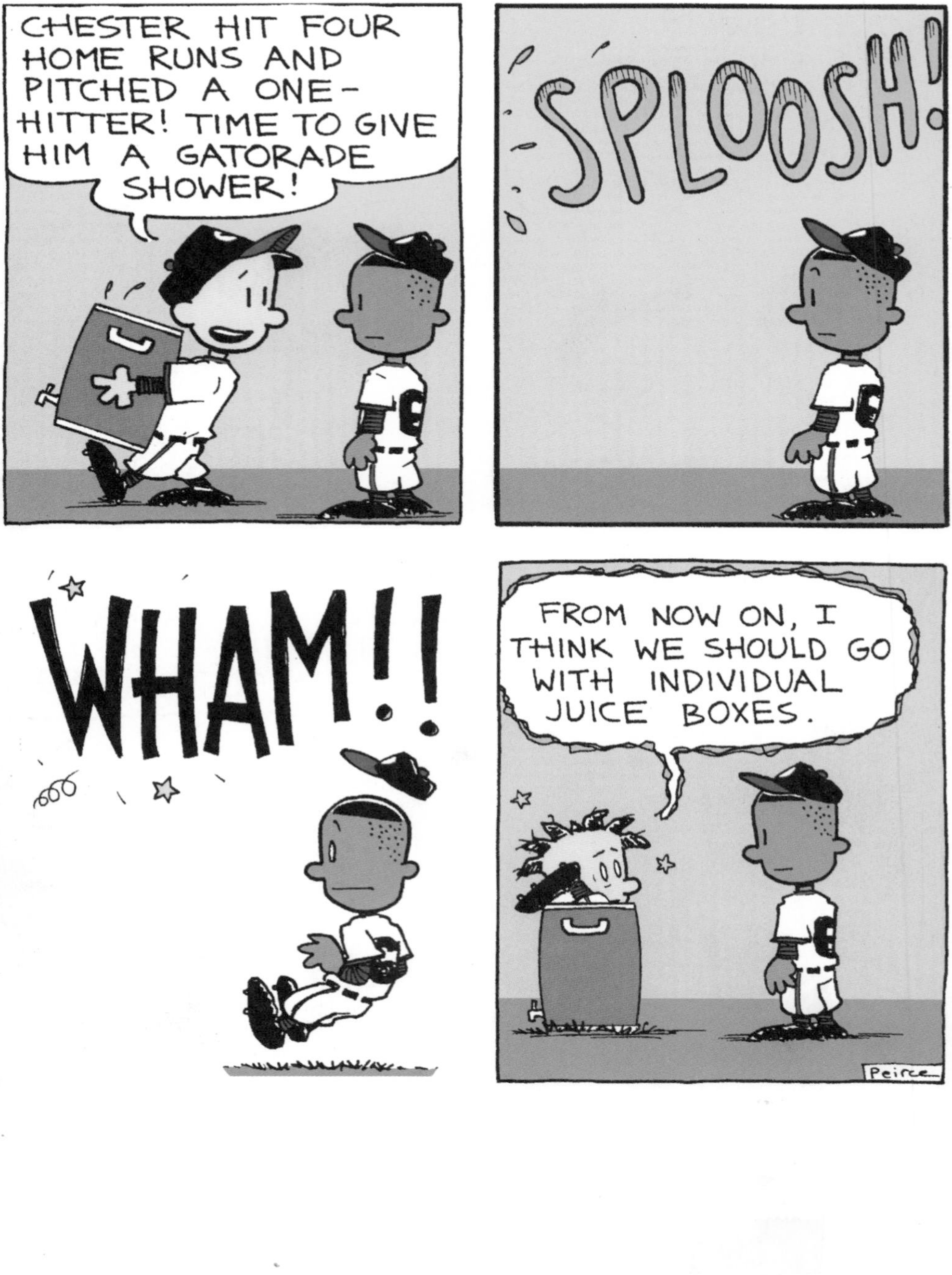

CHESTER HIT FOUR HOME RUNS AND PITCHED A ONE-HITTER! TIME TO GIVE HIM A GATORADE SHOWER!
SPLOOSH!
WHAM!!
FROM NOW ON, I THINK WE SHOULD GO WITH INDIVIDUAL JUICE BOXES.
Peirce

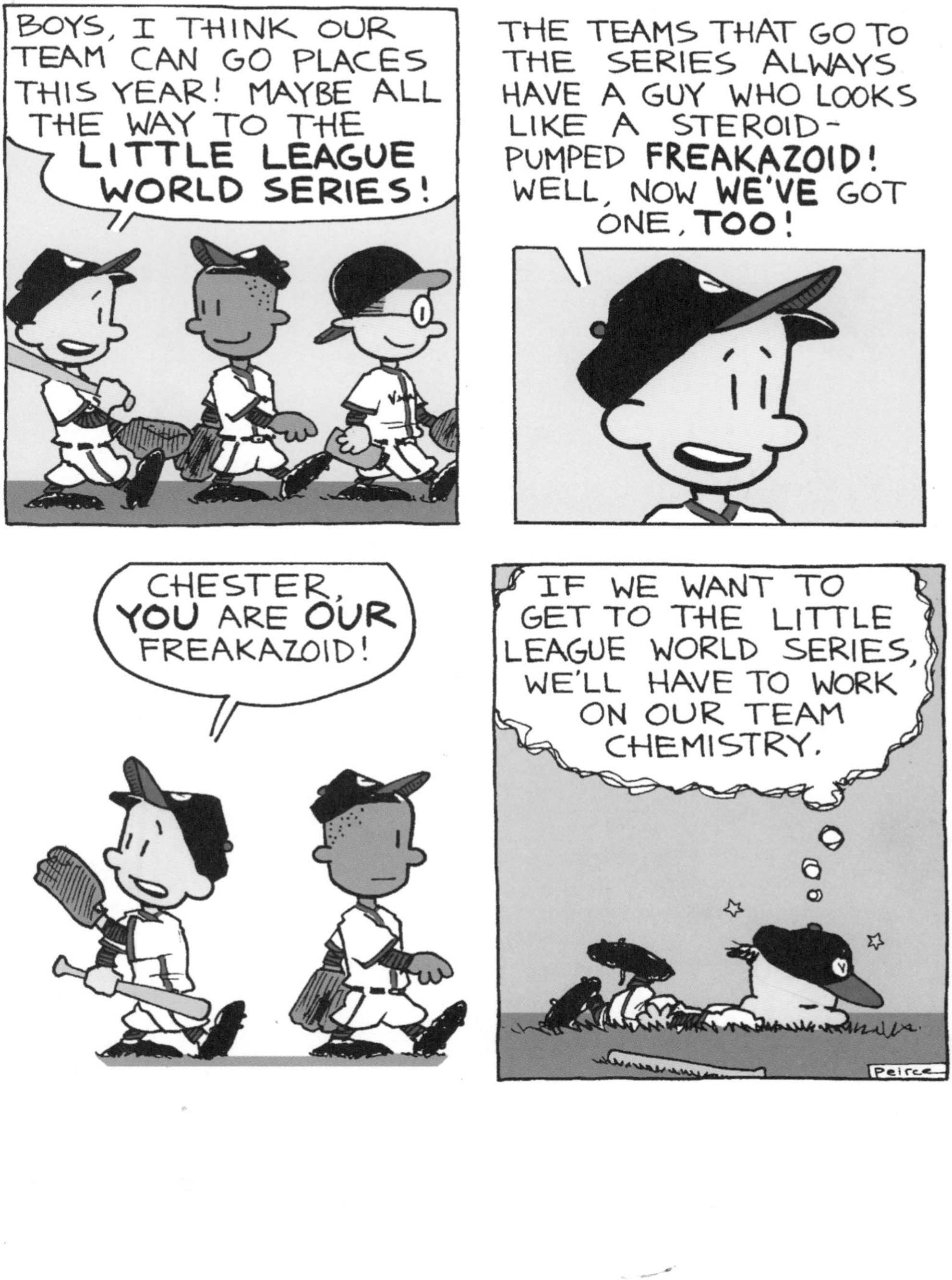
BOYS, I THINK OUR TEAM CAN GO PLACES THIS YEAR! MAYBE ALL THE WAY TO THE **LITTLE LEAGUE WORLD SERIES!**
THE TEAMS THAT GO TO THE SERIES ALWAYS HAVE A GUY WHO LOOKS LIKE A STEROID-PUMPED **FREAKAZOID!** WELL, NOW **WE'VE** GOT ONE, **TOO!**
CHESTER, **YOU** ARE **OUR** FREAKAZOID!
IF WE WANT TO GET TO THE LITTLE LEAGUE WORLD SERIES, WE'LL HAVE TO WORK ON OUR TEAM CHEMISTRY.
Peirce

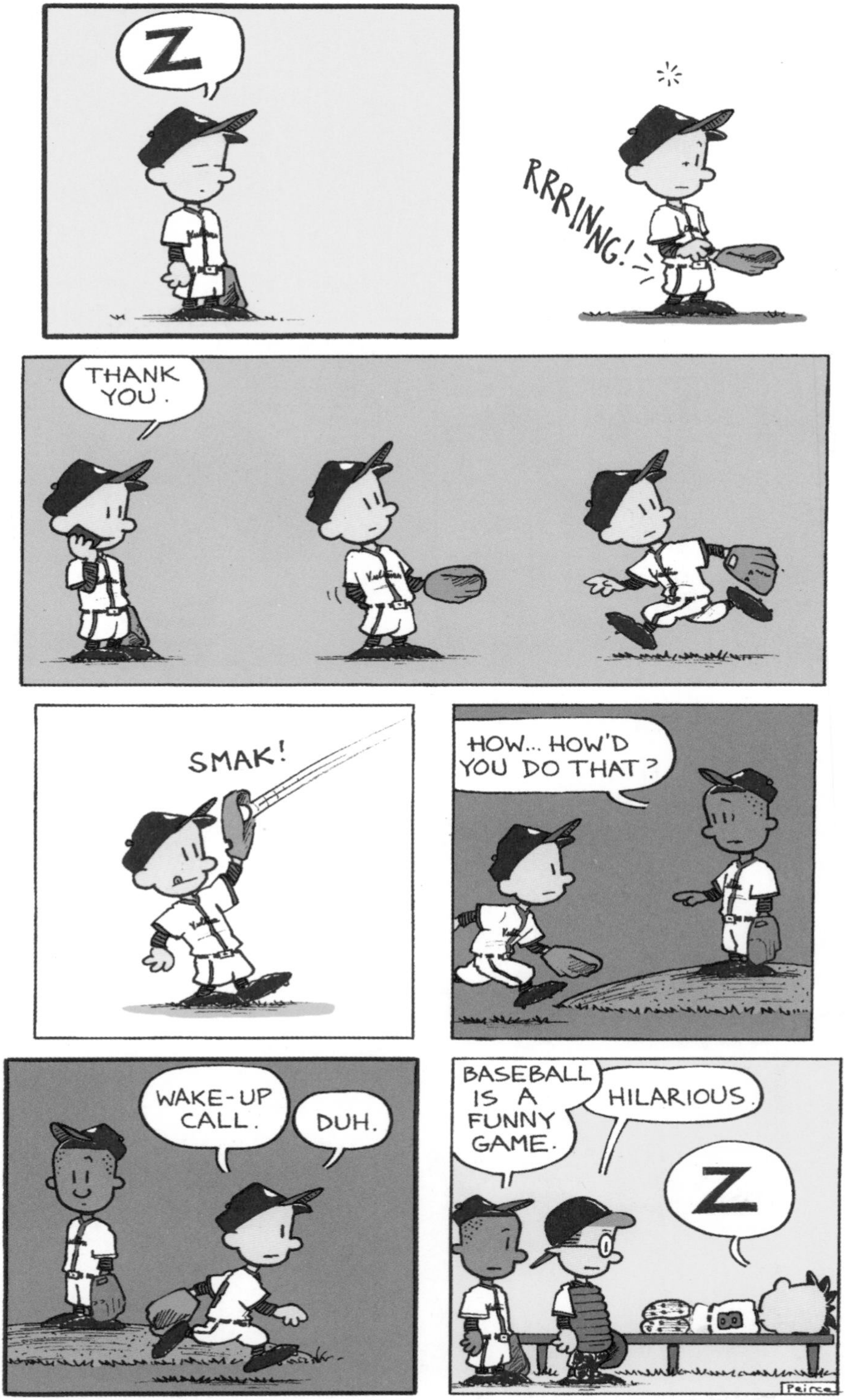
Z
RRRINNG!
THANK YOU.
SMAK!
HOW... HOW'D YOU DO THAT?
WAKE-UP CALL.
DUH.
BASEBALL IS A FUNNY GAME.
HILARIOUS.
Z
Peirce

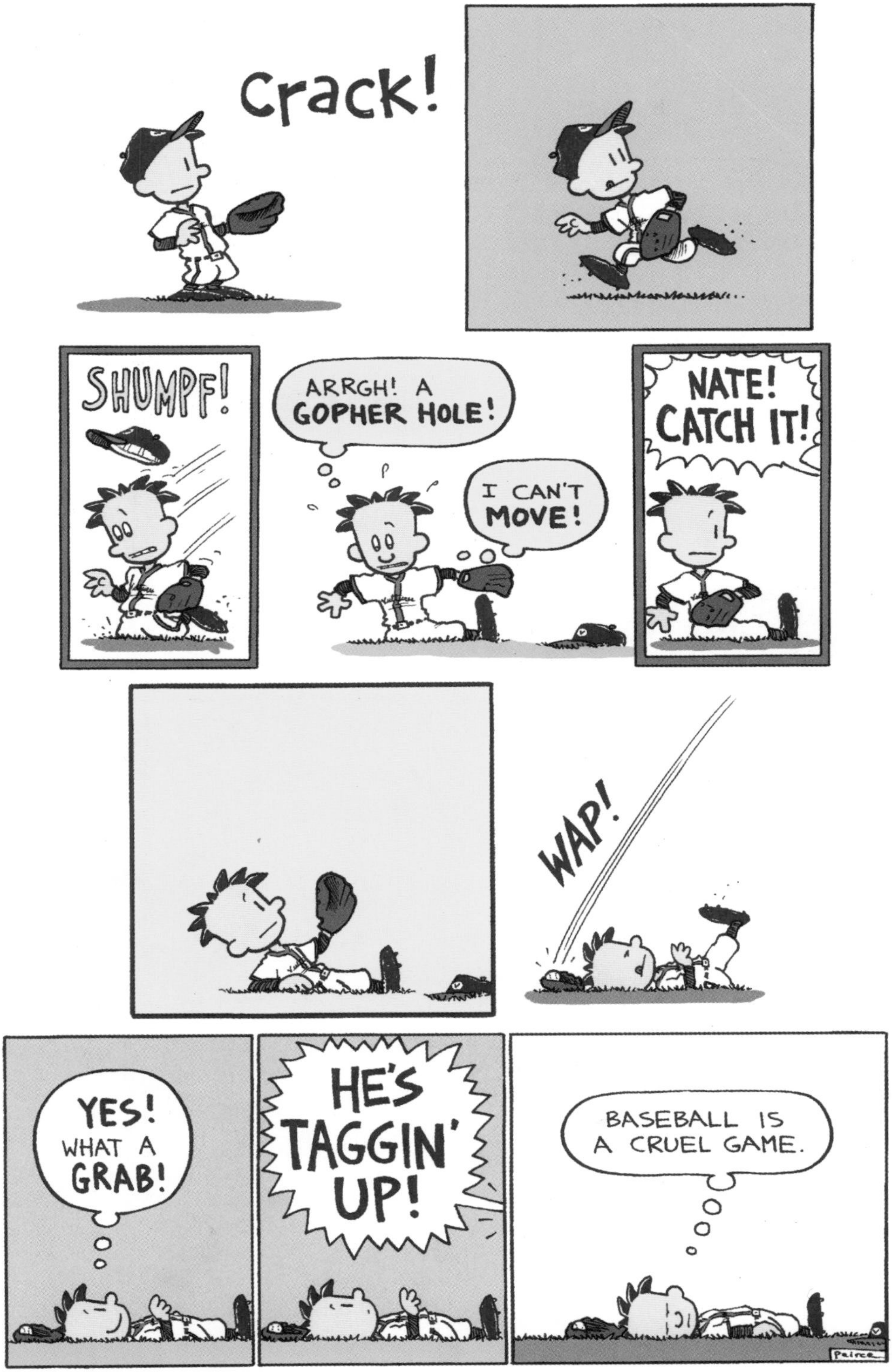
Crack!
SHUMPF!
ARRGH! A GOPHER HOLE!
I CAN'T MOVE!
NATE! CATCH IT!
WAP!
YES! WHAT A GRAB!
HE'S TAGGIN' UP!
BASEBALL IS A CRUEL GAME.
Peirce

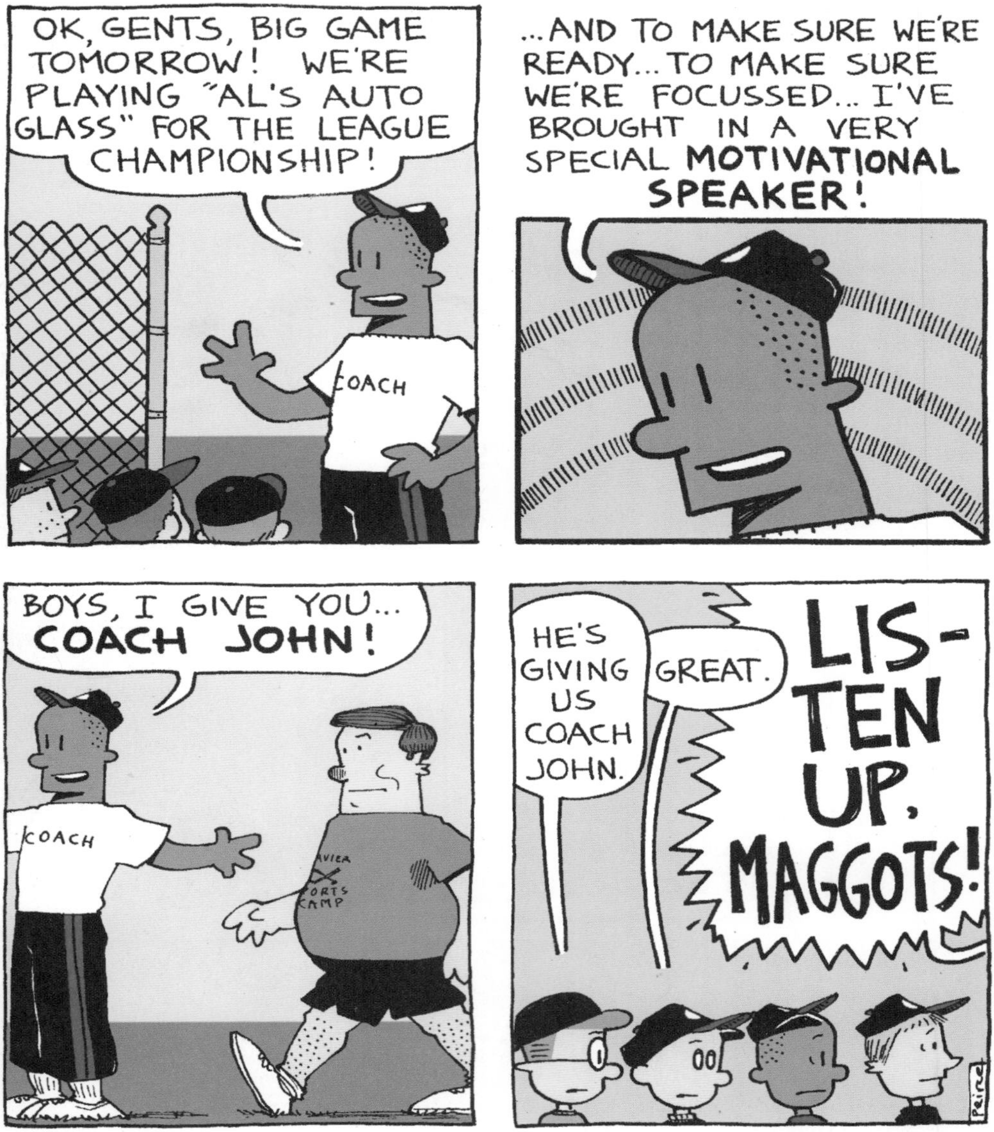
OK, GENTS, BIG GAME TOMORROW! WE'RE PLAYING "AL'S AUTO GLASS" FOR THE LEAGUE CHAMPIONSHIP!
COACH
...AND TO MAKE SURE WE'RE READY... TO MAKE SURE WE'RE FOCUSSED... I'VE BROUGHT IN A VERY SPECIAL **MOTIVATIONAL SPEAKER!**
BOYS, I GIVE YOU... **COACH JOHN!**
COACH
HE'S GIVING US COACH JOHN.
GREAT.
LIS-TEN UP, MAGGOTS!
Peirce

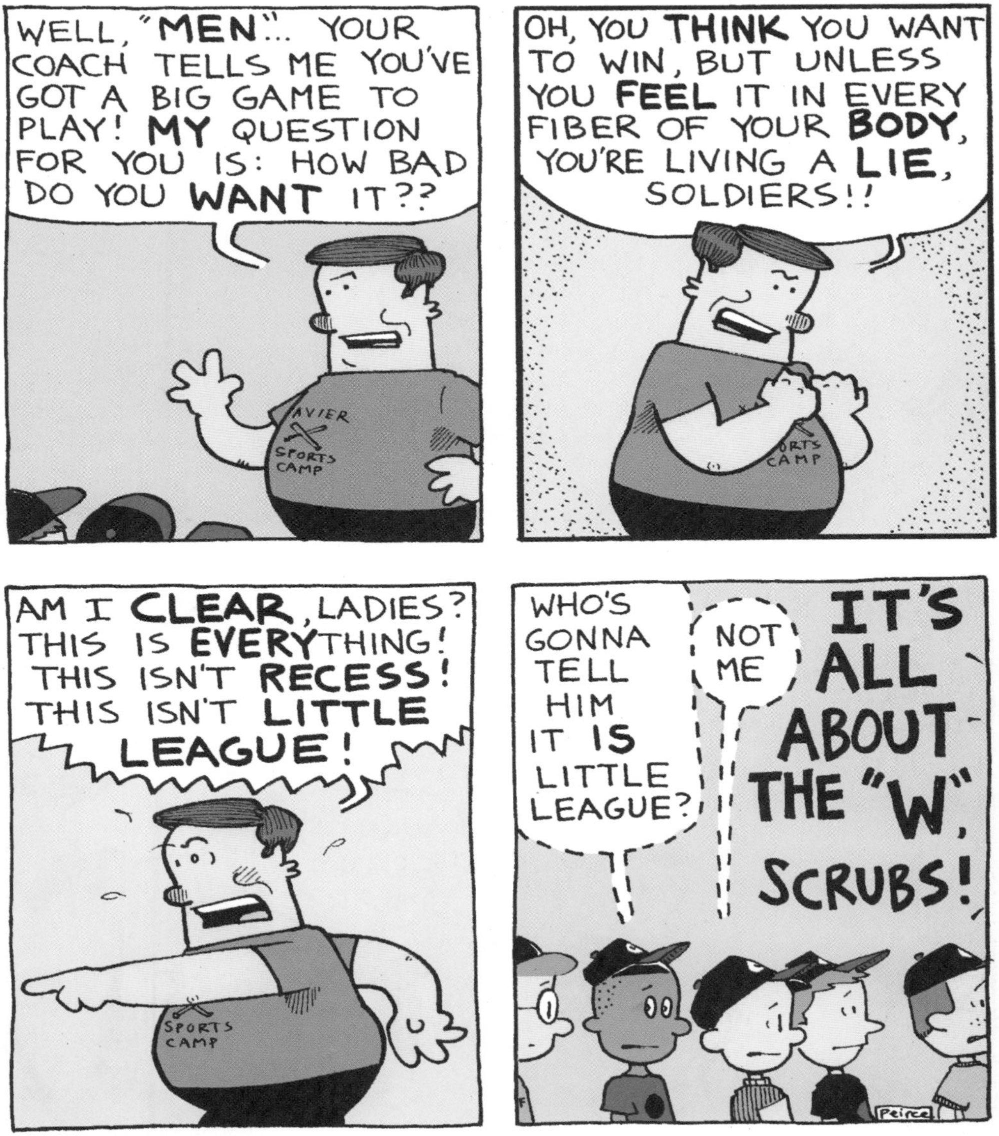

WELL, "MEN"... YOUR COACH TELLS ME YOU'VE GOT A BIG GAME TO PLAY! MY QUESTION FOR YOU IS: HOW BAD DO YOU WANT IT??
AVIER SPORTS CAMP
OH, YOU THINK YOU WANT TO WIN, BUT UNLESS YOU FEEL IT IN EVERY FIBER OF YOUR BODY, YOU'RE LIVING A LIE, SOLDIERS!!
ORTS CAMP
AM I CLEAR, LADIES? THIS IS EVERYTHING! THIS ISN'T RECESS! THIS ISN'T LITTLE LEAGUE!
SPORTS CAMP
WHO'S GONNA TELL HIM IT IS LITTLE LEAGUE?
NOT ME
IT'S ALL ABOUT THE "W", SCRUBS!
Peirce

I'M NOT HAPPY WITH WHAT I SEE HERE, GENTLEMEN! I DON'T SEE THE DESIRE! I DON'T SEE THE HUNGER!
XAVIER SPORTS CAMP
YOU THERE! WRIGHT! DO YOU HAVE THE HUNGER?
YES! YES! I HAVE THE HUNGER!
THEN SHOW ME! SHOW ME!!
Peirce
HOW?... HOW??
EAT SOME-THING, MAN.
WANT A GRANOLA BAR?

READY FOR THE BIG GAME?
AM I EVER! WE'RE GONNA WIN! I CAN FEEL IT!
I HAVEN'T WON A CHAMPIONSHIP SINCE WAY BACK IN TEE BALL!
TEE BALL? THERE WERE NO CHAMPIONS IN TEE BALL!
SURE THERE WERE! MY TEAM WON THE TITLE!
I DON'T THINK SO, NATE! THEY DON'T EVEN KEEP SCORE IN TEE BALL!
BUT... BUT COACH KEVIN GAVE US TROPHIES!...
DUDE, EVERYONE GOT TROPHIES!
THIS IS SAD, MAN.
PEIRCE

THINK WE CAN BEAT "AL'S AUTO GLASS"? THOSE GUYS ARE **GOOD!**

I DUNNO. IT'LL BE TOUGH.

GUYS! **GUYS!**

THIS GAME'S IN THE **BAG!** WE'VE GOT **CHESTER** PITCHING, REMEMBER?

HE'LL ABSOLUTELY **MOW 'EM DOWN!** CHESTER'S A FREAK OF NATURE! HE'S SUPERMAN! HE'S **UNSTOPPABLE!**

CHESTER HAS CHICKEN POX.

NO!!

CHESTER HAS CHICKEN POX?
NO PROBLEM! ANTHONY CAN PITCH!
NO, ANTHONY'S ON A CAMPING TRIP WITH HIS SCOUT TROOP.
COA
OH. WHAT ABOUT JOEL?
JOEL HAS A VIOLIN RECITAL TODAY.
UH... OK... THERE'S MATT, RIGHT?
MATT HAD TO GO TO HIS AUNT'S GRADUATION FROM MASSAGE SCHOOL.
ALL RIGHT, THIS IS GETTING STUPID.
CAN I PITCH?
COACH
Peirce

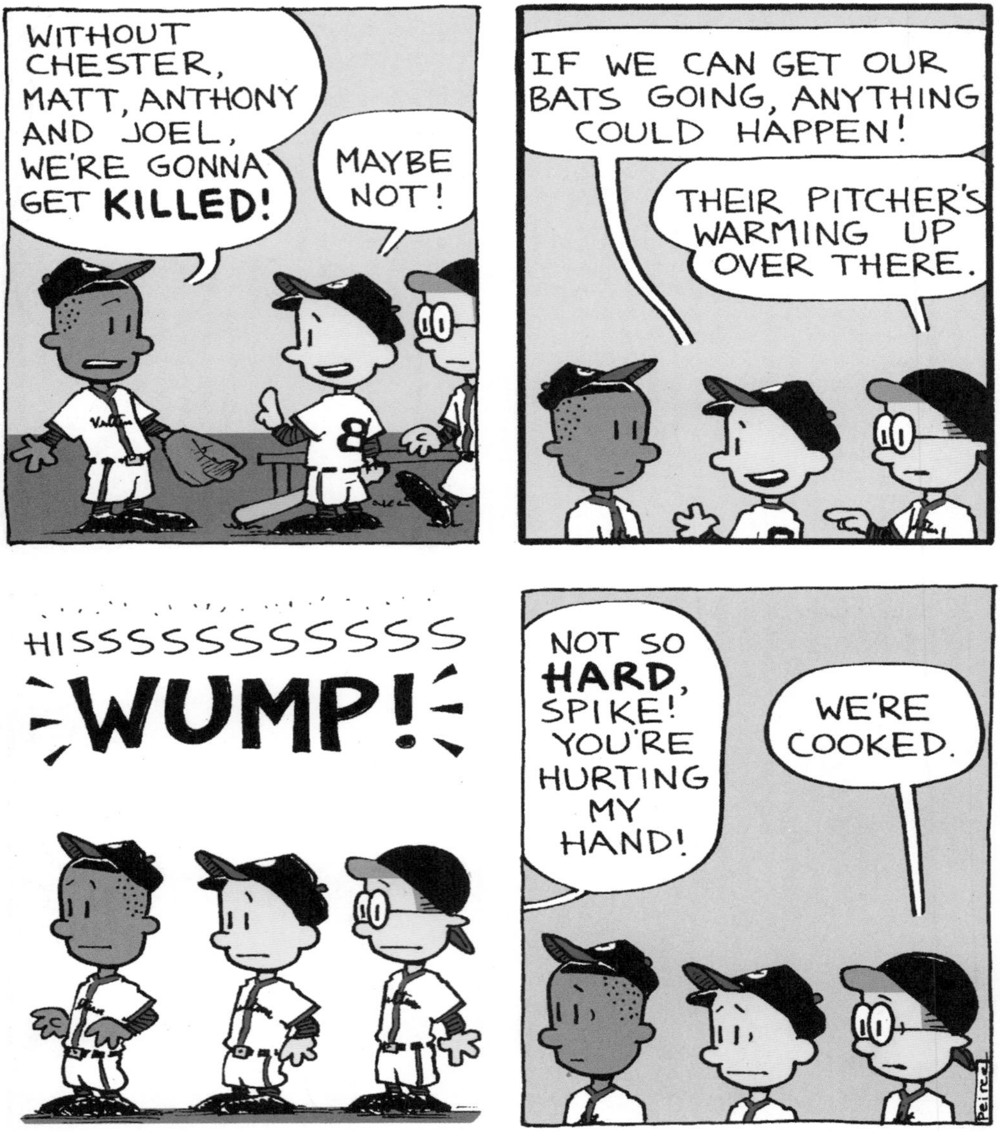
WITHOUT CHESTER, MATT, ANTHONY AND JOEL, WE'RE GONNA GET **KILLED**!
MAYBE NOT!
IF WE CAN GET OUR BATS GOING, ANYTHING COULD HAPPEN!
THEIR PITCHER'S WARMING UP OVER THERE.
HISSSSSSSSSSSS
WUMP!
NOT SO **HARD**, SPIKE! YOU'RE HURTING MY HAND!
WE'RE COOKED.
Peirce

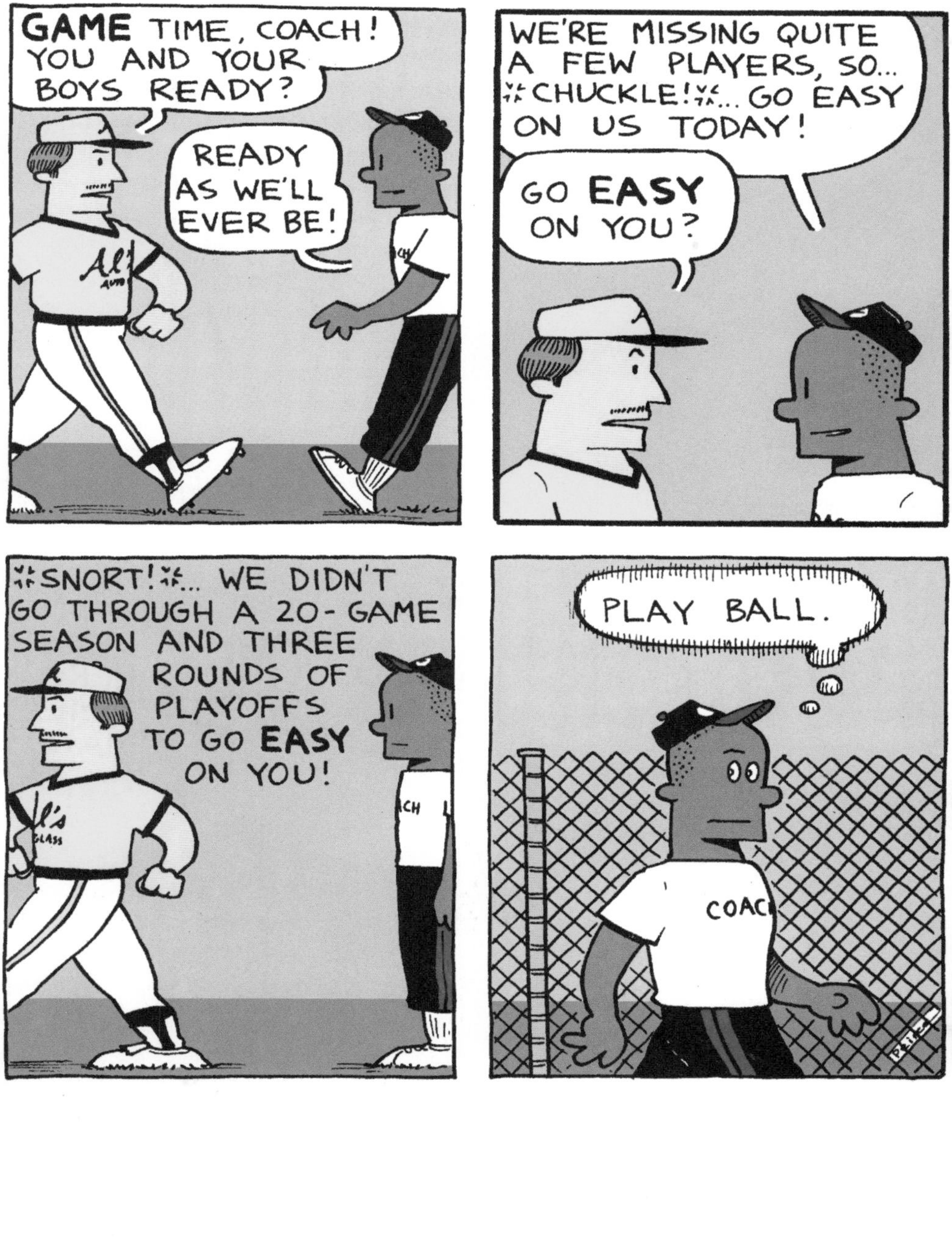
GAME TIME, COACH! YOU AND YOUR BOYS READY?
READY AS WE'LL EVER BE!
WE'RE MISSING QUITE A FEW PLAYERS, SO... *CHUCKLE!*... GO EASY ON US TODAY!
GO EASY ON YOU?
SNORT!... WE DIDN'T GO THROUGH A 20-GAME SEASON AND THREE ROUNDS OF PLAYOFFS TO GO EASY ON YOU!
PLAY BALL.
COAC

ALL RIGHT, BOYS... WE'RE A BIT SHORT-HANDED TODAY. IN FACT, WE'VE ONLY GOT NINE PLAYERS.
COACH
THAT MEANS THAT EACH OF YOU WILL HAVE TO PLAY THE WHOLE GAME! EVEN THOSE OF YOU WHO HAVEN'T PLAYED MUCH THIS YEAR!
IF WE WANT TO WIN THE CHAMPIONSHIP, ALL OF YOU WILL HAVE TO STEP UP AND PLAY MISTAKE-FREE BALL!
THAT MEANS YOU, CHAD.
ME?
IT'S HERO TIME, MAN.
Peirce

POW!
WOW. THAT WAS CRUSHED. I'VE NEVER SEEN A BALL HIT THAT FAR.
HE DIDN'T HIT IT THAT GOOD. IT WAS JUST A POP FLY THAT GOT CAUGHT BY THE WIND.
CAUGHT BY THE WIND? THAT BALL REACHED THE TENNIS COURTS!
I'M TRYING TO KEEP YOUR SPIRITS UP, MAN. WORK WITH ME.
GOOD JOB, TEDDY. NICE MEATBALL.
Peirce

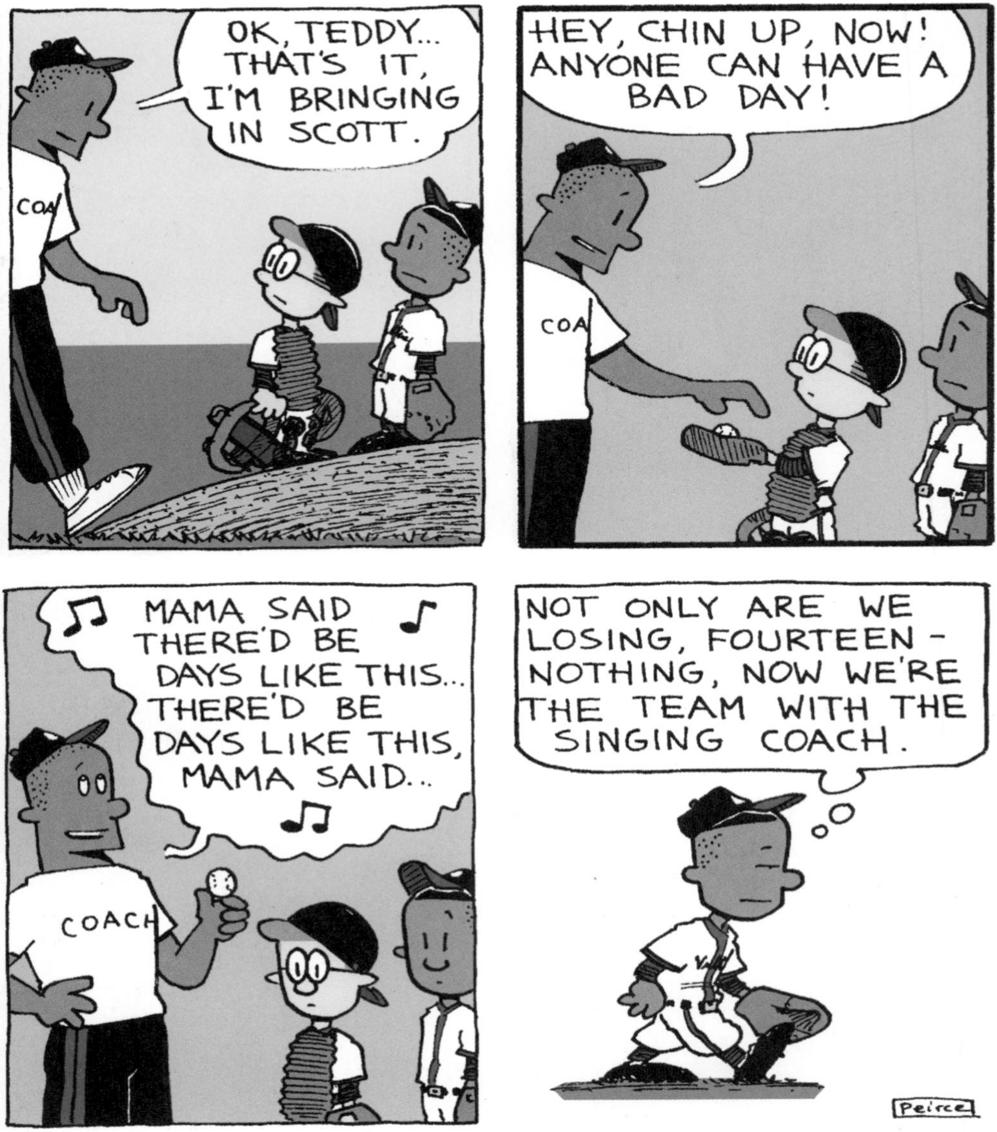
OK, TEDDY... THAT'S IT, I'M BRINGING IN SCOTT.
COA
HEY, CHIN UP, NOW! ANYONE CAN HAVE A BAD DAY!
COA
MAMA SAID THERE'D BE DAYS LIKE THIS... THERE'D BE DAYS LIKE THIS, MAMA SAID...
COACH
NOT ONLY ARE WE LOSING, FOURTEEN-NOTHING, NOW WE'RE THE TEAM WITH THE SINGING COACH.
Peirce

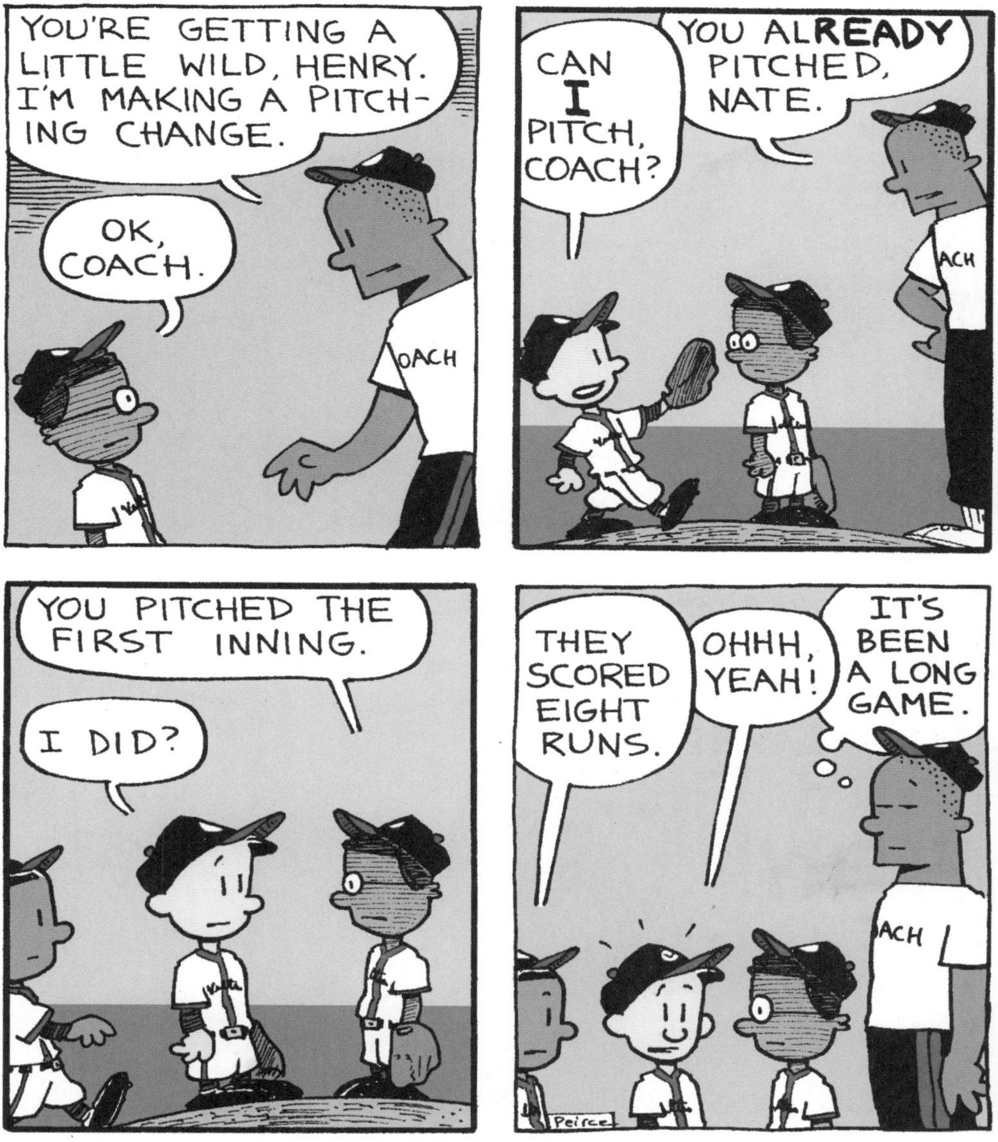
YOU'RE GETTING A LITTLE WILD, HENRY. I'M MAKING A PITCHING CHANGE.
OK, COACH.
OACH
CAN I PITCH, COACH?
YOU ALREADY PITCHED, NATE.
ACH
YOU PITCHED THE FIRST INNING.
I DID?
THEY SCORED EIGHT RUNS.
OHHH, YEAH!
IT'S BEEN A LONG GAME.
ACH
Peirce

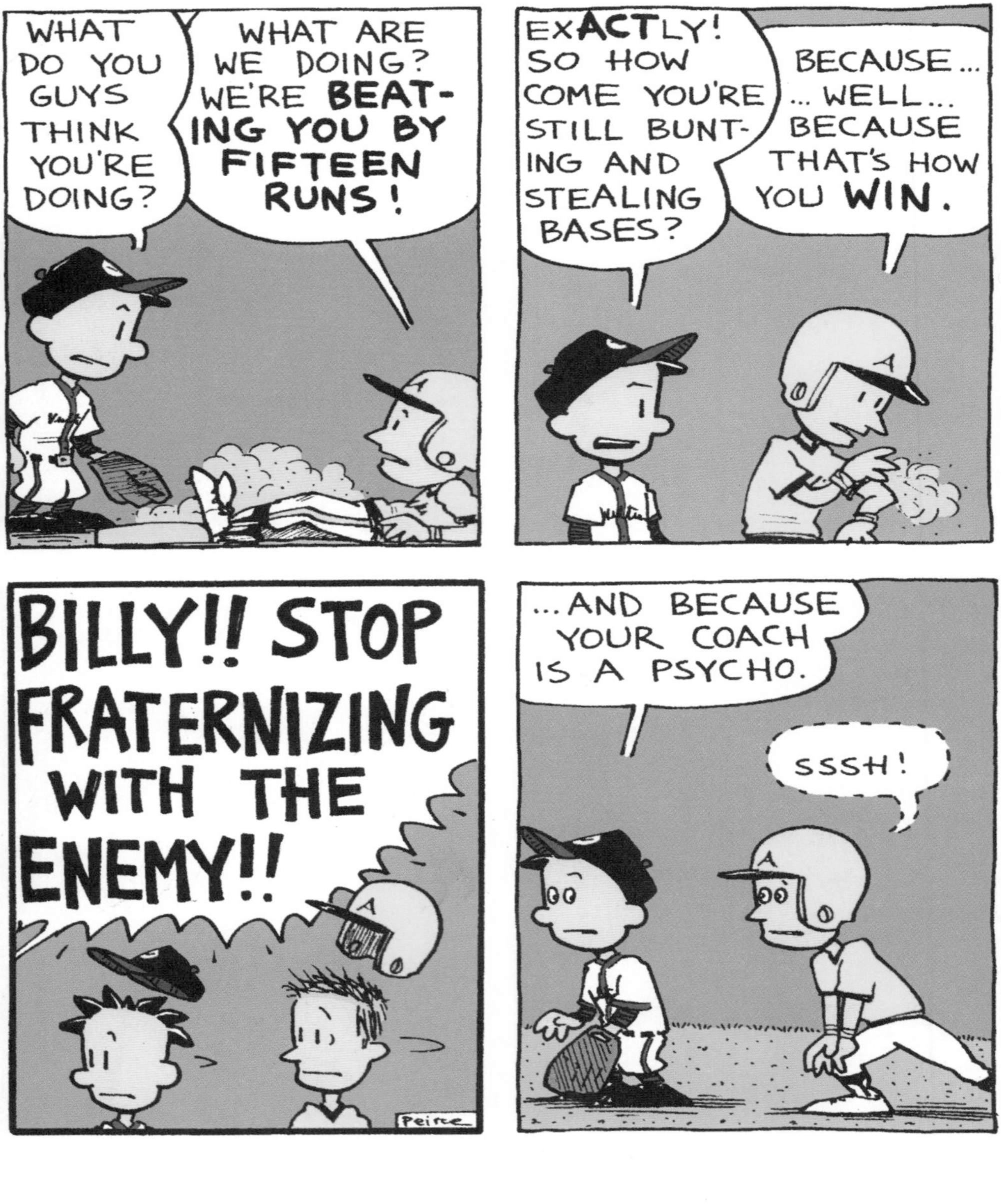
WHAT DO YOU GUYS THINK YOU'RE DOING?
WHAT ARE WE DOING? WE'RE **BEATING YOU BY FIFTEEN RUNS!**
EX**ACT**LY! SO HOW COME YOU'RE STILL BUNTING AND STEALING BASES?
BECAUSE... ...WELL... BECAUSE THAT'S HOW YOU **WIN.**
BILLY!! STOP FRATERNIZING WITH THE ENEMY!!
Peirce
...AND BECAUSE YOUR COACH IS A PSYCHO.
SSSH!

SNICKER! WE'RE DE**STROY**ING YOU GUYS!

YEAH?

WELL, **IF** WE WEREN'T MISSING OUR BEST PITCHER, AND **IF** OUR BEST HITTER WASN'T ON A CAMPING TRIP, AND **IF** TEDDY HADN'T JUST THROWN THE BALL OVER THE BACKSTOP...

...AND **IF** CHAD HADN'T COMMITTED THOSE FIVE ERRORS IN THE FIRST INNING, AND **IF** I'D REMEMBERED TO WEAR MY LUCKY SOCKS, THEN **WE** WOULD BE DE-STROYING **YOU** GUYS!

RIGHT.

"HYPOTHETICAL TRASH TALKING" IS KIND OF LAME, BUT SOMETIMES IT'S ALL YOU'VE GOT.

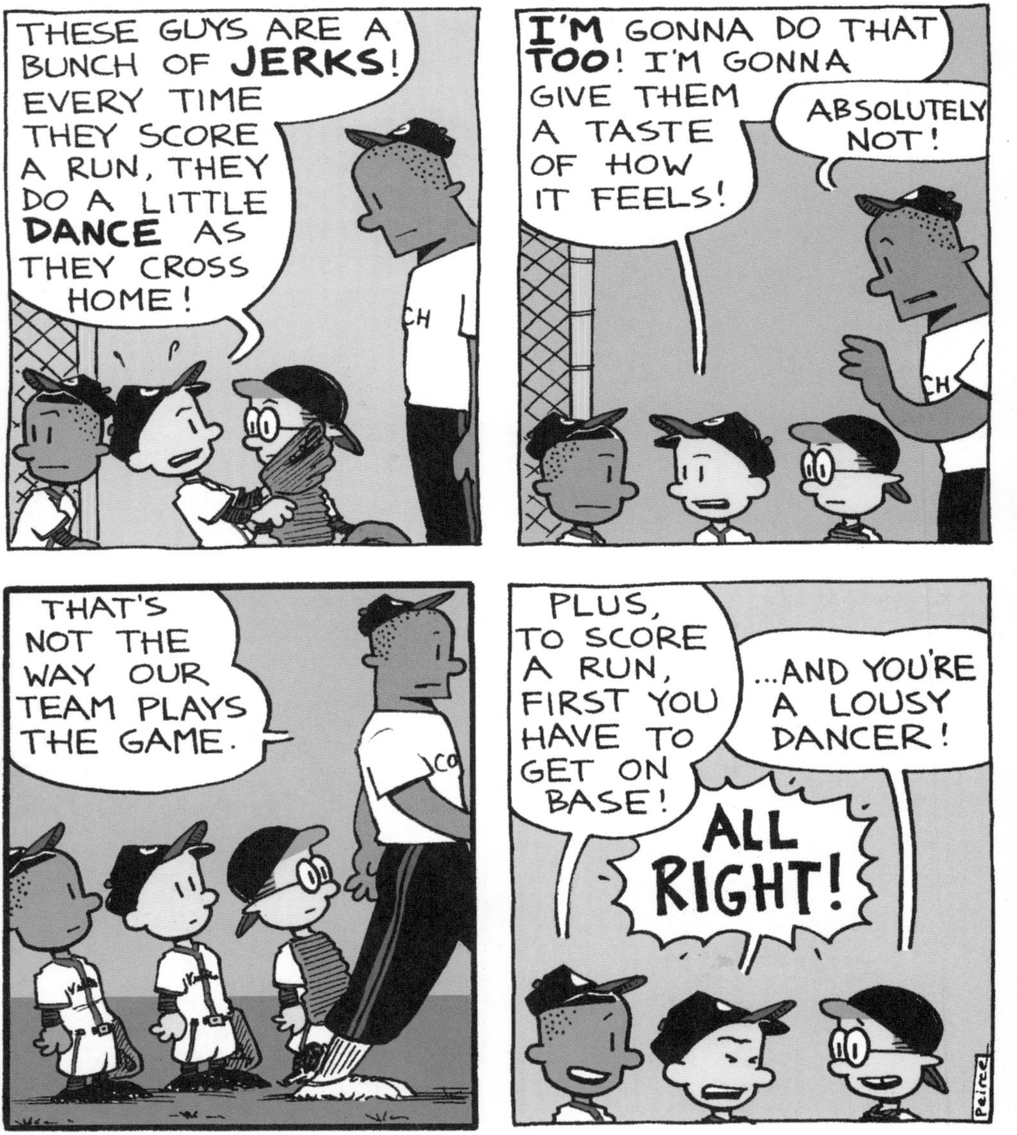
THESE GUYS ARE A BUNCH OF **JERKS**! EVERY TIME THEY SCORE A RUN, THEY DO A LITTLE **DANCE** AS THEY CROSS HOME!
I'M GONNA DO THAT **TOO**! I'M GONNA GIVE THEM A TASTE OF HOW IT FEELS!
ABSOLUTELY NOT!
THAT'S NOT THE WAY OUR TEAM PLAYS THE GAME.
PLUS, TO SCORE A RUN, FIRST YOU HAVE TO GET ON BASE!
...AND YOU'RE A LOUSY DANCER!
ALL RIGHT!
Peirce

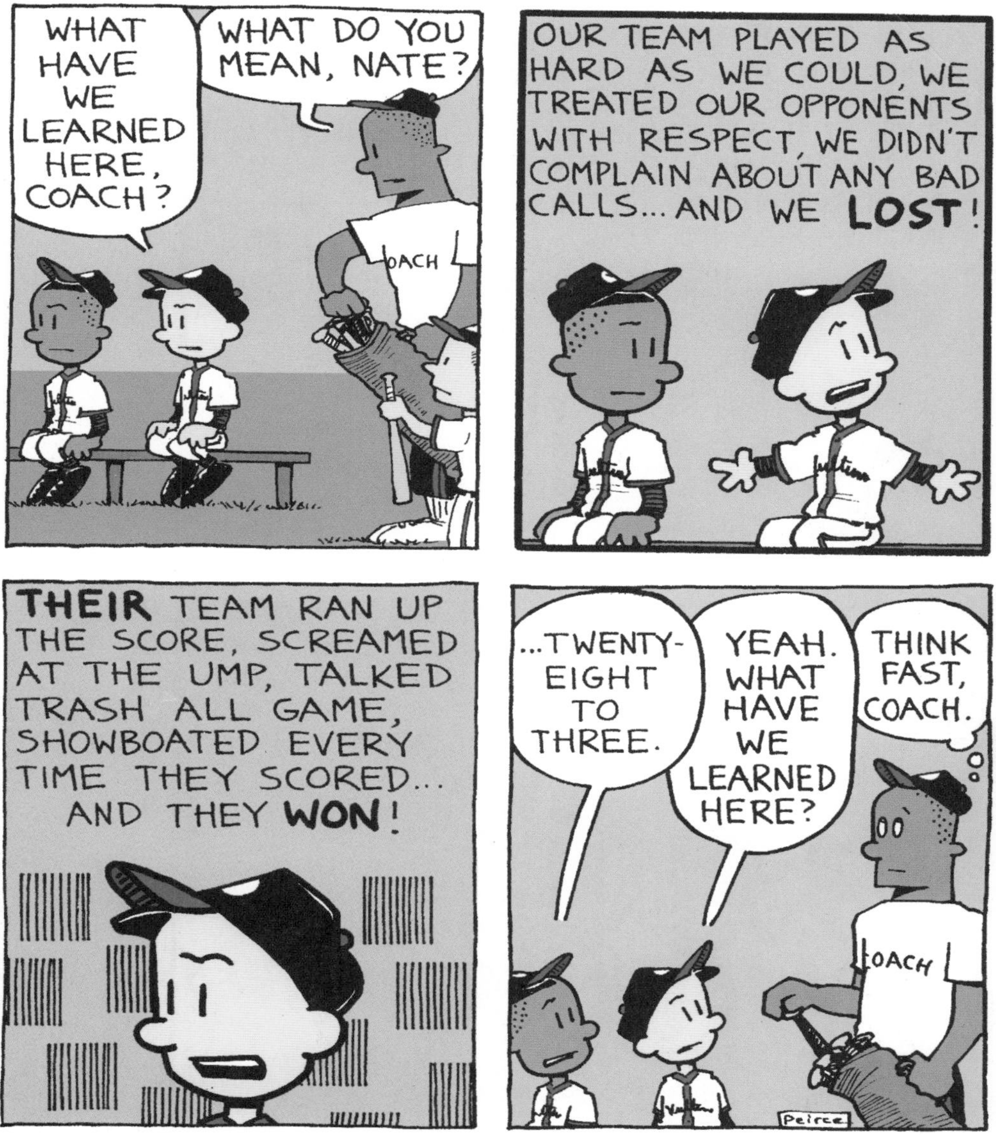
WHAT HAVE WE LEARNED HERE, COACH?
WHAT DO YOU MEAN, NATE?
OACH
OUR TEAM PLAYED AS HARD AS WE COULD, WE TREATED OUR OPPONENTS WITH RESPECT, WE DIDN'T COMPLAIN ABOUT ANY BAD CALLS... AND WE **LOST**!
THEIR TEAM RAN UP THE SCORE, SCREAMED AT THE UMP, TALKED TRASH ALL GAME, SHOWBOATED EVERY TIME THEY SCORED... AND THEY **WON**!
...TWENTY-EIGHT TO THREE.
YEAH. WHAT HAVE WE LEARNED HERE?
THINK FAST, COACH.
OACH
Peirce

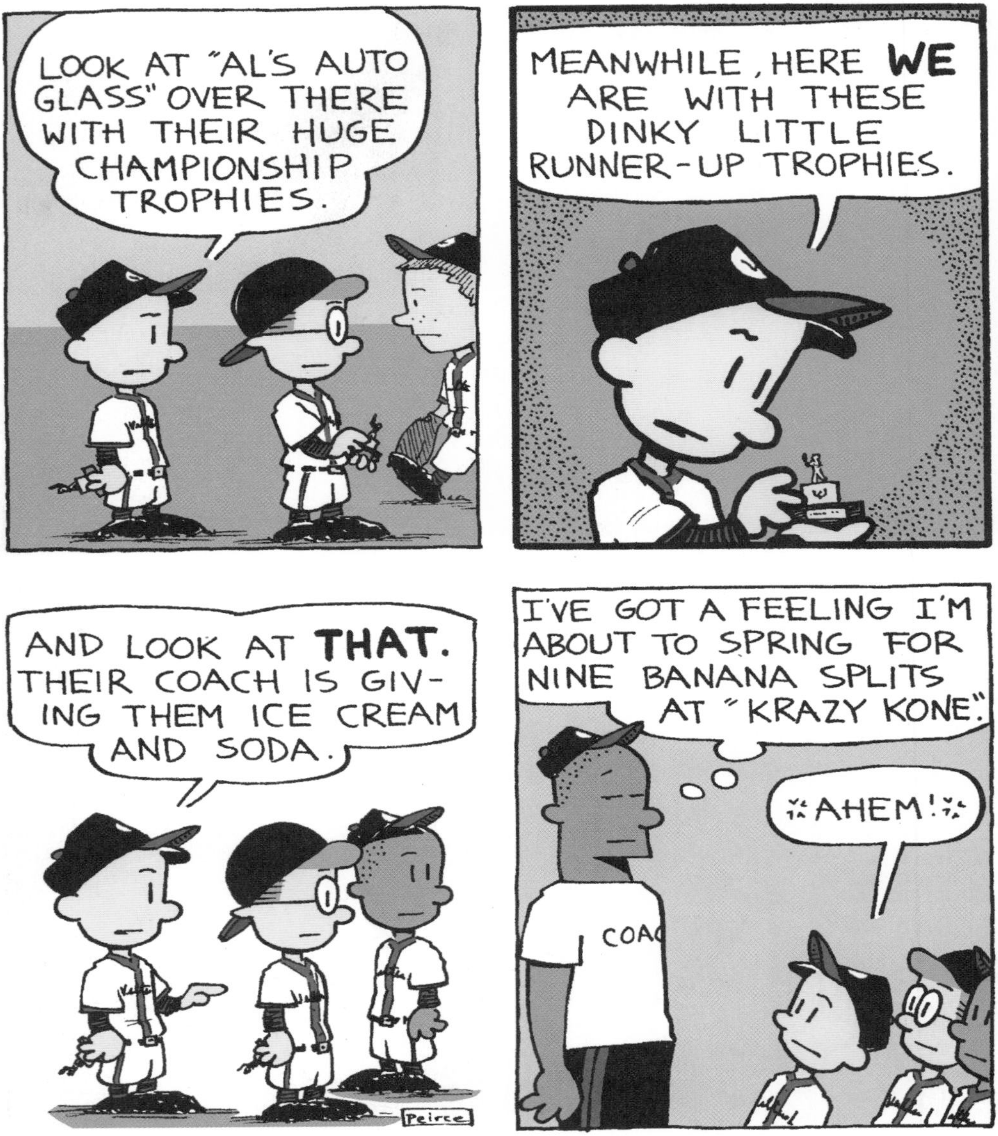
LOOK AT "AL'S AUTO GLASS" OVER THERE WITH THEIR HUGE CHAMPIONSHIP TROPHIES.
MEANWHILE, HERE **WE** ARE WITH THESE DINKY LITTLE RUNNER-UP TROPHIES.
AND LOOK AT **THAT.** THEIR COACH IS GIVING THEM ICE CREAM AND SODA.
Peirce
I'VE GOT A FEELING I'M ABOUT TO SPRING FOR NINE BANANA SPLITS AT "KRAZY KONE".
AHEM!
COAC

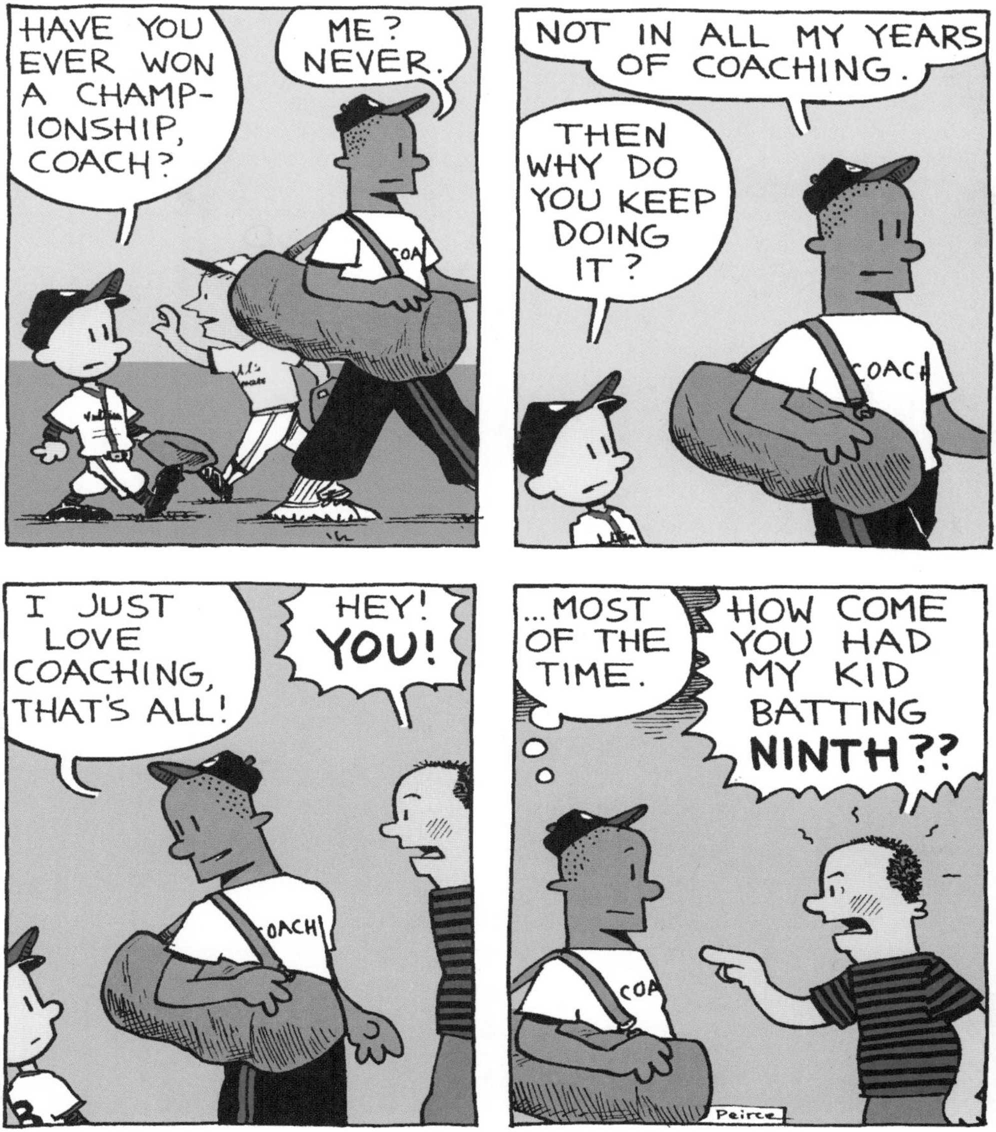
HAVE YOU EVER WON A CHAMPIONSHIP, COACH?
ME? NEVER.
NOT IN ALL MY YEARS OF COACHING.
THEN WHY DO YOU KEEP DOING IT?
I JUST LOVE COACHING, THAT'S ALL!
HEY! YOU!
...MOST OF THE TIME.
HOW COME YOU HAD MY KID BATTING NINTH??
Peirce

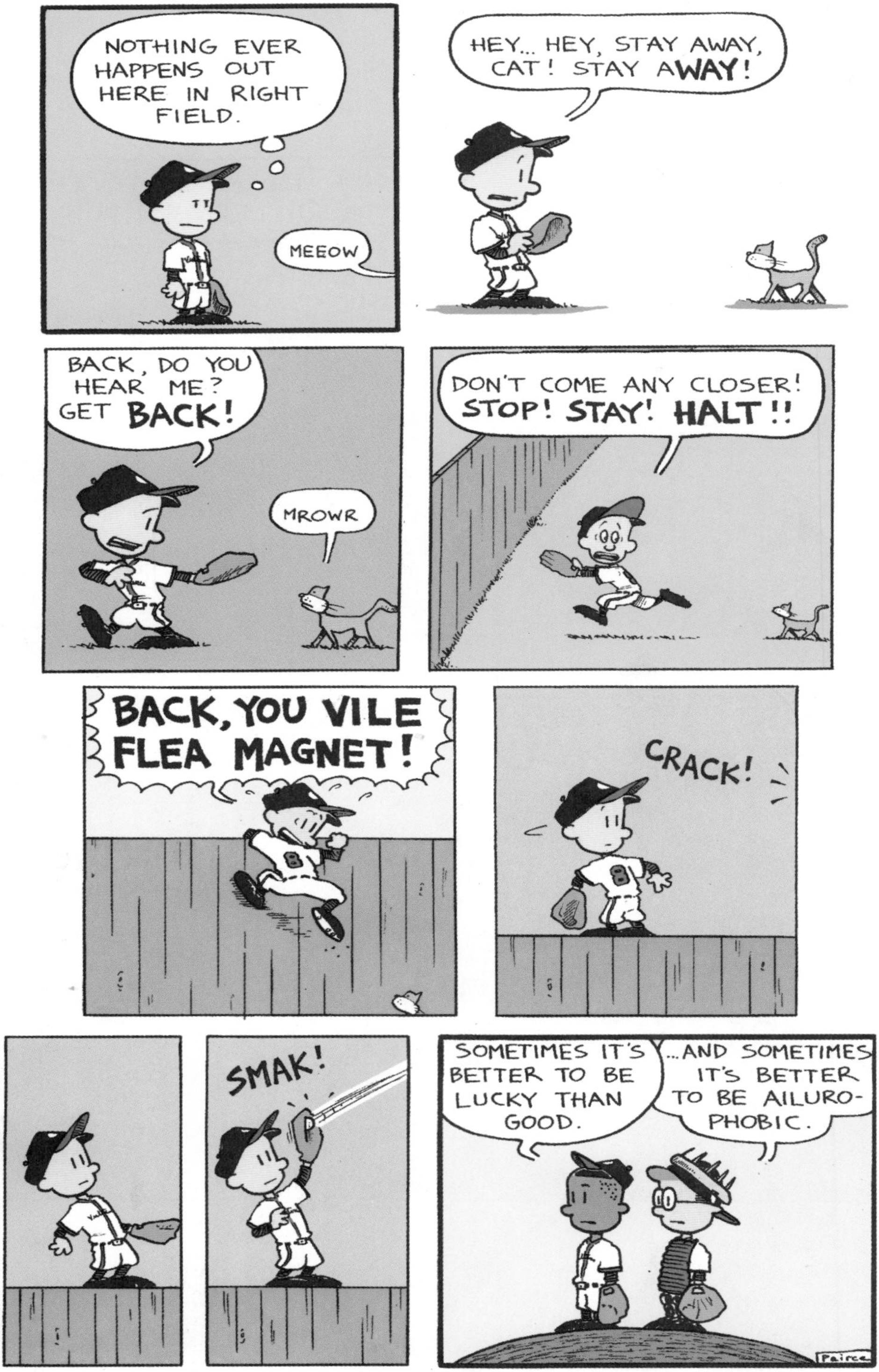
NOTHING EVER HAPPENS OUT HERE IN RIGHT FIELD.
MEEOW
HEY... HEY, STAY AWAY, CAT! STAY AWAY!
BACK, DO YOU HEAR ME? GET BACK!
MROWR
DON'T COME ANY CLOSER! STOP! STAY! HALT!!
BACK, YOU VILE FLEA MAGNET!
CRACK!
SMAK!
SOMETIMES IT'S BETTER TO BE LUCKY THAN GOOD.
...AND SOMETIMES IT'S BETTER TO BE AILURO-PHOBIC.
Pairce

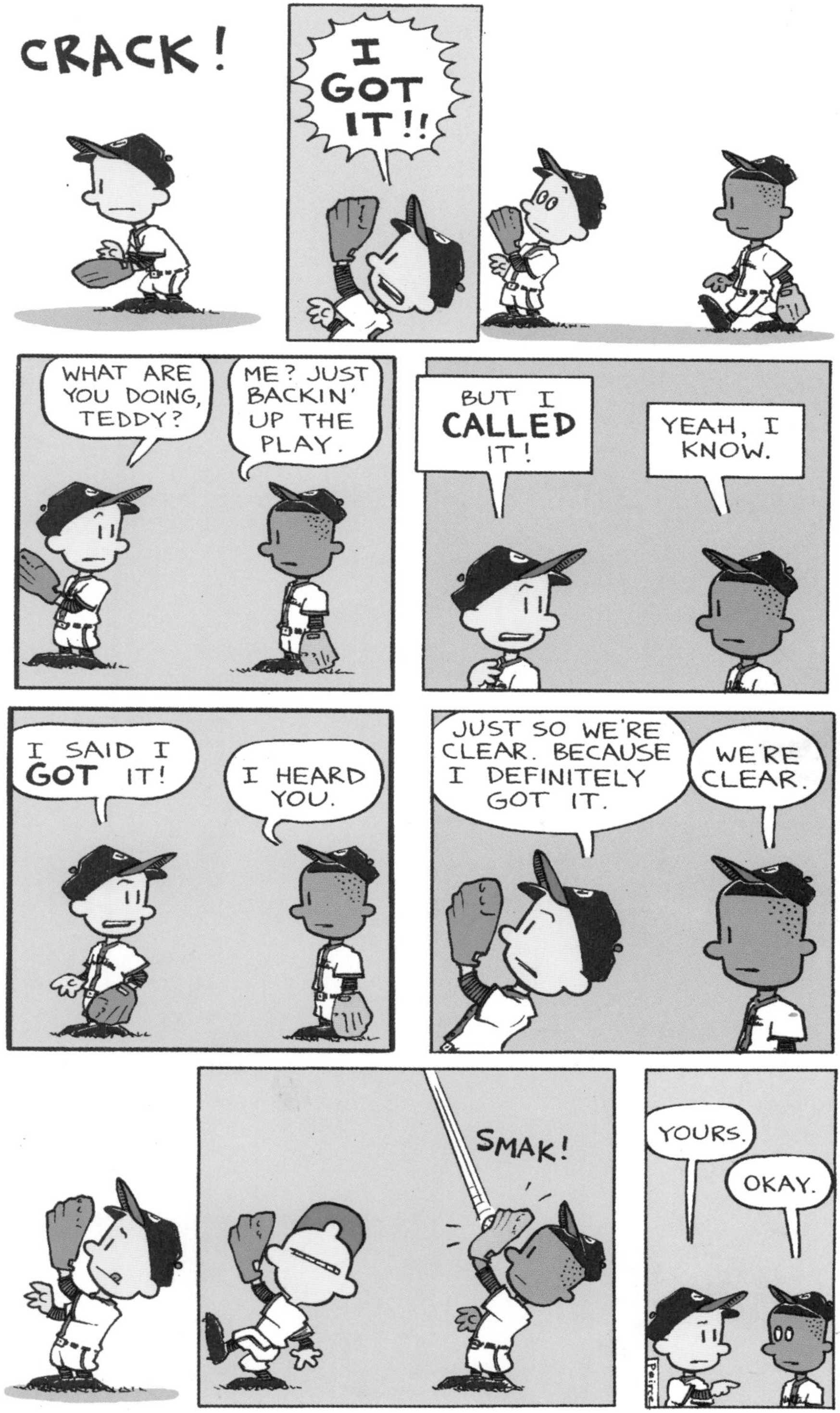
CRACK!
I GOT IT!!
WHAT ARE YOU DOING, TEDDY?
ME? JUST BACKIN' UP THE PLAY.
BUT I CALLED IT!
YEAH, I KNOW.
I SAID I GOT IT!
I HEARD YOU.
JUST SO WE'RE CLEAR. BECAUSE I DEFINITELY GOT IT.
WE'RE CLEAR.
SMAK!
YOURS.
OKAY.
Peirce

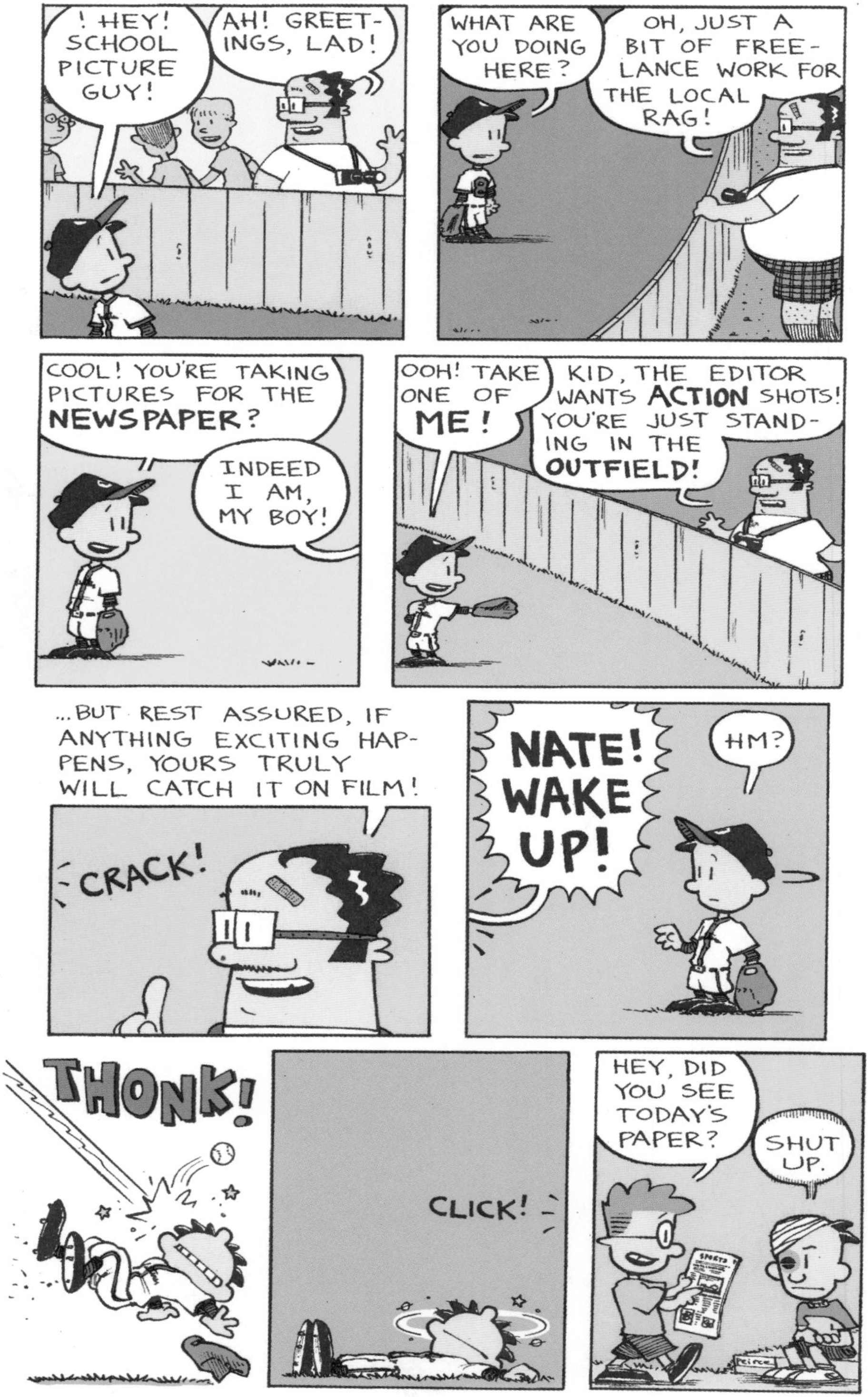

! HEY! SCHOOL PICTURE GUY!
AH! GREETINGS, LAD!
WHAT ARE YOU DOING HERE?
OH, JUST A BIT OF FREE-LANCE WORK FOR THE LOCAL RAG!
COOL! YOU'RE TAKING PICTURES FOR THE NEWSPAPER?
INDEED I AM, MY BOY!
OOH! TAKE ONE OF ME!
KID, THE EDITOR WANTS ACTION SHOTS! YOU'RE JUST STANDING IN THE OUTFIELD!
...BUT REST ASSURED, IF ANYTHING EXCITING HAPPENS, YOURS TRULY WILL CATCH IT ON FILM!
CRACK!
NATE! WAKE UP!
HM?
THONK!
CLICK!
HEY, DID YOU SEE TODAY'S PAPER?
SHUT UP.

HI, COACH!
HELLO, BOYS! READY FOR ANOTHER SEASON?
COACH
YUP! I THINK WE'RE GONNA BE TOUGH TO BEAT THIS YEAR!
ME, TOO! ESPECIALLY WITH OUR NEW ADDITION!
COACH
NEW ADDITION?
COACH JOHN WILL BE HELPING US!
COACH
DEFINE "HELPING."
AWRIGHT, LADIES!! TIME TO SWEAT OFF THAT WINTER FLAB!!
COACH
Peirce

MY DAD TOOK ME TO THE BATTING CAGE YESTERDAY, AND I WAS SWINGING PRETTY GOOD AGAINST THE PITCHING MACHINE!
PITCH-ING MACHINE?
PITCHING MACHINES THROW IT RIGHT OVER THE PLATE EVERY TIME! THAT'S NO WAY TO PREPARE FOR GAME CONDITIONS!
WE DIDN'T HAVE PITCHING MACHINES WHEN I WAS COMING UP! WE DIDN'T HAVE FANCY-PANTS COMPOSITE BATS EITHER!
...AND HELMETS! WE DIDN'T HAVE HELMETS!
NOK
NOK
THAT EXPLAINS A FEW THINGS.
PEIRCE

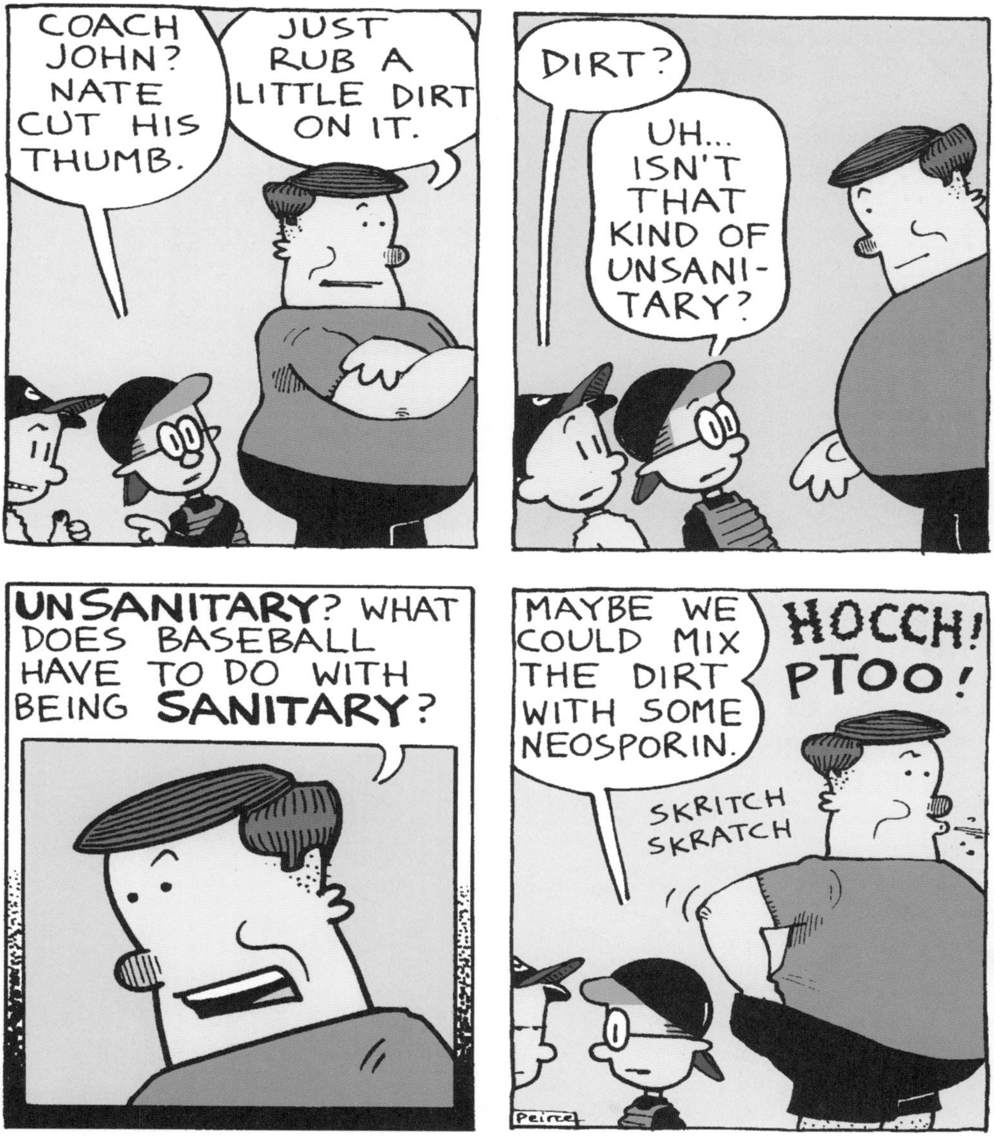
COACH JOHN? NATE CUT HIS THUMB.
JUST RUB A LITTLE DIRT ON IT.
DIRT?
UH... ISN'T THAT KIND OF UNSANI- TARY?
UNSANITARY? WHAT DOES BASEBALL HAVE TO DO WITH BEING SANITARY?
MAYBE WE COULD MIX THE DIRT WITH SOME NEOSPORIN.
HOCCH! PTOO!
SKRITCH SKRATCH
Peirce

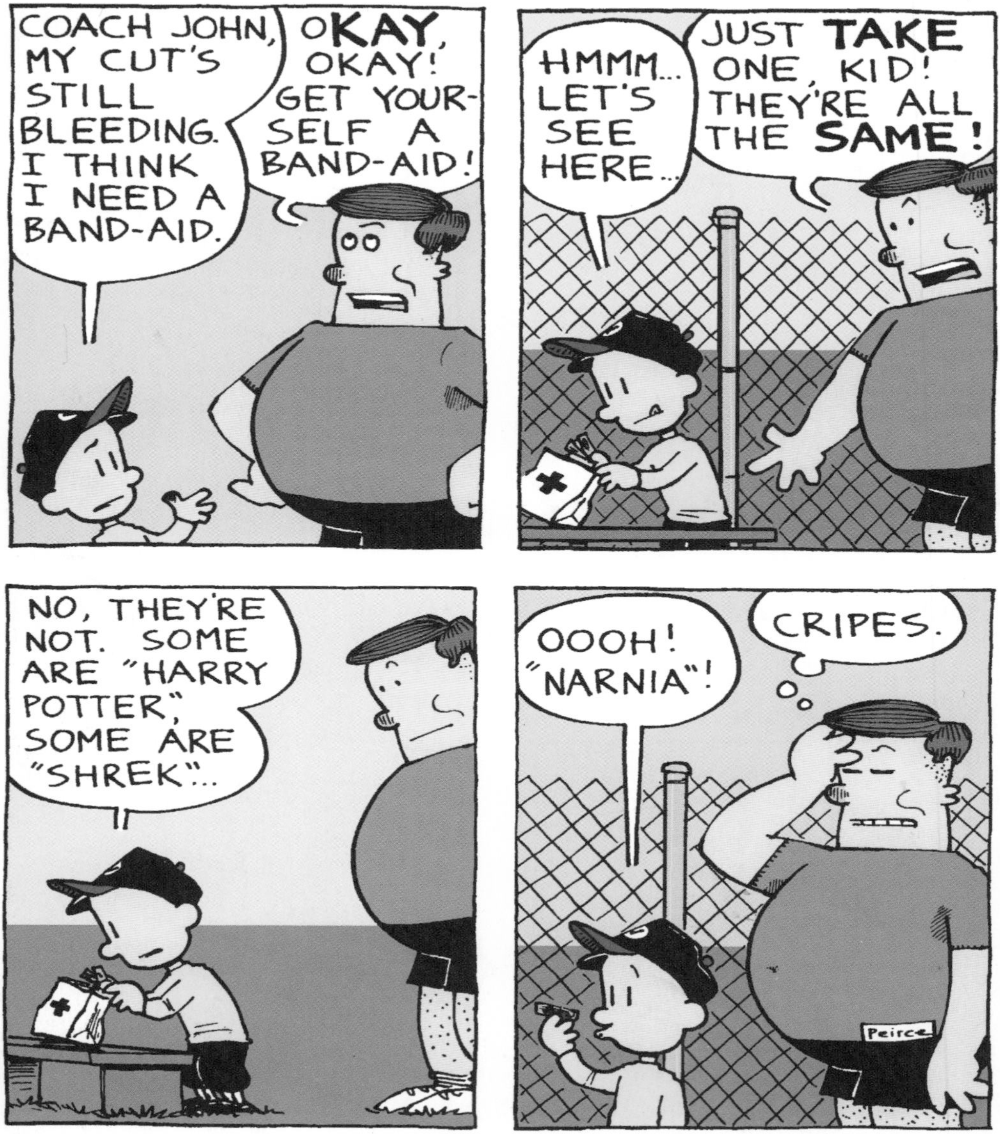
COACH JOHN, MY CUT'S STILL BLEEDING. I THINK I NEED A BAND-AID.
OKAY, OKAY! GET YOURSELF A BAND-AID!
HMMM... LET'S SEE HERE...
JUST TAKE ONE, KID! THEY'RE ALL THE SAME!
NO, THEY'RE NOT. SOME ARE "HARRY POTTER," SOME ARE "SHREK"...
OOOH! "NARNIA"!
CRIPES.
Peirce

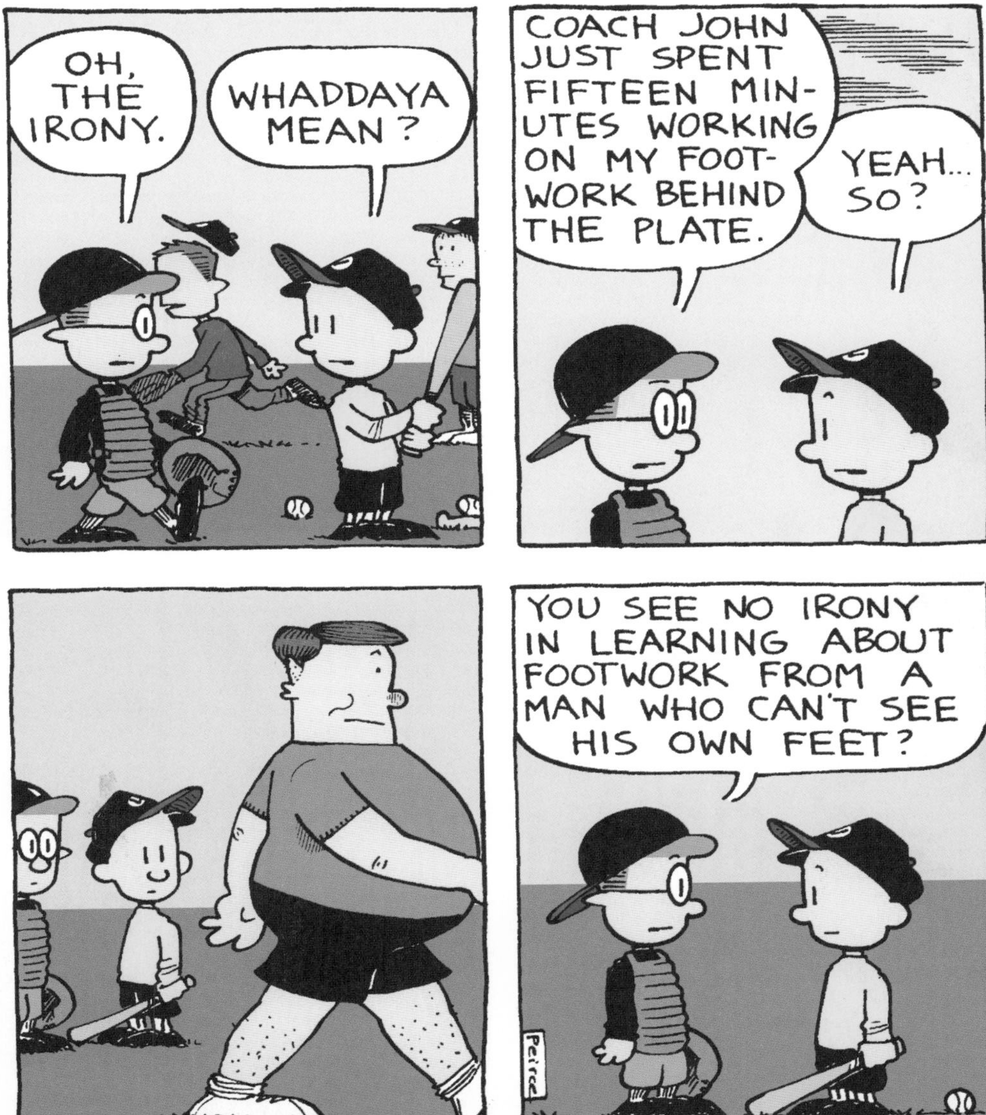
OH, THE IRONY.
WHADDAYA MEAN?
COACH JOHN JUST SPENT FIFTEEN MIN- UTES WORKING ON MY FOOT- WORK BEHIND THE PLATE.
YEAH... SO?
YOU SEE NO IRONY IN LEARNING ABOUT FOOTWORK FROM A MAN WHO CAN'T SEE HIS OWN FEET?
Peirce

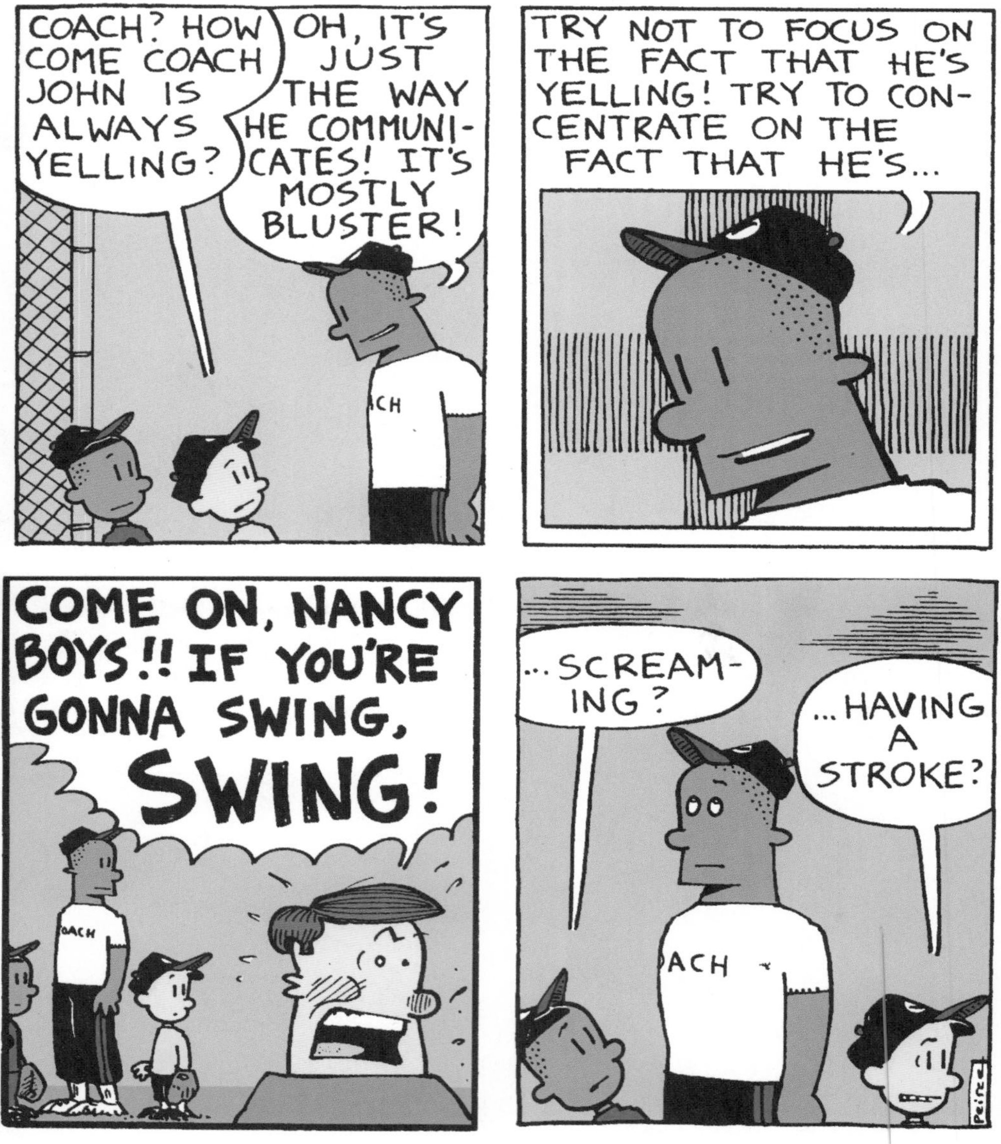
COACH? HOW COME COACH JOHN IS ALWAYS YELLING?
OH, IT'S JUST THE WAY HE COMMUNICATES! IT'S MOSTLY BLUSTER!
ACH
TRY NOT TO FOCUS ON THE FACT THAT HE'S YELLING! TRY TO CONCENTRATE ON THE FACT THAT HE'S...
COME ON, NANCY BOYS!! IF YOU'RE GONNA SWING, SWING!
OACH
...SCREAMING?
...HAVING A STROKE?
ACH
PEIRCE

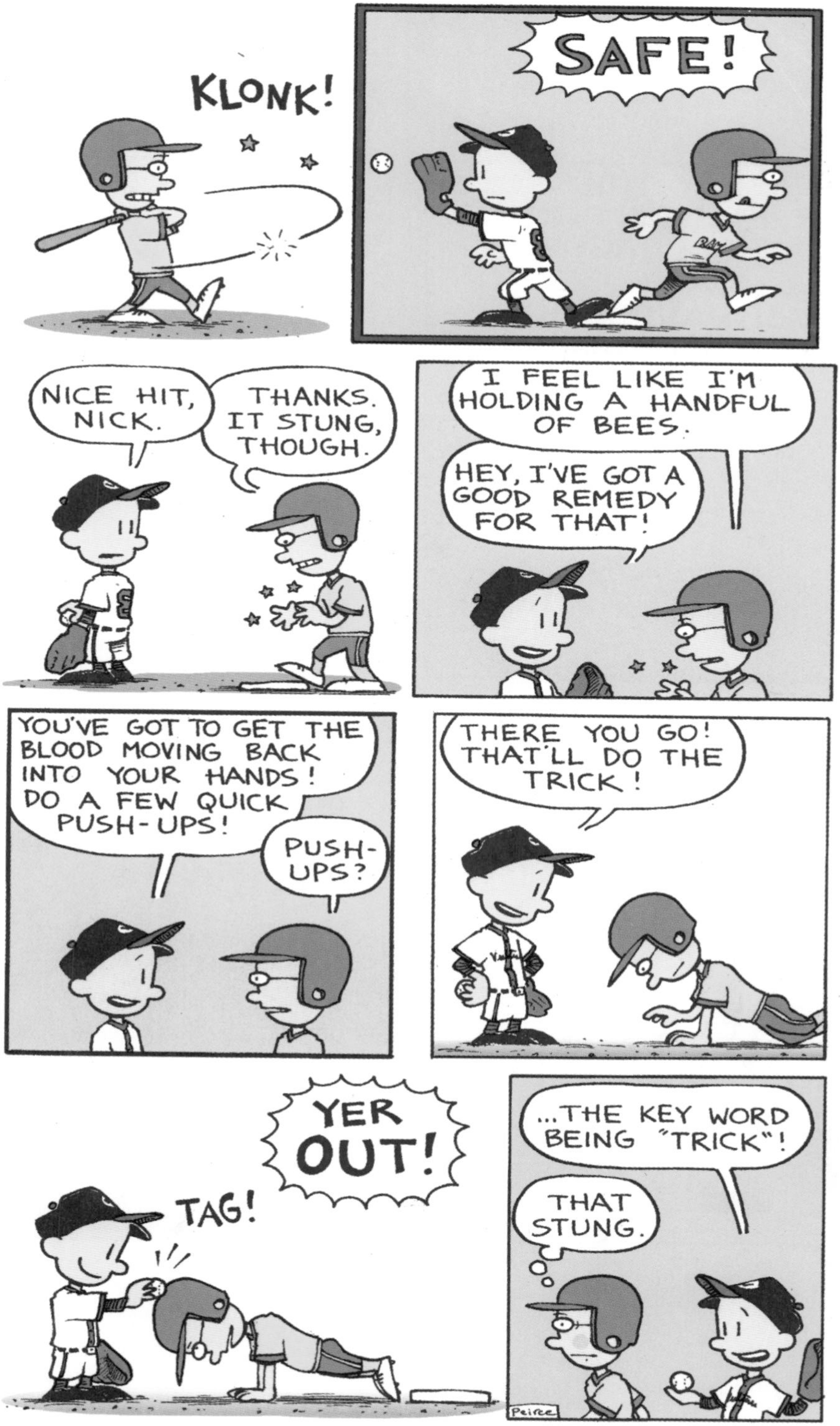
KLONK!
SAFE!
NICE HIT, NICK.
THANKS. IT STUNG, THOUGH.
I FEEL LIKE I'M HOLDING A HANDFUL OF BEES.
HEY, I'VE GOT A GOOD REMEDY FOR THAT!
YOU'VE GOT TO GET THE BLOOD MOVING BACK INTO YOUR HANDS! DO A FEW QUICK PUSH-UPS!
PUSH-UPS?
THERE YOU GO! THAT'LL DO THE TRICK!
YER OUT!
TAG!
...THE KEY WORD BEING "TRICK"!
THAT STUNG.
Peirce

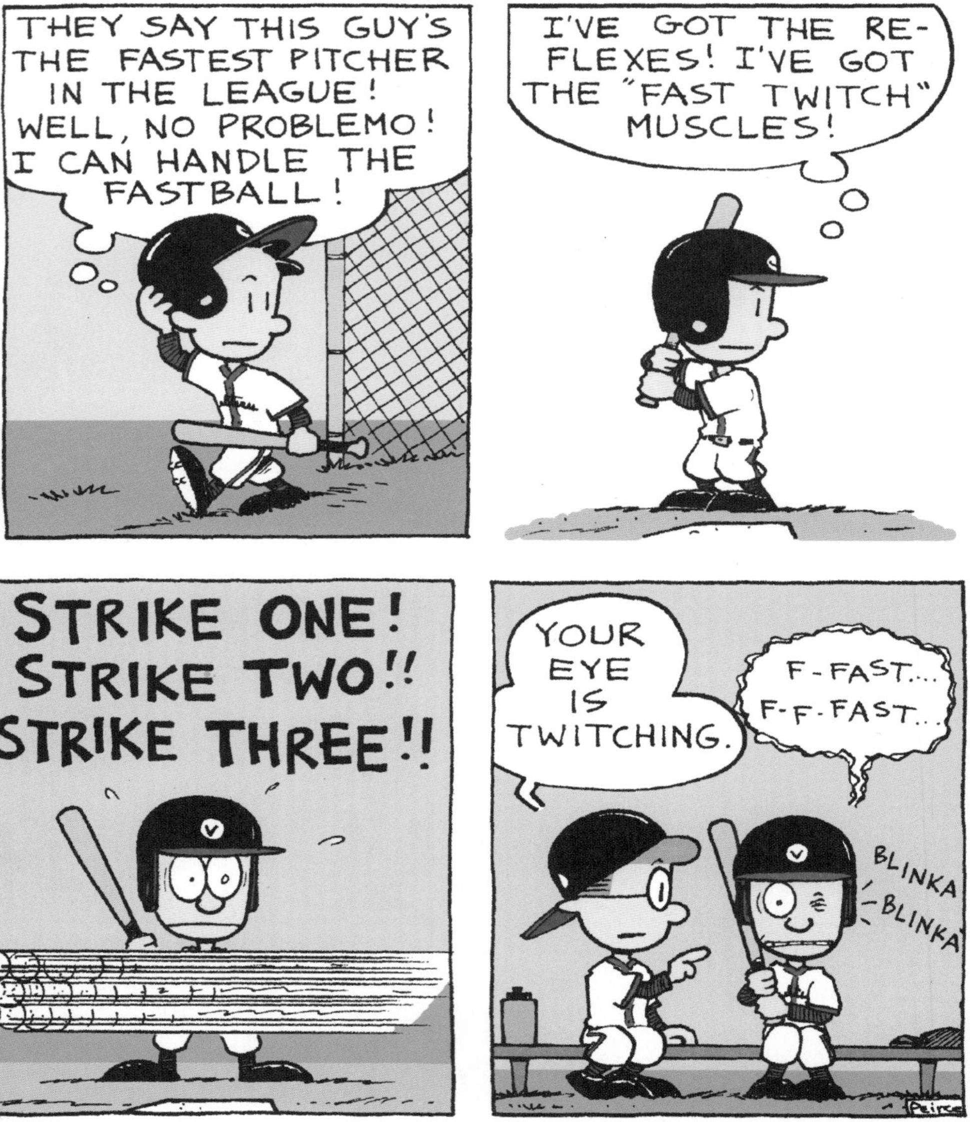
THEY SAY THIS GUY'S THE FASTEST PITCHER IN THE LEAGUE! WELL, NO PROBLEMO! I CAN HANDLE THE FASTBALL!
I'VE GOT THE RE-FLEXES! I'VE GOT THE "FAST TWITCH" MUSCLES!
STRIKE ONE! STRIKE TWO!! STRIKE THREE!!
YOUR EYE IS TWITCHING.
F-FAST... F-F-FAST...
BLINKA BLINKA
Peirce

OKAY, I WAS A LITTLE SLOW IN MY FIRST AT BAT...
THIS TIME, I'LL START MY SWING A LITTLE BIT...
WUMP!
...EARLIER.
STRIKE ONE.
Peirce

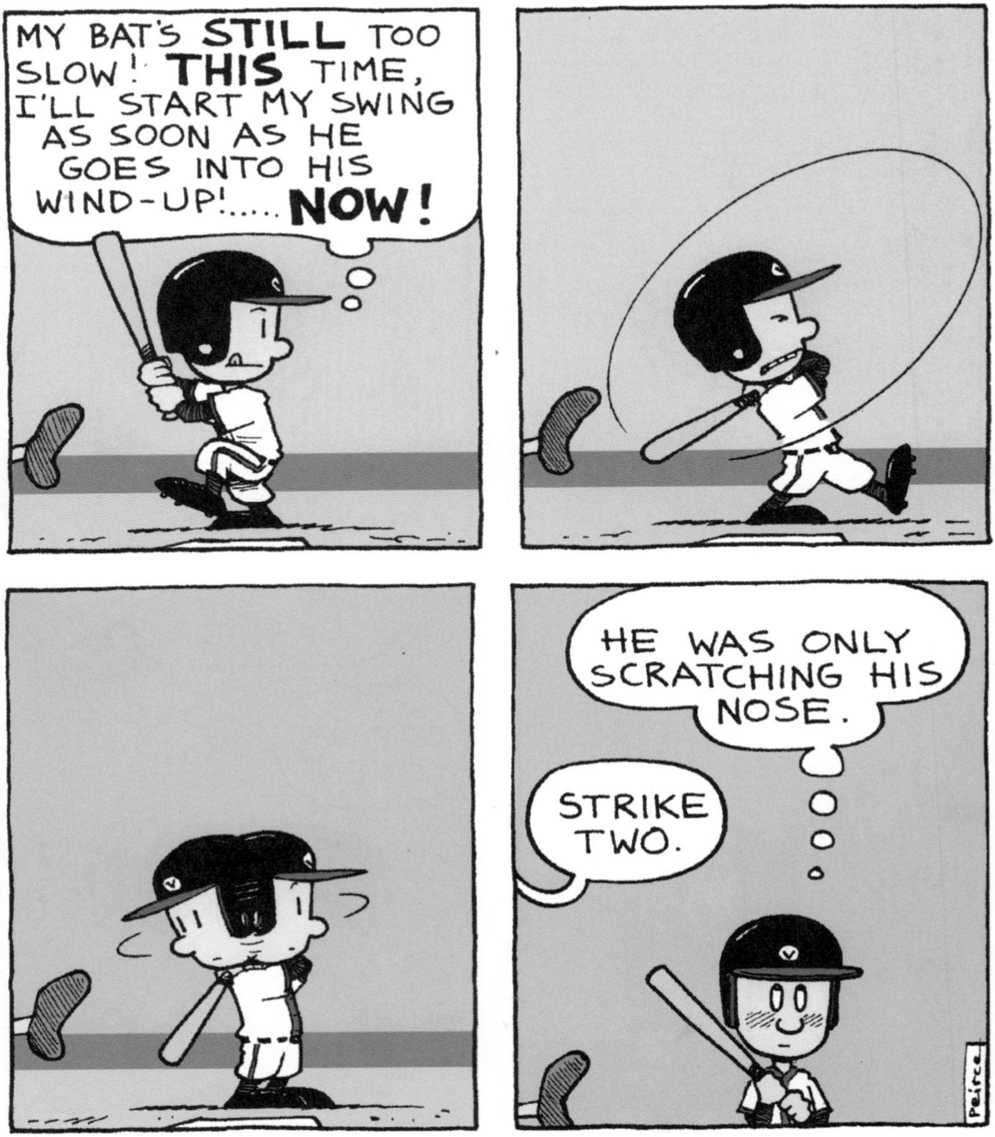
MY BAT'S STILL TOO SLOW! THIS TIME, I'LL START MY SWING AS SOON AS HE GOES INTO HIS WIND-UP!..... NOW!
HE WAS ONLY SCRATCHING HIS NOSE.
STRIKE TWO.
peirce

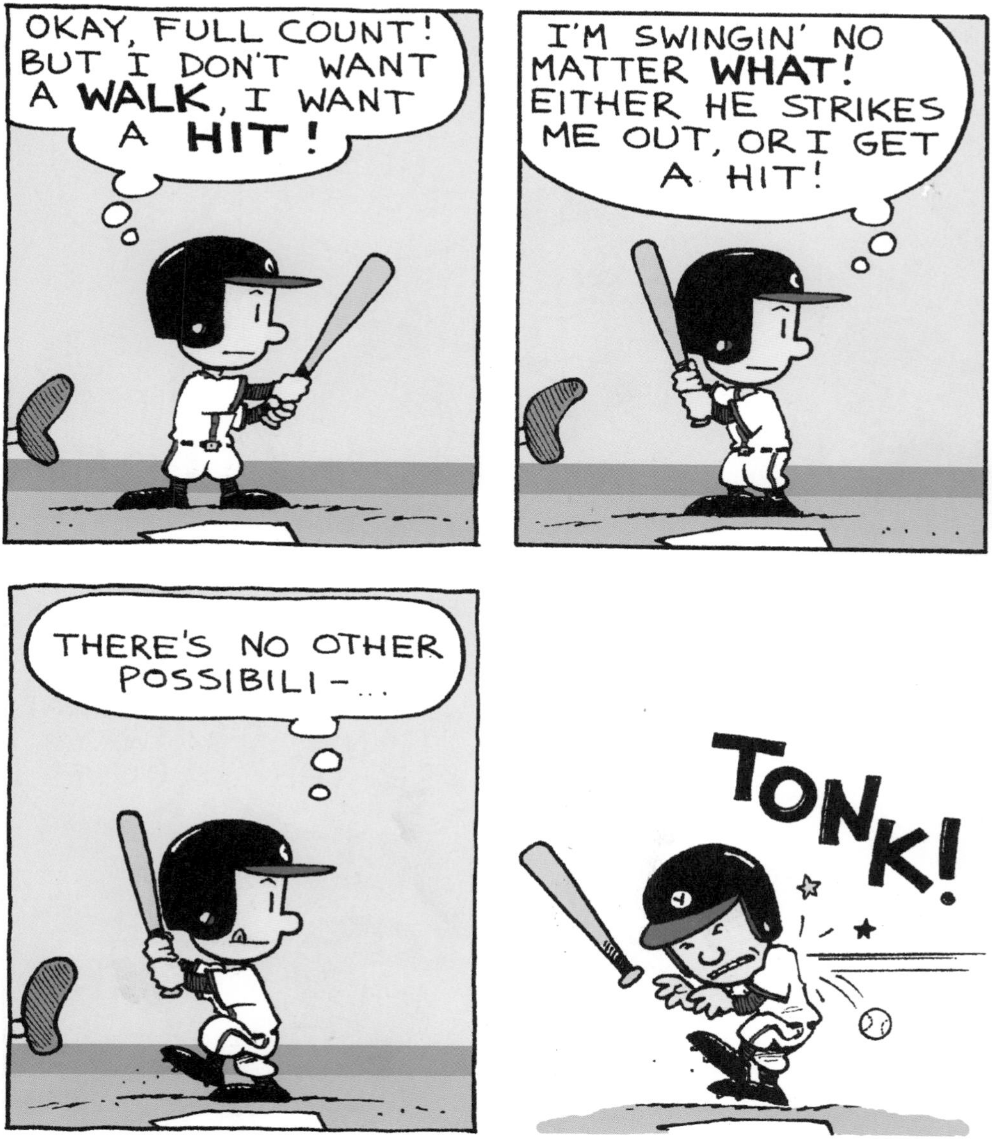
OKAY, FULL COUNT! BUT I DON'T WANT A WALK, I WANT A HIT!
I'M SWINGIN' NO MATTER WHAT! EITHER HE STRIKES ME OUT, OR I GET A HIT!
THERE'S NO OTHER POSSIBILI-...
TONK!

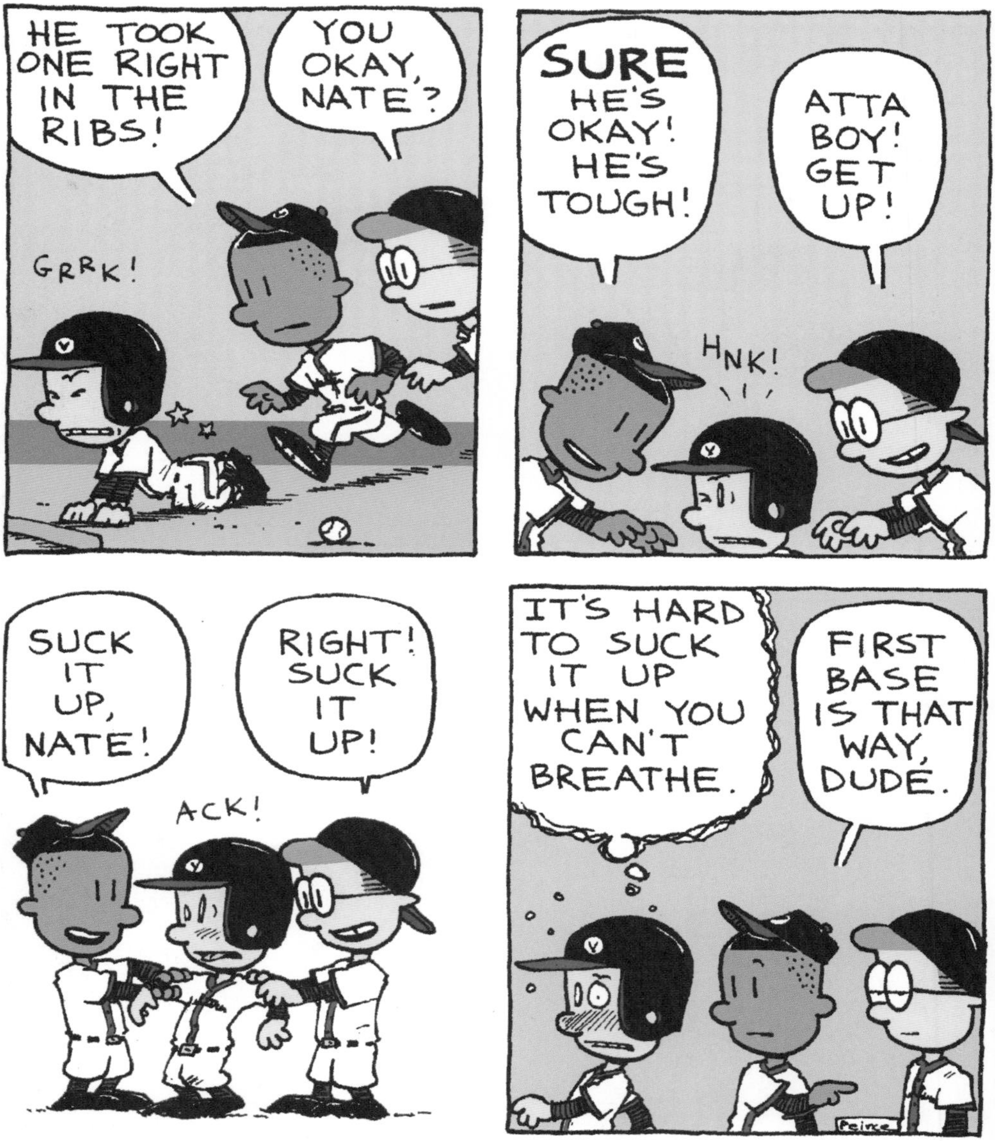
HE TOOK ONE RIGHT IN THE RIBS!
YOU OKAY, NATE?
GRRK!
SURE HE'S OKAY! HE'S TOUGH!
ATTA BOY! GET UP!
HNK!
SUCK IT UP, NATE!
RIGHT! SUCK IT UP!
ACK!
IT'S HARD TO SUCK IT UP WHEN YOU CAN'T BREATHE.
FIRST BASE IS THAT WAY, DUDE.
Peirce

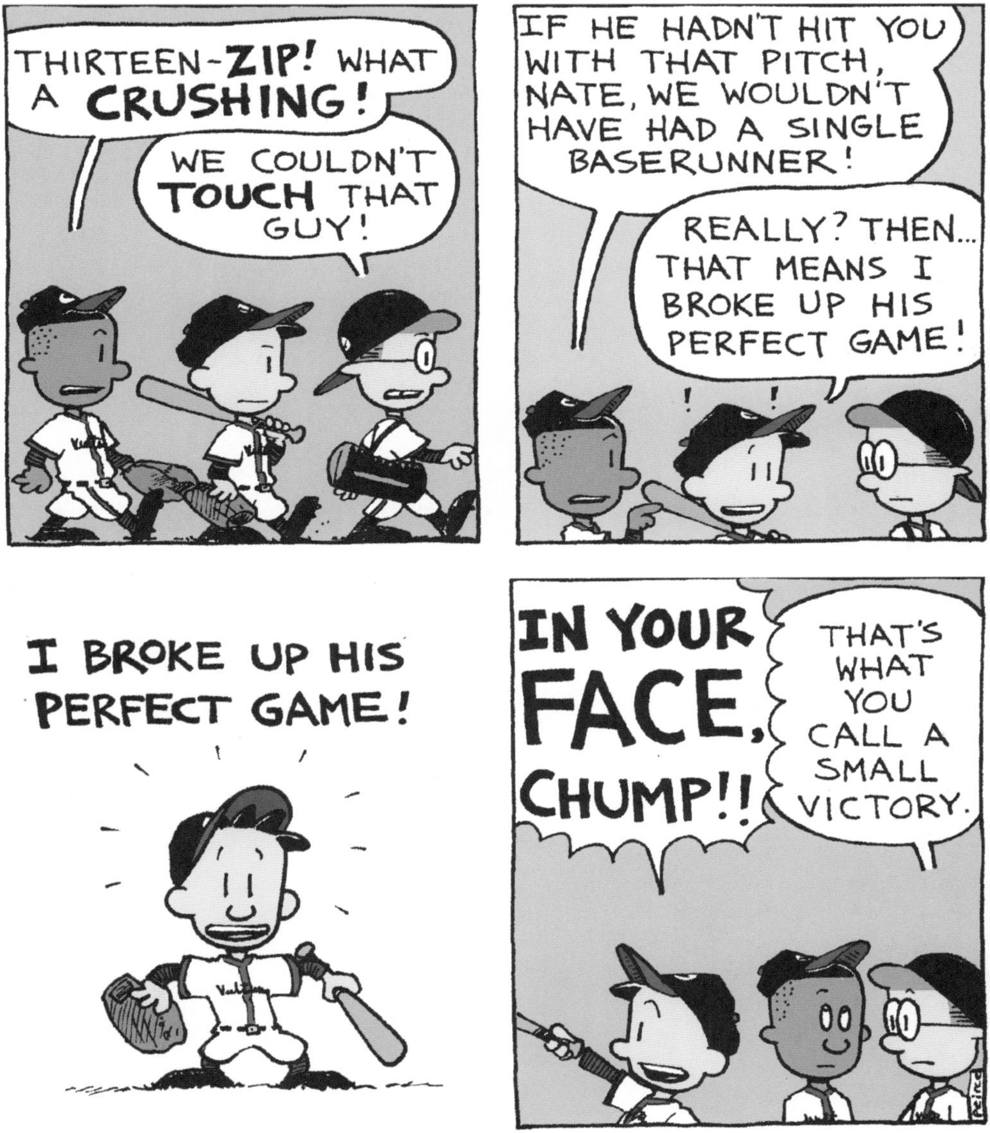
THIRTEEN-ZIP! WHAT A CRUSHING!
WE COULDN'T TOUCH THAT GUY!
IF HE HADN'T HIT YOU WITH THAT PITCH, NATE, WE WOULDN'T HAVE HAD A SINGLE BASERUNNER!
REALLY? THEN... THAT MEANS I BROKE UP HIS PERFECT GAME!
! !
I BROKE UP HIS PERFECT GAME!
IN YOUR FACE, CHUMP!!
THAT'S WHAT YOU CALL A SMALL VICTORY.
PEIRCE

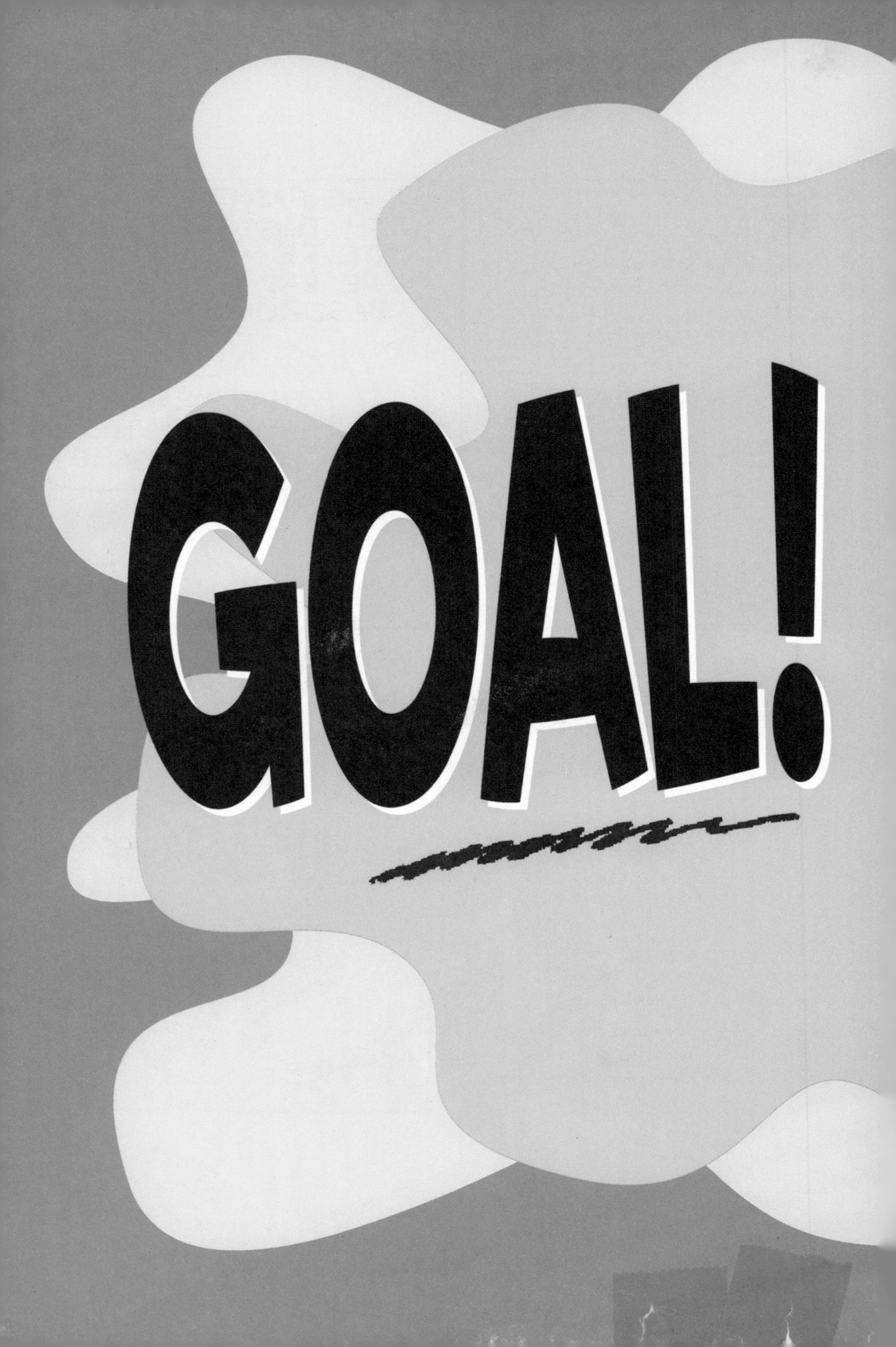
GOAL!

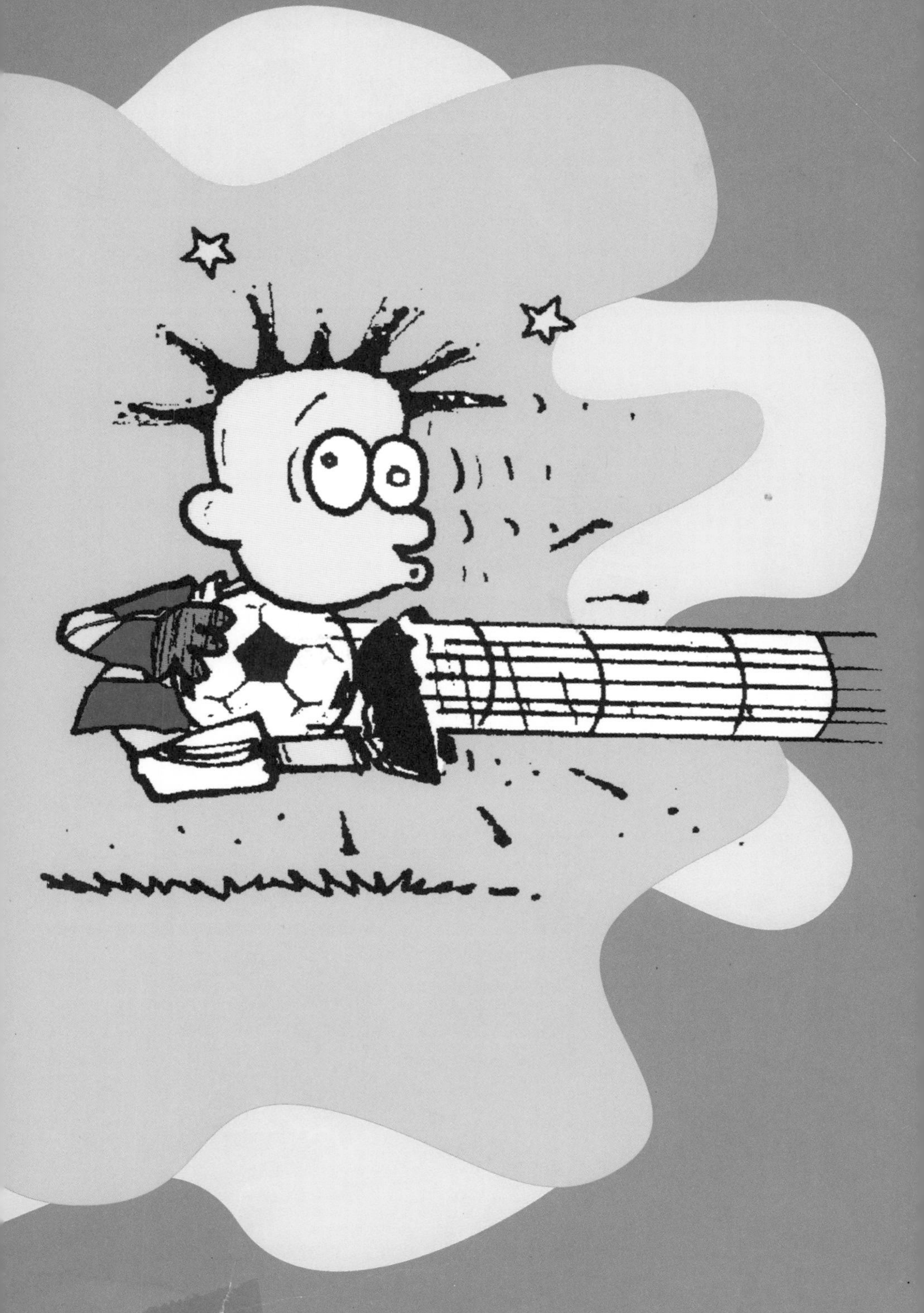

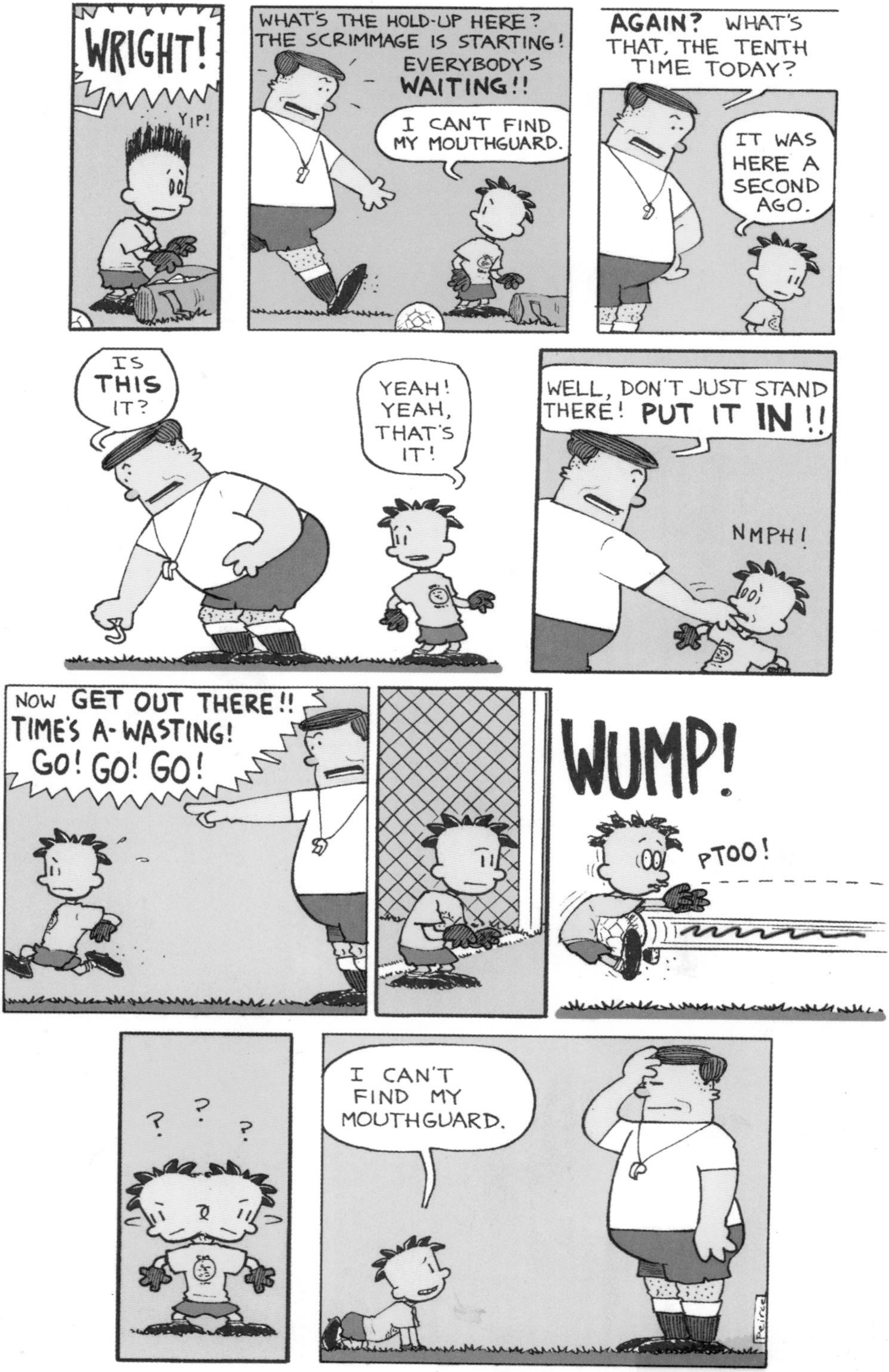
WRIGHT!
YIP!
WHAT'S THE HOLD-UP HERE? THE SCRIMMAGE IS STARTING! EVERYBODY'S WAITING!!
I CAN'T FIND MY MOUTHGUARD.
AGAIN? WHAT'S THAT, THE TENTH TIME TODAY?
IT WAS HERE A SECOND AGO.
IS THIS IT?
YEAH! YEAH, THAT'S IT!
WELL, DON'T JUST STAND THERE! PUT IT IN!!
NMPH!
NOW GET OUT THERE!! TIME'S A-WASTING! GO! GO! GO!
WUMP!
PTOO!
? ? ?
I CAN'T FIND MY MOUTHGUARD.
Peirce

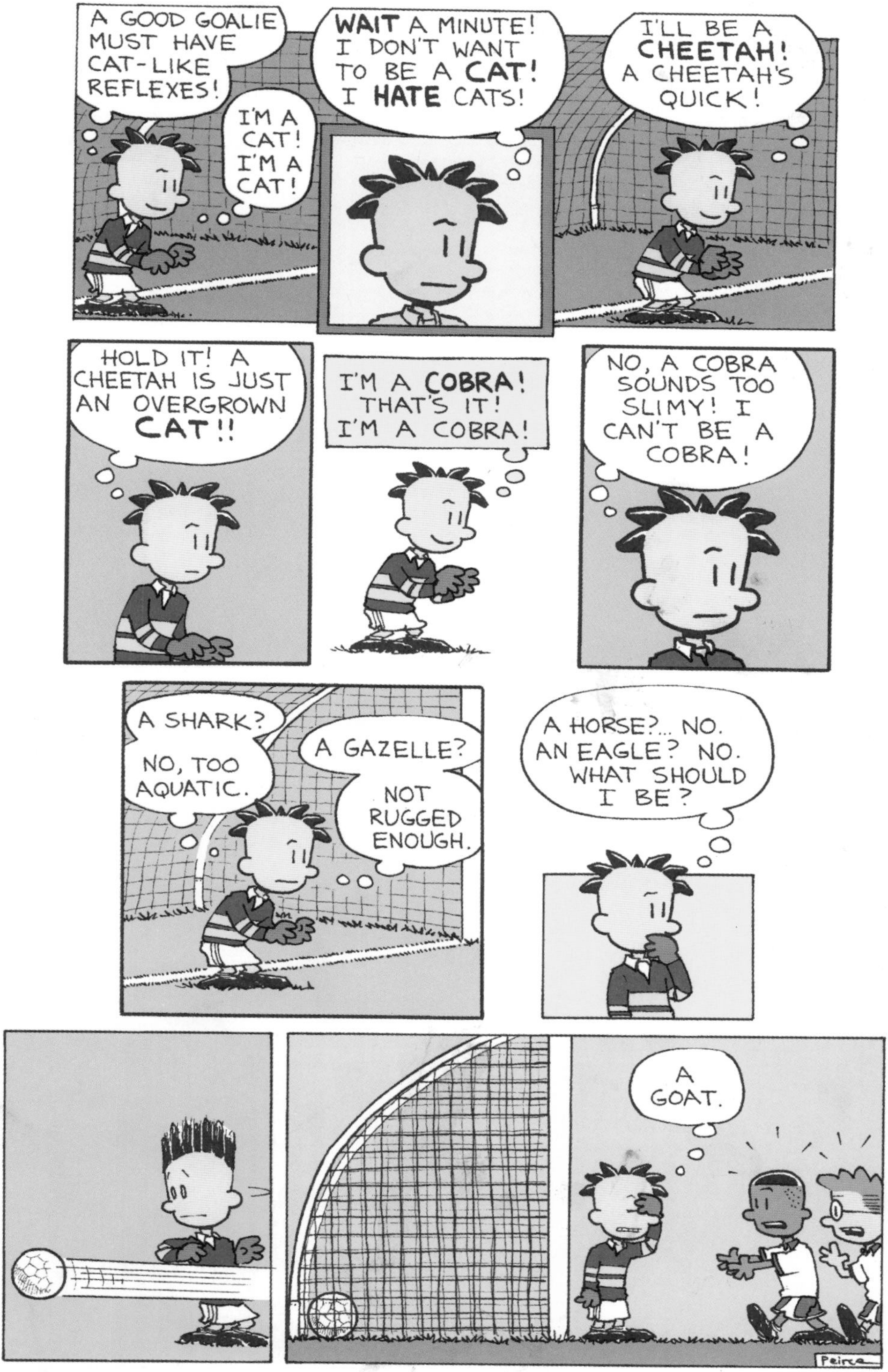
A GOOD GOALIE MUST HAVE CAT-LIKE REFLEXES!
I'M A CAT! I'M A CAT!
WAIT A MINUTE! I DON'T WANT TO BE A CAT! I HATE CATS!
I'LL BE A CHEETAH! A CHEETAH'S QUICK!
HOLD IT! A CHEETAH IS JUST AN OVERGROWN CAT!!
I'M A COBRA! THAT'S IT! I'M A COBRA!
NO, A COBRA SOUNDS TOO SLIMY! I CAN'T BE A COBRA!
A SHARK?
NO, TOO AQUATIC.
A GAZELLE?
NOT RUGGED ENOUGH.
A HORSE?... NO. AN EAGLE? NO. WHAT SHOULD I BE?
A GOAT.
Peirce

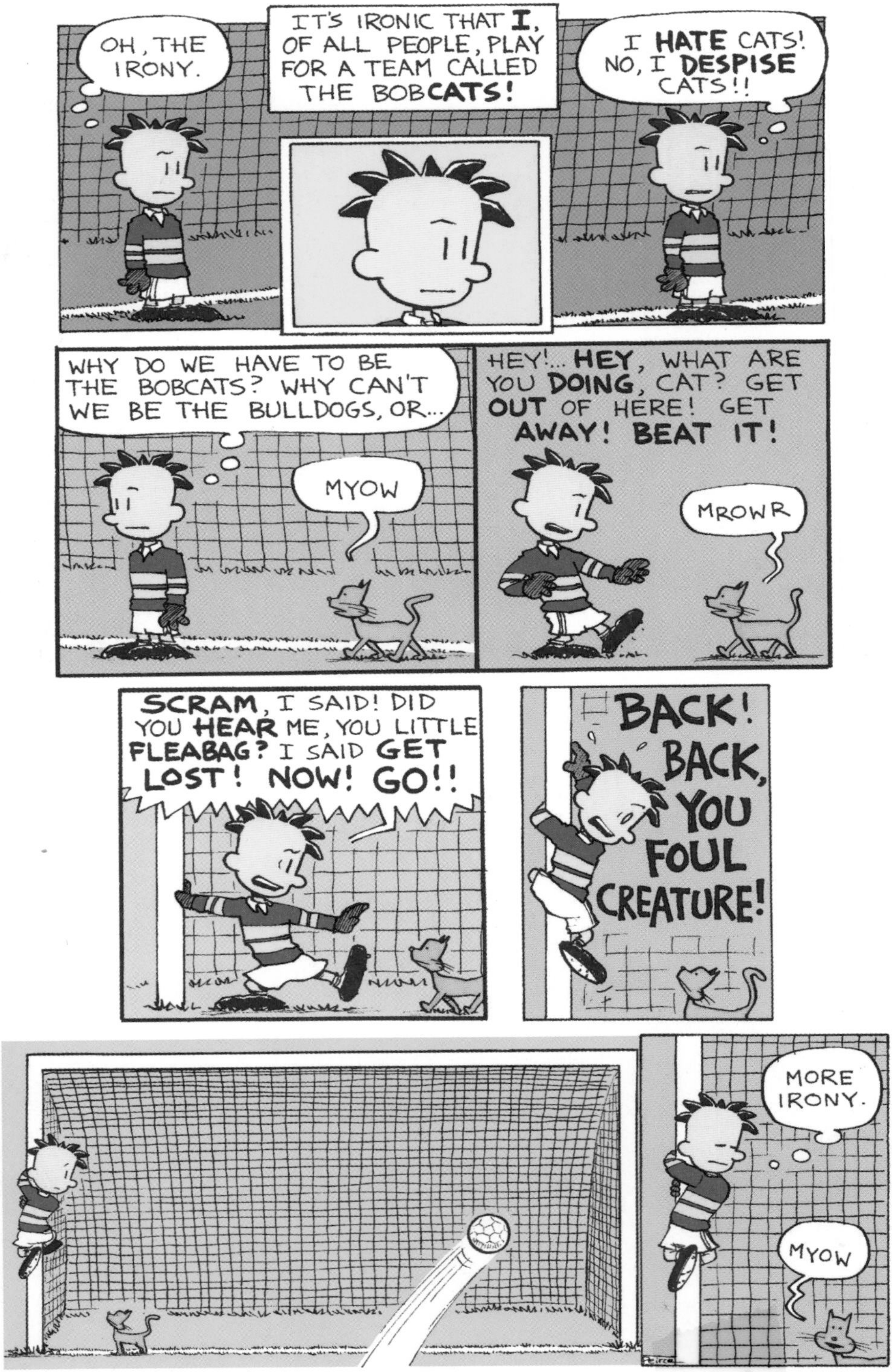
OH, THE IRONY.
IT'S IRONIC THAT I, OF ALL PEOPLE, PLAY FOR A TEAM CALLED THE BOBCATS!
I HATE CATS! NO, I DESPISE CATS!!
WHY DO WE HAVE TO BE THE BOBCATS? WHY CAN'T WE BE THE BULLDOGS, OR...
MYOW
HEY!... HEY, WHAT ARE YOU DOING, CAT? GET OUT OF HERE! GET AWAY! BEAT IT!
MROWR
SCRAM, I SAID! DID YOU HEAR ME, YOU LITTLE FLEABAG? I SAID GET LOST! NOW! GO!!
BACK! BACK, YOU FOUL CREATURE!
MORE IRONY.
MYOW

HEY, HEY! WHAT ARE YOU DOING?
YOU'RE NOT SUPPOSED TO TRY TO SCORE DURING WARM-UPS, FRANCIS YOU IDIOT! THE POINT IS TO LOOSEN UP THE GOALIE!
6
THIS TIME, SHOOT IT RIGHT AT ME!
CAN I HAVE AN ICE PACK?
COACH
Peirce

THESE LAST FEW MINUTES BEFORE THE GAME STARTS ARE WHEN I GET INTO MY "FOCUS ZONE."
MY REFLEXES ARE HONED TO A RAZOR-SHARP EDGE! I'M SUPER-ALERT, SUPER-AWARE! NOTHING ESCAPES MY HAWK-LIKE GAZE!
YOU'VE GOT A HUGE GLOB OF PEANUT BUTTER STUCK ON YOUR FACE.
HOW EMBARRASSING.
PLUS, I THINK YOU PUT YOUR SHORTS ON BACKWARD.
Peirce

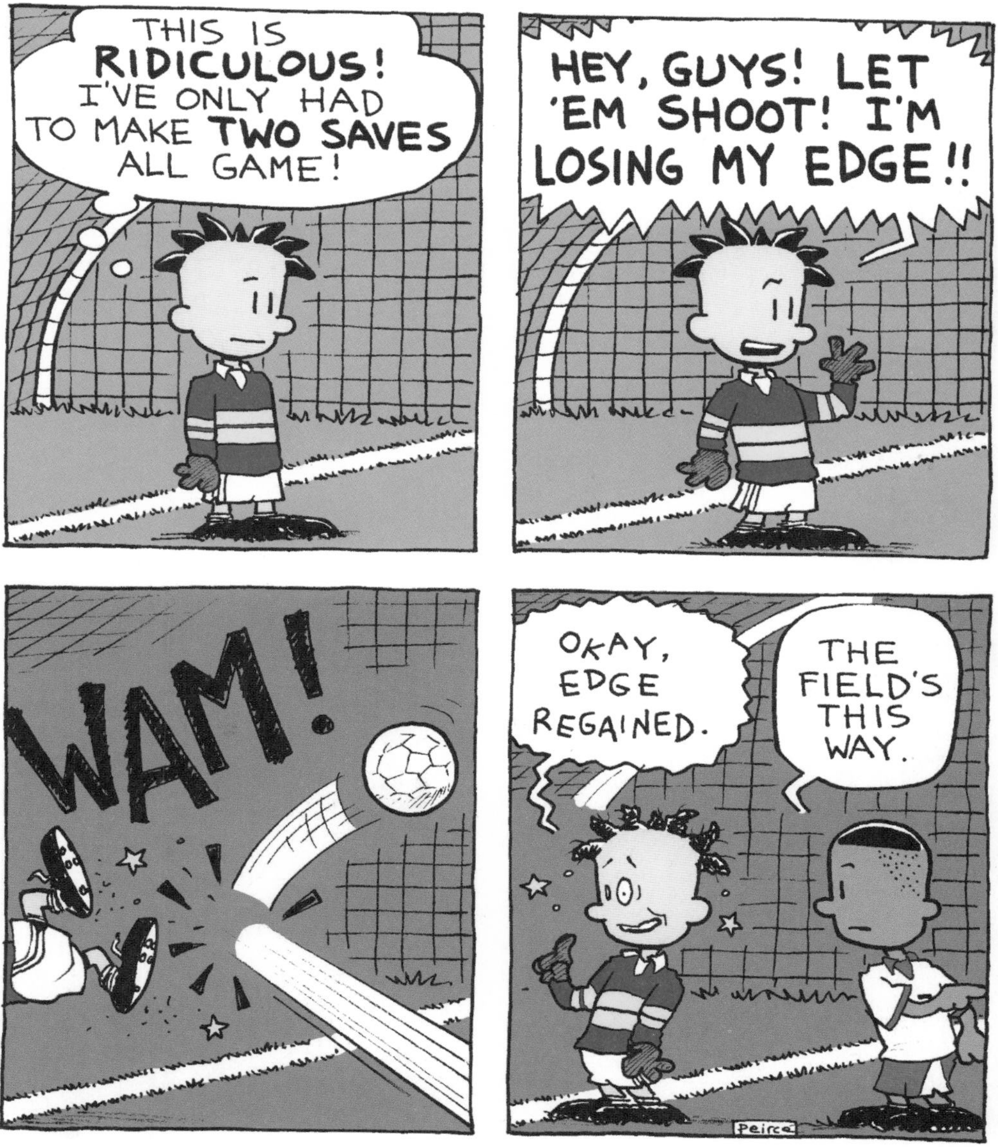
THIS IS RIDICULOUS! I'VE ONLY HAD TO MAKE TWO SAVES ALL GAME!
HEY, GUYS! LET 'EM SHOOT! I'M LOSING MY EDGE!!
WAM!
OKAY, EDGE REGAINED.
THE FIELD'S THIS WAY.
Peirce

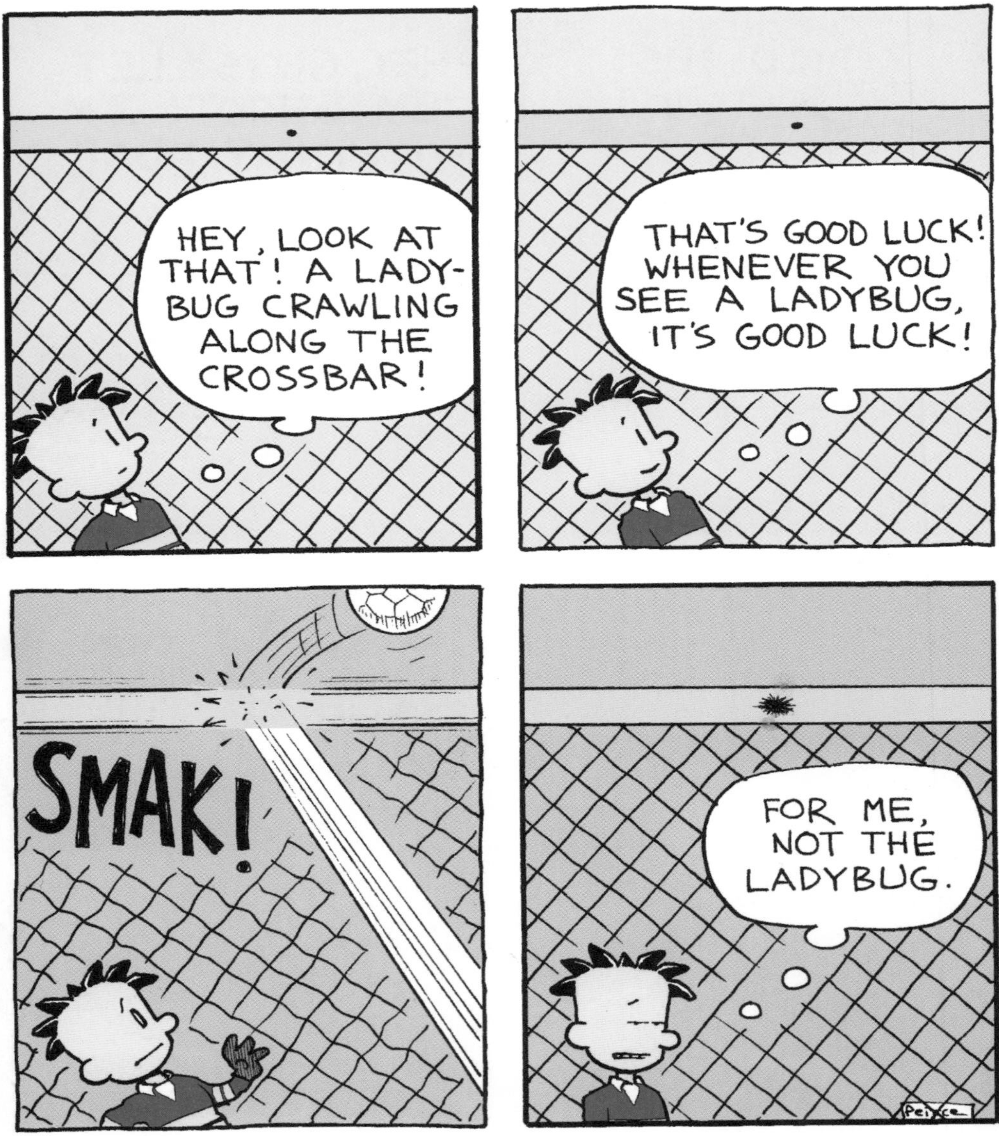
HEY, LOOK AT THAT! A LADYBUG CRAWLING ALONG THE CROSSBAR!
THAT'S GOOD LUCK! WHENEVER YOU SEE A LADYBUG, IT'S GOOD LUCK!
SMAK!
FOR ME, NOT THE LADYBUG.
PEIRCE

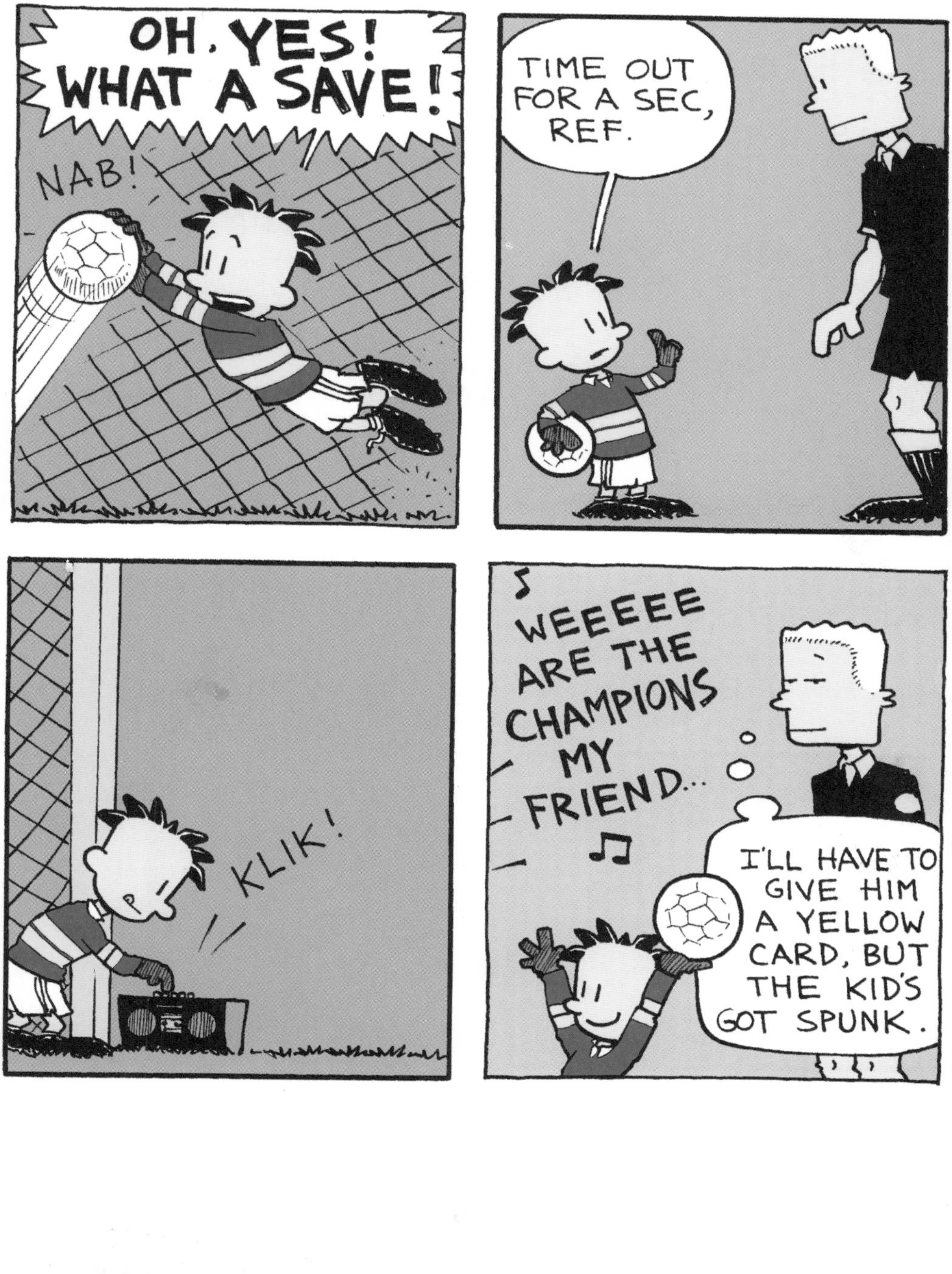
OH, YES! WHAT A SAVE!
NAB!
TIME OUT FOR A SEC, REF.
KLIK!
WEEEEE ARE THE CHAMPIONS MY FRIEND...
I'LL HAVE TO GIVE HIM A YELLOW CARD, BUT THE KID'S GOT SPUNK.

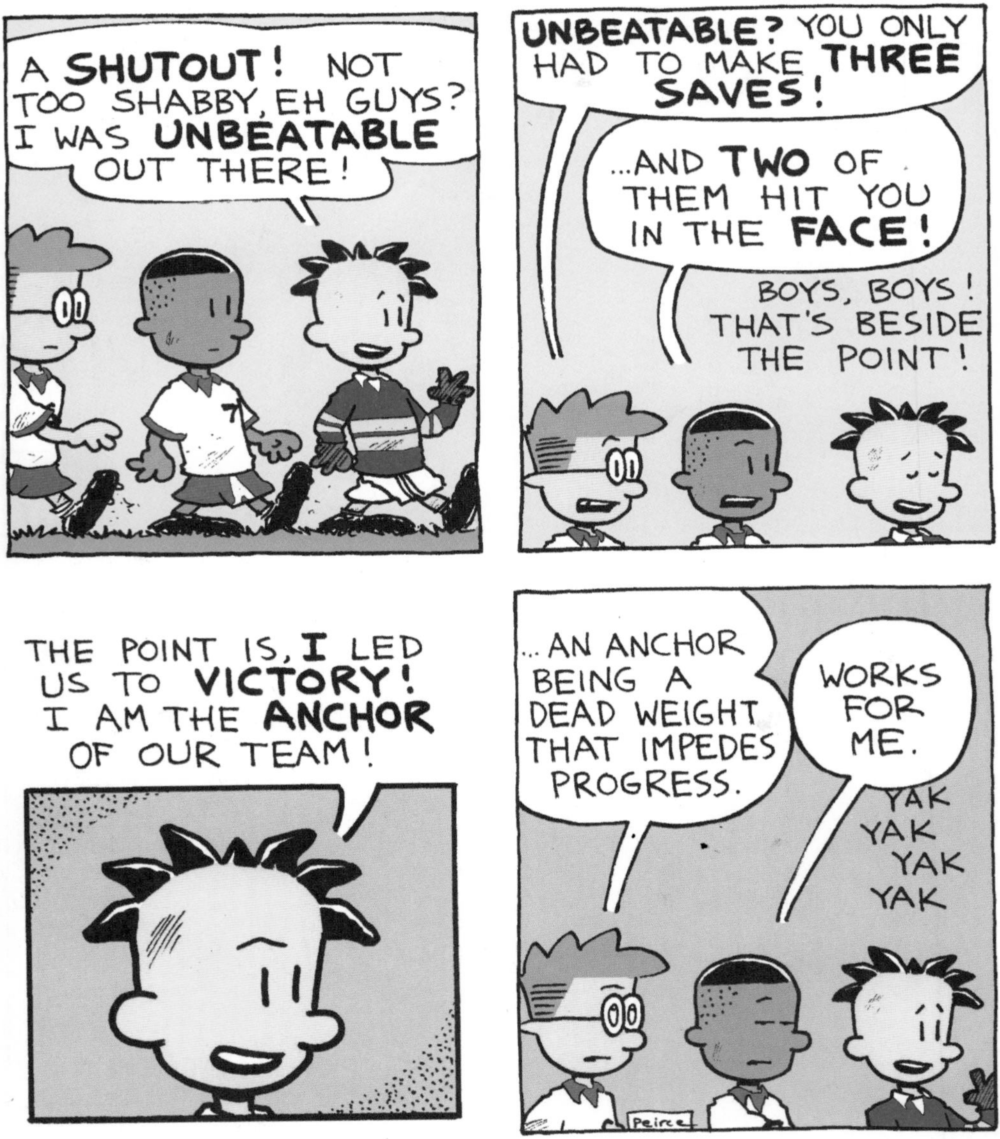
A SHUTOUT! NOT TOO SHABBY, EH GUYS? I WAS UNBEATABLE OUT THERE!
UNBEATABLE? YOU ONLY HAD TO MAKE THREE SAVES!
...AND TWO OF THEM HIT YOU IN THE FACE!
BOYS, BOYS! THAT'S BESIDE THE POINT!
THE POINT IS, I LED US TO VICTORY! I AM THE ANCHOR OF OUR TEAM!
...AN ANCHOR BEING A DEAD WEIGHT THAT IMPEDES PROGRESS.
WORKS FOR ME.
YAK YAK YAK YAK
Peirce

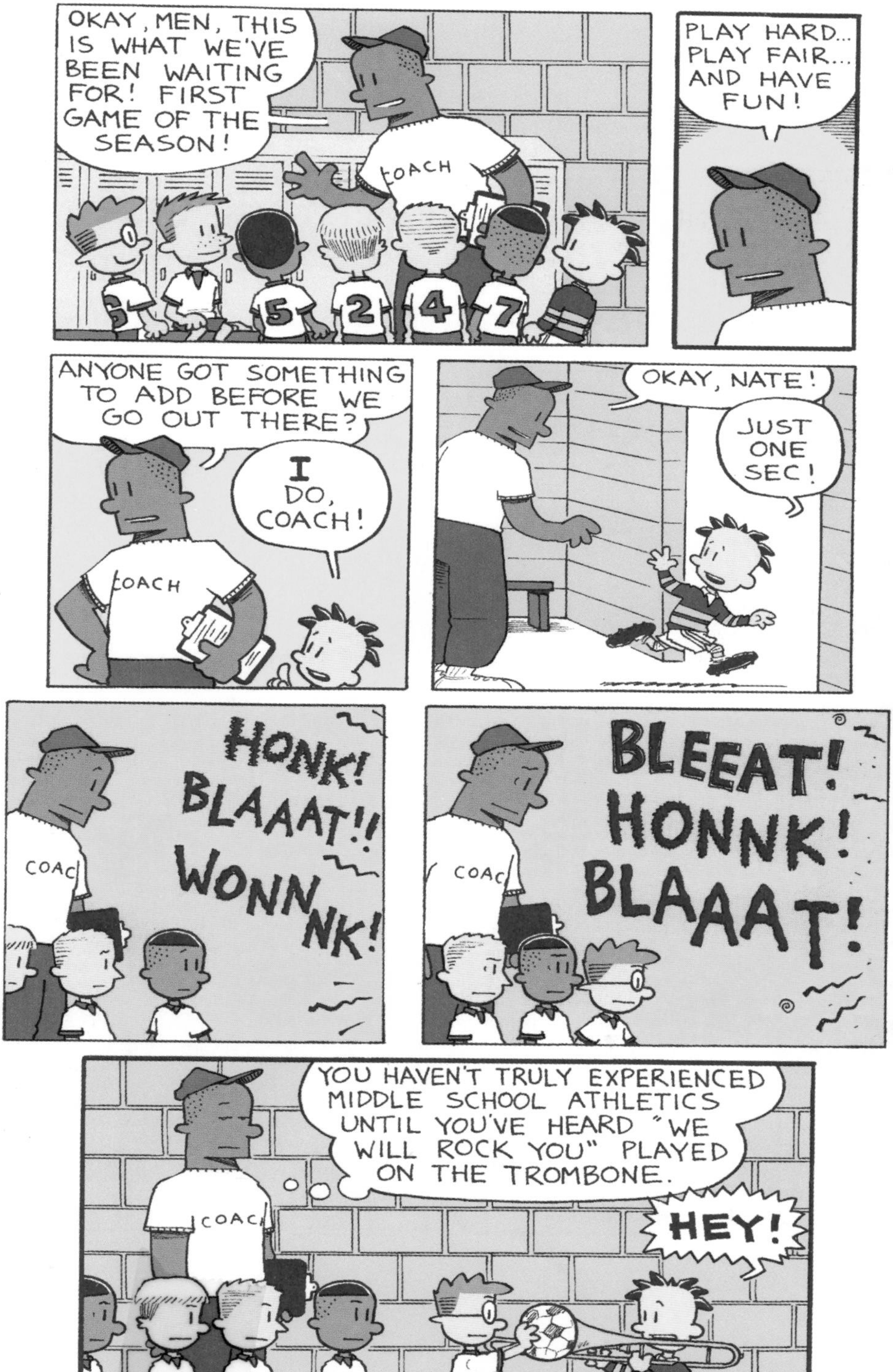
OKAY, MEN, THIS IS WHAT WE'VE BEEN WAITING FOR! FIRST GAME OF THE SEASON!
COACH
5
2
4
7
PLAY HARD... PLAY FAIR... AND HAVE FUN!
ANYONE GOT SOMETHING TO ADD BEFORE WE GO OUT THERE?
I DO, COACH!
COACH
OKAY, NATE!
JUST ONE SEC!
HONK! BLAAAT!! WONNNK!
COAC
BLEEAT! HONNK! BLAAAT!
COAC
YOU HAVEN'T TRULY EXPERIENCED MIDDLE SCHOOL ATHLETICS UNTIL YOU'VE HEARD "WE WILL ROCK YOU" PLAYED ON THE TROMBONE.
COAC
HEY!
Peirce

WHAT HAPPENED?
WHADDAYA MEAN, WHAT HAPPENED? CURTIS JUST GOT HACKED!
COACH
5
6
DIDN'T YOU SEE IT?
NO.
I GUESS I WASN'T REALLY PAYING ATTENTION TO THE GAME.
ALWAYS A GOOD QUALITY IN A GOALIE.
WHAT'S THE SCORE?
Peirce

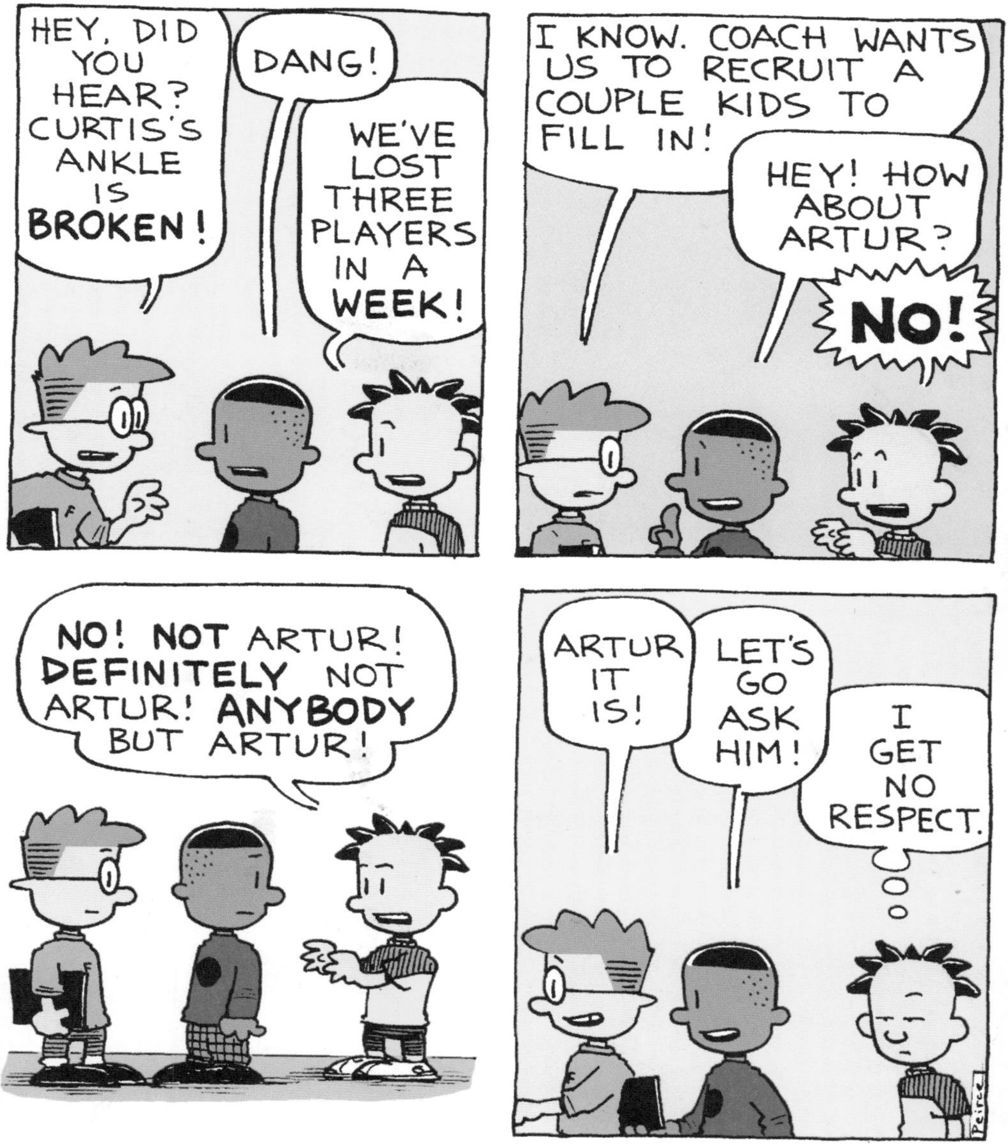

HEY, DID YOU HEAR? CURTIS'S ANKLE IS **BROKEN**!
DANG!
WE'VE LOST THREE PLAYERS IN A **WEEK**!
I KNOW. COACH WANTS US TO RECRUIT A COUPLE KIDS TO FILL IN!
HEY! HOW ABOUT ARTUR?
NO!
NO! NOT ARTUR! **DEFINITELY** NOT ARTUR! **ANYBODY** BUT ARTUR!
ARTUR IT IS!
LET'S GO ASK HIM!
I GET NO RESPECT.
Peirce

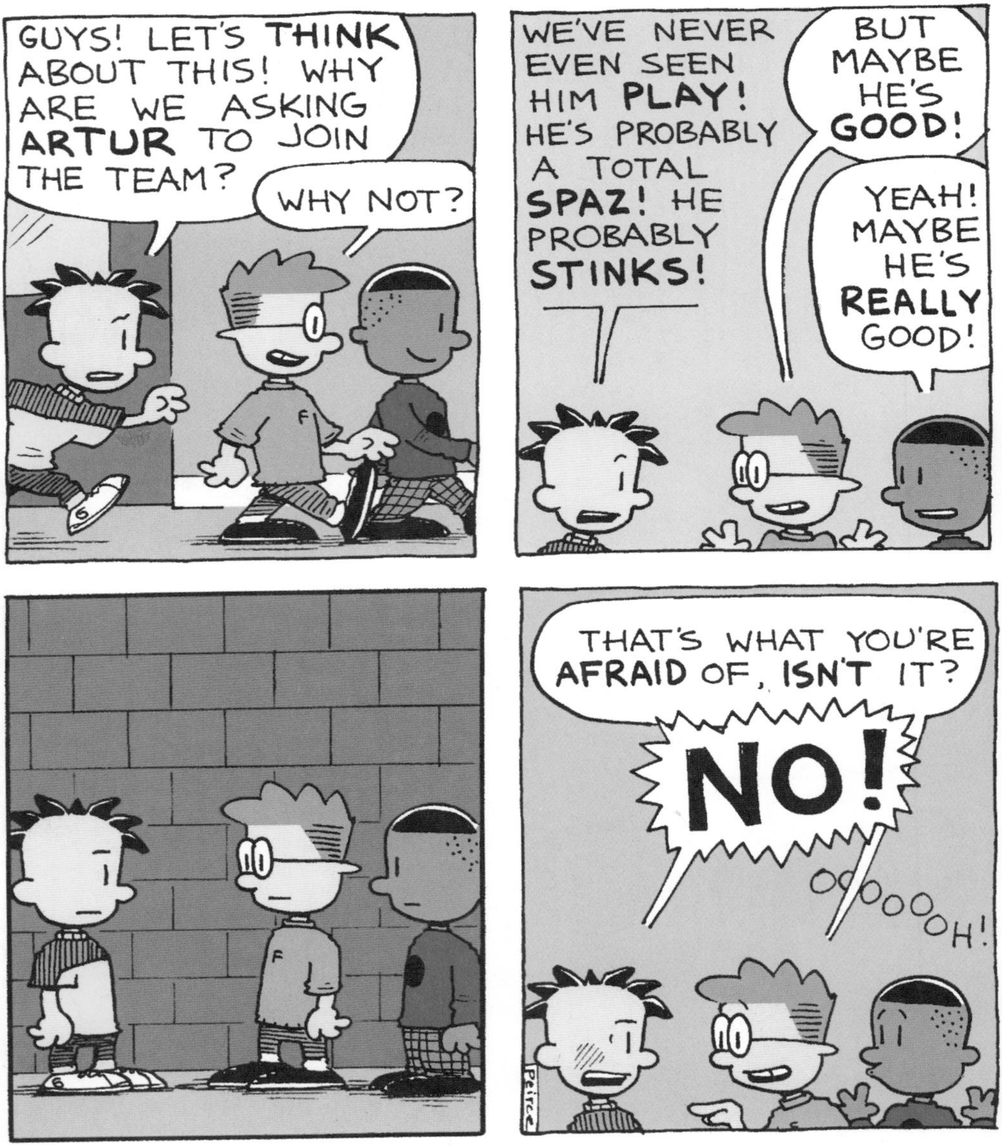
GUYS! LET'S THINK ABOUT THIS! WHY ARE WE ASKING ARTUR TO JOIN THE TEAM?
WHY NOT?
WE'VE NEVER EVEN SEEN HIM PLAY! HE'S PROBABLY A TOTAL SPAZ! HE PROBABLY STINKS!
BUT MAYBE HE'S GOOD!
YEAH! MAYBE HE'S REALLY GOOD!
THAT'S WHAT YOU'RE AFRAID OF, ISN'T IT?
NO!
OOOOOOOH!
Peirce

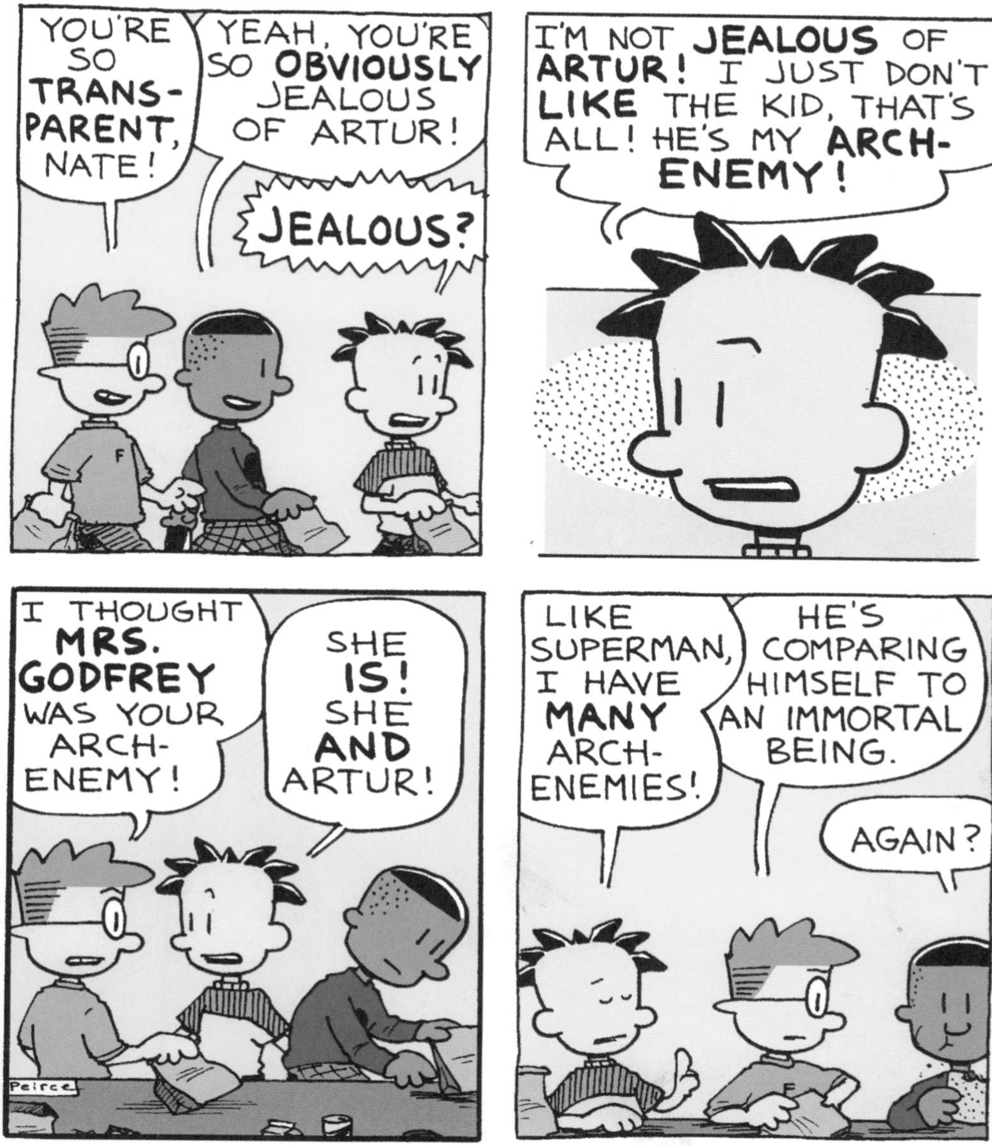

YOU'RE SO TRANSPARENT, NATE!
YEAH, YOU'RE SO OBVIOUSLY JEALOUS OF ARTUR!
JEALOUS?
I'M NOT JEALOUS OF ARTUR! I JUST DON'T LIKE THE KID, THAT'S ALL! HE'S MY ARCH-ENEMY!
I THOUGHT MRS. GODFREY WAS YOUR ARCH-ENEMY!
SHE IS! SHE AND ARTUR!
Peirce
LIKE SUPERMAN, I HAVE MANY ARCH-ENEMIES!
HE'S COMPARING HIMSELF TO AN IMMORTAL BEING.
AGAIN?

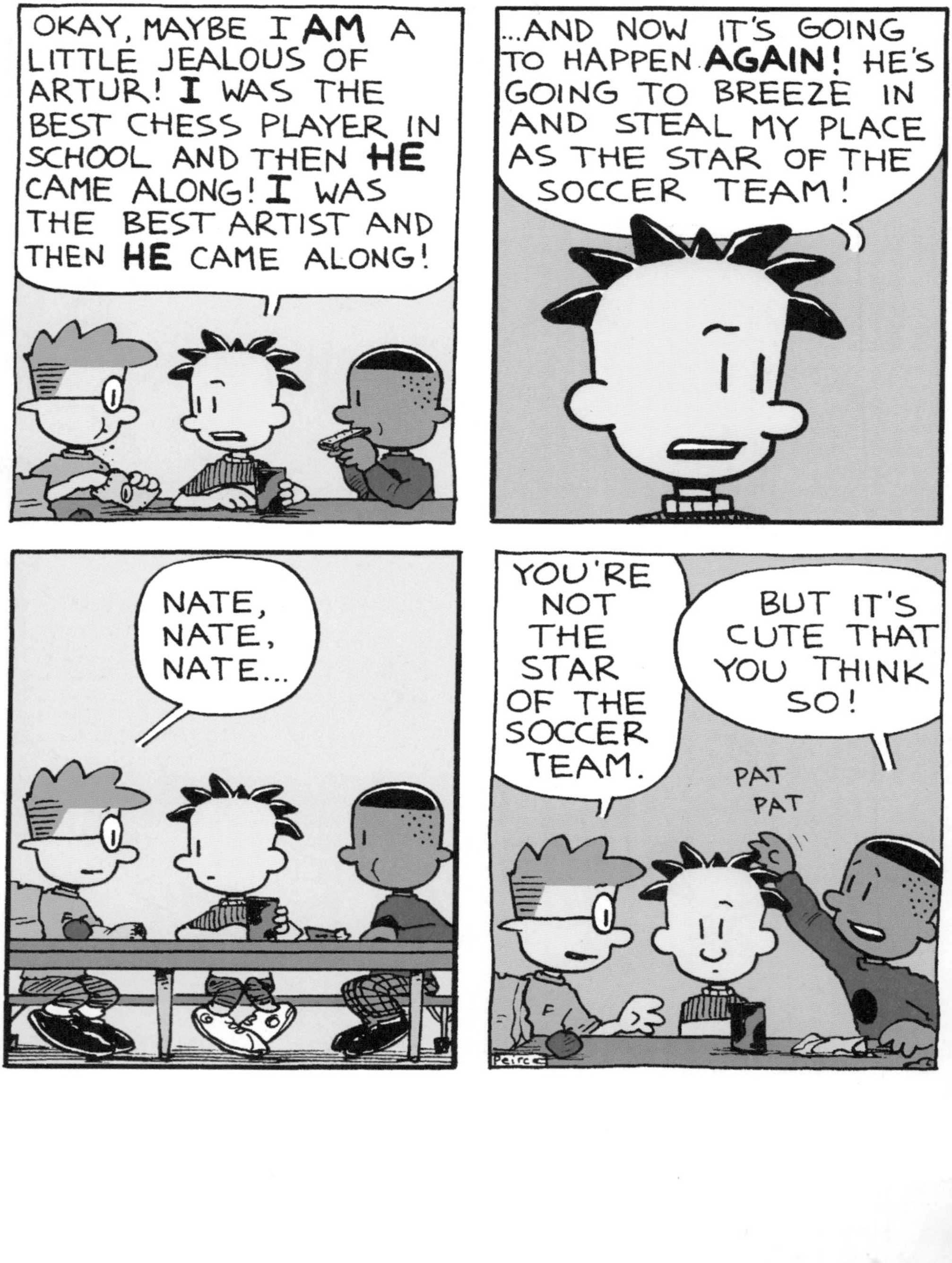
OKAY, MAYBE I **AM** A LITTLE JEALOUS OF ARTUR! **I** WAS THE BEST CHESS PLAYER IN SCHOOL AND THEN **HE** CAME ALONG! **I** WAS THE BEST ARTIST AND THEN **HE** CAME ALONG!
...AND NOW IT'S GOING TO HAPPEN **AGAIN!** HE'S GOING TO BREEZE IN AND STEAL MY PLACE AS THE STAR OF THE SOCCER TEAM!
NATE, NATE, NATE...
YOU'RE NOT THE STAR OF THE SOCCER TEAM.
BUT IT'S CUTE THAT YOU THINK SO!
PAT PAT
Peirce

ARTUR! ARTUR!
WE NEED YOUR HELP!
NO NO NO NO
HALLO
ARTUR! DO YOU PLAY SOCCER?
NO NO NO NO NO NO
SORRY, FELLOWS. DO NOT PLAY "SOCCER."
YES!
IN MY COUNTRY, IS CALLED "FOOTBALL".
NO NO NO NO NO NO
Peirce

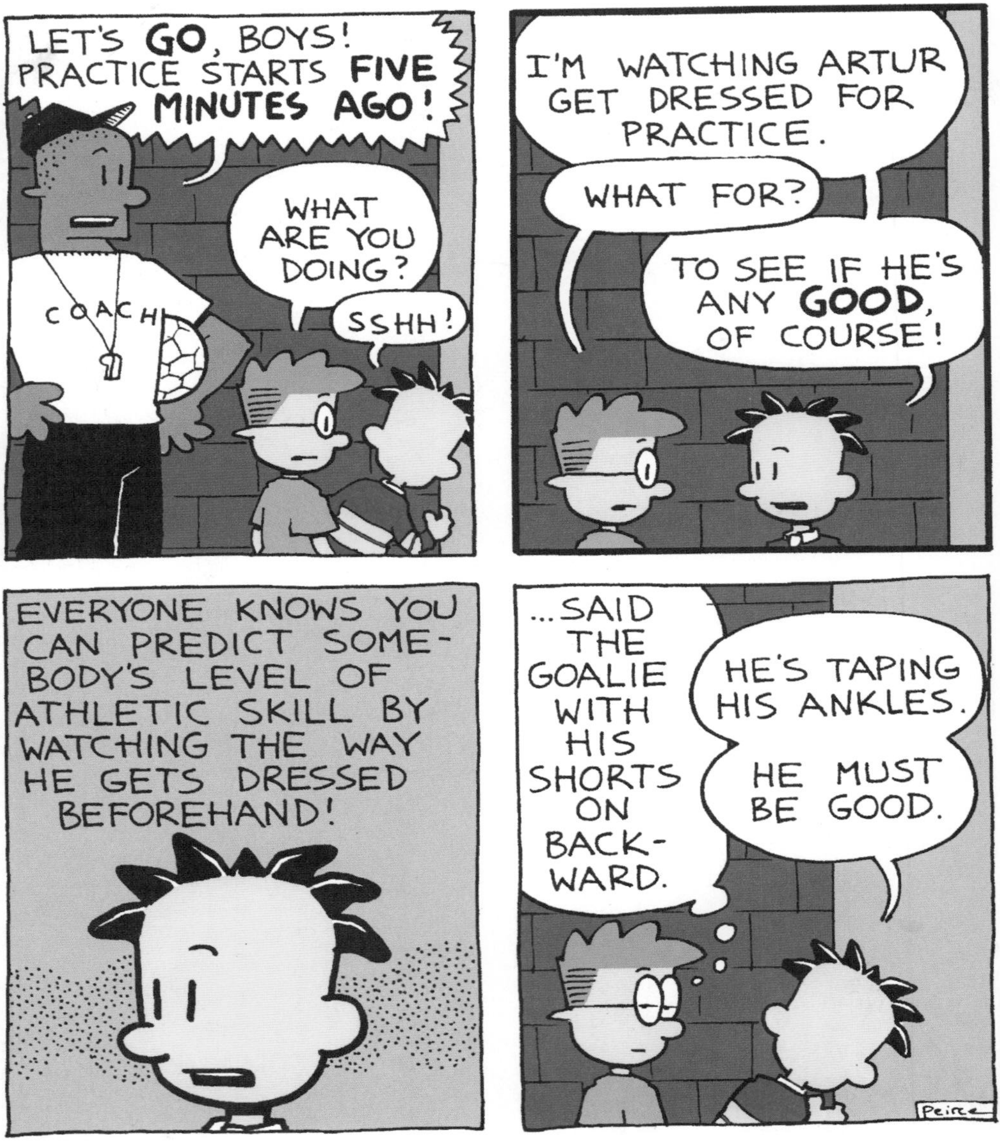
LET'S GO, BOYS! PRACTICE STARTS FIVE MINUTES AGO!
COACH
WHAT ARE YOU DOING?
SSHH!
I'M WATCHING ARTUR GET DRESSED FOR PRACTICE.
WHAT FOR?
TO SEE IF HE'S ANY GOOD, OF COURSE!
EVERYONE KNOWS YOU CAN PREDICT SOME-BODY'S LEVEL OF ATHLETIC SKILL BY WATCHING THE WAY HE GETS DRESSED BEFOREHAND!
...SAID THE GOALIE WITH HIS SHORTS ON BACK-WARD.
HE'S TAPING HIS ANKLES.
HE MUST BE GOOD.
Peirce

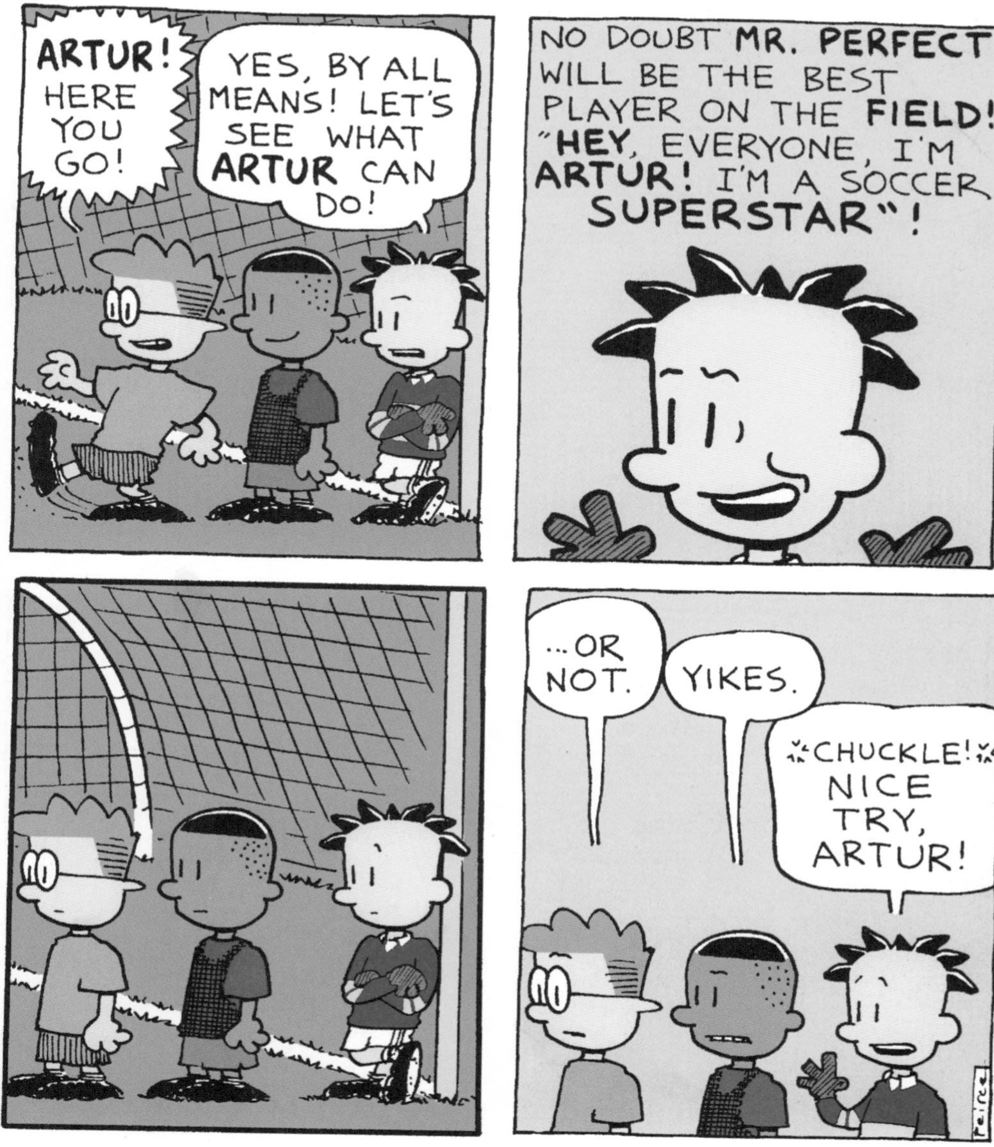
ARTUR! HERE YOU GO!
YES, BY ALL MEANS! LET'S SEE WHAT ARTUR CAN DO!
NO DOUBT MR. PERFECT WILL BE THE BEST PLAYER ON THE FIELD! "HEY, EVERYONE, I'M ARTUR! I'M A SOCCER SUPERSTAR"!
...OR NOT.
YIKES.
CHUCKLE! NICE TRY, ARTUR!
peirce

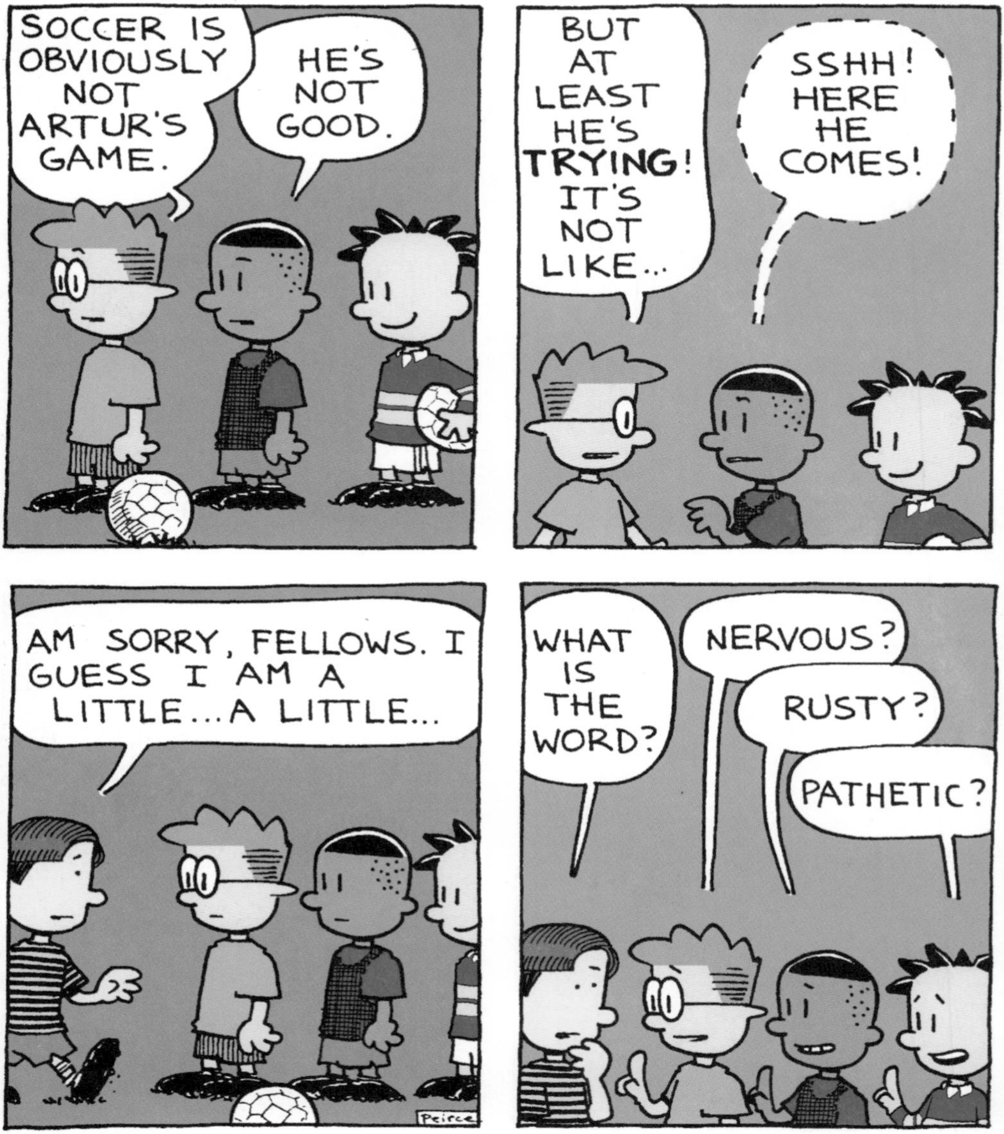
SOCCER IS OBVIOUSLY NOT ARTUR'S GAME.
HE'S NOT GOOD.
BUT AT LEAST HE'S **TRYING**! IT'S NOT LIKE...
SSHH! HERE HE COMES!
AM SORRY, FELLOWS. I GUESS I AM A LITTLE... A LITTLE...
Peirce
WHAT IS THE WORD?
NERVOUS?
RUSTY?
PATHETIC?

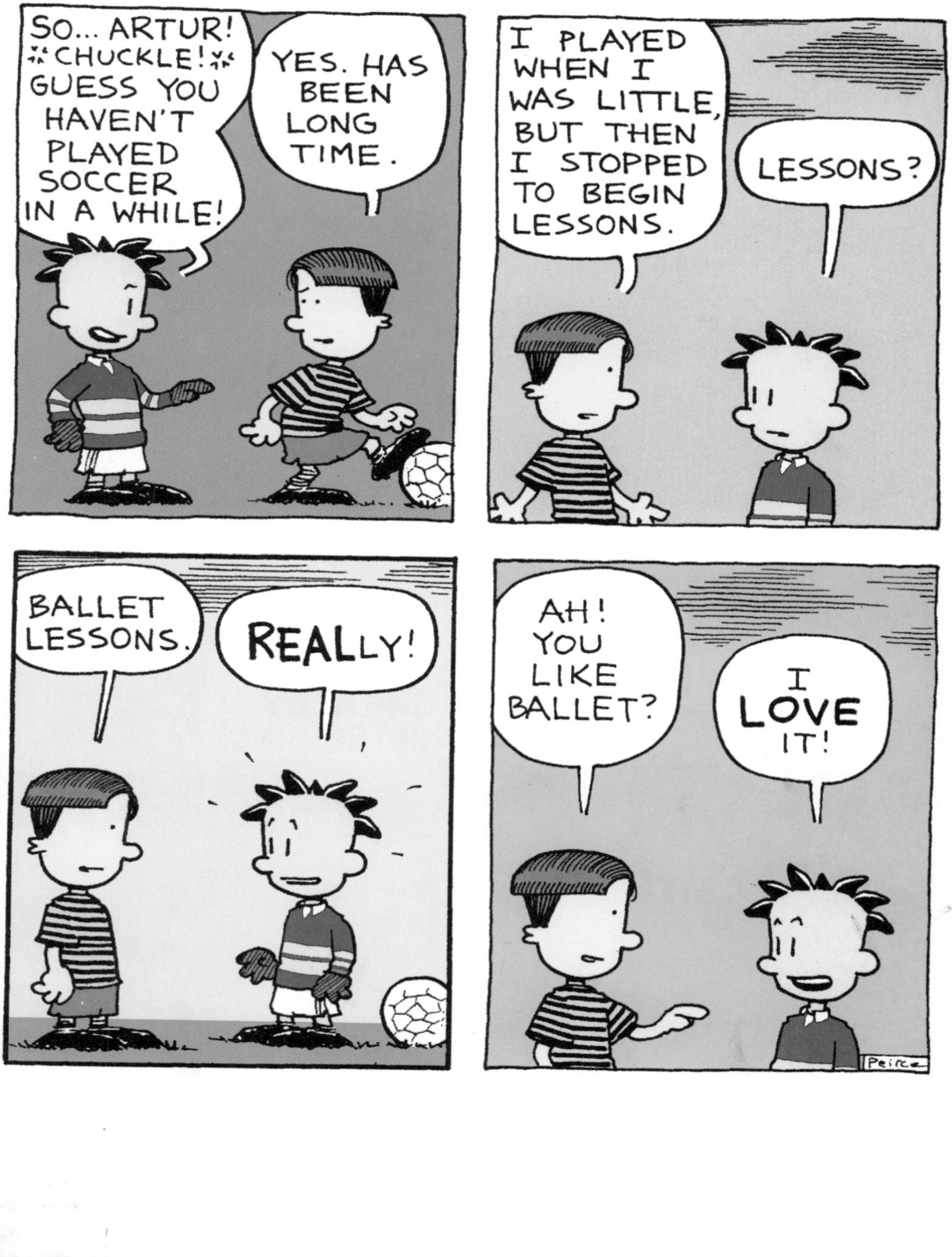
SO... ARTUR! *CHUCKLE!* GUESS YOU HAVEN'T PLAYED SOCCER IN A WHILE!
YES. HAS BEEN LONG TIME.
I PLAYED WHEN I WAS LITTLE, BUT THEN I STOPPED TO BEGIN LESSONS.
LESSONS?
BALLET LESSONS.
REALLY!
AH! YOU LIKE BALLET?
I LOVE IT!
Peirce

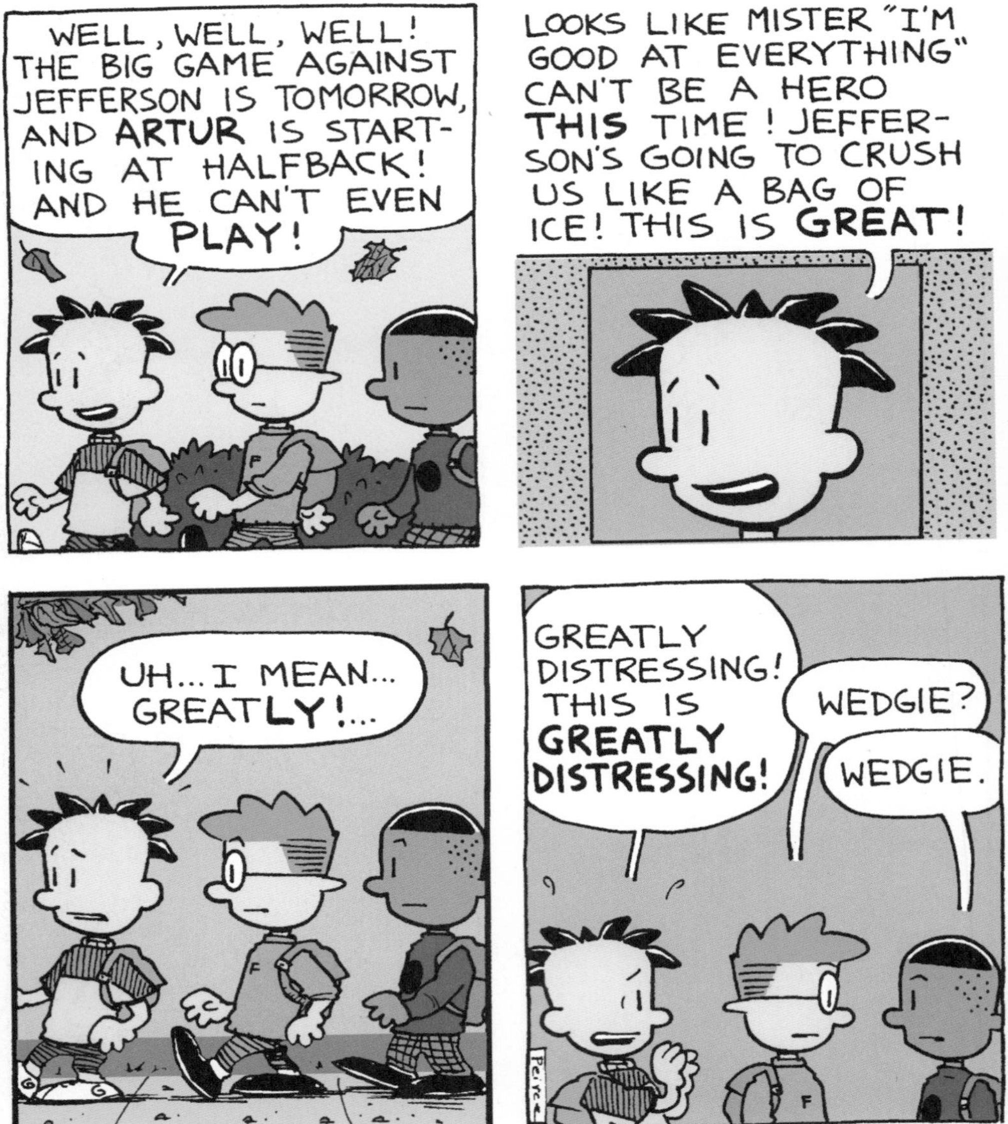
WELL, WELL, WELL! THE BIG GAME AGAINST JEFFERSON IS TOMORROW, AND ARTUR IS STARTING AT HALFBACK! AND HE CAN'T EVEN PLAY!
LOOKS LIKE MISTER "I'M GOOD AT EVERYTHING" CAN'T BE A HERO THIS TIME! JEFFERSON'S GOING TO CRUSH US LIKE A BAG OF ICE! THIS IS GREAT!
UH... I MEAN... GREATLY!...
GREATLY DISTRESSING! THIS IS GREATLY DISTRESSING!
WEDGIE?
WEDGIE.
Peirce

GAME TIME!
HOW YOU DOIN', ARTUR? A LITTLE NERVOUS?
YES. A LITTLE.
LOOK, ARTUR, YOU'RE NOT A VERY GOOD SOCCER PLAYER! THAT'S **OKAY!** NOBODY EX-**PECTS** YOU TO BE GOOD!
JUST TRY TO ACT LIKE YOU HAVE A CLUE! THE REST OF THE TEAM WILL COVER UP FOR YOUR OBVIOUS INCOMPETENCE!
WE DO THAT EVERY GAME FOR OUR GOALIE!
YEAH!
HEY! **HEY!**
Peirce

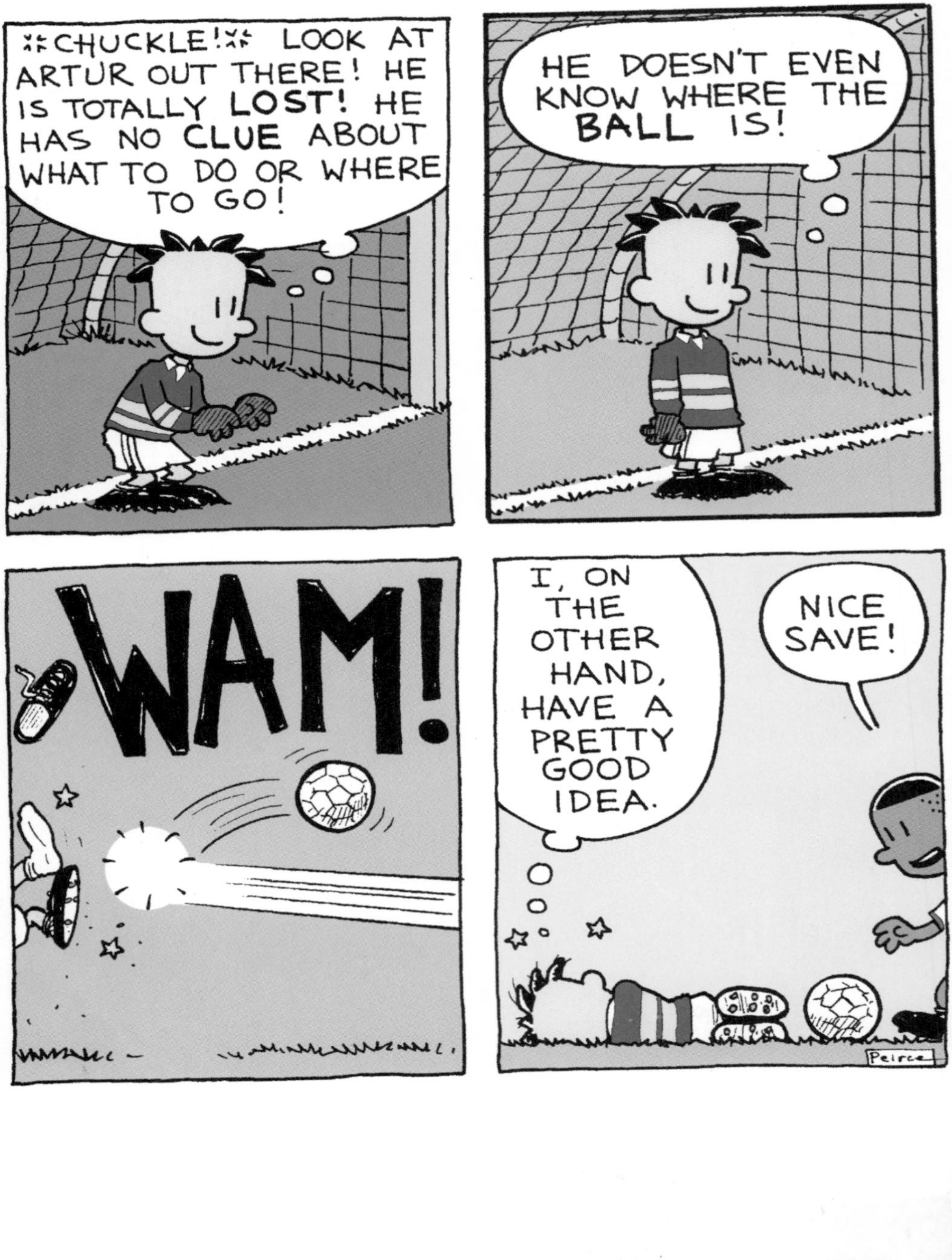

CHUCKLE! LOOK AT ARTUR OUT THERE! HE IS TOTALLY LOST! HE HAS NO CLUE ABOUT WHAT TO DO OR WHERE TO GO!
HE DOESN'T EVEN KNOW WHERE THE BALL IS!
WAM!
I, ON THE OTHER HAND, HAVE A PRETTY GOOD IDEA.
NICE SAVE!
Peirce

COME ON, BOBCATS! LET'S GO!!
CLAP CLAP CLAP
LET'S GO, FRANCIS! LET'S GO, TEDDY! LET'S GO, MATT! LET'S GO, KEVIN!
LET'S GO, ARTUR.
LET'S GO, ANDY! LET'S GO, ERIC! LET'S GO, BRIAN!...
Peirce

COME ON, GUYS! THERE'S LESS THAN A MINUTE LEFT!
TIME FOR SOMEBODY TO PUT ONE IN THE NET! TIME FOR SOMEBODY TO BE A HERO!
CLAP CLAP CLAP
THE CREAM RISES, BOYS! THE CREAM RISES!
EXCUSE, PLEASE. WHAT IS "THE CREAM RISES"?
ARTUR! HEADS UP!
Peirce

?
Peirce

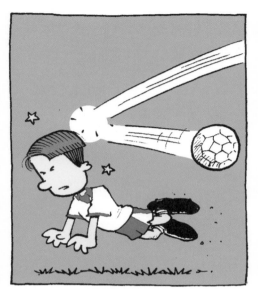

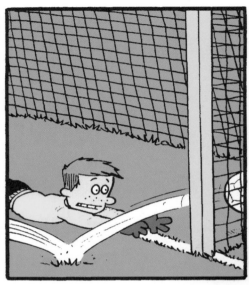

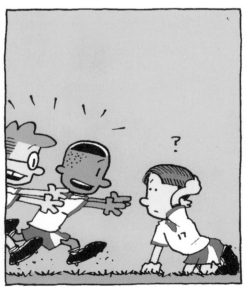

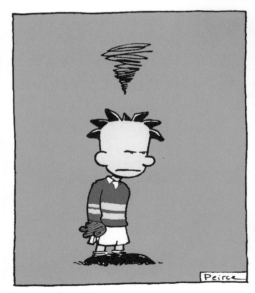

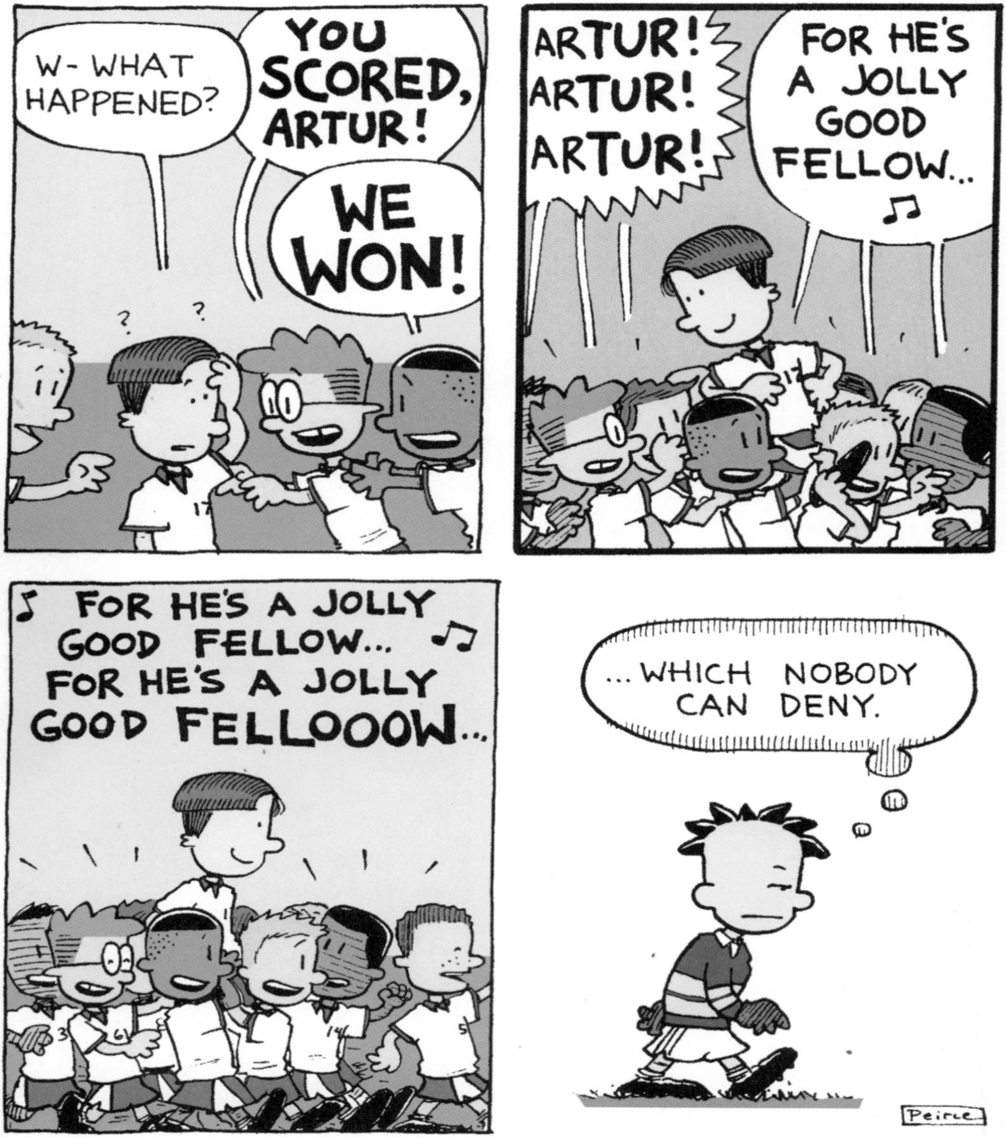
W- WHAT HAPPENED?
YOU SCORED, ARTUR!
WE WON!
ARTUR! ARTUR! ARTUR!
FOR HE'S A JOLLY GOOD FELLOW...
FOR HE'S A JOLLY GOOD FELLOW... FOR HE'S A JOLLY GOOD FELLOOOW...
...WHICH NOBODY CAN DENY.
Peirce

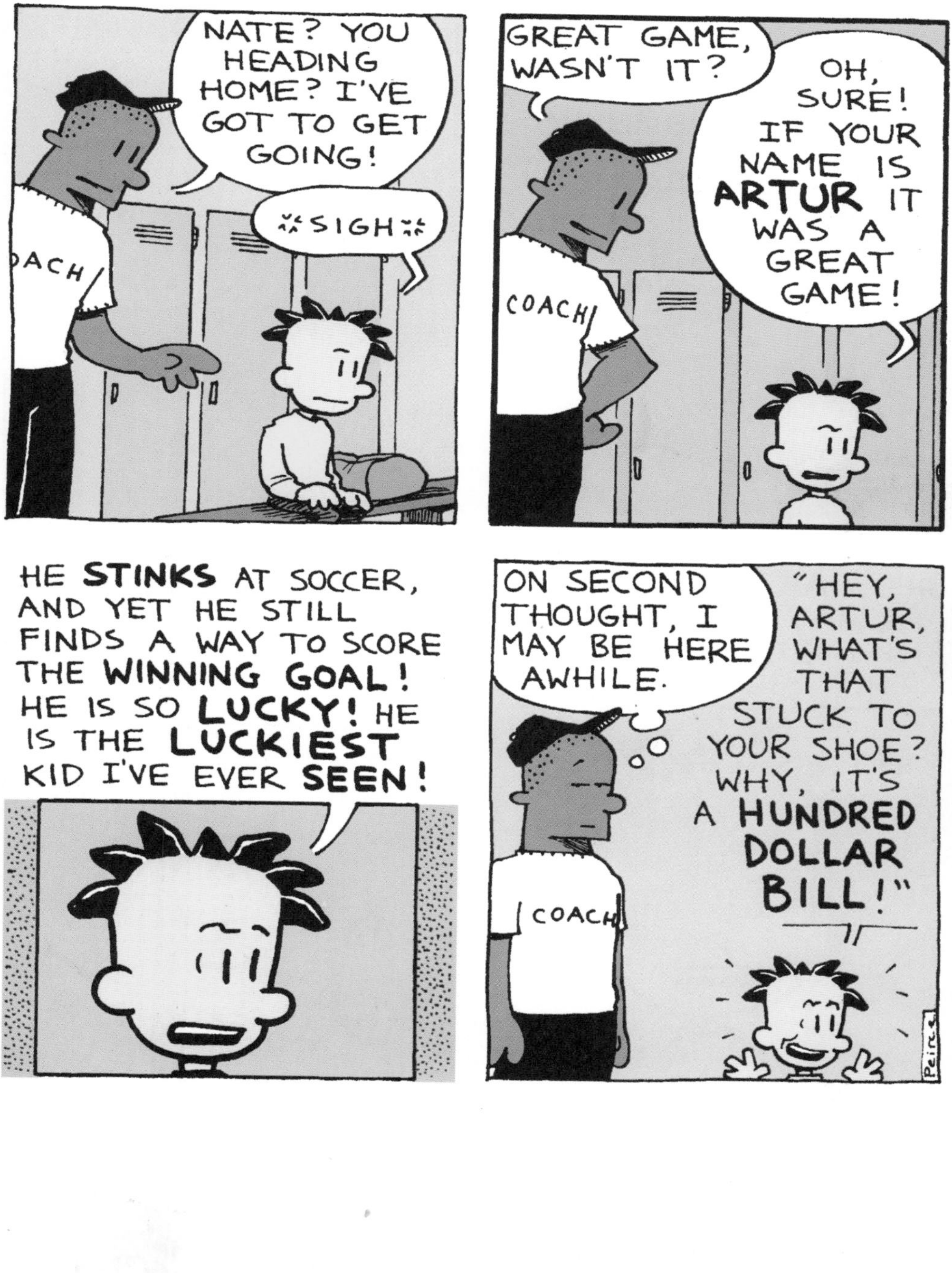
NATE? YOU HEADING HOME? I'VE GOT TO GET GOING!
SIGH
COACH
GREAT GAME, WASN'T IT?
OH, SURE! IF YOUR NAME IS **ARTUR** IT WAS A GREAT GAME!
COACH
HE **STINKS** AT SOCCER, AND YET HE STILL FINDS A WAY TO SCORE THE **WINNING GOAL**! HE IS SO **LUCKY!** HE IS THE **LUCKIEST** KID I'VE EVER **SEEN**!
ON SECOND THOUGHT, I MAY BE HERE AWHILE.
"HEY, ARTUR, WHAT'S THAT STUCK TO YOUR SHOE? WHY, IT'S A **HUNDRED DOLLAR BILL**!"
COACH
Peirce

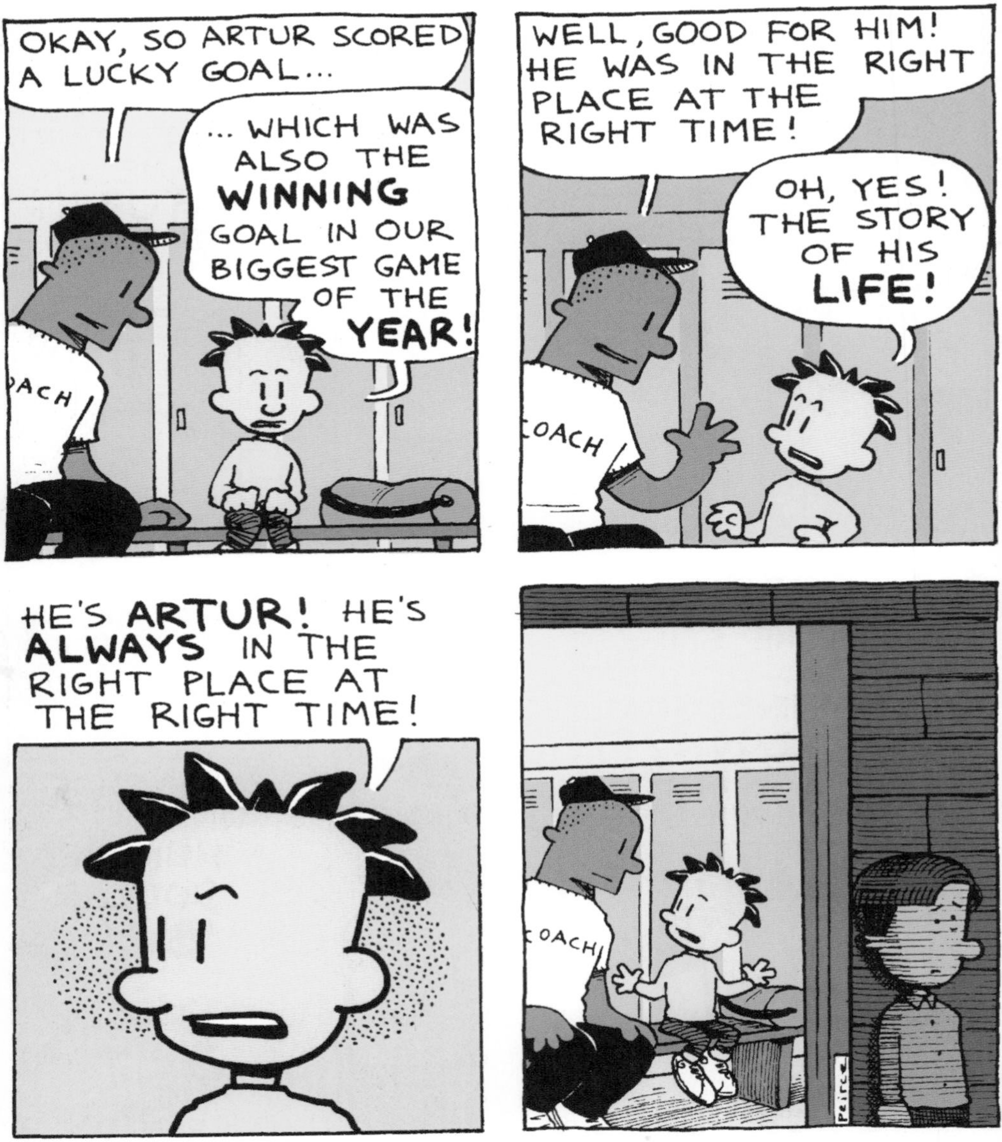
OKAY, SO ARTUR SCORED A LUCKY GOAL...
... WHICH WAS ALSO THE WINNING GOAL IN OUR BIGGEST GAME OF THE YEAR!
COACH
WELL, GOOD FOR HIM! HE WAS IN THE RIGHT PLACE AT THE RIGHT TIME!
OH, YES! THE STORY OF HIS LIFE!
COACH
HE'S ARTUR! HE'S ALWAYS IN THE RIGHT PLACE AT THE RIGHT TIME!
COACH
Peirce

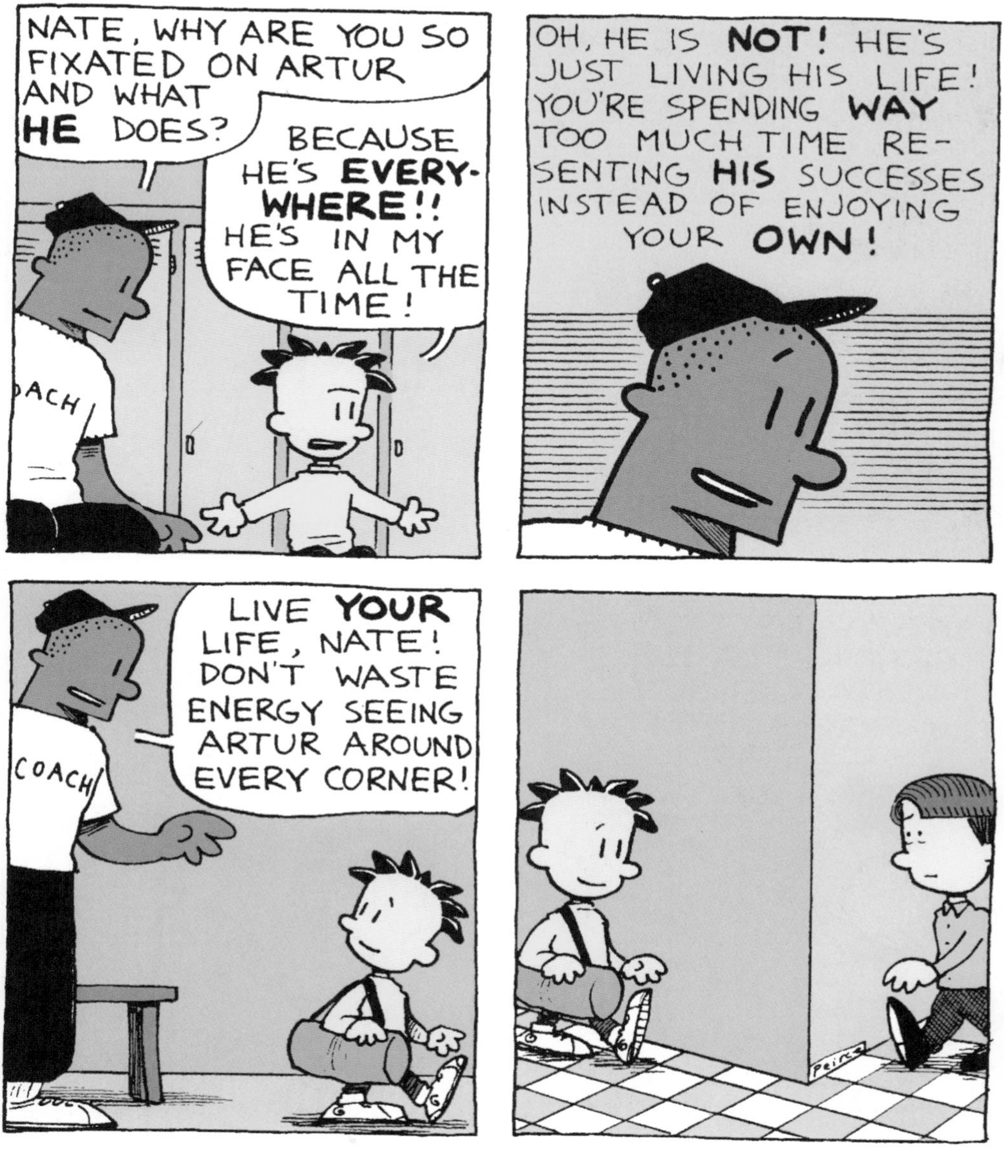
NATE, WHY ARE YOU SO FIXATED ON ARTUR AND WHAT **HE** DOES?
BECAUSE HE'S **EVERY-WHERE!!** HE'S IN MY FACE ALL THE TIME!
COACH
OH, HE IS **NOT!** HE'S JUST LIVING HIS LIFE! YOU'RE SPENDING **WAY** TOO MUCH TIME RE-SENTING **HIS** SUCCESSES INSTEAD OF ENJOYING YOUR **OWN!**
LIVE **YOUR** LIFE, NATE! DON'T WASTE ENERGY SEEING ARTUR AROUND EVERY CORNER!
COACH
Peirce

!!
ARTUR!
HALLO, NATE.
I WAS JUST... UH... I WAS HANGING OUT A LITTLE BIT... JUST TALKING WITH COACH.
ANYWAY... WELL!... IT'S GETTING LATE. I GOTTA GET HOME FOR SUPPER.
SEE YOU TOMOR...
WHY DO YOU HATE ME?
Peirce

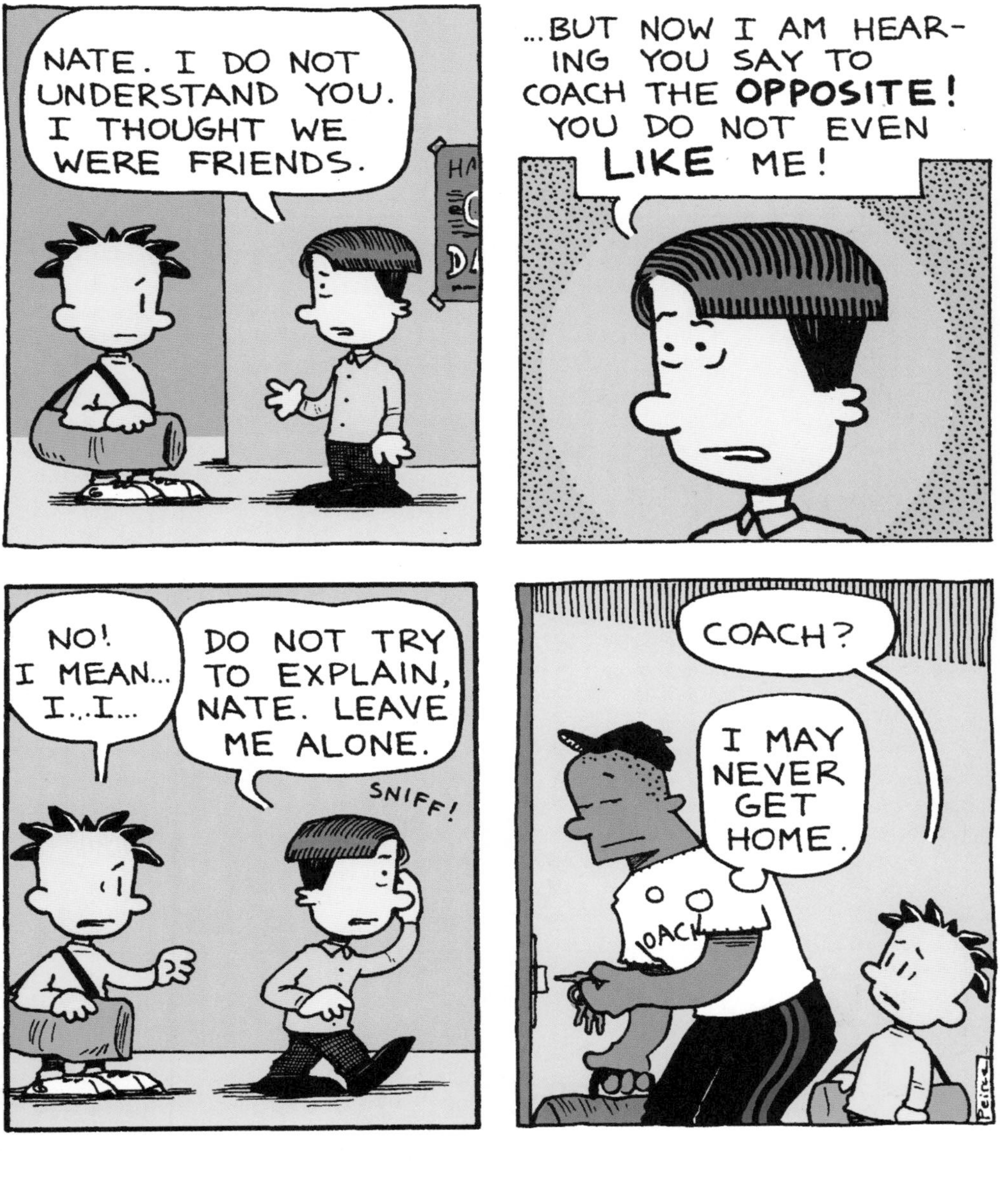
NATE. I DO NOT UNDERSTAND YOU. I THOUGHT WE WERE FRIENDS.
...BUT NOW I AM HEARING YOU SAY TO COACH THE OPPOSITE! YOU DO NOT EVEN LIKE ME!
NO! I MEAN... I...I...
DO NOT TRY TO EXPLAIN, NATE. LEAVE ME ALONE.
SNIFF!
COACH?
I MAY NEVER GET HOME.
Peirce

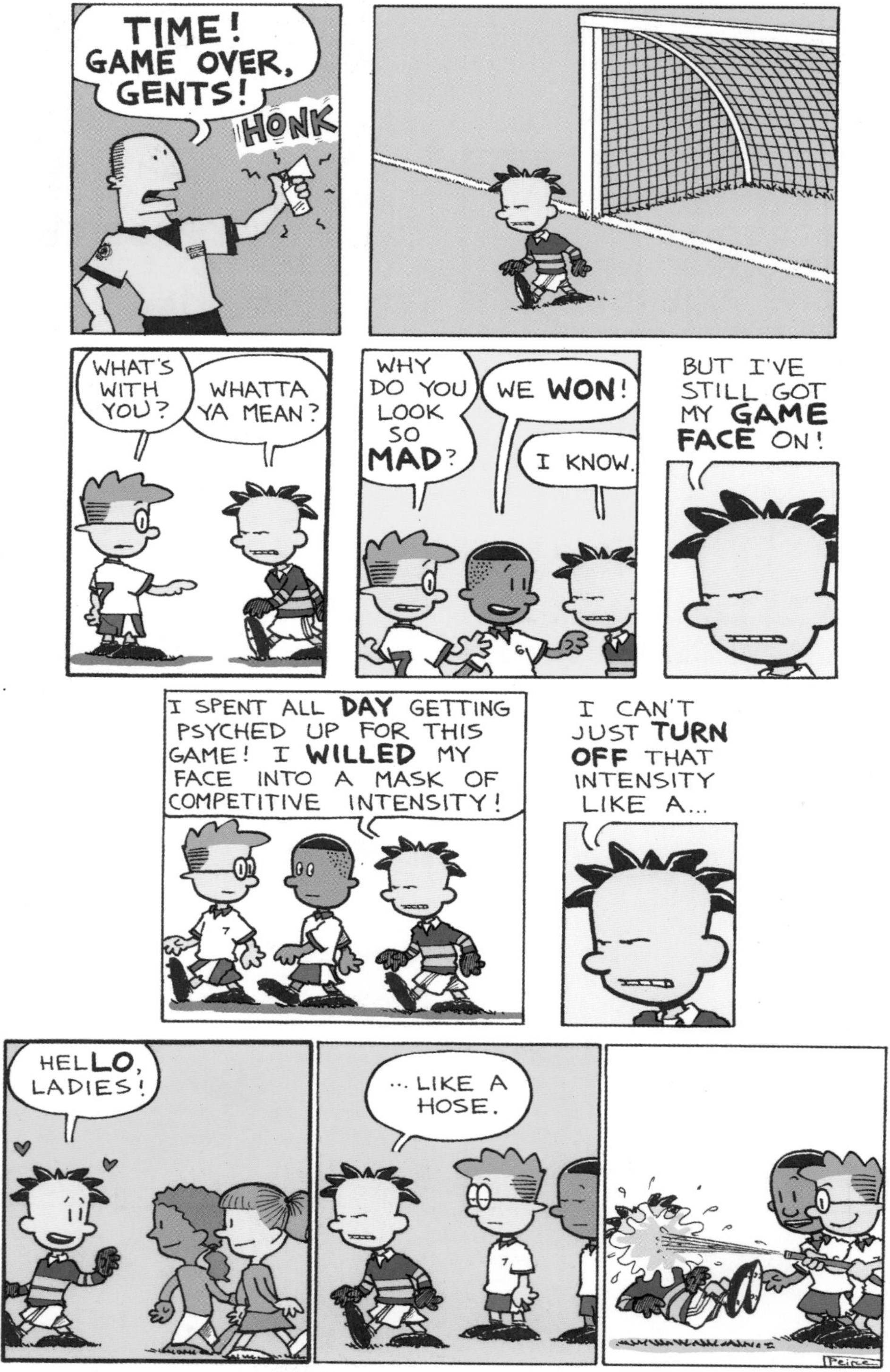

TIME! GAME OVER, GENTS!
HONK
WHAT'S WITH YOU?
WHATTA YA MEAN?
WHY DO YOU LOOK SO MAD?
WE WON!
I KNOW.
BUT I'VE STILL GOT MY GAME FACE ON!
I SPENT ALL DAY GETTING PSYCHED UP FOR THIS GAME! I WILLED MY FACE INTO A MASK OF COMPETITIVE INTENSITY!
I CAN'T JUST TURN OFF THAT INTENSITY LIKE A...
HELLO, LADIES!
...LIKE A HOSE.
Peirce

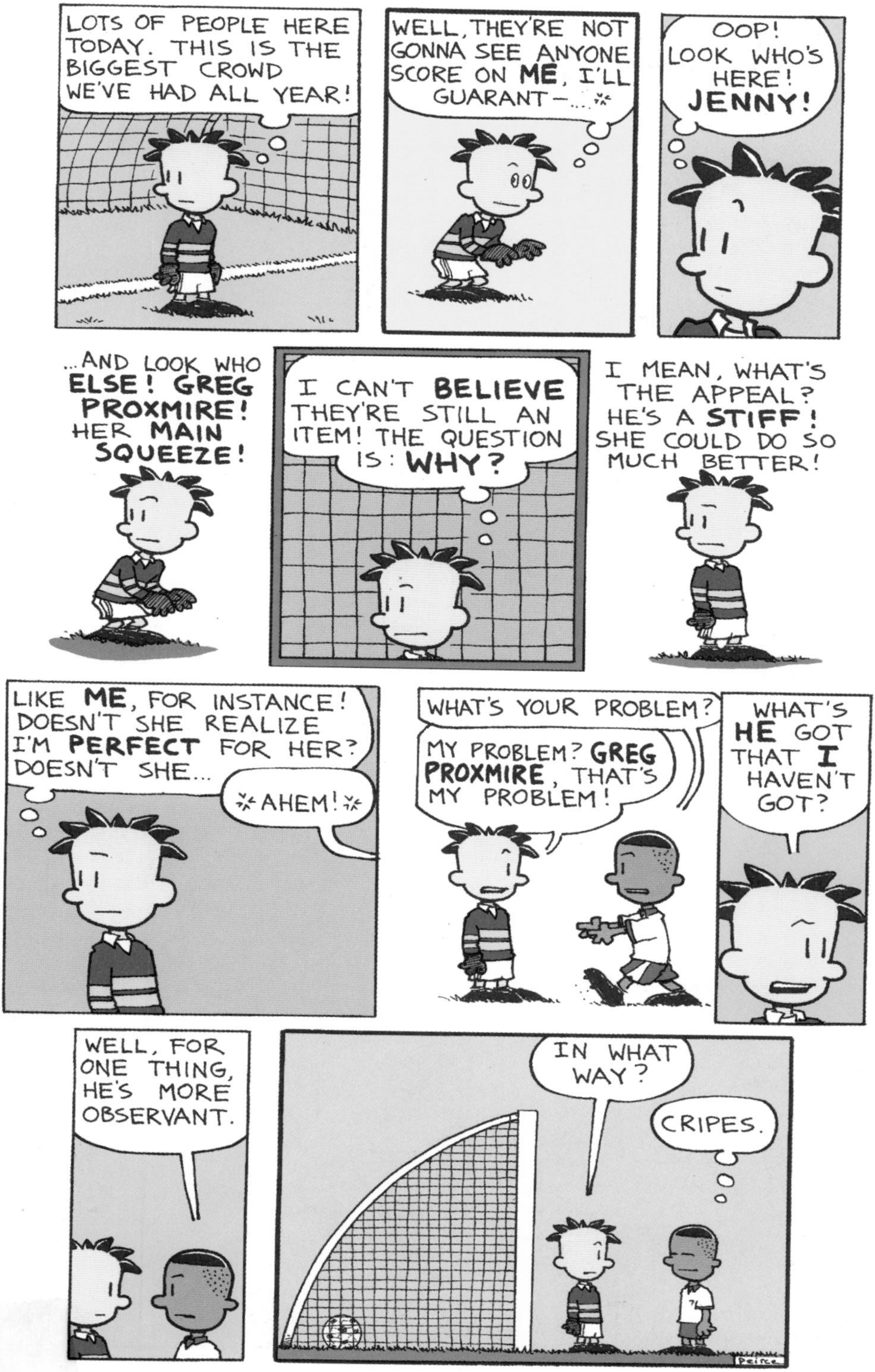

LOTS OF PEOPLE HERE TODAY. THIS IS THE BIGGEST CROWD WE'VE HAD ALL YEAR!
WELL, THEY'RE NOT GONNA SEE ANYONE SCORE ON **ME**, I'LL GUARANT—...
OOP! LOOK WHO'S HERE! **JENNY!**
...AND LOOK WHO **ELSE! GREG PROXMIRE!** HER **MAIN SQUEEZE!**
I CAN'T **BELIEVE** THEY'RE STILL AN ITEM! THE QUESTION IS: **WHY?**
I MEAN, WHAT'S THE APPEAL? HE'S A **STIFF!** SHE COULD DO SO MUCH BETTER!
LIKE **ME**, FOR INSTANCE! DOESN'T SHE REALIZE I'M **PERFECT** FOR HER? DOESN'T SHE...
AHEM!
WHAT'S YOUR PROBLEM?
MY PROBLEM? **GREG PROXMIRE**, THAT'S MY PROBLEM!
WHAT'S **HE** GOT THAT **I** HAVEN'T GOT?
WELL, FOR ONE THING, HE'S MORE OBSERVANT.
IN WHAT WAY?
CRIPES.
Peirce

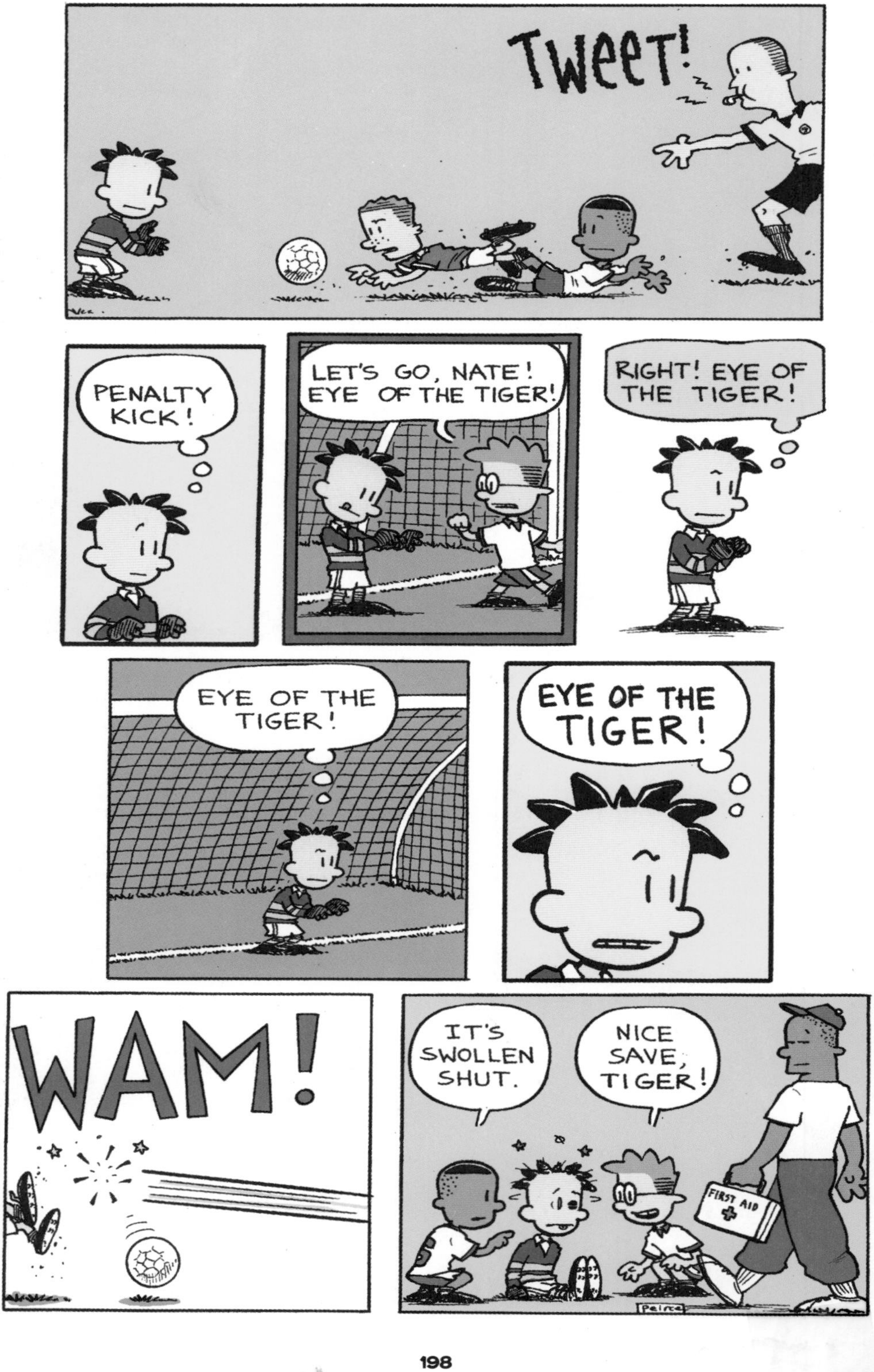
TWEET!
PENALTY KICK!
LET'S GO, NATE! EYE OF THE TIGER!
RIGHT! EYE OF THE TIGER!
EYE OF THE TIGER!
EYE OF THE TIGER!
WAM!
IT'S SWOLLEN SHUT.
NICE SAVE, TIGER!
FIRST AID

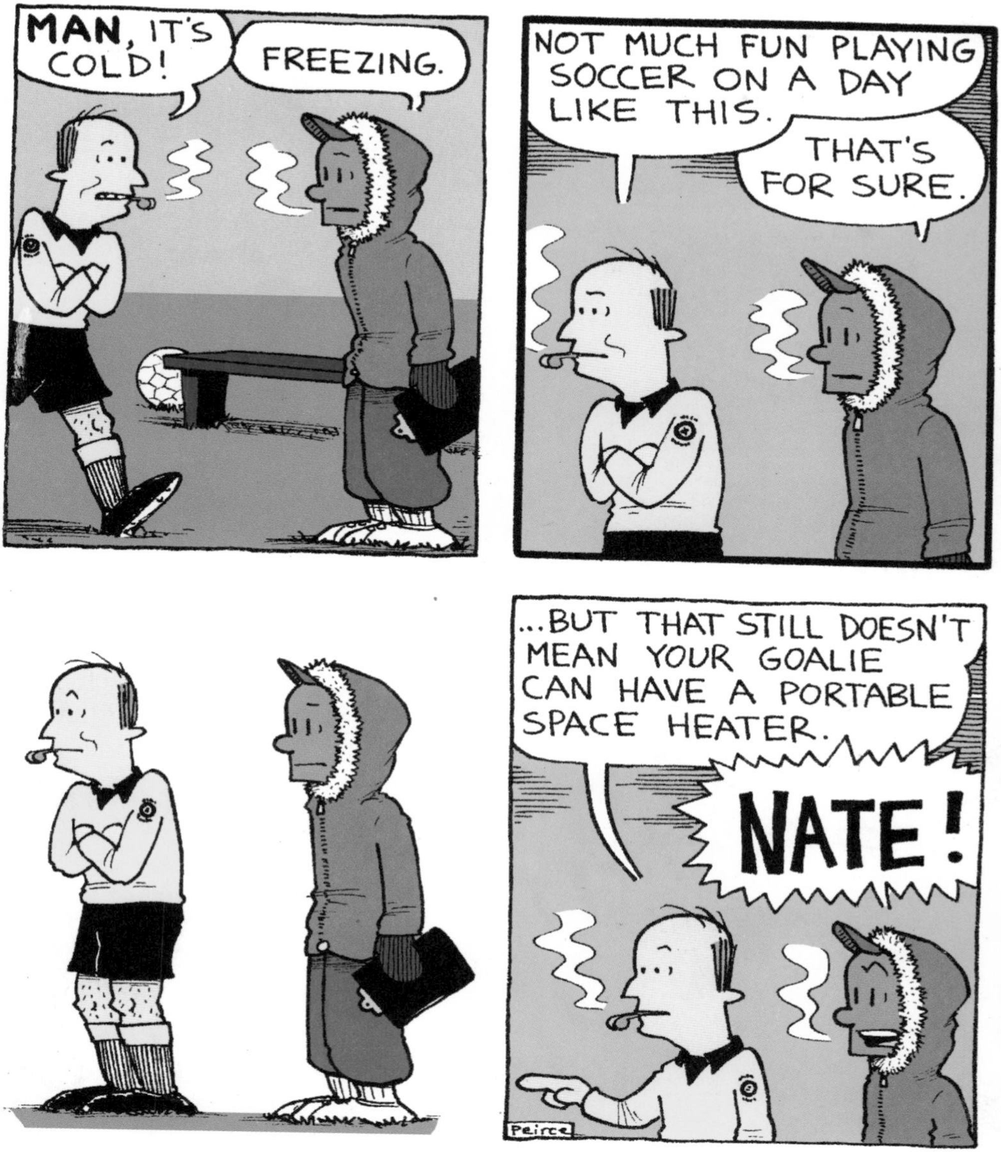
MAN, IT'S COLD!
FREEZING.
NOT MUCH FUN PLAYING SOCCER ON A DAY LIKE THIS.
THAT'S FOR SURE.
...BUT THAT STILL DOESN'T MEAN YOUR GOALIE CAN HAVE A PORTABLE SPACE HEATER.
NATE!
Peirce

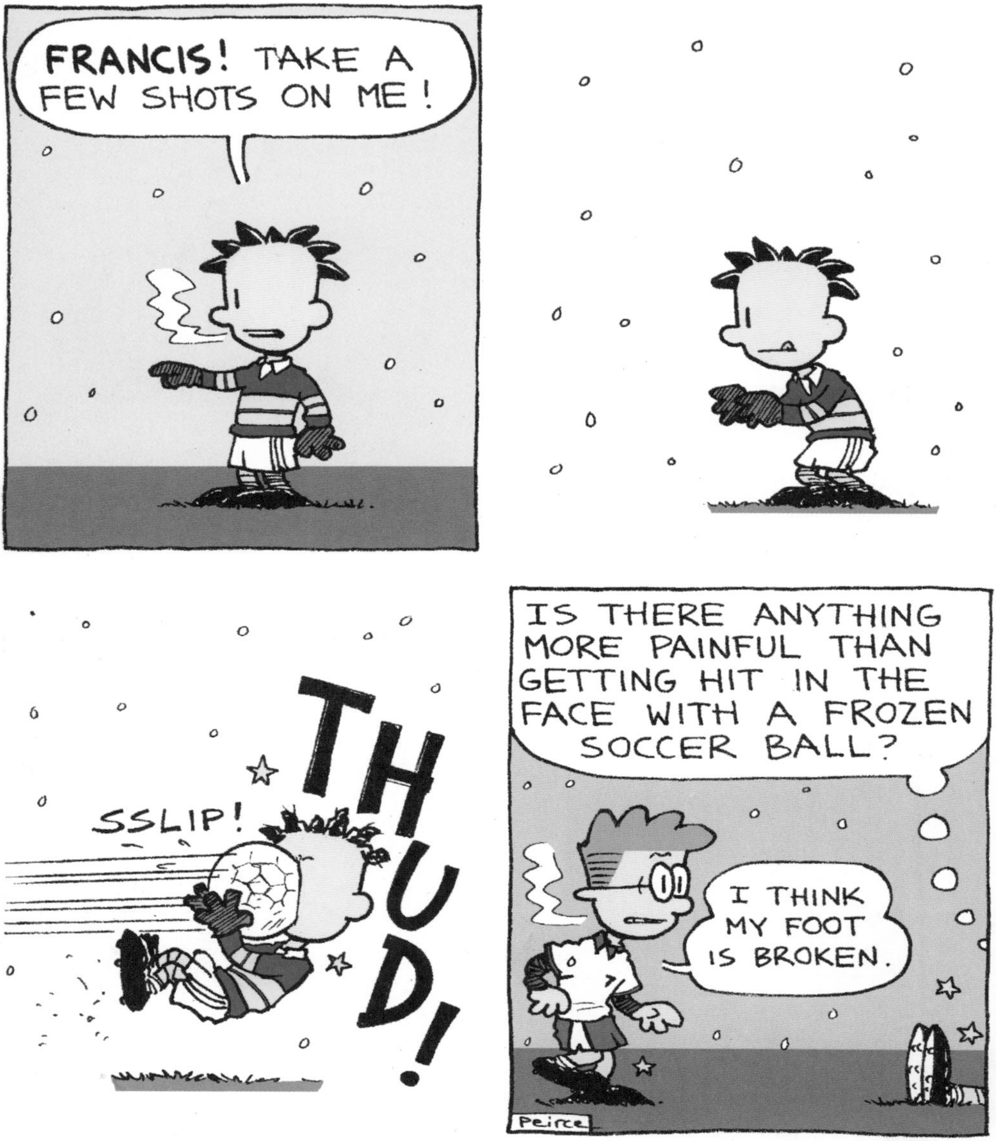
FRANCIS! TAKE A FEW SHOTS ON ME!
SSLIP!
THUD!
IS THERE ANYTHING MORE PAINFUL THAN GETTING HIT IN THE FACE WITH A FROZEN SOCCER BALL?
I THINK MY FOOT IS BROKEN.
Peirce

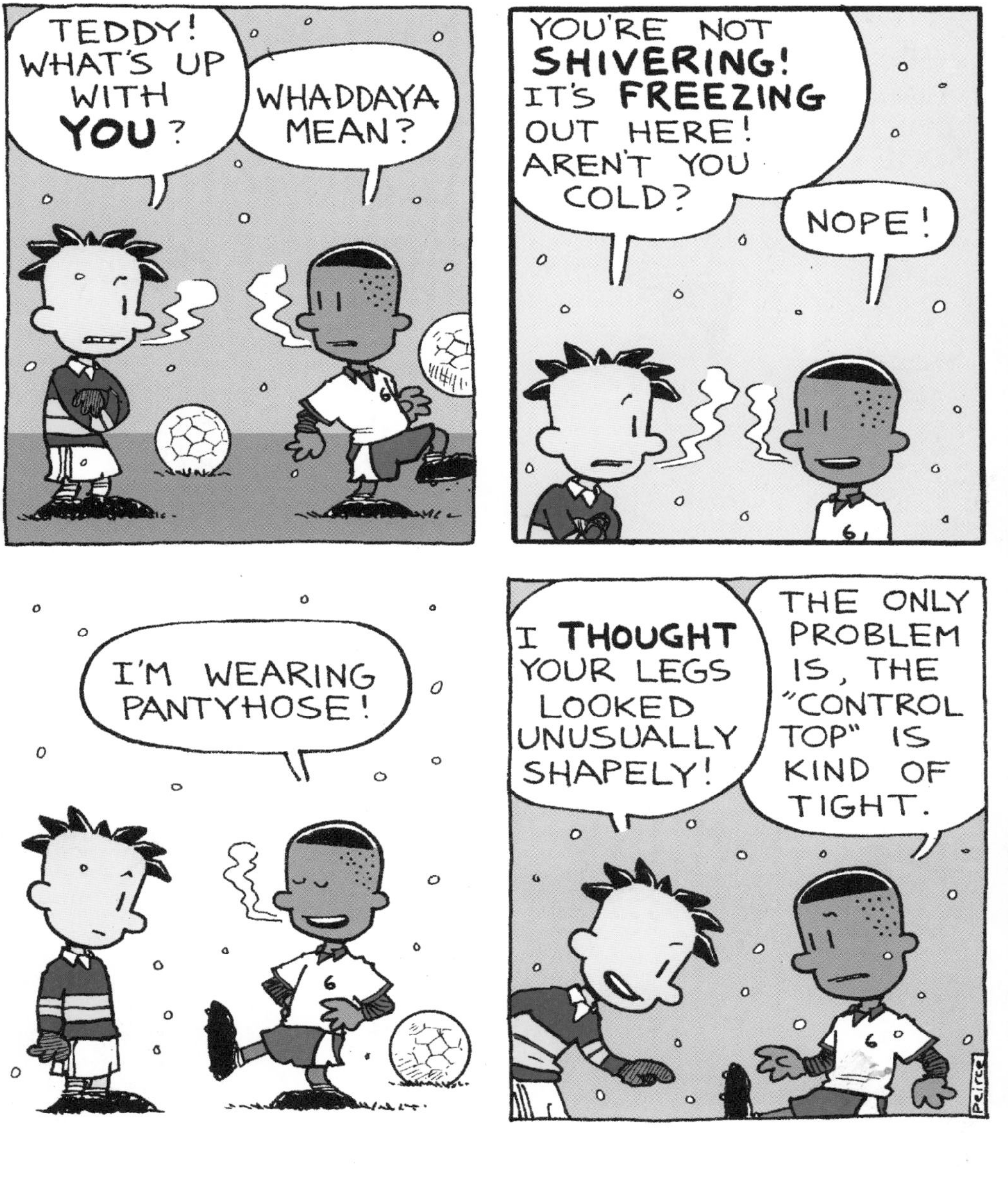
TEDDY! WHAT'S UP WITH **YOU**?
WHADDAYA MEAN?
YOU'RE NOT **SHIVERING**! IT'S **FREEZING** OUT HERE! AREN'T YOU COLD?
NOPE!
I'M WEARING PANTYHOSE!
I **THOUGHT** YOUR LEGS LOOKED UNUSUALLY SHAPELY!
THE ONLY PROBLEM IS, THE "CONTROL TOP" IS KIND OF TIGHT.
PEIRCE

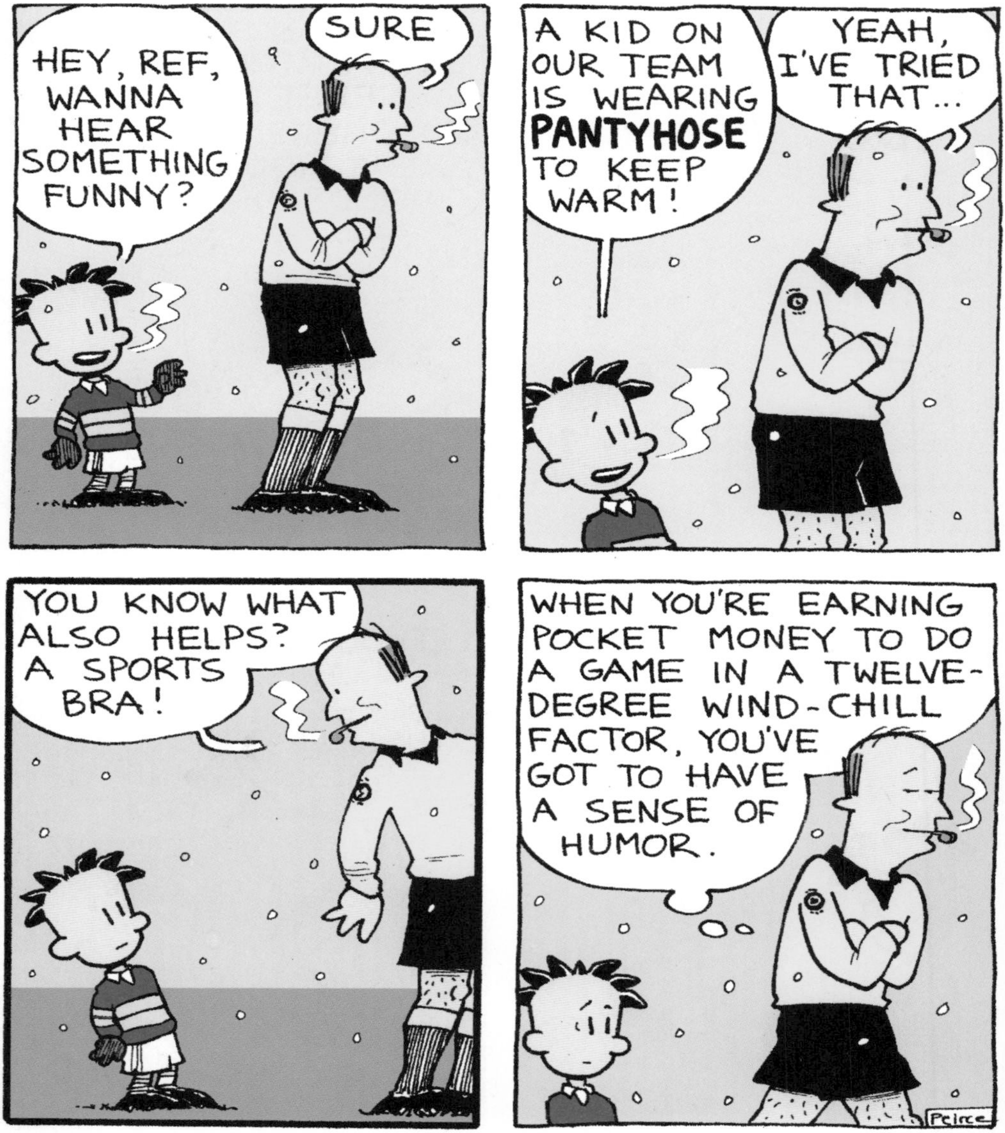
HEY, REF, WANNA HEAR SOMETHING FUNNY?
SURE
A KID ON OUR TEAM IS WEARING **PANTYHOSE** TO KEEP WARM!
YEAH, I'VE TRIED THAT...
YOU KNOW WHAT ALSO HELPS? A SPORTS BRA!
WHEN YOU'RE EARNING POCKET MONEY TO DO A GAME IN A TWELVE-DEGREE WIND-CHILL FACTOR, YOU'VE GOT TO HAVE A SENSE OF HUMOR.
Peirce

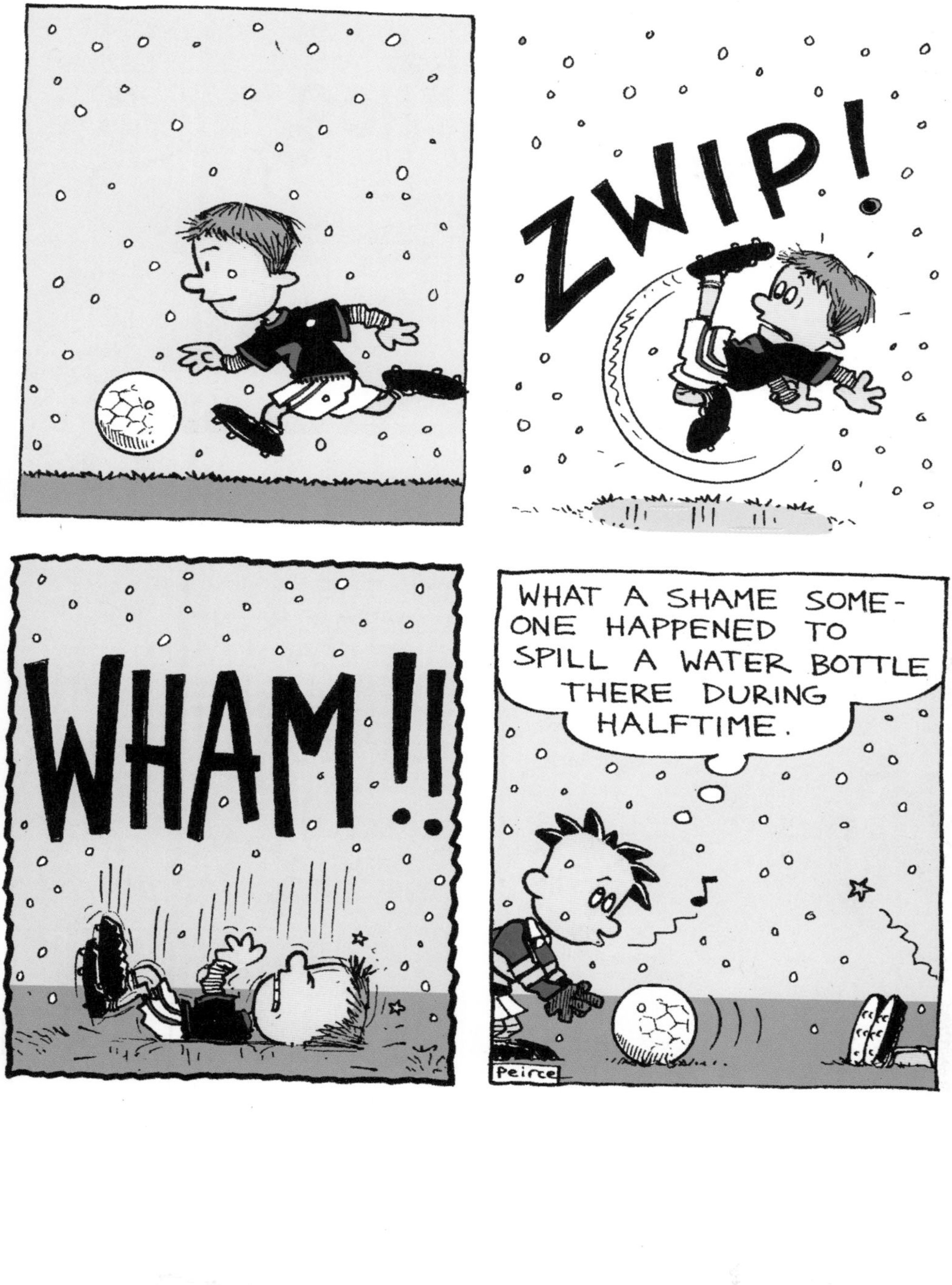
ZWIP!
WHAM!!
WHAT A SHAME SOME-ONE HAPPENED TO SPILL A WATER BOTTLE THERE DURING HALFTIME.
Peirce

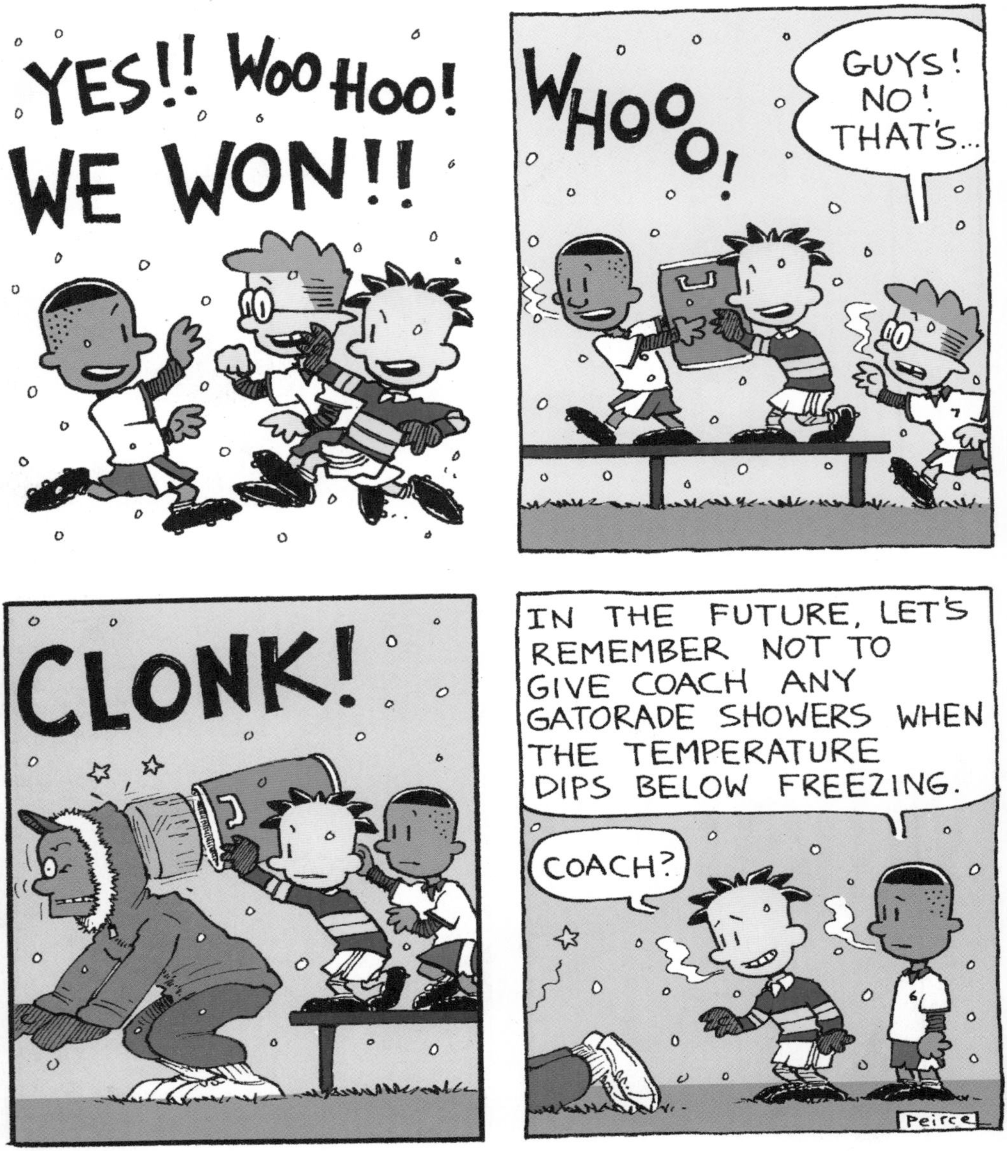
YES!! WOO HOO! WE WON!!
WHOOOO!
GUYS! NO! THAT'S...
CLONK!
IN THE FUTURE, LET'S REMEMBER NOT TO GIVE COACH ANY GATORADE SHOWERS WHEN THE TEMPERATURE DIPS BELOW FREEZING.
COACH?
Peirce

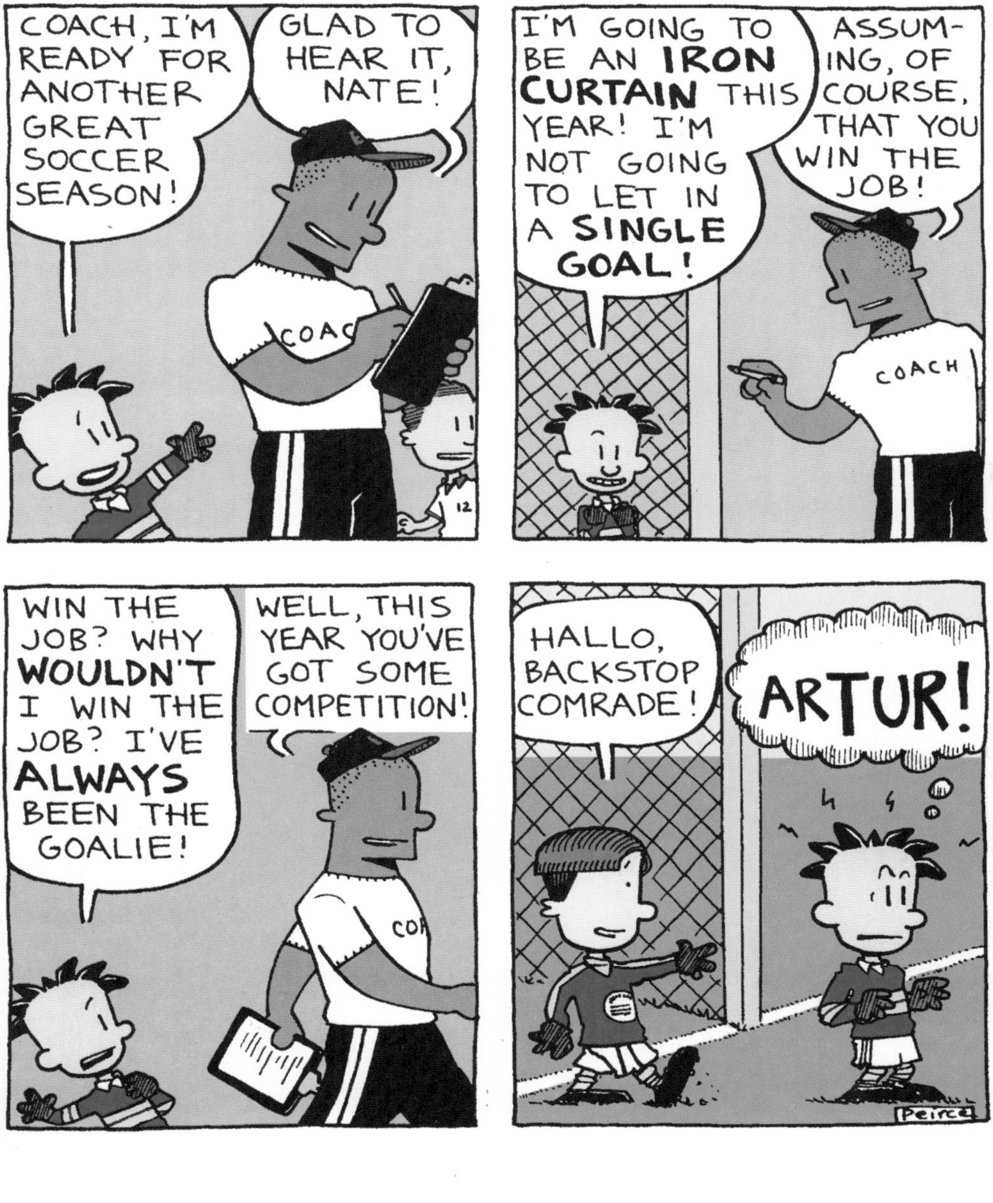

COACH, I'M READY FOR ANOTHER GREAT SOCCER SEASON!
GLAD TO HEAR IT, NATE!
COACH
12
I'M GOING TO BE AN **IRON CURTAIN** THIS YEAR! I'M NOT GOING TO LET IN A **SINGLE GOAL**!
ASSUMING, OF COURSE, THAT YOU WIN THE JOB!
COACH
WIN THE JOB? WHY **WOULDN'T** I WIN THE JOB? I'VE **ALWAYS** BEEN THE GOALIE!
WELL, THIS YEAR YOU'VE GOT SOME COMPETITION!
HALLO, BACKSTOP COMRADE!
ARTUR!
Peirce

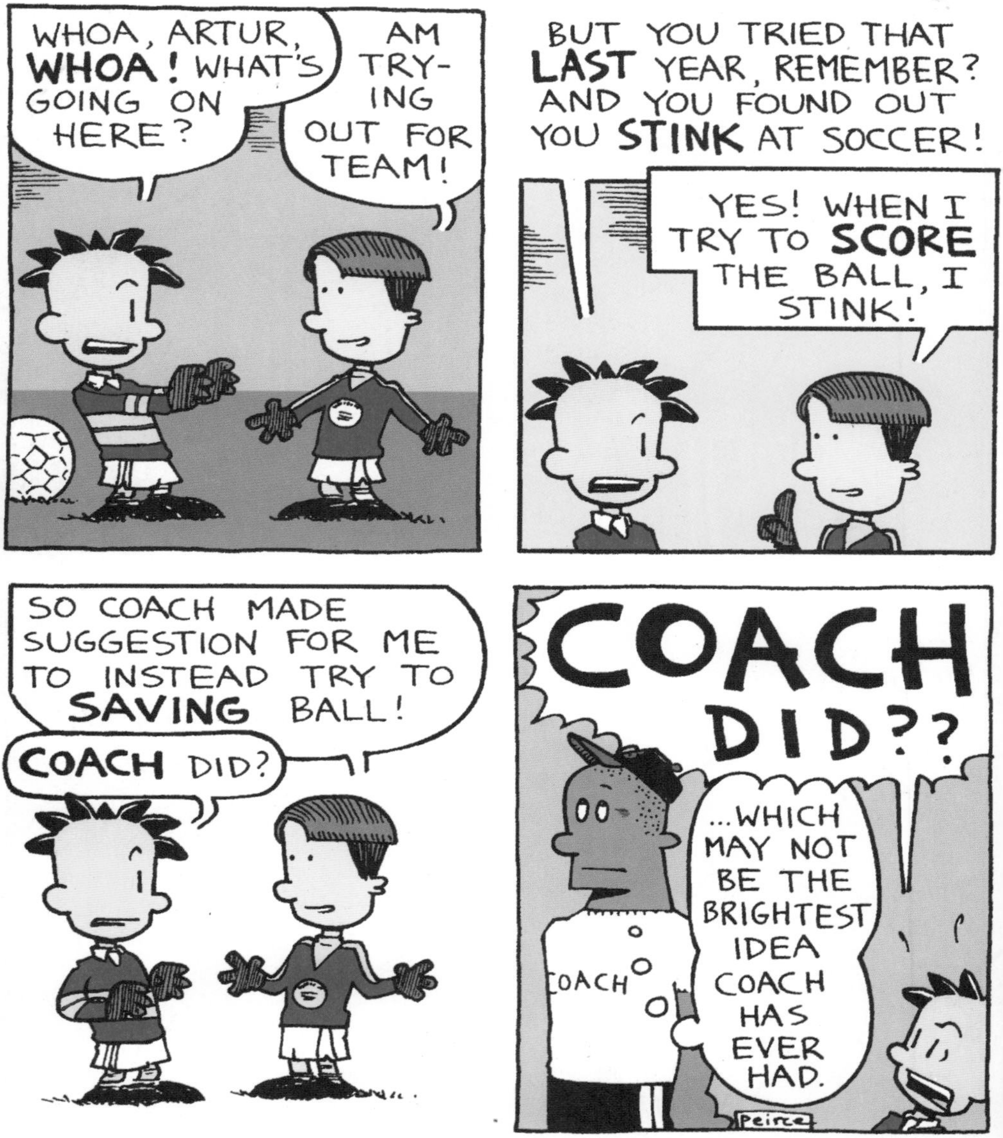
WHOA, ARTUR, WHOA! WHAT'S GOING ON HERE?
AM TRY-ING OUT FOR TEAM!
BUT YOU TRIED THAT LAST YEAR, REMEMBER? AND YOU FOUND OUT YOU STINK AT SOCCER!
YES! WHEN I TRY TO SCORE THE BALL, I STINK!
SO COACH MADE SUGGESTION FOR ME TO INSTEAD TRY TO SAVING BALL!
COACH DID?
COACH DID??
...WHICH MAY NOT BE THE BRIGHTEST IDEA COACH HAS EVER HAD.
COACH
Peirce

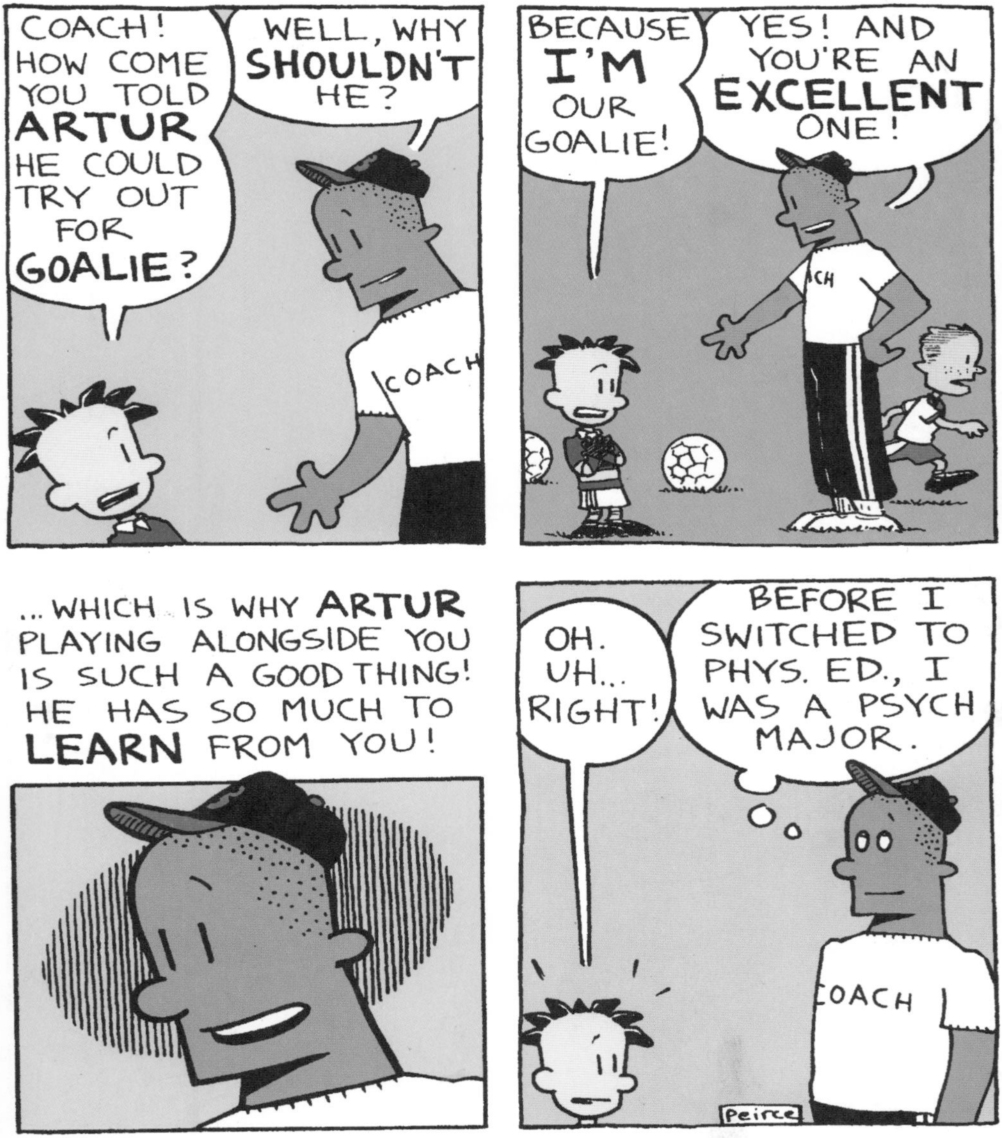
COACH! HOW COME YOU TOLD ARTUR HE COULD TRY OUT FOR GOALIE?
WELL, WHY SHOULDN'T HE?
COACH
BECAUSE I'M OUR GOALIE!
YES! AND YOU'RE AN EXCELLENT ONE!
...WHICH IS WHY ARTUR PLAYING ALONGSIDE YOU IS SUCH A GOOD THING! HE HAS SO MUCH TO LEARN FROM YOU!
OH. UH... RIGHT!
BEFORE I SWITCHED TO PHYS. ED., I WAS A PSYCH MAJOR.
OACH
Peirce

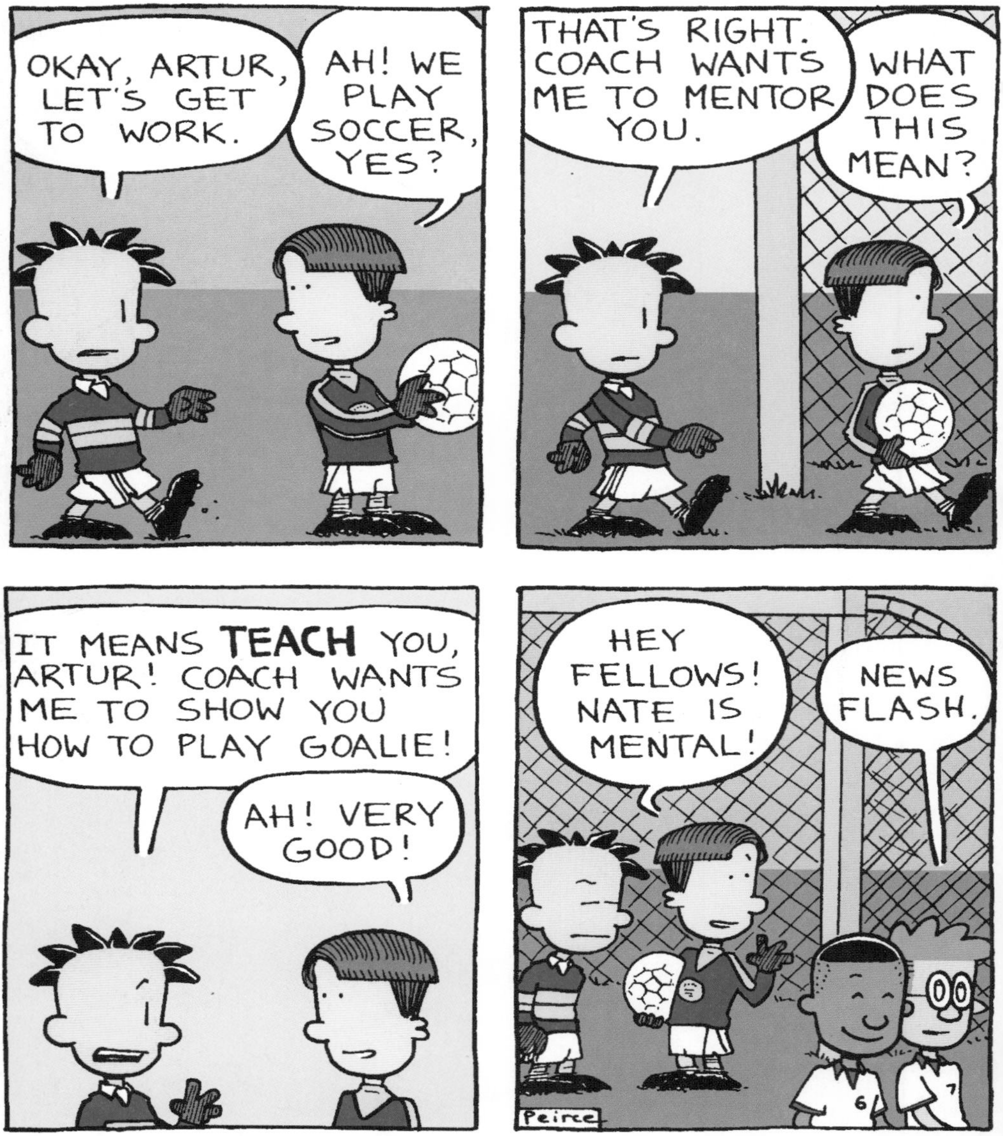
OKAY, ARTUR, LET'S GET TO WORK.
AH! WE PLAY SOCCER, YES?
THAT'S RIGHT. COACH WANTS ME TO MENTOR YOU.
WHAT DOES THIS MEAN?
IT MEANS **TEACH** YOU, ARTUR! COACH WANTS ME TO SHOW YOU HOW TO PLAY GOALIE!
AH! VERY GOOD!
HEY FELLOWS! NATE IS MENTAL!
NEWS FLASH.
Peirce

OKAY, ARTUR, WATCH CAREFULLY! FOR A GOALIE, THE MOST IMPORTANT THING IS TO HAVE A GOOD WARM-UP!
OKAY, GUYS, WARM ME UP!
DOOF!
I AM CONFUSED. HOW YOU TO GET WARM WITH COLD ICE ON FACE?
SHUT UP, ARTUR.
Peirce

NO!
NO!
NO!
ARTUR, WHAT ARE YOU DOING? YOU'RE SUPPOSED TO STOP THE BALLS, NOT GET OUT OF THE WAY!
YES, BUT SHOTS ARE MOVING VERY FAST!
IF I LET BALL TO HIT ME, IT WILL HURT!
IF YOU'RE DETERMINED TO FIND A PLACE ON THE TEAM FOR ARTUR, MAY I SUGGEST THE ALL-IMPORTANT ROLE OF EQUIPMENT MANAGER?
OACH
Peirce

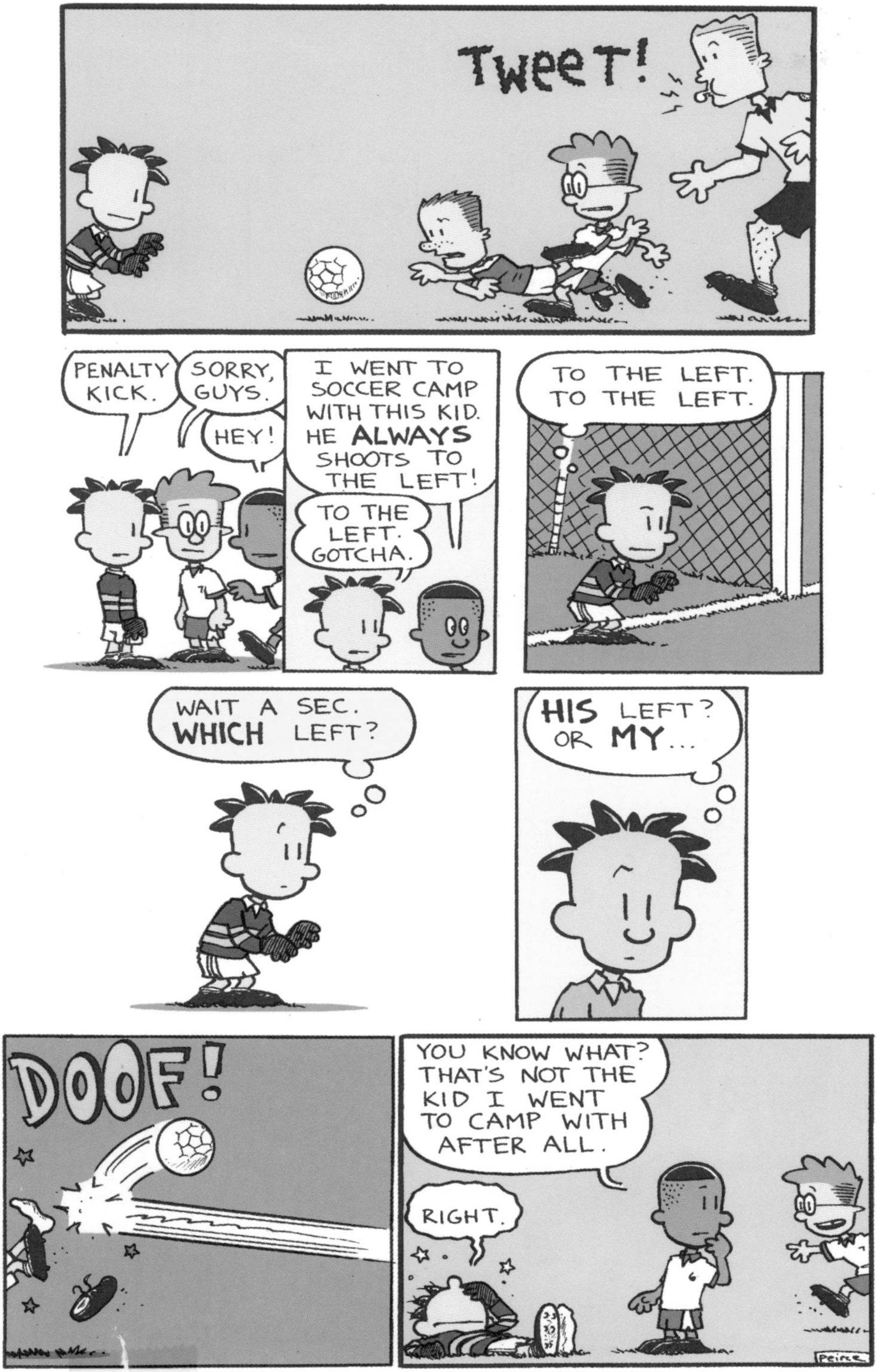
TWEET!
PENALTY KICK.
SORRY, GUYS.
HEY!
I WENT TO SOCCER CAMP WITH THIS KID. HE **ALWAYS** SHOOTS TO THE LEFT!
TO THE LEFT. GOTCHA.
TO THE LEFT. TO THE LEFT.
WAIT A SEC. **WHICH** LEFT?
HIS LEFT? OR **MY**...
DOOF!
YOU KNOW WHAT? THAT'S NOT THE KID I WENT TO CAMP WITH AFTER ALL.
RIGHT.
Peirce

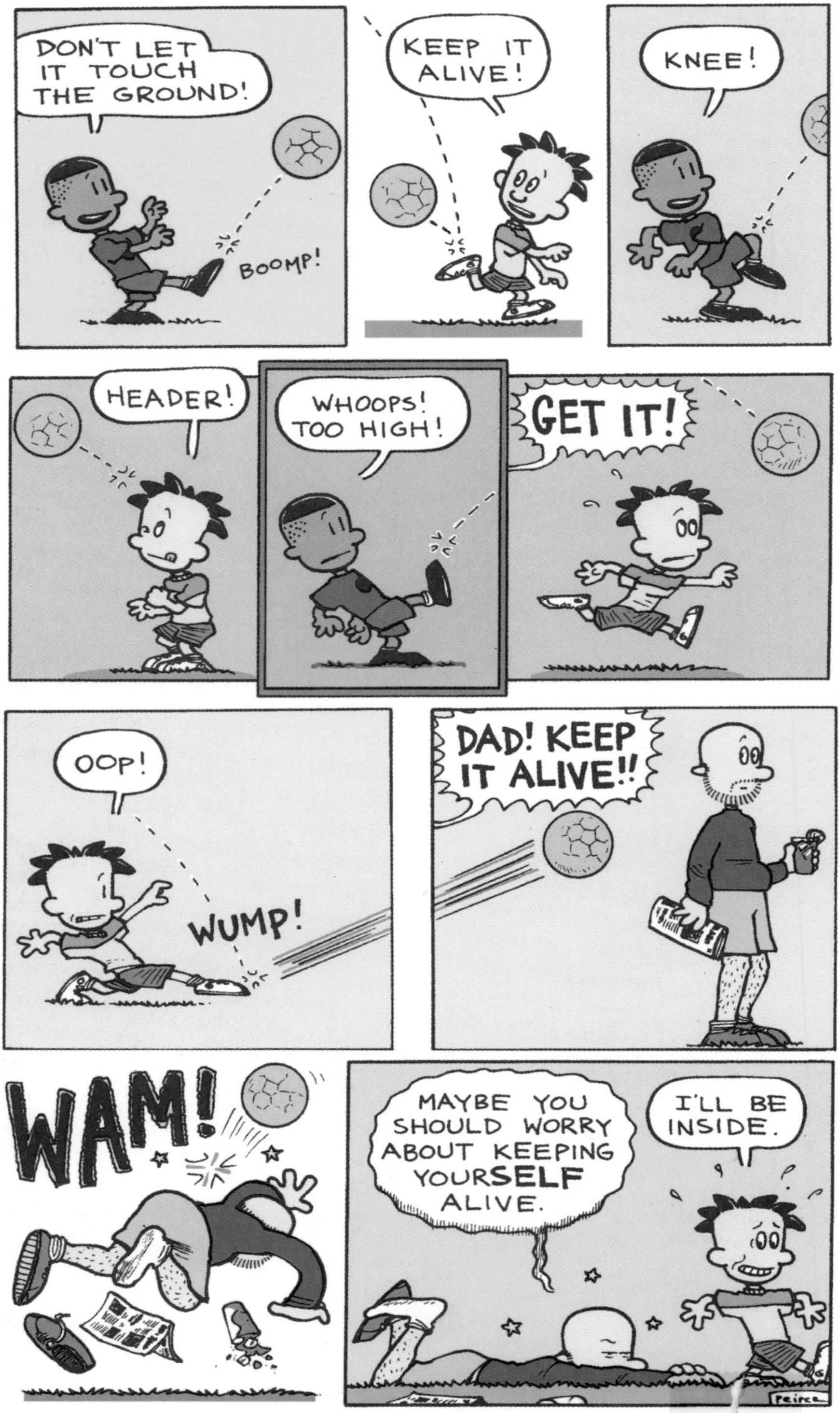
DON'T LET IT TOUCH THE GROUND!
BOOMP!
KEEP IT ALIVE!
KNEE!
HEADER!
WHOOPS! TOO HIGH!
GET IT!
OOP!
WUMP!
DAD! KEEP IT ALIVE!!
WAM!
MAYBE YOU SHOULD WORRY ABOUT KEEPING YOURSELF ALIVE.
I'LL BE INSIDE.
Peirce

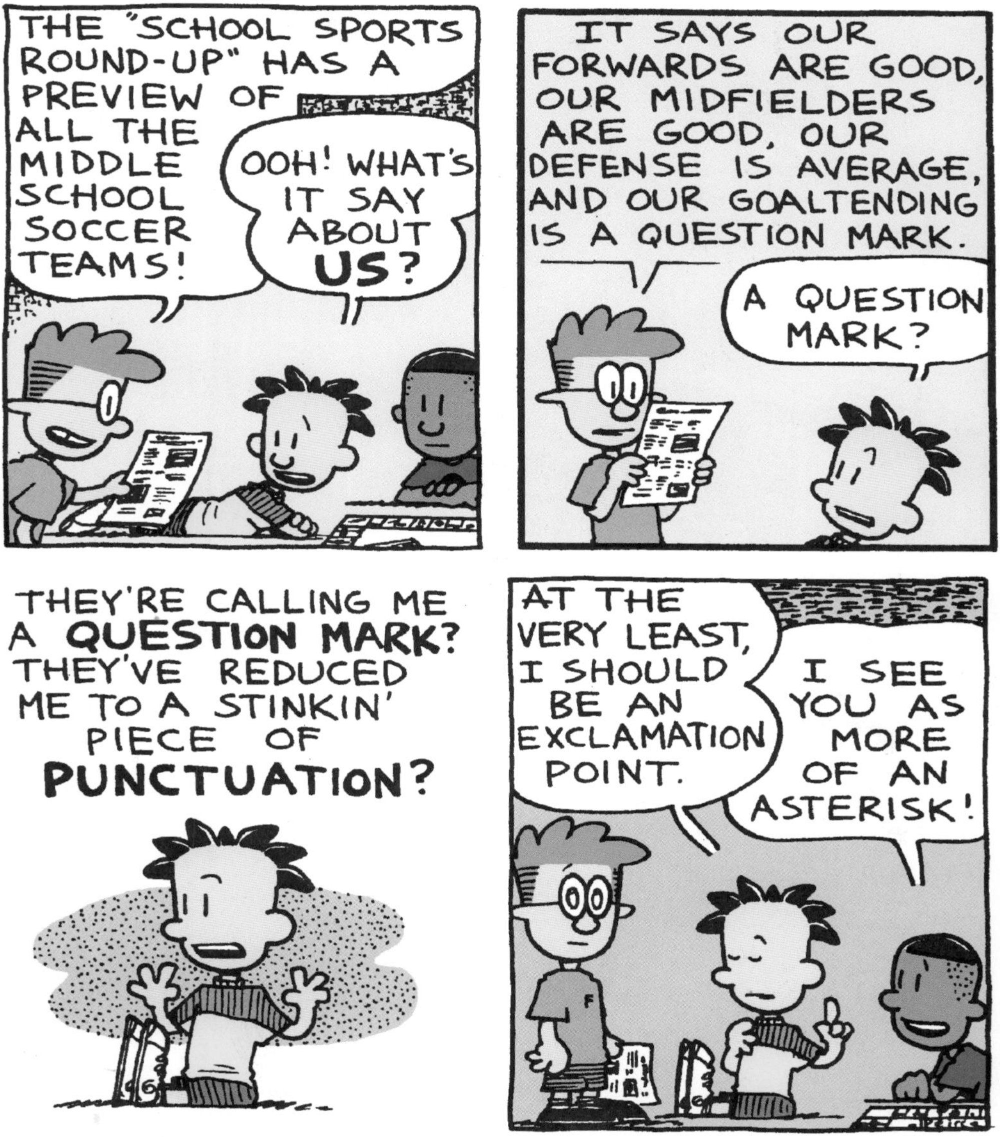
THE "SCHOOL SPORTS ROUND-UP" HAS A PREVIEW OF ALL THE MIDDLE SCHOOL SOCCER TEAMS!
OOH! WHAT'S IT SAY ABOUT US?
IT SAYS OUR FORWARDS ARE GOOD, OUR MIDFIELDERS ARE GOOD, OUR DEFENSE IS AVERAGE, AND OUR GOALTENDING IS A QUESTION MARK.
A QUESTION MARK?
THEY'RE CALLING ME A QUESTION MARK? THEY'VE REDUCED ME TO A STINKIN' PIECE OF PUNCTUATION?
AT THE VERY LEAST, I SHOULD BE AN EXCLAMATION POINT.
I SEE YOU AS MORE OF AN ASTERISK!

I NEED A NICK-NAME.
YEAH?
YEAH! OUR FORWARDS CALL THEMSELVES "STRIKE FORCE"! OUR DEFENDERS ARE "THE BEEFY D"!
AS OUR GOALKEEPER, I HAVE NO IDENTITY! I NEED A NICKNAME!
HOW ABOUT "PINHEAD"?
A SOCCER NICK-NAME!
IT WORKS FOR SOCCER!
Peirce

WE'RE TRYING TO THINK UP A NICKNAME FOR NATE.
A **SOCCER** NICKNAME! TO HIGH-LIGHT MY VITAL ROLE AS OUR GOALIE!
HOW ABOUT "DOOF"?
DOOF??
THAT'S THE WORST NICKNAME I'VE EVER **HEARD**! WHY WOULD I CALL MYSELF SOME-THING STUPID LIKE...
DOOF!
PEIRCE

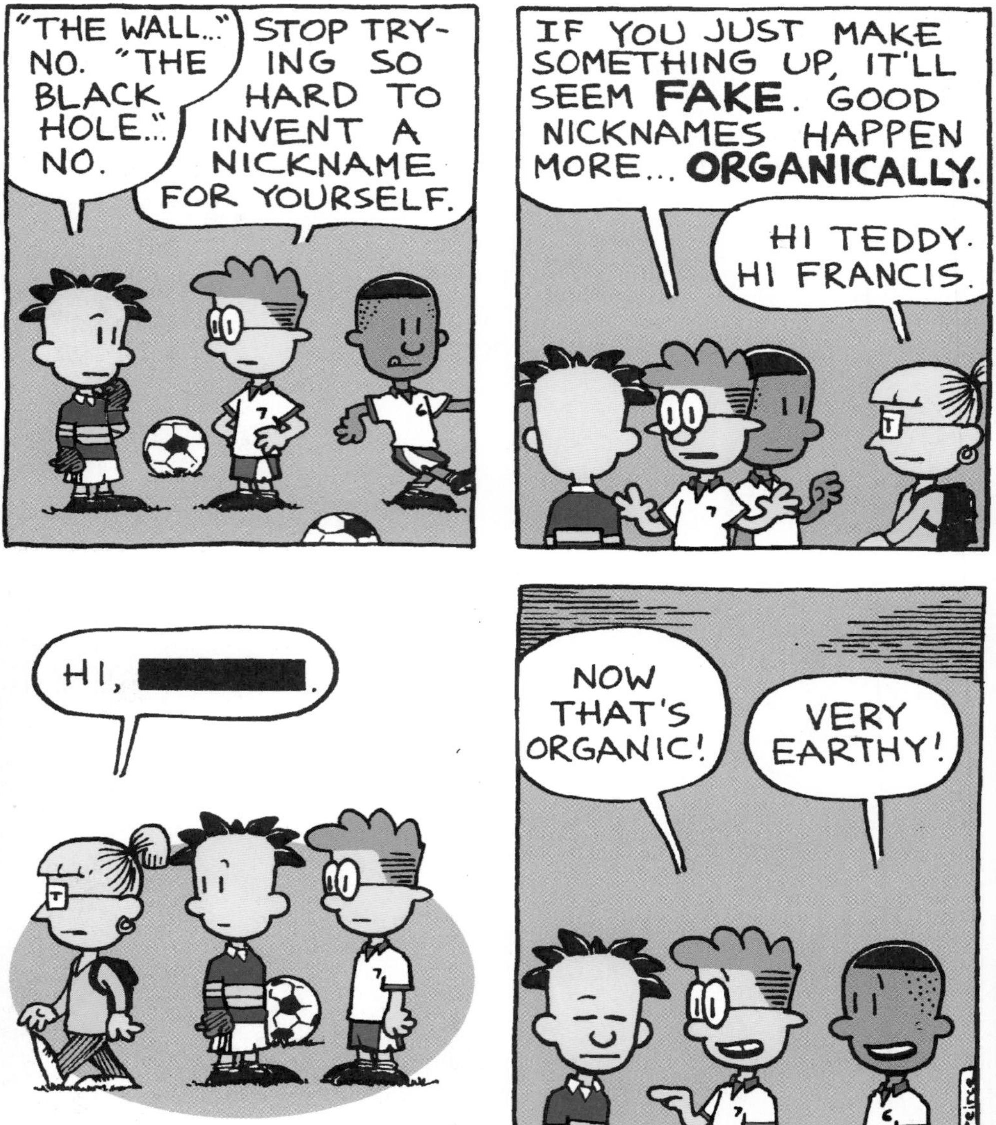
"THE WALL..." NO. "THE BLACK HOLE..." NO.
STOP TRYING SO HARD TO INVENT A NICKNAME FOR YOURSELF.
IF YOU JUST MAKE SOMETHING UP, IT'LL SEEM **FAKE**. GOOD NICKNAMES HAPPEN MORE... **ORGANICALLY**.
HI TEDDY. HI FRANCIS.
HI, [redacted].
NOW THAT'S ORGANIC!
VERY EARTHY!
Peirce

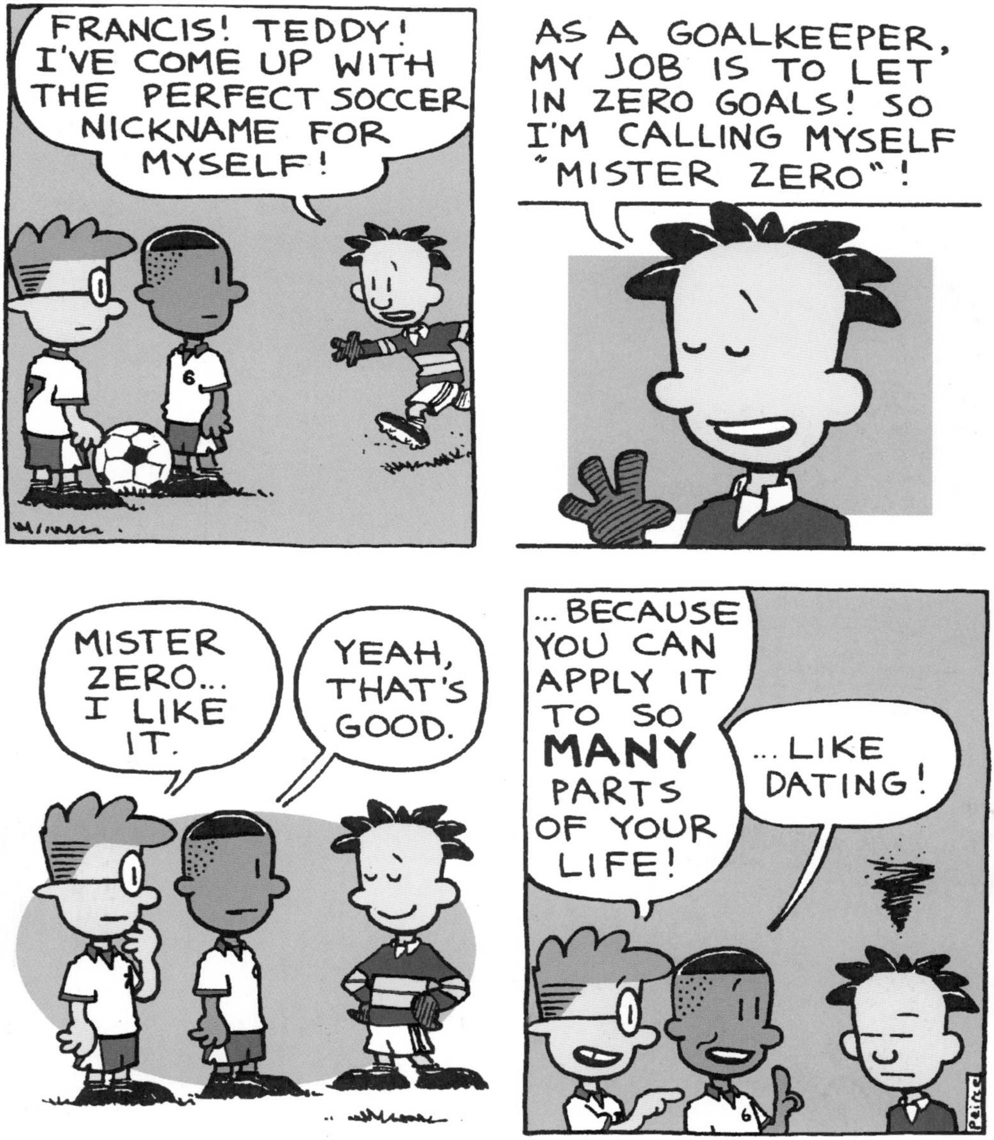
FRANCIS! TEDDY! I'VE COME UP WITH THE PERFECT SOCCER NICKNAME FOR MYSELF!
AS A GOALKEEPER, MY JOB IS TO LET IN ZERO GOALS! SO I'M CALLING MYSELF "MISTER ZERO"!
MISTER ZERO... I LIKE IT.
YEAH, THAT'S GOOD.
...BECAUSE YOU CAN APPLY IT TO SO **MANY** PARTS OF YOUR LIFE!
...LIKE DATING!
PEIRCE

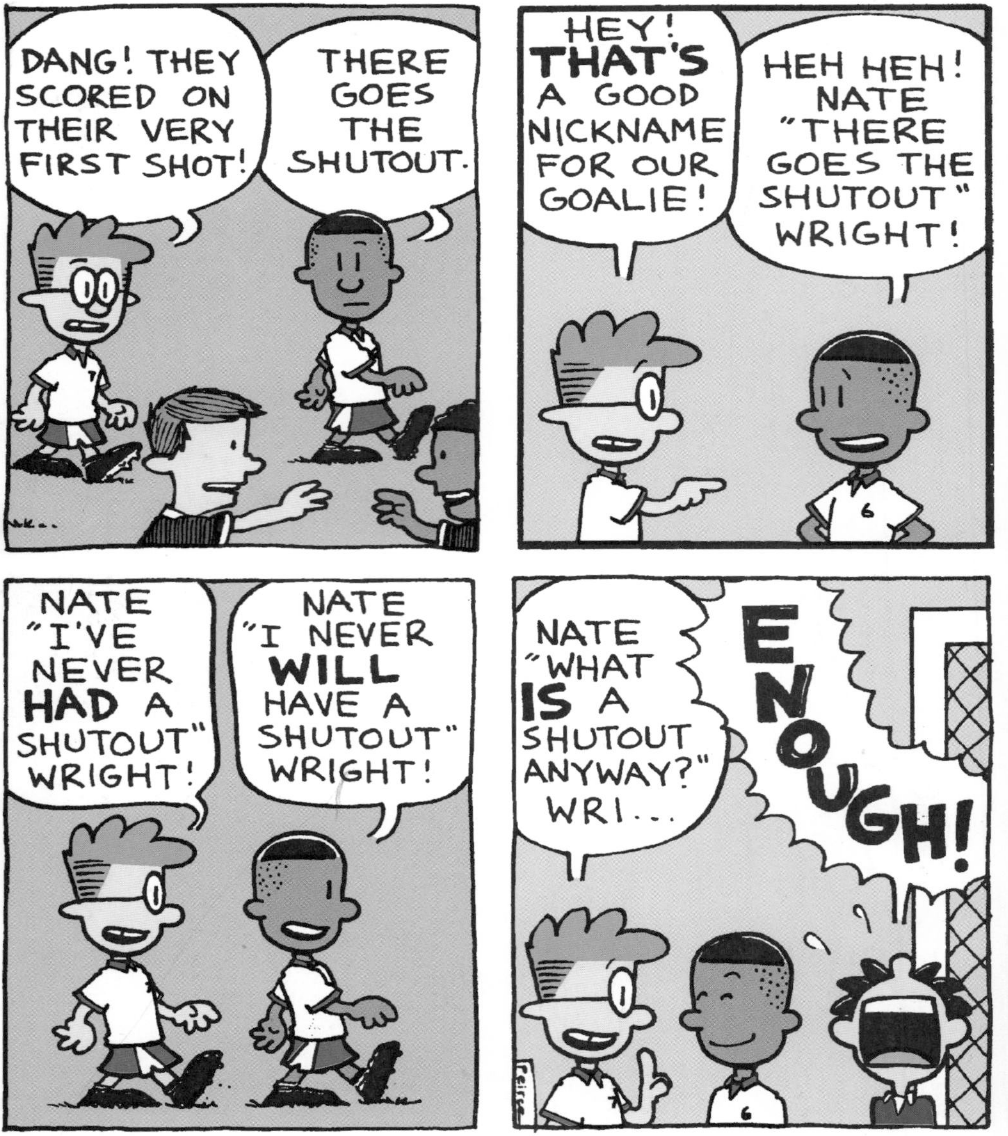
DANG! THEY SCORED ON THEIR VERY FIRST SHOT!
THERE GOES THE SHUTOUT.
HEY! **THAT'S** A GOOD NICKNAME FOR OUR GOALIE!
HEH HEH! NATE "THERE GOES THE SHUTOUT" WRIGHT!
NATE "I'VE NEVER **HAD** A SHUTOUT" WRIGHT!
NATE "I NEVER **WILL** HAVE A SHUTOUT" WRIGHT!
NATE "WHAT **IS** A SHUTOUT ANYWAY?" WRI...
ENOUGH!

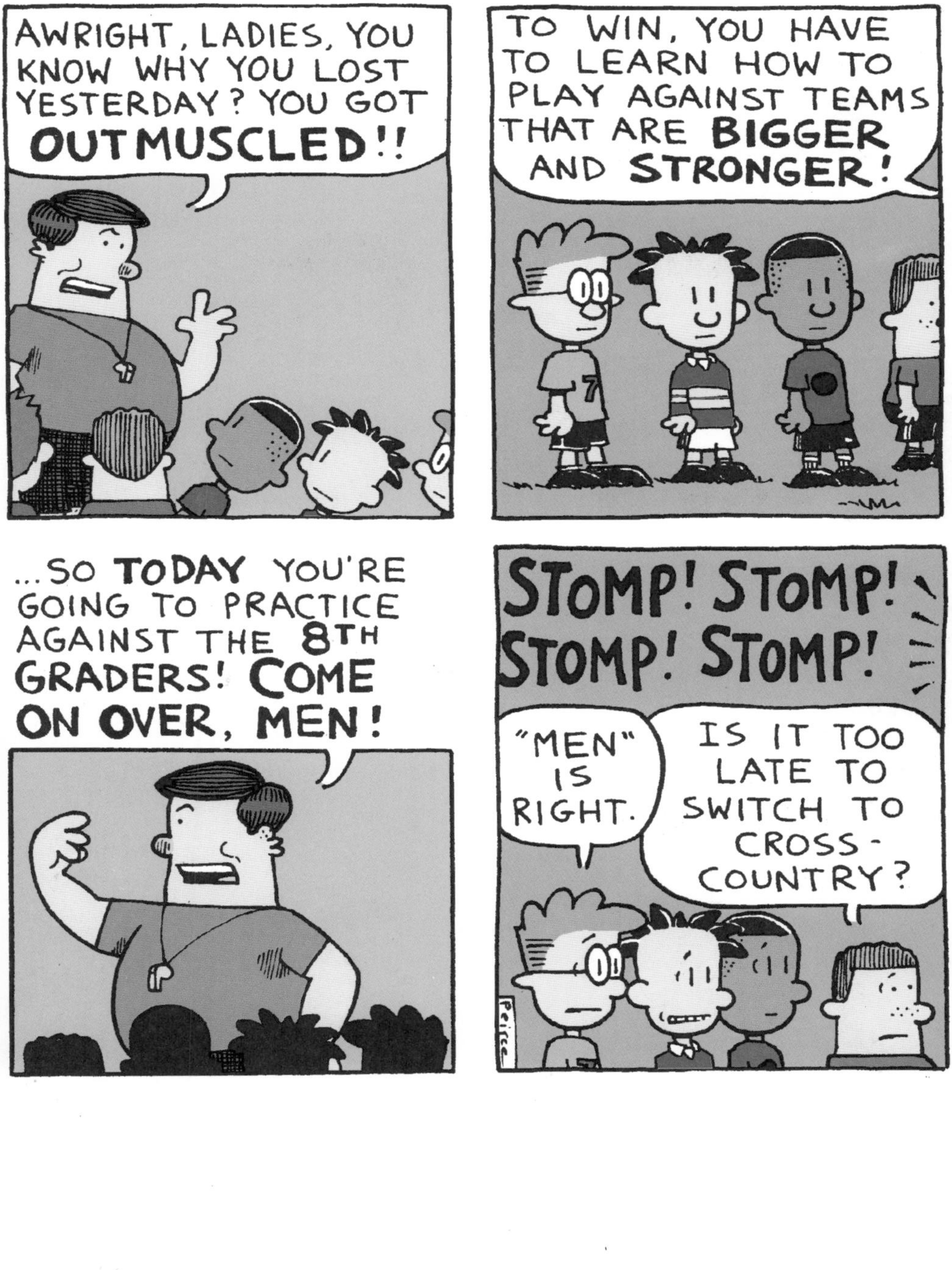
AWRIGHT, LADIES, YOU KNOW WHY YOU LOST YESTERDAY? YOU GOT OUTMUSCLED!!
TO WIN, YOU HAVE TO LEARN HOW TO PLAY AGAINST TEAMS THAT ARE BIGGER AND STRONGER!
7
...SO TODAY YOU'RE GOING TO PRACTICE AGAINST THE 8TH GRADERS! COME ON OVER, MEN!
STOMP! STOMP! STOMP! STOMP!
"MEN" IS RIGHT.
IS IT TOO LATE TO SWITCH TO CROSS-COUNTRY?
Peirce

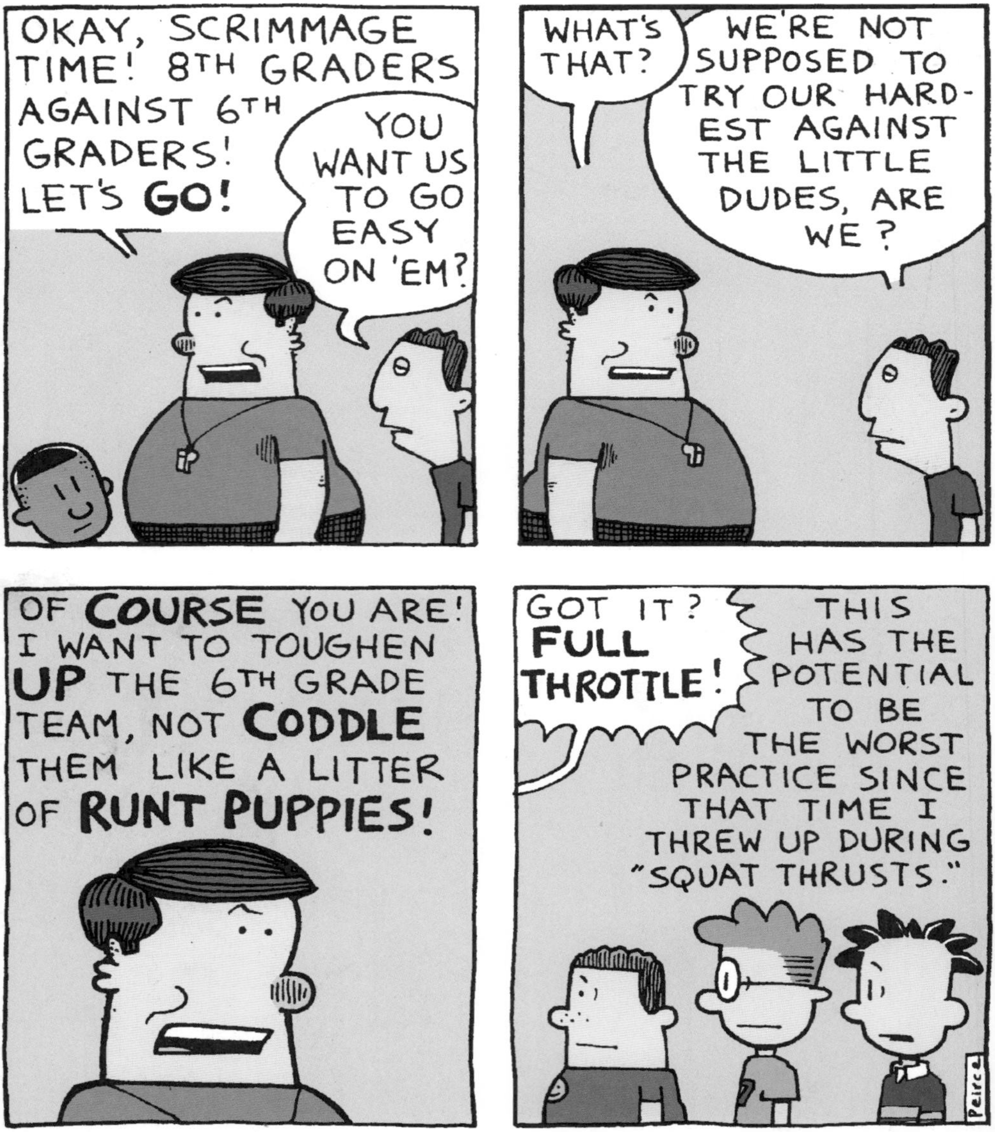
OKAY, SCRIMMAGE TIME! 8TH GRADERS AGAINST 6TH GRADERS! LET'S GO!
YOU WANT US TO GO EASY ON 'EM?
WHAT'S THAT?
WE'RE NOT SUPPOSED TO TRY OUR HARDEST AGAINST THE LITTLE DUDES, ARE WE?
OF COURSE YOU ARE! I WANT TO TOUGHEN UP THE 6TH GRADE TEAM, NOT CODDLE THEM LIKE A LITTER OF RUNT PUPPIES!
GOT IT? FULL THROTTLE!
THIS HAS THE POTENTIAL TO BE THE WORST PRACTICE SINCE THAT TIME I THREW UP DURING "SQUAT THRUSTS."
Peirce

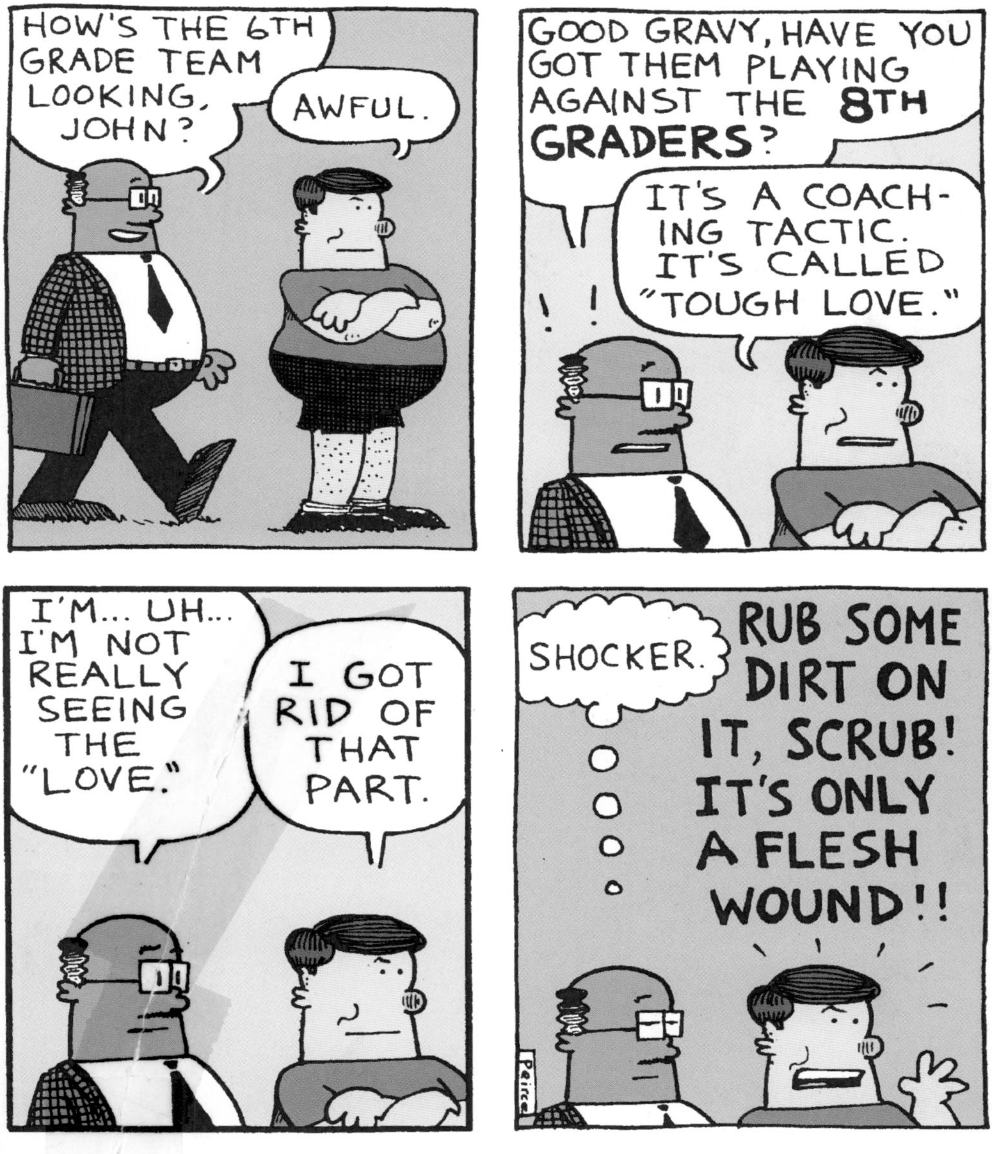
HOW'S THE 6TH GRADE TEAM LOOKING, JOHN?
AWFUL.
GOOD GRAVY, HAVE YOU GOT THEM PLAYING AGAINST THE **8TH GRADERS**?
IT'S A COACH-ING TACTIC. IT'S CALLED "TOUGH LOVE."
! !
I'M... UH... I'M NOT REALLY SEEING THE "LOVE."
I GOT RID OF THAT PART.
SHOCKER.
RUB SOME DIRT ON IT, SCRUB! IT'S ONLY A FLESH WOUND!!
Peirce

OKAY, SO THE 8TH GRADERS ARE BIGGER AND STRONGER! WE'LL BEAT 'EM WITH SPEED!
HEADS UP. COMIN' THROUGH.
I'LL TAKE THAT.
MUST BE NICE TO HAVE LONG LEGS.
I WOULDN'T KNOW.
Peirce

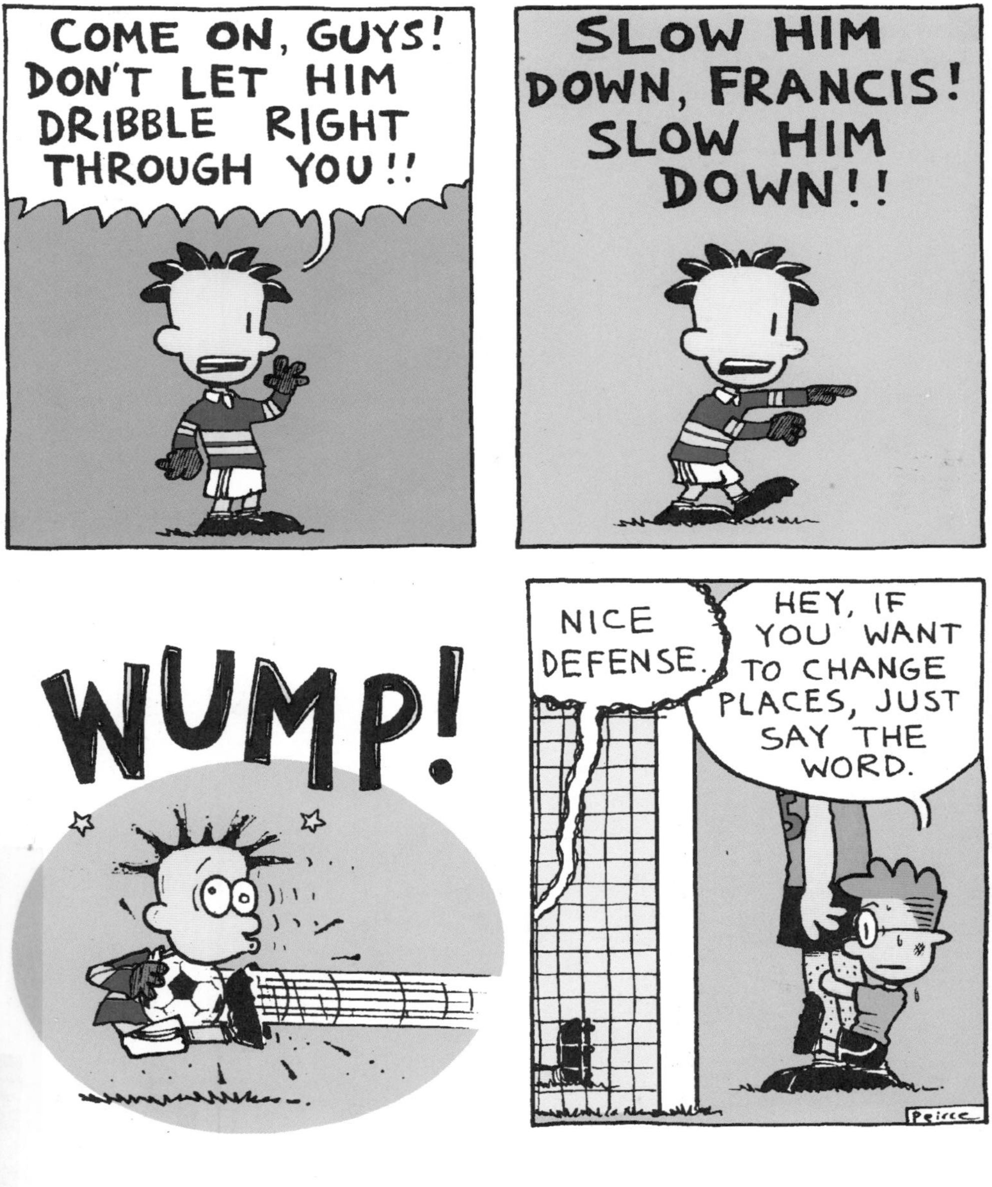
COME ON, GUYS! DON'T LET HIM DRIBBLE RIGHT THROUGH YOU!!
SLOW HIM DOWN, FRANCIS! SLOW HIM DOWN!!
WUMP!
NICE DEFENSE.
HEY, IF YOU WANT TO CHANGE PLACES, JUST SAY THE WORD.
Peirce

THE 8TH GRADERS HAVE SCORED SO MANY TIMES, I'VE LOST COUNT!

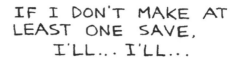

IF I DON'T MAKE AT LEAST ONE SAVE, I'LL... I'LL...

WHAM!

I WAS GOING TO SAY, "I'LL LOSE ALL RESPECT FOR MYSELF," BUT NEVER MIND.

Peirce